their
freefall
at
last

JULIE OLIVIA

Author's Note

Their Freefall At Last is the fourth book in the *Honeywood Fun Park* Series.

While this book can be read as a standalone novel, it is **HIGHLY recommended** to read this book **AFTER** enjoying the first three books in the series. This book is a series finale.

Please be advised that this book is a **slow burn, open-door** romance, meaning there is **on-page** sexual content. Mature readers only.

Finally, Bennett and Ruby's story is filled with funny and heart-warming moments, but there is also a decent amount of angst. Be kind to your heart when you read, friends. I promise I only write happy endings.

Enjoy your visit to Honeywood!
    xo Julie O.

For all the guests of Honeywood Fun Park.
Thank you for loving this silly little piece of my heart.

Playlist

"Best Friend" - Rex Orange County
"You're On Your Own, Kid" - Taylor Swift
"Daddy Issues" - The Neighbourhood
"Let's Fall in Love for the Night" - FINNEAS
"Please, Please, Please, Let Me Get What I Want" - The
Smiths
"Hunger of the Pine" - alt-J
"The Past and Pending" - The Shins
"I Kissed Someone (It Wasn't You)" - dodie
"Jolene" - Dolly Parton
"Never Blue" - Maggie Jean Martin
"Glimpse of Us" - Joji
"Nothing Better" - The Postal Service
"when the party's over" - Billie Eilish
"The One That Got Away" - The Civil Wars
"Prime" - Roan Martin
"Alone" - Trampled By Turtles
"Say Yes" - Elliott Smith
"At Last" - Etta James
"We'll Meet Again" - She & Him

Honeywood
FUN PARK

1. The Bee-fast Stop
2. The Beesting
3. Bumblebee Greenhouse
4. Bumblebee's Flight
5. Buzzard of Death
6. Canoodler
7. The Grizzly
8. Little Pecker's Joyride
9. The Romping Meadow
10. Honey Pleasure Stage
11. Security Office
12. Main Office
13. The Great Forest Journey

Prologue
Ruby

My one job is to make sure the groom doesn't run away, and I'm failing at it.

I've ripped open every door in this white-paneled church and passed by every hanging cross at least three times. But between searching in the empty groomsmen room, through the small reception hall filled with roses, and behind every silk curtain—I'm desperate, okay?—there is no sign of my big man with tattoos.

A few guests side-eye me as I shuffle past the open chapel doors. I give a tiny wave, the kind that says, *Isn't this an exciting day with absolutely nothing going wrong at all?* They don't wave back.

"Doesn't talk much, does she?" one of them stage-whispers as they turn back around to face the altar.

People whisper around me a lot, like because I'm quieter, that means I can't hear either. It doesn't matter whether I'm thirty or thirteen, whether they're strangers or my own parents, adults have never considered me consequential.

I try door after door, silently opening and closing until I

finally tear open the last door in the church, and that's exactly where I find him. My best friend, the groom on this hectic day, sits in the corner of the small storage closet, holding his head in both of his large palms, right beside where the mop bucket meets the squeegees.

He doesn't look so good. Well, he does—that tux cost a pretty penny not to look amazing. But he also seems ... sad.

Bennett is a classic Roman statue brought to life with a carved jaw and rough, defined hands. Even when he releases his head from his palms, swiveling his eyes to me, the light from the hall illuminates their dark brown color, a color so pure and deep that I could swim in its depths. Or drown in them.

I muster up every bit of courage I have in my heart and lean against the doorframe.

"Hey, Pirate. You've got a show in five."

Bennett blinks for a moment before darting his eyes behind me and then back. I nod in understanding, stepping into the tight space and snicking the door shut.

I've been told that's weird—my and Bennett's whole mind-reading thing. Our friends don't like playing Guess Who with us anymore. They're convinced we cheat. I don't know how to tell them that I know who he picked based on the twitches of his large hands or the way the small scar on his lip tilts to the side.

Bennett gives me a weak smile that doesn't tilt the scar. Which means he's not doing okay. Or that he didn't pick Bill in Guess Who. It's a toss-up.

"I shouldn't be seeing you," he says.

"Well, the good thing is that it won't be bad luck."

He flexes his fist, the little veins on the back rippling with the motion. His jaw shifts, and he focuses on the shelves instead of me.

2

"Sit with me?" he murmurs, almost to himself.

Without thinking, I let out the smallest, "Mmhmm," and slide down across from him, aware of the messy floor but ignoring it. Just like I'm aware of the way he seems very interested in the spray bottles beside him instead of leaving this closet, but I'm choosing to ignore that too.

"So cozy," I say, tracing my fingers over the broom handle beside me. "Really love what you've done with the place."

Bennett centers a look at me. And, God, that stare—that *stare*—is something that punches me right in the chest. A mix between intense concentration and ache. This expression is normally reserved for when he watches rom-coms, like *When Harry Met Sally, 13 Going on 30,* or *My Best Friend's Wedding.*

On second thought, scratch those references.

Now's not the time for thinking. We've got five minutes until this wedding starts.

I clear my throat. "So, did you hear about the two cell phones that got married?"

He blinks, opens his mouth, then shuts it.

"What?" he asks.

"Did you hear about the two cell phones that got married?"

He blinks again.

Oh no, I've stunned the man.

"Psst." I hold my hand up to the side of my mouth and lower my voice to a whisper. "It's a joke. Play along."

Slowly but surely, Bennett finally smiles.

There we go.

It's hard to describe how gorgeous my best friend's smile is, and I'm not even sure words could do it justice. It's like happiness fills his chest up like a balloon, inflating his smile,

3

until it finally bursts through him from the inside out. Sometimes, it's so big that it makes his eyes squint. That's the smile that warms me to my core. The smile that feels like home.

"No," Bennett says with a chuckle. That low, beautiful chuckle that rumbles in my chest as much as it probably does his. "Tell me, what happened to the cell phones that got married, Rubes?"

I inhale like a drumroll and say, "I heard the *reception* was amazing."

Bennett instantly barks out a laugh, genuine and full-bodied. Loud. Much louder than I'm capable of, which I've always admired about him. His laugh is debatably better than his smile.

He reaches his hand up for a high five, and I slap his palm. Totally routine. Totally normal.

"So, why the closet?" I ask. "Nervous about all the people out there?"

I could tell him that half the wedding party is looking for him, but there's no need to put that on him right now.

"Nah," he says. "Got a stain on my shirt." He exhales a moaning sigh, fiddling with the towels on the shelf. "No stain-remover pens in here though."

I look at his shirt. There is no stain.

"It'll be fine," he continues. I lift my eyebrows in sarcastic disbelief, and he chuckles again. "And this groom right here is gonna be fine too."

"Y'know, 'The Groom Is Fine' could definitely be a song title."

"Oh, it would have to be on a mix CD."

"Called *Songs about Forever*?" I suggest.

He looks wistfully at the ceiling. "I can hear the commercial now."

"Airs at midnight or two in the morning, right?"

"Wakes you up from your sleep on the couch."

"Celine Dion is the headliner." I wave my hand around. "Or Etta James!"

Bennett bites his lip and fists the air. "Now, *that's* what I call music."

My best friend laughs, but the low sound fades as our joking bit dies out.

"Yeah," I say. "You're gonna be fine. Now, let's get back out there, huh?"

Bennett blows out an exhale before tilting his head to the side with a gentle smile.

I bet he's thinking, *Thanks, Parrot.* I know because this expression is the same one that's always admired my jokes. It's the same one that's wished me *happy birthday* for most of my life. The one that always finds me across the room when everyone has forgotten I'm there.

A familiar, slimy thought curls around my heart and gives a tight squeeze.

My Bennett.

I pull my lips in. I wish I could take the thought back, elbow-drive it deeper into my brain, close the door, lock it, and swallow the key. Because, just like I can read my best friend's thoughts, I'm almost certain he read mine.

"Oh, Rubes ..."

Bennett reaches out his hand, sliding the palm up my bare wrist. It feels important, but all moments with Bennett are significant. He is the consistent bookmark to all the fantastic, exciting, and wonderfully miserable moments in my life.

Every memory with Bennett matters. And I couldn't lock up that thought if I tried.

I made myself swear to hold it together today, but I'm

now Alice falling down the rabbit hole. Barreling into the depths of my heart. Through the locks and dead bolts and chairs propped against doorknobs. Right to the truth of it all.

I am currently in love with, have always been in love with, and will continue to be in love with my best friend, Bennett Walker Shaw. I don't know when it started, and I don't know when it will end. But, God, it'd better be soon.

Because in five minutes, his bride-to-be will greet him in a beautiful white gown with *forever* on her lips.

Except that bride won't be me.

I could try to pinpoint where my mess started, but I'm not sure where I'll land in our patchworked timeline.

Maybe it's best to go back to the beginning. Back to when the meaning of love was simply defined by a small-town theme park and that beautiful, messy-haired boy.

Part I

1
Ruby

Twenty-Three Years Before
Ruby & Bennett are Seven Years Old

"You're going in. Big girls don't cry."

"But, Daddy ..."

"Amelia, let's not do this today, okay? Your mom is running late."

She is.

I know because Daddy jumped our car right onto the curb, making Mama scream, "RICHARD!" But she still had a smile, which meant she liked that he was making a big deal out of it.

Daddy holds out my Buzzy the Bear backpack. I sniffle and grab it slowly because, if I don't, they'll think I have *attitude*. And if I have attitude, I might have to actually stay here.

Other kids laugh and run past us from Honeywood Fun

Park's gates, their backpacks jangling with key chains and untied sneakers.

I want to go home.

Mama is filling out paperwork at the sign-in table. She told me Honeywood Fun Park would be exciting. But so far, there're too many new people, the morning sun is too bright, and the roller coaster I can sort of see through squinted eyes is way too tall.

Like, *way* too tall.

I now get what Daddy meant at dinner last night.

"I'm telling you, Amelia is not gonna ride the roller coasters," Daddy said.

"She's seven," Mama said. "What seven-year-old doesn't want to ride roller coasters?"

Sometimes, I wonder if I have superpowers because Mama and Daddy say a lot of things like I'm not there. But one time, I tested it by slamming my fork on my plate, and Daddy shook his head at me with the scary eyebrows, so I guess I'm not invisible.

"You promise not to be scared, honey?" he asked me, glancing down to my uneaten veggies and back up.

I nodded because not agreeing would only get more questions.

"It'll be fun," Mama said, showing me a piece of paper about the day camp at Honeywood, where they were sending me for my birthday week. She said there would be a scavenger hunt, arts and crafts, where we'd color pictures of Queen Bee, *and* we would be meeting the *real* Buzzy the Bear.

I was excited because I loved Buzzy the Bear and I loved scavenger hunts.

But then we got here, and I saw my first roller coaster. The crisscrossing blue bars were so high up that I couldn't see the top through the sunbeams, and then a big train flew over the track faster than any of my Hot Wheels. It was so loud that I had to cover my ears.

I'm not excited anymore.

Daddy looks at me, his jaw doing that grinding thing. The thing that says he's thinking about what to say, and it will probably be something not fun.

"Why are you scared?" he asks.

I point to the roller coaster, and Mama lets out a sigh.

Daddy rubs Mama's back, and she leans her head on his shoulder. Even though he's not next to me, I feel better. I like it when he hugs Mama. I like that when she's stressed, he smiles. Like her being exhausted is funny. And sometimes, she smiles back, but that's because she loves him so much. I can just tell.

He pinches the seam of his pants, tugs them up, and crouches down in front of me.

"Hey, look at me," he says, tipping my chin up. "We need to have courage, remember? We've talked about that."

"Mmhmm."

"Use your words, Amelia."

"Yes, sir."

"You're here to have fun. That's what you wanted, right?"

"Yes, sir."

Then, he lowers his voice to a whisper. "And you'll talk to other kids? Make friends?"

I feel like *making friends* is all we've talked about ever since I brought my yearbook home a couple weeks ago. Daddy opened it, stared, then flipped to the back cover and stared again. Lots of staring and concentrating.

"Did they not have yearbook signing time?"

I didn't answer.

11

He shut the book. "Amelia, who is your best friend?"

Easy question.

"Moose."

Our giant white dog lifted his head up when he heard his name. His lazy ear flopped over, and that would have been funny if Daddy wasn't doing that jaw-shifting thing.

He clicked his tongue. "Besides Moose."

I shrugged, and he sighed.

"Isn't there someone you talk to every day?"

I felt bad that I didn't have an answer then, and I feel bad again now.

I had a friend when I first got to school, but she invited someone else to be our third friend after the second week. I liked it at first because I didn't have to talk much and I could just listen to their conversations. But then I started hearing about slumber parties I hadn't been invited to, and honestly, I liked reading books instead, where I didn't hear jokes I was left out of.

But I've really been wanting to watch *A Bug's Life*, and it'd be nice to have someone other than Moose, who barks at the screen the whole time.

"Amelia?" Daddy asks, tucking a strand of hair behind my ear. "Do you hear me? Are you gonna make friends today?"

"Yes, sir."

"And you're gonna speak up if you have questions?"

"Yes, sir."

"Tell the truth." His mouth twitches into a smile, and he winks.

I get that fluttery feeling in my chest, like a bird taking flight. I like Daddy's winks, and he normally only winks at Mama.

"Okay," I whisper.

"Okay what?"

"I'll make friends."

I almost smile. Almost. But then another roller coaster roars, and I grip Daddy's hand.

A man with a thick mustache sitting behind the sign-in table laughs.

I don't see what's so funny.

"And what's your name?" he asks.

"Sullivan," I answer.

Daddy always taught me to say our last name first. It's faster, and it won't bother the other people waiting behind us. There's nobody behind me right now, but it's best to be safe than sorry.

"Come again?" Mustache Man leans over the table with his ear cupped in his palm.

"Amelia Ruby Sullivan," Mama says for me, which is good because I don't like talking louder. It always feels like I'm yelling, but if I don't, nobody will hear me.

The man chuckles, looking only at me and not Mama before disappearing behind the table, then reappearing with a sticker, like some magician. Maybe he's part of the park, too, but I don't remember any magicians in Honeywood. And so far, the park is exactly like the books and movies they're based off of.

The ground is that bumpy stone kinda walkway, and there's a fountain with a statue of Buzzy the Bear in the middle. Tall trees line the park edges, and every wooden building looks straight out of the *Birds, Bees, and Bears* books I read all the time. I even know the music playing through the speakers. It's the theme from the *Honeywood* movie.

"Here's your name tag," Mustache Man says. "Stick it on your shirt, okay?"

I watch Mama sign some stuff on a clipboard before running a hand over my head.

"Don't forget to eat all your lunch, Amelia."

Suddenly, my body feels twitchy, and that awful bird in my chest wants out.

They're actually leaving.

"Mama ..."

"And the carrots," Daddy adds. "Especially the carrots."

"Y-yes, sir. But, Mama, can I—"

Mama holds out a single finger, her eyebrows turning in with worry. "Amelia, please, I'm gonna miss my flight."

I nod fast and lower my head so she can't see that I'm about to cry. I know it would only make her upset.

Mama works a lot. Daddy once said the airport was her first home and we were the vacation home. Mama looked really sad after that, but she didn't say he was wrong. She doesn't normally argue with Daddy, especially not when he winks afterward. She once said his winks could resolve wars, whatever that meant.

With a final kiss on my hair from Mama and a pat on the head from Daddy, they turn to leave, clacking every step of the way until they disappear out the iron gate.

"Amelia?" Mustache Man asks.

I sniff, turning back to him.

"You see the woman waving? That's Mrs. Stanley. You'll be in her group, okay? And, hey, I promise you'll have a good time."

I follow his finger point to a small group huddled in a blue-duct-taped square. The woman standing with the clipboard has one of those bowl haircuts with bangs all the way around her head, and she's already squinting at my name tag when I walk over.

"You must be ... Amelia Ruby."

I nod because I know you should never correct adults. I only go by my first name, Amelia, but the sticker lists both my first and middle names. Even if I wanted to correct her, she wouldn't hear me anyway.

The bangs-hair lady, Mrs. Stanley, says I can take a seat anywhere. I scan the crowd. Everyone here already has someone they're talking to, so I choose the far corner of the taped-off square, where nobody is. I plop on the ground, and I can feel the stinging behind my nose again.

Big girls don't cry.

I. Do. Not. Cry.

"Are you about to cry?"

I jump at the voice.

A boy is beside me, staring at my very wet eyes.

Where did he come from?

I've seen this boy at the lunch line in my school. He's the boy with the crooked teeth, who's always laughing.

The boy with the hair.

No other boys in our school have hair past their ears, but this boy does. It's messy and tangled, and it kind of looks like that one time I knocked over the black paint at day care. I liked how it looked on my paper with curly strokes and a wildness I couldn't have purposefully painted if I tried. This boy has the same pretty look to him.

Can boys be pretty?

"No," I whisper.

"What?" he asks, slipping down the brick wall to sit next to me.

"No," I repeat a little louder. The words wobble out of me. "I'm not crying."

He blinks at me. "My mom says it's okay to cry. And that I should help if someone is crying."

"My daddy says big girls don't cry."

15

His face scrunches up. "Well, my mom says everyone cries."

"Do you cry?"

"Sometimes."

He blinks at me, as if waiting for me to respond, but when I don't—because I cannot believe *boys* cry—he rips his name tag off his shirt and folds it in half. He starts tearing it into tinier pieces, and he looks like he's concentrating pretty hard on it. His mouth twists to the side as he thinks, and there's a little freckle beside his lip. I kinda like it. It's not gross, like my billions of freckles. Then, I notice he has a scratch on his ear. No, a small hole.

Are his ears pierced?

When he looks back to me, I instantly look away. Mama and Daddy tell me it's rude to stare, and here I am, being the rudest person ever. But this boy has *holes in his ears.* He reminds me of Captain Hook in *Peter Pan.* I always rewatch his scenes the most.

I peek at him. He's still looking at me. I jerk my eyes away again.

"I like your hair," he says. "It's like fire."

"It's not fire."

"But it looks like it."

"It's orange."

"I like oranges," he says. "I promise I won't eat your hair though. But I could. It's *that* orange."

He's been leaning in closer the more we talk. And by the end of his orange speech, he's really, really close to me.

"You're quiet," he says.

"I'm sorry."

He shakes his head. "It's okay. My mom would like you. She says I should be more quiet."

"Why?"

"She says I tell too many people she waxes her lips."

He has a toothy grin, but it's kind. I giggle. "Why does she do that?"

"I don't know."

He twists his mouth to the side, and the little flapping bird wings in my heart barrel through me.

He goes back to ripping his name tag.

"I like your hair too," I blurt out because I miss his talking. "You look like a pirate."

His eyebrows scrunch in, and I shake my head.

Oh no. That was rude.

"I mean ... that's not ..."

But then his mouth twitches into a smile, like my daddy's does. Except my daddy's teeth are straight and white, and this boy's bottom teeth are out of his mouth more than the top, and one of his front teeth is missing.

"I *am* a pirate."

My mouth falls open, and the energy inside me bubbles up into another giggle.

"No, you're not."

"Yes, I am."

"Where's your boat?"

He shrugs and rips another piece off his name tag. "At home. In the woods."

"Oh."

"You can be a pirate with me if you want."

"No thank you," I say because Mama would want me to be polite and Daddy wouldn't want me to steal and drink *boobs* or whatever it's called.

"Why not?" he asks.

"They're the bad guys."

"Oh." He squints into the sun. "Well, you can be my parrot then. They're not bad, like, ever."

17

"A parrot?"

"Parrots don't talk as much." Another rip of the name tag. "And you don't talk much either." His head jerks to me. "Is that okay?" His eyebrows are pulled in again. "I don't mean that you're my sidekick or anything. Mom says girls should never be sidekicks."

I think I like his mama.

"It's okay," I say. "I like parrots."

And, slow as a wave brushing onto the beach, he smiles back to me with his crooked little teeth.

"Good," he says. "I like parrots too."

Then, out of nowhere, like energy finally releasing from me, I call out, "Caw!"

The boy laughs, head back, hair shaking, gripping his stomach. I've never seen such happiness, and it's infectious. Suddenly, I'm laughing too.

"You're funny," he says.

I'm funny.

"All right, children!"

I jump at the loud adult voice. I almost forgot where we were. There are more kids around us now, and Mrs. Stanley is outside the taped-off square with her clipboard held up to her glasses dipping at the end of her nose.

"Before we get started ... it looks like we have two birthdays coming up!"

Oh no.

No, no, no.

I slide down the brick wall. I don't want people to know it's my birthday because then they stare and sing "Happy Birthday" and I hate it.

"Amelia!" Mrs. Stanley looks around. "Wait, where'd she go?"

This is horrible.

"Amelia?" she repeats.

"Here," I say, but the word comes out like a whisper, and nobody looks my way.

I glance to my right, where the boy is now staring me down with blinking eyes. I wonder if he's embarrassed to be sitting next to the birthday girl who can't talk loud enough. I would be.

But then he cups his hands to his mouth and yells, "She's over here!"

Mrs. Stanley finally finds me. I give a small wave, and her wave is somehow smaller. Adults do that wave a lot.

"Everyone say, 'Happy birthday, Amelia!' "

"Happy birthday, Amelia!"

Even though everyone else yells it, the boy next to me whispers, "Happy birthday."

I feel giddy, like I've emptied a bottle of glitter into my stomach, and I can't shake it off.

"Thanks for not yelling," I say, smiling.

"You're welcome, Parrot. Why didn't you tell her where you were?"

"She couldn't hear me. Nobody can."

His bottom teeth poke out between his lips before they pull into a wider grin. "*I* can."

"Perfect!" Mrs. Stanley says, tapping her clipboard. "Okay, and our other birthday is ... Ben Shaw!"

The boy twists his head away, shooting his hand into the air. "Here! And my name is Bennett. Not Ben."

I gasp. This boy *corrected* her? Doesn't he know you can't correct adults?

"I'm sorry, Bennett." Mrs. Stanley uncaps the pen with her teeth and scribbles something on her clipboard. "But look! Both of our birthdays are already sitting together! Everyone say, 'Happy birthday, Bennett.' "

"Happy birthday, Bennett," we all say, including me, and I try to say it as loud as I can, just for him.

She claps. Some other kids do too. But I just stare at his pretty smile and soft hair.

"You don't like your name?" I ask him.

His face scrunches. "Ben is my dad's name," he mumbles.

It's the first time his face looks weighed down, and I don't think I like it very much. Not seeing his crooked teeth makes him seem like the bad kind of pirate instead of my good pirate.

"I can call you Bennett," I say. "If you want."

Bennett's teeth peek through his lips again, like the crack in a doorway to his smile. I return the look because I like being the one who nudged that doorway open.

"Okay," he says. "And I can call you something else too. If you want."

I open my mouth to tell him to call me Amelia, just like my mama would want me to do, but then I stop. If this boy can get other people to call him something different, then I can too. I like the idea of having a secret with the pirate boy.

I glance down at my name tag displaying both my first name and my middle name, then say, "Call me Ruby."

His hand shoots out and grabs mine. I gasp because I definitely didn't try to shake his hand, but then I realize he's just holding it. My body might explode. I've never held hands with someone other than my parents before. Bennett's hand is warm.

"Do you want to sit next to me on rides today?" he asks.

"Oh. I ..."

I pause. I can't say I'm *scared*. Not when he thinks I'm a super-cool parrot with a cool new name.

But I think I take too long to say something back

because he quickly adds, "You don't have to. I just figured since we're birthday buddies, y'know?"

"Birthday buddies," I say, giggling because it sounds funny.

Birthday buddies with Bennett.

His mouth tips into another grin, and when it does, it's the biggest one yet. So big that it makes his eyes squint. Like he's staring right into the sun.

"Yeah," he agrees. "Birthday buddies."

I don't think roller coasters would be so bad with my birthday buddy, so I squeeze his hand and say, "Okay."

I have a feeling it won't be the last time I agree to something Bennett says.

2

Bennett

Twenty-One Years Before
Ruby & Bennett are Nine Years Old

"Bennett's here?"

I can hear Mr. Sullivan through the door, but I don't think he knows. He's trying to talk over Moose's wild barks.

"Richard, just open the door."

"Is she going somewhere with him?"

"His mother is grilling out for their birthdays."

"I thought Brittney worked nights?"

More barking.

"Richard, open the door for the child."

The front door opens with a jerky crack. Ruby's dad—a man with a thick black beard and even thicker eyebrows—stands in the doorway. I think he's trying to smile down at me, but it looks difficult for him.

My fist clenches tighter over the roses in my hand.

"Can Ruby come out to play, sir?"

I know to use the word *sir* around him. It's not that Mr. Sullivan makes me nervous—Mom said no adults should make me feel that way. But Ruby's dad is the one person who can ground her, and if he does that, then we can't eat cake and watch that bug movie that Ruby always likes to see on her birthday.

Moose shoves his head side to side to make room between Mr. Sullivan's legs and the doorframe. His great, big tongue is lolling out, heaving musty breaths and drooling onto the hardwood.

Mr. Sullivan calls over his shoulder, "Amelia! Bennett is here!"

We stand there in uncomfortable silence, like we always do. I learned really quick that nobody in Ruby's family talks much. I've only been inside the Sullivan house once, but I got goose bumps from its unusually pristine floor. I had to shush my sneakers from squeaking too loud.

The sound of flip-flops smack on clean hardwood and then my best friend appears.

Ruby's ginger hair is normally long and straight but, today, it's wrapped up into two cheesy-looking bread rolls on either side of her head.

She power-walks to the door—because you don't run in the Sullivan household—and slings her pink backpack over her shoulder.

Mr. Sullivan pats her head. "Back by five, honey. We have that event tonight, and you've gotta get in your dress."

"Yes, sir."

Ruby's parents always throw her a big birthday dinner party in some fancy building that isn't their house. She's told me she never knows anyone there, except for her cousins or her dad's assistant, Miranda. I'm never invited.

"Good. Have fun, you two."

23

He narrows his eyes at me. I don't know why he does that, but it makes me feel weird. Sometimes, I wish I could sneer right back at him. See how he likes it.

We cross the street to walk through Miss Lisa's yard, circling around her picket fence. Ruby's neighborhood is different from mine. The yards don't have cars in them, and the gates always look freshly painted. Plus, Miss Lisa has an in-ground pool, which is wild because I only know kids with above-ground ones.

We shimmy through the trees behind Miss Lisa's house and empty into the small trail between our neighborhoods.

I shove my fistful of flowers toward her. "Uh, happy birthday, Parrot. Mom says girls like flowers."

"They do?"

"You don't?"

Ruby's shoulders rise, and she giggles. "I don't know."

"Good. They're boring anyway." I draw my finger into a hook. "Let's play pirates instead. Yarr! Status report, matey!"

Ruby gives her little parrot-like squawk before tucking the flowers into the backpack's side pocket.

"What's the news?" I ask.

"Map!" she caws.

"Map?" I drop my hook. "Wait, what map?"

Grinning, Ruby rips off her backpack and reaches in, pulling out a curled piece of paper, held by a pink scrunchie. She hands it to me, and when I uncurl it, I smile so wide that it almost hurts.

My best friend is the freaking coolest.

Ruby drew Cedar Cliff. There's her neighborhood, mine, our school, the woods we're in with the creek and the big tree, and Honeywood Fun Park in the corner of town. She even drew Moose in her backyard.

It looks awesome.

"Whoa, is that *treasure?*" I poke at the large X in my living room. *MY living room!*

"Yarr!" she says with a giggle.

"Yarr!" I echo. "Thar be booty!"

I run to the big tree—our pirate ship—and hold out my hand for her to climb on. But when her foot doesn't land in my palm, I turn around. Ruby's face is bright red.

"What?" I ask.

"Bennett, you can't say that."

"Say what?"

"That word," she says, her voice getting quieter.

"Booty?"

She giggles in response. One time, her dad caught us saying the word *ass* and instantly grounded her. Not being able to play outside for a couple of days scared her into not saying related words. Even *booty*.

She walks over and lifts a foot into my palm. I boost her up to the branch in our pirate ship, then climb up after her.

To see her face turn red, I whisper, "Booty."

"Bennett!"

"What?! It means, like, gold and treasure and stuff." I scoot closer to her. "Nobody can hear us. You can say it too."

Mom says, sometimes, you can see a hamster running on the wheel in someone's head when they think, and Ruby's hamster is flying. She always does this when she's considering whether to break rules. They're not actual rules, but she has a list in her head of what she can and can't say. Sometimes, she says the can't-say words when she's around me. Especially when we're in the magic tree ship.

"Say it," I say. "Come on, Rubes. *Booty.*"

She squints, and I copy the look, making her giggle.

"Okay. Booty!" she caws.

"Aha! Yarr!" I yell, hooking my finger again.

She erupts into a fit of giggles, which has me laughing too, and then, because we're both laughing, I laugh more. We can't stop until both our cheeks and bellies hurt.

Finally, I curl open the map again. "So, what is it?"

"It's a secret."

"But we don't keep secrets."

"No, but ... it's a secret."

"Wait. Is it my birthday gift?"

She nods, and instantly, I hop out of the tree.

"Well, I wanna go get it!"

"But the ship!" She waves her arms in the air. "We've just set sail!"

"But booty!"

Ruby lets out a, "Shush," and I grin, wrapping my arms around her waist to help her off the branch.

Twigs snap under our sneakers as we run through the woods. Once we reach my backyard's chain-link fence, I lift the lock and let her through first.

My yard isn't as big as Ruby's or as neat, and even though it's summer, the ground is still covered in crunching leaves and old branches from last fall. But the smell of barbecue is rising from the grill, and Mom's rock music is roaring from the house, which is definitely more awesome than Ruby's quiet, echoey house that smells like cleaning supplies.

We run up the back porch steps and slide open the glass door to an irritated, "Just this once, Ben."

Ruby and I halt at the sound.

It's my mom talking on the phone. She exhales. I can hear her pacing in the kitchen with her bare feet sticking to the linoleum and the phone's cord rattling against the wall as she moves.

"I know what I said. But, hey, maybe next time, don't knock someone up at sixteen and then—" She stops midsentence. "What responsibility? You're off, living your life on the back of a motorbike, and I'm here—" Another pause. "I'm only asking for one birthday. One. That's it."

Ruby's hand takes mine and squeezes.

We both know who Mom is talking to.

She's talking to my dad.

I've never met my dad. Not that I can remember anyway.

Sometimes, Mom shows me a Polaroid from her memory box, and she'll tilt her head to the side and say, "Y'all look so similar," but all I see is a tattooed stranger holding my mom's hand.

She gets a weird smile on her face when she looks at that specific photo, like the faded colors of the picture pull into her, making her look faded too.

I don't know my dad, but I never want to if that's how people look when they're around him for too long.

"Hey," Ruby whispers.

"Yeah?"

"Why did the chicken cross the road?"

I smile. "Why?"

"It was a *fowl* day."

I let out another laugh. This is the best thing about Ruby. She knows the perfect time to tell the funniest jokes.

I don't hear the rest of the conversation because Mom's music is loud, but I do hear the phone clanging on the receiver. She comes around the corner.

"Oh! Hey there, kiddos!"

Mom is all smiles, holding grill tongs over her shoulder.

She's even got her "face on" with her thick eyelashes and maroon lips. Her favorite Journey shirt is tucked into her ripped denim shorts. She always says that outfit makes her feel like a rock star.

She playfully snaps the tongs at Ruby before pulling her in for a hug. "Happy birthday, my precious gemstone. Get anything good this year?"

"Books."

"Books? Good. Books are good." Mom slides open the back door and opens the grill. Smoke wafts out, filling the air with a charred smell. "Gotta stay smart. It'll keep you out of trouble."

Mom mentions trouble a lot, especially to Ruby. Her three cardinal rules are: never have too much fun at parties, never laugh at jokes that aren't funny, and all boys with motorcycles are automatically bad news.

Before she can go off on her typical trouble speech, I hold up my map. "Is there something in the living room for me?"

Mom curls her lips in and winks at Ruby. "I don't know. Maybe."

I scramble inside. I look everywhere for my hidden booty, and I finally find it in a yellow folder behind the bookshelves. My name is scrawled on the front in Ruby's handwriting below a giant X. I open it, and inside is a packet of Pokémon cards and a drawing. I skip past the cards and take the drawing out. It's a roller coaster. I love Ruby's roller coasters. I love them even more when she designs them for me.

"Awesome," I breathe. "Thank you."

I hear the sliding door open again, and Mom comes into the living room.

"Oh, wow," she says, putting a hand on Ruby's shoulder. "This one turned out so good."

"Ruby's smart," I say.

Ruby's face gets all pink, and she winds her hands together. "I named it The Bennett."

I gasp. "Hell yeah!"

My mom snaps her fingers. "Bennett Shaw, no foul language in my household, mister."

"*Fowl*," I whisper to myself with a giggle.

"It has three loops," Ruby says. "And the drop is, like, three hundred feet. And after that, it goes underground. For thirty minutes."

Mom nods slowly. "Wow," she says, dragging out the word. "I might vomit, but I'd at least give it a whirl once. Oh! Have your parents taken you to see The Grizzly yet, Rubes?"

She shakes her head. "The Grizzly?"

"Honeywood added a new roller coaster, kiddo. It's got their tallest drop so far."

Ruby gasps. I gasp too. Mom gasps, but I think she does it just to be funny.

"They did? Mom, can we go? Can we go?"

"Maybe. I'll see if I can get time off, all right?"

"Can I come too?" Ruby asks. "Mama's been away a lot, and Dad's been really busy with work."

"You can come with us whenever we go," Mom says, bumping her hip against Ruby's shoulder. "I'll even buy your ticket."

Her lips pull into a secret smile in my direction. Mom was just talking about how expensive our electric bill was the other day, so I know that's a huge deal.

"Cool. Dad says he spends a lot of money on his assistant and that we can't buy much right now."

Mom pauses in place, grill tongs snapping closed. "His assistant?"

"Miranda."

"Right," Mom says, dragging out the word. "Uh-huh. Miranda. Okay. Is ... your mom friends with Miranda?"

Ruby shrugs. "I guess?"

I don't know why Mom looks confused, but she walks away and slides open the back door.

"What's wrong with Miranda?" Ruby asks me.

I shrug. Ruby's dad's assistant is always at their house when Ruby's mom travels for work. It's not that weird.

We play pirates until lunch when Mom brings out two cakes—one for each of us. She tells us to make a wish before we blow out our candles. I never know what to wish for, so I just hope for Ruby's wish to come true instead.

We eat our cake while we watch *A Bug's Life* because it's Ruby's favorite movie to see, and I hold her hand because it's my favorite thing to do.

"Hey, what did you wish for?" I ask.

"To find real buried treasure."

So smart.

"I would have never thought of that," I say. "I like that."

"Thanks." Her voice is so quiet that I almost don't hear it. Ruby doesn't like compliments.

"I liked my booty today."

"Shh. Your mom will hear you."

"Booty."

She giggles. "Bennett!"

I squeeze her hand with a laugh, and she instantly squeezes back.

3

Ruby

Twenty Years Before
Ruby & Bennett are Ten Years Old

So, that's *The Grizzly.*

Honeywood Fun Park's new roller coaster towers over us like a behemoth, glistening with an orange track and polished wood. I can already smell it too—all Honeywood coasters have that type of scent, like used brakes and rubber that reminds me of hot summers and damp boat rides. As the train rumbles over the track, taking the first edge with a jarring turn that has riders screaming with joy, my pulse races.

Where the heck is Bennett?

Miranda puts a hand on my shoulder. I jump.

"You okay?" she asks.

"Mmhmm."

This isn't my first roller coaster. I've ridden The Beesting with its free-falling drop, Bumblebee's Flight with its continuous loops, and even the purple terror that is Buzzard of Death. I've designed more coasters than that, too, with steeper falls and more loops. The bigger and badder, the better. All of my sketchbooks are packed with wild ideas. But riding them is a different story if my best friend isn't here to hold my hand the whole time.

We've waited one year to finally ride The Grizzly because Bennett's mom couldn't find time away from work. I ended up begging my dad to take us instead.

"Well then, are you getting on?" Dad asks.

"I'm waiting on Bennett."

Miranda smirks.

Dad's assistant is a working businesswoman, just like my mom, except she travels way less. She always looks a little angry, and the only soft thing about her is her angelic blonde hair.

Dad, standing on the other side of her with his hands in his pockets, blows out air. "You'd think he could be here on time."

"His mom works a lot," I say.

I rise to my tiptoes to look through the crowd. It's hot in Honeywood today. The blacktop radiates through the soles of my sneakers, and beads of sweat already trickle down my back. I place my hand to my temple to block out the sun, but I halt when I see someone staring back at me.

But not just someone.

Michael Waters.

Michael is one year older than me and really, *really* cute. He's tall, and he has freckles all along his nose that somehow make him look nice even though they make me look really stupid. His dark hair even does that swooping thing that I've only ever seen on MTV.

And, holy cow, he's looking *right at me.*

His mouth pulls into a slow, lazy smile, like he can't be bothered to lift the other side of his lips too. It's so effortless. It's so *cool*. My chest feels like it's filled with glitter. I'm a kaleidoscope of nerves.

"Who's that?" Miranda says, nudging me. "You like him?"

My head jerks to her. She's staring at Michael too, head tilted to the side in that beautiful way of hers that I couldn't imitate even if I tried.

"What?" I scoff. "No."

Dad's eyebrows pull in. I can feel my face heat, and I wonder if the sun has already burned me that fast. I swear I put on sunscreen.

"Oh, come on, Ruby." Miranda snickers. "He's totally cute."

I shift from foot to foot. Well, *of course* he's cute. He's *Michael* with his black hair and blue eyes and every-day-of-the-week football jerseys. And he's looking at *me*.

I jump at the sound of a loud squeal, and some girl runs past us, long, beautiful legs extending into a run, before she barrels into Michael's arms. Her skin is dark and smooth—not bombarded with dumb freckles or caked in layers of sunscreen.

He wasn't looking at me at all.

"Oh," Miranda says.

Yeah. *Oh.*

But just before I turn away, I finally see someone else sidestepping through the crowd. It's a much more familiar face, and any of the shimmering in my chest that shone for Michael gets ramped up to a billion when I see my best friend.

Bennett has no idea where he's going. He's looking through the arms of an older man in suspenders, glancing around a stroller, and stumbling into a scene where a man is on one knee in front of a woman. His hands fall by his sides in frustration. When Bennett tries to apologize, he accidentally knocks over a cup on the fountain's ledge, fumbles it, and places it back.

My best friend is a mess, but my mouth still twitches into a smile.

"It's a crush, Ruby," Miranda says. "It's totally normal."

A crush? On Bennett?

But then I notice she's still staring at Michael.

Oh.

Well, that's not right. I don't have a crush on Michael, do I? Not when I get those same weird feelings around Bennett, and I know for a fact that I definitely don't *like*, like him. He's my best friend—not a *crush*.

"You should tell him, girlie," she says.

A nervous laugh bubbles out of me like a shaken soda can.

"Michael? No, no, no."

She straightens her spine, spreading her palms over the fabric of her skirt. "Take what you want in life. That's what I do." Her eyes cut over to my dad when she says it.

I look back out in the crowd, and Bennett's already running toward us with the biggest grin.

Bennett got braces this summer, and now, every time he smiles, green little bubbles stare back at me. When he first got them, we wanted to see how many pieces of spaghetti we could wind through them, but when his mom saw us with the box of noodles, she instead gave us her sewing kit and sat with us while I threaded Bennett's teeth with pink string. We couldn't stop laughing for an hour.

"Hey, Rubes." He's out of breath after running to us,

pushing his fingers through his messy black hair that now falls around his neck like a lion's mane.

He's gotten taller. I don't remember when it happened, but one day, my neck started hurting from looking at him so long, and I realized we weren't the same height anymore.

"You're late," I observe. "You okay?"

His hand is on my lower back, steadying me closer to him so he can hear my words when I speak. I like how he smells today. He has some unique blend of his mom's coffee and pancake syrup and sweat, but under all of that, Bennett's hair always smells like strawberries.

He sighs. "Sorry. Mom couldn't get off work in time."

"Oh. It's okay. That stinks though."

Bennett waves his hand at me. "It's fine. Anyway, happy birthday!"

"Happy birthday to you too!"

"Mom has your carrot cake at the house whenever you want."

I squint. "Did you eat some of it?"

"With these?" he says, poking his braces. "No way. Carrots would get all stuck."

"You don't fool me, rabbit," I tease.

He barks out a laugh with his head tilted back. "Got me."

My stomach feels like glitter all over again.

A crush.

No, Miranda is wrong. This isn't what a crush feels like.

I glance over at Michael, still leaning against the queue line for The Grizzly with his hands in his pockets, looking up with the arc of his neck pointing to the sky.

I pull in a sharp inhale, and it takes a moment to swallow.

Now, *that* might be a crush.

"All right, children, we doing this or not?" Dad asks.

I stiffen for a moment, but Bennett nudges me to enter The Grizzly's queue.

"Go on, Rubes."

"You first."

"Chicken."

"Baby."

"Scaredy-cat."

We both run through, trying to race to the end of the line. After waiting another hour, we finally get on the ride, and Bennett sits next to me, as promised. My hands grip the lap bar, and right when we jolt forward, he takes my hand in his.

The Grizzly turns out to be wonderful, full of swoops and dips and everything I imagine a perfect roller coaster would be. I'm convinced whoever made it is a genius. I'm convinced even more that I want to be a genius designer too.

The sun exhausts us after we ride The Grizzly one more time, so we run to The Canoodler instead since it's indoors and cool. I lean my head on Bennett's shoulder, just like my mom does to my dad. I see why she does; it's relaxing. I don't remember some of the ride because I drift off a little. And when I open my eyes, Bennett has his head on top of mine, so I wonder if he fell asleep too.

Once we've ridden everything at least once—and The Grizzly four times—Dad, Miranda, and I shuffle into the car. I wave at Bennett, who's getting into his mom's car as we pull out of the lot.

Dad's eyes dart up to the rearview mirror. "So, how was today, honey?"

"Good," I say.

"And what was your favorite part?"

I smile again, but my cheeks hurt from all the smiling

I've done today. All I can think about is Bennett. Riding The Grizzly, screaming on The Beesting, eating too many pancakes, and then my nap on his shoulder.

"I slept with Bennett."

There's a screech. My seat belt jerks forward. Our car comes to a halt in the middle of the road. There's a honk behind us.

"You *what?!*"

I suddenly realize what I said and how it sounded, but all I hear is Miranda cackling in the front seat.

4

Ruby

Eighteen Years Before
Ruby & Bennett are Twelve Years Old

My hands are too slobbery to hold my fork, but that's the price I pay for feeding Moose under the table. And it's not like I was going to eat anyway.

It's quiet at our dinner table, just the sound of clinking utensils on plates as my parents do not talk for the third night in a row. I even showed them my perfect report card, which I was positive would cheer them up, but nobody even cracked a smile.

Moose's massive head nudges my leg. I take a chunk of my chicken and tuck it under the tablecloth again.

"Amelia, stop feeding the dog."

My head snaps up. Mom's lips are pursed.

Busted.

Mom doesn't normally have such a harsh look. But lately, something has changed.

My dad halts his fork halfway to his mouth. "Do you not like chicken anymore?" he asks.

"She doesn't like anything, Dick."

Mom started with this new nickname. She says it's a short version of Richard, and when Bennett and I looked it up on the internet, we found she was right. But I also know what else that word means.

I know because, years ago, Bennett and I looked that word up after some kid in class called another kid a *dick*. Unfortunately, our search also pulled up pictures of misshapen hot dogs, which I also now know are penises.

However, at the time, Bennett snapped out of the browser window before I could get a better look. He acted super weird for the rest of the afternoon. It took one hour of watching wrestling for him to finally chill out and explain to me what I had seen.

His mom overheard us and said, "All men don't just have dicks; they are dicks too. Except you, kiddo."

Bennett held a fist in the air, as if in solidarity.

There were too many mysterious dicks that day.

"Can I be excused?" I ask.

Mom observes my plate, scouring it from edge to edge, like she's trying to clean it with her eyes. I don't know why; her plate has more food than mine.

"You haven't eaten anything."

"Yes, I have."

"If she doesn't wanna eat, she doesn't wanna eat," Dad says.

Mom's head swivels to him, and in a very low, almost-hushed whisper—even though I can totally hear her—she hisses, "Why? So she can look skinny, like Miranda?"

The whole dinner vibe shifts. Dad buries his face in his palms. Mom twists her jaw, like she's prepping for a hot dog–eating competition. Or like maybe she's ready to bite off Dick's dick.

Mom has been bringing up Miranda a lot lately, as if she were some ghost in our home that wouldn't carry on to the afterlife. Sure, Miranda spends a lot of time with Dad, but she's also his assistant.

"I'll take the plates," I say because I really don't want to be in here if they're starting to fight.

Moose follows me into the kitchen with his nose in the air, tongue lolling out. After I pass through the swinging doors, I drop him a spare piece of chicken. I'm only human.

I pick up the phone beside the toaster, dialing my only lifeline.

It rings a few times before I hear Bennett's low tone say, "Hey, you."

You.

Bennett's voice has gotten lower over the summer, so when he says it like that, it almost sounds like a cat's purr or something. I love it every single time.

"Red alert," I whisper. "We've got *dick* talk going on over here."

"What?" His voice cracks.

"My mom and dad are fighting."

"Oh. Ha. Right. Still?"

"It's bad tonight."

"Is your mom still not eating?"

"Yeah. Well, sort of. Barely." I walk across the kitchen. The tip-taps of Moose's nails follow me.

"And did *you* eat?" Bennett asks.

"This isn't about me."

"It's always about you."

I roll my eyes even though I know he can't see it. Maybe he'll be able to feel it.

Bennett snorts. "You're rolling your eyes, aren't you?"

"So hard, it hurts."

"Rubes."

"I'll have you know that Moose ate very well."

"Ah, come on."

"I wasn't hungry!"

"No, your parents just can't cook," he says. "Come over here."

I look at the clock on the wall, but I don't know why I bother.

"Not a chance," I say. "It's late. And I gotta study."

"It's the middle of summer."

"Like that matters."

It doesn't. I have a summer reading list a mile long and practice problems my dad assigned me so I can test into advanced math classes in the fall. Plus, even if I had completed everything, I'm not allowed to go to Bennett's after a certain time. Period. Dad said it was because of our "growing bodies," which is so dumb. Just because our legs are longer doesn't mean we can't watch a movie together.

"Sneak out."

"Bennett, oh my God, no."

I immediately look at the dining room's double doors. My mom has the hearing of a bat, so I take a few steps to the opposite side of the kitchen.

"But Mom made hot wings," he singsongs.

I deflate onto the floor with my head tilted back against the cabinets.

"I *love* your mom's hot wings."

"I know," he says, and I can practically hear the smile in his voice. "So, sneak out."

"I guess I could ask ..."

"No asking. They'll just say no."

I groan.

From the other room, their voices get louder. Mom says something about *underwear* and *Brittney knew.*

"I can hear them," Bennett says. "Wait, did they mention my mom?"

"Yeah. I don't know what's happening."

"Come over." His voice is even. I don't hear his smile anymore. "Don't take no for an answer."

I laugh. "It's fine."

"If it's getting bad, Mom can take care of you," he says. And then I think I hear him swallow before he adds, "*I* can take care of you."

The familiar glitter—the kind that only appears when Bennett says things like that—slides over my chest and into my stomach. I never know what to say when he gets all boy-like and serious, so I sit on the line in silence.

He sighs. "Be a pirate for once, Rubes. Yarr?"

"I can't."

"Yeah, you can. Say it with me."

"Ha, no."

"Ruby."

"No."

"Rubes. Rubert. Rubothy."

"Fine. Yarr."

"There we go." I can finally hear his smile again. "I'll meet you in Miss Lisa's yard in thirty minutes."

"Maybe."

"Definitely."

I hang up, lean my head back against the wall, and blink up at the ceiling. I pull in a breath. I hold it for a few seconds, then let it out.

It's just a simple question. Maybe they'll be too distracted by their argument to care.

You can ask. You can do this.

Moose blinks up at me.

"I know; I know," I whine. "Have courage. I know."

I push open the double doors to the dining room. Mom and Dad are in different spots. She's standing in the corner with her arms crossed. Dad is still in his seat. His hair is disheveled, as if he's been running his hands through it.

"Hey," I say slowly. "Can I ask a question?"

Mom meets my gaze, and something in it looks different. Maybe it's the fact that her eyes are red or that I can see her hand shaking in the crook of her arm. Maybe it's because her bottom lip is doing that thing where it trembles in place when she's thinking about what to say, like a drum-roll to disappointing words—words like *you can't go to Bennett's house tonight*, which would totally suck but I can feel them in my bones.

Dad is the one who finally speaks. "Amelia, we need to talk."

5

Ruby

I bolt through the woods faster than I ever have before. The flashlight in my hand illuminates trees, then the ground, then branches again. I hate going down this trail by myself, but tonight, I don't care.

I jump over the creek, barrel through the chain-link fence, and rush to the Shaws' basement door—the direct entrance to Bennett's bedroom.

My fist pounds hard on the wood.

"Bennett," I say, but it's a whisper in the night, and my chest aches at the thought of not being heard.

I'm never freaking heard, am I?

The weird mix of emotions—anger, worry, hurt—all gargle inside me. I want to yell. I've never wanted to yell so much in my whole life.

So, I open my mouth and scream, "Bennett!" as my fist raps on the door again.

It's so *loud.*

Footsteps pound inside the house, the basement stairs creak, and through the square window, I see he's finally here. Bennett's eyebrows are pulled together so tightly that there's a distinct line running between them. He fumbles to unlock the dead bolt, then the chain before whipping the door open.

Within seconds, I'm in his arms.

In even less time, he's tugging me tighter, pressing his cheek against mine, and saying, "What's wrong? I thought we were meeting in five more minutes."

"I went through the woods by myself," I murmur against his chest.

His head rears back. "Is everything okay?" His palms rest on either of my cheeks as he tilts my face to his. "Are you all right?"

"Mom is moving out."

An exhale leaves him as he breathes out, "What?"

"They're breaking up." The end of the sentence is warbled as I shove my face back into his chest and cry.

I cry so hard because Bennett has always said it's okay to cry, and I can't imagine not crying right now.

"How the heck can you *break up* when you're married?" I say, but half the words come out as garbled nonsense. I keep saying them anyway. "When you said vows that meant forever? When you laugh together? When they're the person you can count on for everything?"

Bennett's hand strokes my back. "Ruby ..."

I wonder if their relationship flashed before their eyes as they ended it. It did for me. All the times they had sat on opposite sides of the couch but told me it was so I could snuggle between them. When they had stopped sleeping in the same bed, but it was because Dad snored too loud. How they wouldn't kiss when Mom got home from a week of travel, but they had said that was because they needed to clean or make dinner or ...

Lies. So many lies.

Bennett reaches behind me and shuts the door, but he doesn't stop hugging me for one single second.

My person doesn't let me go.

From the stairwell, I hear Brittney yell down, "Everything all right?"

"Everything's fine, Mom," Bennett calls back. "Be up later. Ruby ..."

I shake my head. I can't see anyone but him right now.

"Ruby's just got some homework questions first."

"All right then! I'll get some extra wings on the grill!"

The door closes, and I cuddle closer.

"Want to lie down?" he asks.

I sniff and whimper out a small, "Yes."

Running his hand down my arm and over my wrist, he entwines our fingers together and walks me back to the mattress on the floor. When Bennett moved down to their finished basement, the bed's box spring never fit through the doorway. I like the floor mattress though.

He lies down first, scooting back to the wall of pillows. I crawl on top of him, like I always do, nestling my head onto his chest, settling my torso between his skinny legs. His hand rests on my lower back.

Finally, he sucks in a breath.

"Are you moving out with your mom?" Bennett asks.

"No," I say. "She travels too much. Dad and I are staying here."

He exhales his held breath, followed by a laugh. "Good. I'd hate if you left. Who would tell me jokes?"

I laugh a little, but honestly, I didn't even think about that. The thought of leaving Bennett crawls under my skin. I would miss all of this. Bennett's posters of professional wrestlers or rock bands; the smell of wood and clanking of screws in the corner of the basement, where Bennett tinkers endlessly; and the small, slightly battered brown desk with a computer and RollerCoaster Tycoon installed just for me.

I nestle my head into his chest more.

"What happened?" he asks calmly.

"I don't know. They wouldn't tell me."

"I'm sorry, Rubes."

"It just doesn't make sense. I thought marriage meant forever."

"It does."

I lean my head up. "Was your mom ever married?"

"No," he says.

"Because of your dad?"

"Yeah."

"Did she ever want to be?"

Bennett slowly nods. "She told me one time that she waited for him for a while. She said she isn't anymore, but I think she still might be."

My heart races, sparked by anger and frustration. My emotions are fuming out of me.

"How does it happen?" I ask. "Like, how do two people who love each other finally decide not to?"

Bennett sits there, silent, before shrugging. "I don't know, Rubes."

"It's so unfair," I spit out.

"I've never seen you this angry."

"I'm *so* angry. And you know what? I don't think I want to get married. Ever."

"Why not?"

"It's not worth it," I say. "Marriage ruins love."

"You think?"

"Definitely. I wouldn't marry anyone."

After a few moments, Bennett says, "Well, I'd marry you."

My head whips up, almost as fast as the way my heart is racing.

"What?" I ask.

"I think we could get married."

"But you're my best friend."

A slow smile rises on his face, revealing the green braces beneath his lips.

"Exactly," he says. "Maybe that's the secret. Marrying your best friend or something. Do you wanna get married to me, Ruby?"

That sentence makes my heart, which beat with anger seconds ago, now feel different. Like those little, familiar pieces of sparkling glitter.

I laugh. "You're ridiculous."

"I'm serious," he says. "Why not?"

"Because we're twelve."

"Okay, obviously, we won't get married *now*."

Bennett sits up, and I crawl off him. He pulls his knees to his chest. His smile is getting so big that his eyes start to squint. I see the full range of green tracks on his teeth. He only smiles like that when he's the happiest. I just didn't know the thought of marrying *me* could make him that happy.

"If we're not married when we're old, let's do it," he says.

"When?"

"I don't know. What's an old age?"

"Thirty seems super old."

"Definitely," he says with a laugh. "So, thirty then."

"Well, what if we break up?" I ask. "I could never *not* have you in my life."

He leans forward, placing a palm on the bedsheets between us. My heart jumps.

"Rubes, I would never break up with you once we're married."

The promise hits me in the chest, leaving my nerves sizzling afterward, like fireworks slowly crackling out and disappearing. It's that energy again. The need to *do* something. To be louder. To run down that spooky trail between our houses. To feel the energy flow out of my lungs.

"You promise?" I whisper.

"Here, hang on."

Bennett stands from the bed, walking over to his corner workshop. He digs through the messy toolbox, tossing aside a tape measure, a hammer, a box of nails. It all clatters to the floor, the carpet barely managing to silence it. Whenever Bennett gets an idea, the whole house knows about it.

"You should get a new box," I observe.

"Nah, works just fine," he says. "If it ain't broke, don't fix it. Oh! Here we go."

He rips out a small spool of pink string—the same string we looped through his wires years ago when he first got braces.

"Okay ... what about it?"

Bennett crosses over to me, crawling back onto the bed. He sits on his feet, just like I am, and our knees knock against each other.

"Ow."

"Sorry. Okay, so my mom told me some people get promise rings if they wanna get married later," he says. "So, what if ... we do that too?"

"With string?"

"Sure!"

He's holding the string in the palm of his hand, his grin so wide that it's infectious, and a smile pulls up my cheeks as well.

With a breathy, excited laugh, Bennett pulls the end, sending the spool bouncing to the mattress. He keeps tugging until the string is long, and then he pulls it between his teeth and gnaws until it breaks.

"Gross," I say with a laugh. "Now, I'll have your spit on me."

"Whoops." But he still carries on, wrapping it over and over so the string layers up. "Okay, now, give me your arm."

I hold out my wrist, and his hands slide over mine. The pads of his fingers feel rough. It must be from the constant building and hammering and whatever boy stuff he gets into. But as they slide over my wrist, they're lighter. Gentler. Like he's handling me with care.

I watch him work, thinking about what Miranda said about crushes. How my chest does feel like sparklers are glimmering inside. How maybe crushes are just the people you like having around you.

Bennett's thumb lingers on my wrist bone as he knots my bracelet.

He holds out his palms, as if saying, *Ta-da!*

I twist my wrist around to see the knotted and frayed string. It's haphazard, but it's also very Bennett.

"What do you think?" he asks.

"It's perfect."

His smile beams at me before he picks up the thrown-aside spool and tugs out a fresh piece of string.

"What are you doing?"

"I'm making one for me too."

"Isn't pink too girlie for you?"

"Nothing with you is too anything." He says it so casually, like it's as routine as brushing your teeth or eating breakfast.

Is promising to spend forever with me really that easy?

50

Bennett twirls and tugs the string before biting it off, then loops it around his wrist.

"Can you knot it?" he asks.

"I don't know how."

"I'll walk you through it. Go over the—yep. Then make the—uh-huh. See? You know what you're doing."

The sentence, low and whispering, has me smiling wider. He's always whispering encouragement to me. He's the most supportive person I know. But this feels different.

When I sit back, I look at him. Really look at him. How his cheekbones are a bit more defined than they were last summer. How his shoulders are wider. How his wrists are bony with little veins trialing up his skinny forearms. How he has an Adam's apple that moves when he laughs, which he's doing now, as if this whole process is just another one of our adventures.

We sit there with our wrists side by side, branded by a knotted pink string.

"See? Easy-peasy. And when we're twenty-nine or whatever, I'll propose at Honeywood and everything."

"Why?"

He twists his bracelet around. "I don't know. That's what people do, I think."

"Can I have flowers too?"

"Roses?"

"No. Yuck. They smell."

"They really do," he says, laughing. "So, what flowers do you want?"

"I don't know." I run a thumb over the pink string. "Anything. As long as you handpick it."

"I can do that."

I swallow, twirling the knots of my bracelet and sighing. "You'll never leave me, right?"

His thumb and forefinger land on my chin, and he tilts my head up. My heart catches in my throat when his dark brown eyes meet mine.

"Never. And you'll never leave me either, right?"

"Right."

"Good. Only"—Bennett looks away, counting on his fingers silently—"eighteen more years."

"Not too bad."

"Nah. It'll fly by."

"What do we do until then?"

"I don't know. Wanna watch TV?"

We search for the remote in his messy room, then turn the TV on. Once we do, there's a commercial for those cheesy mixed CDs with a bunch of love songs. Celine Dion. Etta James.

I wonder if these songs will play at our wedding one day.

6

Bennett

Fifteen Years Before
Ruby & Bennett are Fifteen Years Old

"Shop class is nowhere near Robotics."

Ruby's face is pulled tight in concentration, eyes darting from my unfolded class schedule to the school map in her opposite hand. I lean forward, hovering over her as I try to catch a glance too. My long hair cascades around us, creating a secret canopy. She peers up through ginger lashes, a sly smile on her face.

"We're gonna get in trouble."

I grin down at her. "Why do you say that?"

" 'Cause it looks like ... you know what." She uses her delicate finger to part a piece of my hair like curtains. "Yeah, he's totally staring at us again."

I grumble, straightening my posture and pocketing my hands as I lean back on my heels to wave at Ruby's Advanced Placement English teacher. He glares at me with fire in his eyes. I imagine he doesn't like his star student hanging around with the boy in a black band tee and ripped jeans with hair that looks like I'm auditioning for *America's Next Top Biker*—at least, that's what my mom says.

He waves the back of his hand out, as if to say, *Keep moving.*

"Looks like we can walk until ..." Ruby starts, but the words fade into the cacophony of high school chaos—loud voices, a distant whoop, and smacking sneakers with rattling key chains—as someone jogs past us.

"Hey, no running!" Ruby's teacher calls, huffing and clenching fists by his sides as he walks off from his classroom doorway in pursuit.

I take the opportunity to lean down, placing my hand on Ruby's lower back. My hair hangs around us again.

"Sorry, what did you say? It's too loud."

"Or I'm too quiet."

"No, you're perfect. This place just sucks."

"No, it doesn't," she replies with a giggle. "I love school."

I can't help the grin that spreads over my face. "I know you do."

It's only the first week of high school, but Ruby has taken to it like a fish to water. She's already tackling the assigned books for her new slew of advanced classes, including ones not offered to freshmen.

On the first day of school, Ruby's dad, dressed in his golfing best, performed a very pompous, "Paul!" and, "Richard!" exchange with our new principal.

Ruby said they were fraternity brothers back in the day. But while we both scrunched our noses and scoffed at the sight of her dad acting like he owned the place, Ruby's schedule was ultimately adjusted to fit the most exclusive of advanced classes. I guess there's something to be said about your dad having connections.

"C'mon. Let's just go." Ruby laughs, tugging at my free wrist. "We're gonna be late."

I keep my hand on her lower back as we navigate the hallway traffic. Her petite frame allows her just enough room to squeeze through, and then my bulky body follows behind. All week, we've had a small line behind us, other students using our carved path like ducklings.

"Damn, it gets worse every day," I say.

"Language," Ruby whispers, giving me a teasing half-smile.

"Not that one either?"

"Well, if I didn't like the A-word, I'm definitely not gonna like that one."

"I'm just trying it out," I say. "See if I like it."

"You rebel, you. You're gonna be too cool for me one day."

"Impossible. You're in Robotics."

"Hey!"

"I mean that in the best way, Rubes."

"Sure you do."

Robotics *is* super cool.

Ruby stops in front of the Shop class, and I halt behind her.

"Aren't we going to your class first?" I ask.

"Your door is here though."

"Ruby Sullivan, walking me to class? I'm so honored."

She pushes my arm. "Shut up."

I let out a mock gasp. "Ouch."

But when she turns away to blush and I try to mirror her motion to further the joke, I instead catch eyes with Sarah. She's a girl in our grade, and, boy, she changed over the summer. Her legs are longer. Her skin is almost golden. As she walks past, her eyes scan me from head to toe. Her tongue darts out to lick her lips. They're very pink, and for a split second, I wonder how the gloss tastes.

I swallow at the thought, averting my gaze back to Ruby, who stares at me with her mouth hanging open. Her lips are a softer pink than Sarah's.

Wait, when did my best friend's lips get so pink?

"Be less obvious," Ruby says with a snort, digging into her backpack.

"About what?"

"Sarah."

"What about her?"

"Seriously?" Ruby tilts her hip to the side.

I glance at her floral T-shirt, all the way down to her pink Converse. She sure isn't dressed in a low-cut top, like Sarah's, but Ruby's attitude, juxtaposed with all the pink, is enough to make me smile wider.

"You know, you don't think you're cool, but I think you're the coolest, Parrot."

Ruby's face flushes red, blending into her mess of freckles.

"I'm not. But maybe I'll borrow one of your band T-shirts," she teases. "See how the hard-core look feels."

Maybe she doesn't remember, but she already did borrow one of my shirts. This summer, Ruby had to throw on my Red Hot Chili Peppers shirt after we both fell in the creek. My T-shirt swallowed her whole, landing just above her skinny knees and onto freckled thighs that I couldn't tear my eyes away from.

"Maybe not," I find myself saying, running a hand through my tangled hair.

Ruby huffs out a disbelieving breath. "You just don't want me to be cool!"

"I told you, you're already cool."

"No, I'm not. I need a new personality."

I laugh. "A new personality?"

"I don't know. I want some type of change." The energy shifts, and her pink lips turn downward. "Something ... new."

Ruby's been doing this more lately—finding little things about herself to change. First, it was trying out different shoes—from bulky sneakers to Converse. Then, it was wearing pants instead of skirts. Then, it was skirts again or dresses or something called skorts.

And it all started because of—

Oh.

"Ah crap, I forgot," I confess. "Wicked stepmom's moving in this weekend, isn't she?"

"Yep," Ruby mumbles, popping the *P.*

"God. I'm sorry. That's weird."

Ruby's eyes grow wide, and her hand flies in the air. "It *is* weird, right? Like ... Miranda's his *assistant.*"

After her parents' divorce, her dad and Miranda started dating. We don't talk about it much because Ruby tends to shut down when we do, burying her nose in homework or hunching over my computer to build yet another theme park in RollerCoaster Tycoon.

Part of me wonders if the timeline is correct. I have a theory Miranda and Mr. Sullivan started dating *before* the divorce, but I try not to think about that too much.

Miranda is Mr. Sullivan's prized possession. Unless Ruby is getting the highest grade in class, all conversation is turned to Miranda. Something about her captured Mr. Sullivan, and Ruby has been working to get his attention back ever since. I guess if my dad wasn't a total piece of garbage, I'd want the same thing.

I curl my thumb under her matching pink string, placing a hand on the hallway's brick wall behind her. "Okay, new personality then. Oh! I've got an idea. How about we call you Ruby 2.0? That's a cool nickname, right? Fits your Robotics image?"

"Bennett, we're going for cool."

"Robotics is totally cool, Robo-Ruby."

She smiles. "R2-B2."

"The Rube-inator."

"Rube-E."

"Nice."

I raise my hand for a high five. She smacks her hand with mine. And just as our hands meet, I see her eyes wander over my shoulder. Those green eyes get a weird haze to them, and I don't need to look to know why.

Michael.

I follow her gaze to confirm—yep, there he is—then roll my eyes.

Football team captain. Swoopy hair. Blue eyes that look too blue. It's all part of his image. I'm convinced he's secretly an alien, posing as a person. Plus, I think his face looks like a lopsided potato. His cheekbones are too high. His jaw is too curved. I don't know; maybe girls like that kind of thing.

When I turn back to Ruby, I can't see the pink of her lips anymore. They're pulled in.

It's definitely Ruby's kind of thing.

"Earth to Ruby?"

"Hmm? Oh. Right." She shakes her head. "Um, what were we talking about?"

But just when I open my mouth to continue, a body

bumps into me. I twist, accidentally bumping them back-ward again. Books clutter to the floor.

It's a girl with wavy brown hair, pushed back with a headband. She bends to pick up the books. Ruby and I crouch to help her. I grab a binder, littered with various Honeywood Fun Park stickers.

"I'm sorry!" Flustered, she waves her hand around. "I should watch where I'm going."

"Nah, it's fine."

I hand her back what I picked up. So does Ruby.

This girl is tall, maybe only a couple of inches shorter than me. She wears a T-shirt with The Grizzly's logo.

"Honeywood fan?" I ask because I know Ruby wants to, but probably won't.

When it's just me and her, Ruby is confident and loud and the funniest person I know. But new people? It takes a bit of time.

The girl grins. "Big fan. You?"

"She is," I say, throwing a thumb over my shoulder.

"I like your shirt," Ruby comments.

The girl pinches the T-shirt up at the shoulder and looks down at it, as if admiring the design.

"Oh. Thanks!" she says. "Yeah, The Grizzly's my favorite."

Ruby smiles. "Me too."

"Me three," I say, which makes both girls laugh.

"I'm gonna apply to work there this year," the brown-headed girl says. She crosses her fingers. "Well, hopefully."

"Same," I say. "Next year, I mean."

"Are y'all freshman?"

"Guilty," Ruby chimes in, making this girl laugh.

She points to herself. "I'm a sophomore. It gets easier, I promise."

59

"Lore! LORELEI ARDEN!"

The three of us turn at the screams of another girl barreling down the hall, mouth open in a *Muppets*-like gesture, still mid-yell. And she's coming right toward us.

Our new brown-haired pal—I guess, Lorelei?—says, "Oh my God, what's going on?"

And that's when I realize the running girl is crying. Or on the verge of tears. Wetness bubbling up beneath her eyes, red-rimmed with blotchy cheeks. She's looking away from Lorelei, as if she's holding them in. It's such a contrast to how she's dressed. The girl's clothes are black on black on black. Thick black eyeliner. Bulky black shoes. Black fishnets. The only thing not seemingly menacing about her are her pink braces and her long blonde hair—so light that it looks like it belongs on one of Ruby's old Barbie dolls.

"Your brother and his football buddies," she says, gritting her teeth. "And *Michael*."

"What'd he do?" I ask.

The goth girl is having trouble forming words.

"They stole ... I ..."

Lorelei reaches out and strokes her arm. "Quinn, breathe."

The girl—Quinn—nods quickly, sucking in a shaky breath and letting it out less than a second later. But it's overshadowed by a small cough and a wet laugh, as if she's disappointed in herself for getting overwhelmed.

"If you breathe slower, it helps," Ruby says.

Quinn sniffs and wipes the back of her hand across her face. Then, she does exactly as Ruby said—she breathes slower. A couple of seconds in. Then out. At least she isn't laughing at herself anymore.

Her eyes focus on the door Michael just passed through, then back to Lorelei.

"Sorry, I can't believe I'm crying over that jerk," Quinn murmurs.

I shrug. "It's okay to cry."

She eyes me, then Ruby, her eyebrows furrowing into a glare. "Who are you?"

"Sorry, I'm Bennett. This is Ruby."

Quinn shakes her head with a grimace. "Uh, okay. Whatever." Her head swivels back to Lorelei. "Lore, we're skipping class."

"What?" Lorelei hiss-whispers. "Quinn! It's the first week!"

"I can't be in class right now. Look at me! I'm a fucking mess."

Ruby lets out a small peep behind me at the curse word, and I have to cover my mouth to stop from laughing.

Lorelei bites her lip, tilting her head side to side.

"Lore," Quinn whines, her hands slapping together in prayer. "Please."

Lorelei's eyes dart to the clock on the white brick wall.

"Okay. Yes," she whines. "We'll skip. But only this one time!"

"One time," Quinn agrees. "Promise."

She grips Lorelei's arm, tightening like she's her lifeline. Lorelei grips hers back with a weak smile. It reminds me of when Ruby and I hold hands sometimes. I think I might like these two.

"Go to the locker rooms in the basement," I suggest. "I bet the teachers don't check there."

Quinn's eyes roam over me, as if assessing me. A squint here, a snarl there, and finally, she must see something satisfactory because she sniffs out, "Thanks."

"No problem."

This girl might look tough, but the tears say otherwise.

"Do y'all want to come?" Lorelei proposes, looking between me and Ruby even though Quinn is already rolling her eyes in disagreement.

I open my mouth, then close it and let out a breathy chuckle. "Yeah, probably not. I don't think I should be in the girls' locker room."

Lorelei laughs. "Fair. Okay, well, *you* are coming then."

"Wh-what?" Ruby stammers out before her arm is getting tugged forward by Quinn, mumbling, "If we must."

The warning bell chimes through the hallway speakers. Quinn waves her hands in the air.

"Okay. If we're going, let's hurry, team!"

I can see the nerves transform to giddiness in Ruby's eyes. That same look she got wearing Converse for the first time. It's rebellion she's interested in. Her version of it, anyway.

I nudge her with my elbow. "Go."

"No pressure," Lorelei says.

Quinn starts to walk backward. "Nope, tons of pressure. Move it or lose it, lady."

I place my palm on Ruby's lower back and lean down so my hair shrouds us once more. Our own fortress of solitude.

"Be a rebel, cool girl."

Her face flushes again—that light pink that matches her newly pink lips.

She swallows and nods. "Yeah. I can be cool, right?"

"*So* cool."

I hold up my hand for a high five. She slaps my palm.

"Okay," she says. "Let's go."

Our new friend Quinn grabs her arm once more and drags her off. I watch the three of them run until Ruby's panicked giggles disappear around the corner.

Ruby *is* the absolute coolest.

The bell rings.

Looking back down at my schedule, I follow the map until I find the doorway in front of me. A sign above the threshold reads *Shop Class*. And it's the same doorway Michael passed through minutes before.

I groan.

Here we go, I guess.

7

Bennett

I expected Shop class to feel like home, and it passes the test.

There are pegboards on the wall with different tools I'm familiar with and some I'm not, but can't wait to toy with. The floor, while seemingly clean, hides tiny piles of sawdust in the corners, just like my basement at home. There are even half-built birdhouses stored on shelves that look similar to the one I constructed for my mom last summer.

This class might be perfect ... were it not for Michael and his cackling brood of football pals.

The blue-eyed menace is already sitting on the corner of a desk, laughing with his whole chest, like he's giving the funniest stand-up routine and enjoying his own jokes.

Worst comedian ever.

I've never met my dad, but I'm willing to bet he's a lot like Michael. Loud. Full of himself. Punchable.

The rest of his pals are performing fabulous impressions of hyenas, save for a tall guy at the end of their table with his head buried in his palms.

I feel your pain, buddy.

I don't bother walking past; I want to sit at the front of the room anyway. I claim a seat and attempt to read my textbook, but it doesn't block out whatever nonsense is leaving Michael "Potato Face" Waters's mouth.

"The look on her face, I swear," he jeers. "And then you! And your whole, 'Not a chance.' That was even more brutal than me, Arden."

I peer over to see the tall guy shift uncomfortably in his chair, twirling a pen between his fingers.

"Let's drop it, okay?" he mumbles.

"Dude, you know she's in love with you."

"Michael, come on."

The other guys laugh and start up the totally mature chant of, "Landon and Quinn sitting in a tree—"

My body tenses, and I grip my textbook.

Quinn?

"Y'all are seriously five years old," the tall guy I assume is named Landon says. "She dropped her diary. We read it. And what we said was mean and wrong. Let's grow up, okay?"

He whips his pen in his hand harder.

So, that's why Quinn was crying. I don't like it when girls cry. Not because it makes me uncomfortable, but because my mom preaches that's one of men's biggest crimes. If you make a girl cry, you're the problem. And Michael seems like a big problem.

"Ooh, are you planning your wedding?" he continues. "Did *Mrs. Landon Arden* do something to you? Maybe touch your—"

A fist slams on the tabletop. "Hey," Landon snaps. "Shut up. She's my sister's best friend. That's it."

Something tells me Michael didn't want to hear that.

"What did you just say to me, Arden?"

And then, because I'm tired of it all, I also pull in a heavy sigh and say, "You heard him, man."

The room goes quiet. Dead quiet. Maybe it's one thing for someone *in* the group to talk back to Michael, but me? Not so much.

His creepy blue eyes swivel over.

Ah shit.

"I'm sorry, did you say something, freshman?"

Not your monkeys, not your circus. Not your monkeys, not your—

"Sure did," I say, turning at the waist with my arm slung over the chair. "Got a problem with it?"

Michael hops off the table and saunters toward me.

Saunters.

Is the guy serious right now?

Maybe the football king thinks he carries himself with the swagger of John Wayne, but he looks more like a drunken sailor to me. In that moment, I see my dad clear as day—his chin tipped up, his haughty and slimy sneer. It's the attitude of a guy who thinks he's cooler than he actually is.

But then something flashes over Michael's face, and he holds out a pointed finger.

"Wait a second. I know you."

"You know me?" I drawl in a bored tone.

"Yeah. You're the guy who hangs out with that pretty redhead."

It's almost surprising how quickly my face heats. My fingers twitch on the back of the chair. My jaw tightens. And Michael's potato face pulls into a nasty grin.

"Oh, did I touch a nerve? Is that your little girlfriend?"

I blink for a moment.

Ruby? My girlfriend?

I've never connected the two. She's a girl. She's my friend. But all the ancillary things that come with the combination of the words? Not so much.

"She's like a sister to me," I scoff. But even as I say it, the room suddenly seems colder. I can feel every ridge in my chair, every curve of the cool steel leg forming the seat I'm in. I shift and adjust my feet, trying to find a position that feels comfortable again.

His eyes dart to my movement, then back up. "Dude, do you have a sister?"

I glare. "No. What's it matter?"

"Well, *I* have a sister."

"Good for you."

"And she's disgusting," he continues. "I don't look at my gross sister like you do with Red."

Heat starts in my chest and spreads out like molten lava across my shoulders and into my arms. My head swims.

Do I look at Ruby a certain way?

I mean, sure, I appreciate her longer legs now, but I like them because she's faster when we run down the trails together. She has softer skin, but that also is convenient ... for ... something. And her freckles. Well, I've always liked her freckles.

"Maybe you see her like a sister," Michael says, bringing me back. "But I sure don't."

"Michael," Landon says, pushing out from the table.

Michael is getting closer, slowly starting to tower over me. He wouldn't be so threatening if I were to stand up too. He's a big guy with broad football shoulders. But I'm bigger.

"Back up," I growl.

"In fact, I think she's really pretty."

My heart is racing, and my blood is pounding in my skull. I like to think I'm not a fighting kind of guy, but sometimes, people just have punchable faces. And this guy needed a fist in his potato face yesterday.

He leans in. I don't budge. We're almost nose to nose.

"Maybe she needs a real man."

And then the next words burst out of me so fast that I can't even remember when they landed in my thoughts.

"Touch her, and I'll kill you, Mikey."

Michael's head juts back, and he tongues the inside of his cheek before smirking at me like I'm a bug ready to be stomped on.

Give it a try, buddy.

"What the fuck did you just call me?" he asks.

I can hear Ruby's little voice, muttering, *Language!* in my head. I want to laugh, but it seems like the wrong time.

"Are you seriously smiling at me right now, freshman?"

Okay, so maybe I did anyway.

"Michael ..." Landon has gotten up and walked behind him, placing a hand on his shoulder. Michael rolls his arm back, and Landon's hand falls. "Come on, man. You're being a dick."

"You know what?" Michael says, his face getting redder. "Maybe I *will* ask her out. Maybe I'll even peek under those skirts of hers. Maybe I'll see if the carpet matches the—"

What happens next occurs too fast.

My chair shrieks across the floor as I stand. My body tenses as I shove my hands into his shoulders. Michael's shocked face forms a silly little O. A chair clatters as he stumbles into it. Then, his body and the chair hit the ground.

I want to say I don't know why I did it. But I do.

Michael isn't just the guy who insulted my best friend. He's also a glimmer of my dad in that moment. The guy who probably wondered the same thing about my mom at our age. The guy who knocked her up and left. And I don't have time for boys disrespecting *my* girls.

The Shop teacher walks in, hands holding a stack of papers. One look at the scene, and they flutter to the ground.

I sigh, "Fuck."

And Ruby's little voice in my head hisses, *Language!*

8

Bennett

Fourteen Years Before
Ruby & Bennett are Sixteen Years Old

"Oh, look. A code of conduct. Your sworn enemy."

I roll my eyes and lightly swipe the back of my knuckles against Ruby's pointed finger.

She giggles.

"I'm not gonna pick a fight at Honeywood," I say, flipping to the next page of the booklet. "This is my work. I know better."

Ruby traces a finger over the picnic tabletop. "Those words are right out of your mom's mouth."

"Hey, I'm a rule follower now. New leaf, okay?"

"Doubtful."

I glance up at Ruby right as she curls her bottom lip in, and I wonder not for the first time if they get a prettier shade of pink every year.

She sticks out her tongue—even pinker.

I like autumn in Honeywood Fun Park. The slight breeze, the look of the trees shaking off their brown and red leaves, the smell of their all-day pancakes with their limited-time apple-flavored syrup. I'm thrilled to finally be filling out new-hire paperwork, but I can't focus if my best friend keeps distracting me.

Lorelei and Quinn started working at Honeywood last summer, and this fall, I'm finally joining them. I was supposed to apply this past summer, but school took up most of my time. Turns out, not completing homework for every class, except Shop, lands you in summer school. I understand all the concepts; homework is just a waste of time when I could be building stuff instead. Cedar Cliff High curriculum doesn't agree.

I change the subject. "How was girls' day with Miranda?"

Ruby tilts her head to the side, tucking a strand of ginger hair behind her ear, showing off a shimmering gold stud.

"Oh, wow," I say, placing down my pen. "Look at you. Pierced ears."

"Miranda let me."

"She's really going for the Best Mom award, huh?"

"She's winning."

I wince. To her credit, Ruby does too.

"Rubes ..."

"What? I'm allowed to be mean," she mumbles, picking off a loose splinter from the picnic table. "She's the one who left, so ..."

Ruby hasn't seen her mom since last Christmas. Ms. Sullivan was already scarce due to work travel, but once her dad and Miranda tied the knot in an intimate ceremony in Cedar Cliff's white chapel, I think that was the final tipping point for her to start a completely separate life from her ex-husband. Now, all Ruby receives are postcards or envelopes with free key chains from work conferences her mom attends.

"It's fine," Ruby says quickly, giving a weak smile.

I can tell she's trying to ignore her feelings because if she discusses her mom too much, then her feelings transform to anger, and even though she gets feisty when she's angry and I kind of like that, I know she hates the feeling. So, when Ruby gets to this point where she can no longer carry her own emotions, I try to shoulder some for her.

"It's not fine," I correct. "On the bright side ... I guess my mom can finally give you all her old jewelry now. She'll love that. And they look great!"

I reach up and trace my thumb over the new gold stud. Ruby sucks in a breath.

"Oh, sorry, does that hurt?" I ask.

"No."

I pull my hand away anyway. Another one of Mom's lessons is that if someone looks uncomfortable, you don't keep doing what you're doing.

"Dad didn't like them," Ruby admits.

"No?"

"No, but when Miranda said it was her idea, he was immediately fine with it."

"Dang," I say, heaving an exhale. "Rough day, Parrot. We've got the mom and dad double-whammy comments."

"I'm on a roll."

"What kind of roll?" I offer because I know it'll lead to a joking bit, and I love her imagination.

"A sushi roll, obviously. With spicy tuna and cucumbers."

"You are a little spicy sometimes."

I smile. She returns the gesture before looking out across the grassy lawn. It's crowded with Honeywood guests enjoying the nice weather on checkered blankets. Even the parents have their fanny packs tossed to the side and shorts rolled up their thighs.

A breeze whips past, brushing a strand of ginger hair across Ruby's freckled cheek. It catches on her eyelashes, coated in a layer of black mascara, which she started wearing this past summer—a direct influence from Quinn.

While I miss seeing Ruby's pretty lighter lashes, there's also something about this new makeup that gives her an intense quality. It's as if the ferocity she has bottled up inside is getting time to shine.

Her solemn expression falls. "Oh no. Don't look now."

"Why?" I follow Ruby's line of sight, and the hair on my neck immediately stands up. Every bit of calm I have gets sucked right out of me. "Oh. Him."

Michael is standing across the midway, holding up his hand in a wave.

Ruby, her face now bright red, waves back. I do not.

Mikey has developed a rhythm when he sees us together. He'll toss a vicious glare at me, narrow-eyed, and then, like a light switch, he stares at my best friend with some half-raised smile that makes him look like Elvis. Or one of Honeywood's broken animatronics with a twitching eye and hanging jaw.

It's absurd.

But Ruby, with her bitten bottom lip, falls for it every time.

Every. Single. Time.

What the hell is the appeal?

Michael is tall, but so am I.

He has black hair, but so do I.

So do I.

It's not like I want Ruby looking at *me* or anything.

73

She's my best friend. But when she stares at Michael like his eyes have the answers to the universe, I want to push him all over again. And I might, too, if I knew my mom wouldn't ground me for three months afterward, like she had the last time.

Ruby leans her chin on her freckled knees again. Like little wisps of thoughts flow from her mind to mine, I can tell she's dreaming about his hair or eyes or whatever other heartthrob thing she thinks about.

Why Michael, of all people?

If it were anyone else, I don't think I'd care. It's the fact that it's *Michael*.

Quinn told us her side of the story when Michael stole her diary in the middle of the hallway. Apparently, Landon —Lorelei's brother—wasn't any better in the moment even if he did try to defend her in Shop class. Ruby, being a good friend, listened to Quinn with agreeable nods. But I think something about that story only captivated her more. Michael was no longer the football star, but the *bad boy*.

But I was the one who got detention, so aren't I *bad* too?

I flip open my employee booklet again.

No, I don't *want* to be the bad boy. Who cares if my best friend stares at me? I sure don't.

A hand slaps on the table, and we both jump.

"God, are you almost done with the paperwork yet?" Quinn takes a long slurp through her straw. "We've already ridden The Grizzly fifty bajillion times today. I need backup to convince Lorelei to ride something else."

"That last line *was* way too long," Lorelei chimes in. They both take a seat on the table—Lorelei on the seat across from me and Quinn climbing cross-legged on the tabletop. "You know, I think if they had a different queue system ..."

Quinn snorts. "Pitch it to Freddy at the next meeting."

Apparently, the general manager of Honeywood, Fred Louder—my boss now—is very receptive to suggestions. I just wish I could grow a mustache as thick as his. No dice yet.

Quinn bare-hands a single pancake from her black overalls pocket and rips into it with her teeth. "Whar to nehxt?"

Lorelei laughs, and I would, too, but from the corner of my eye, I see Michael walking past us again.

Okay, seriously, is he a stalker or something?

My eyes flash to Ruby, who has already clocked him.

Quinn's nose scrunches up. "Gross. Don't think about him, Rubes. He's trouble."

"I heard he broke up with Meghan," Lorelei says.

"So?" Quinn sneers, tearing off another bite of pancake.

"Well"—curiously, Lorelei's face reddens—"I heard it was because she didn't have ... y'know."

Ruby blinks. "Didn't have what?"

Lorelei quickly points at herself. All of us blink at her. Exhaling, she points at herself again. What's she pointing at? Her Grizzly T-shirt?

Ruby and I exchange a look.

"Boobs," Quinn blurts out. "She means boobs, guys."

"Oh!" Ruby and I chorus together.

Oh.

A ball of energy bounces through me, and my face suddenly feels like it's on fire.

Boobs.

Quinn barks out a laugh. "Embarrassed, Benny?"

"Ha. No."

I glance to Ruby again, but she's not looking back this time. Instead, she's staring down at her own chest.

Oh.

I forget my friends have boobs. We went to the community pool this past summer, and Quinn and Lorelei wore bikinis, and their boobs were just *there*, moving and just *existing* as my friends cannonballed into the pool. Ruby was forced to stay at home to finish her summer reading. But now, as I stare at The Beesting or the amphitheater or the Buzzy the Bear statue—literally anywhere but at my best friend—I wonder what *she* would look like in a bikini.

I shouldn't be thinking about her like that. There are other girls to imagine. Sarah. Stacey. Sadie. Some other S name.

Ruby doesn't say anything, but she does cross her arms over herself.

Something is wrong. I know my best friend. I also know she won't talk about her feelings with anyone but me.

"Hey," I say, folding my paperwork in half and tucking it into my back pocket. "I could use a break. I bet there's no line for The Canoodler. Let's go there."

"Ugh," Quinn groans. "That's a boring ride."

I knew she'd say that.

"Then, just me and Ruby will go. Right, Rubes?"

Ruby looks like she's fallen out of a dream, blinking up at me. "Huh? Yeah, sure."

"Well, I'd like to ride The Grizzly again," Lorelei says. "Quinn?"

Quinn groans but hops off the picnic table. "Fine, fine. One more time. But that's it! Then no more. Promise me."

But Lorelei, in her Grizzly T-shirt, gives a noncommittal, "*Mmhmm.*"

I snort a laugh.

Yeah, that won't be their last ride.

Our two groups part ways and, aside from our sneakers hitting the blacktop, it's silent between Ruby and I. A weird awkwardness that seeps into my bones and fingers. I'm not sure why though.

No, I am.

It's the thought of *boobs*.

Is that what Ruby's thinking about too?

I place my hand on her lower back and lean down. "Everything okay, Rubes?"

"Yep." The word is quick.

"Bzzt!" I say, making the sound of a game-show buzzer. "Wrong. Try again."

She tries to fight back a smile and keeps walking with her arms crossed.

"Really," she says, "I'm fine."

"I'm very persistent."

"Bennett."

"Ruby."

"I just wanna ride The Canoodler."

"All right then. And no talking too? Got it."

"Bennett ..."

But I make the motion of zipping my mouth closed and throwing away the key, making her bite her bottom lip to hold back laughter. Though I don't understand why she won't just let herself have fun.

We walk past The Bee-fast Stop, past the employee offices, and around the corner to The Canoodler. We quietly wind through the queue line ropes and step into an empty boat. It bobs side to side before the bored operator presses a button, and we roll off the moving platform and into the water.

Our lonely boat is no less quiet, just the lapping of water hitting against the outside. Once we cross into the tunnel, it's pitch-black, and I can't see a dang thing, except the occasional glow of a projector on the tunnel walls, displaying excerpts of the *Honeywood* movie.

There's a reason this ride has no line. It's basically a promotional ride for the movie. But it's always been our favorite. Ruby and I have ridden it so many times that we try to recite the next line before the recorded narrator says it.

But when I mouth the words, *In a world* ... Ruby doesn't follow along.

Her arms hold tighter over her body.

"Okay, I can't be quiet," I plead. "What's wrong?"

Her shoes squeak in the boat as she adjusts in her seat. "I don't wanna talk about it."

"Why?" I laugh. "You tell me everything."

"Not everything."

"Yeah, you do."

She doesn't respond.

"Rubes—"

"Do you think boob size matters?"

My face grows red hot. I immediately regret asking anything.

I scoot around in my seat, causing the boat to roll side to side in the water. "I ... I don't know."

"Do you think I'm flat?"

"What?" My voice cracks.

"You know ... flat as a board."

I try to move again, but my sneakers slip loudly against the slick boat floor.

Is she flat-chested? I've always liked Ruby's figure. I worry, sometimes, she gets a little too small around the waist, but Ruby has never liked food all that much. But I like Ruby, tiny frame and all.

"No," I say.

"No, as in I'm not flat?"

"No. You're perfect. Don't let anyone else tell you different, okay?"

"But ... I mean, you like Sarah's boobs, don't you?"

"I don't know. I don't really ... I mean—"

"She wears low-cut shirts."

Sarah *does*, and that little line of cleavage makes my heart race faster, but whenever Ruby smiles at me, I feel the same, so why does it matter whether I like Sarah's boobs?

I don't answer Ruby. I kick my feet up on the front of the boat and tongue my cheek.

"Can I tell you something and you promise not to get mad?" Ruby asks.

"I'd never be mad at you."

"You look mad."

"It's too dark to see me."

"I can feel that you're mad," she says.

"I'm just ... it doesn't matter. What's up?"

My brain is too fuzzy to be mad—too filled with thoughts of how Sarah's and Ruby's chests are not the same, but I like how Ruby looks when she lies on my mattress when we play video games. I like how, when the air-conditioning kicks on and she hasn't gotten up to get a blanket yet, her breasts pucker a little until they form tiny pebbles and—

"I just ... I wonder if Michael would ever notice me with ... these."

I shake my head. "What? Michael?!"

"I know," she whines. "I know you don't like him. But—"

"Is it his Elvis look?"

"His Elvis look?"

"Yeah. The whole lip thing."

"I ... I don't know. His lips are nice, I guess."

My stomach twists. "His lips are gross. *Your* lips are nice."

There's a small silence when I realize what I just said.

"You think my lips are nice?" Ruby whispers, the words almost echoing off the tunnel walls.

I shrug. "Sure."

"Sure?"

"Yeah. They're ... pink."

"Oh."

I clear my throat. This is too weird. And I don't like when my stomach twists around her.

"So, like, you think his lips are nice?" I ask.

I hear her swallow. "Sure. I don't think kissing him would be so bad."

Kissing?

Who said anything about kissing?

I move once more, causing the boat to shift and my untied shoelaces to snap against the bottom of the boat.

I don't like the idea of her kissing Michael. Not one bit. I don't want him to do anything with her. I could be okay with her kissing Landon because he's Lorelei's brother and he's cool. But not *Michael*.

"Are you mad?" she asks.

"No. Maybe. I don't know. It's Michael. It'd be terrible."

"Terrible? You think I'd be bad at kissing?"

"No," I rush out to say. "No. I didn't say that. I meant, *he* would be—this is coming out wrong. Listen, if you'd be bad, I would be too," I say, letting the words fall out of me in a mess. "I've never kissed anyone."

She inhales. "You haven't?"

"I tell you everything. Of course I haven't. We're in the same boat."

"Literally, yes," Ruby says, kicking the interior of our literal boat.

We both laugh, and the mood almost returns to our usual light banter. So, why does my chest still feel tight?

"So ... you're seriously thinking about kissing Michael?"

"Maybe," she says tentatively. "If he'd kiss me back."

I hate this. This boat ride is supposed to be *our* ride, and here we are, talking about my best friend kissing potato-faced Michael of all people.

I don't want her pink lips on his.

I want Ruby's lips on mine.

That—that right there—breaks my brain.

I don't want that, do I?

Do I?

No, I'm only thinking that because she's *my* best friend and it feels wrong for anyone else to take her first kiss or make her feel self-conscious about her chest or whatever else matters to her.

I'm protective of her. I always have been. But I'm just doing my best-friend duty, which is why the next words barrel out of me before I realize what's happening.

"What if we just knock it out now?"

It's dead quiet. Silent like the grave. Even the lapping water and the ride's narrator sound a thousand miles away.

Ruby's soft voice whispers out a small, "You want to kiss me?"

"I mean, I don't want ..." I scratch behind my head. "*Blegh.* Rubes, it's just a first kiss. That way, we know it won't suck when we kiss other people."

"Well, sure, yeah, I totally want to kiss you after you made that gross sound."

"Heh. Sorry. But ... I don't know ... what if we try?"

"Bennett, I've seen the way you eat hot wings."

I bark out a laugh. "That makes me a bad kisser?"

She bursts into a fit of giggles again. And I laugh, too, but it's forced because I'm freaking serious. And I feel like I'm grasping at straws because the only thought in my head is, *I want to kiss my best friend.* But the ride is coming to an end, so if we don't do it now, we won't do it at all, and I can't —I cannot—have her kissing Michael before me.

"Okay, let's kiss," she says.

I freeze. "Okay?"

"Yeah," she says. "Just, y'know, to be sure we're good."

"Do we close our eyes?"

"Yep."

"Cool."

"Bennett, are you okay?"

I nod even though she can't see me. "Yep. I'm perfect. Let's do this."

It hits me all at once that I have zero idea how you kiss a person. Do we just mash our faces together? Do I pucker my lips tight? When we touch, do I just open and close my mouth over and over?

I reach out my hand to cup her head because I think I saw someone do that in a movie once. My hand collides with something wet.

"Ouch! Bennett! My eye!"

"Sorry!"

I attempt to put my hand on her face again, and this time, I succeed. I do the same on the other side, feeling the softness of her hair cascade over the back of my hand. I pull her face closer. Ruby lets out a small breath of air, and I smell the minty scent of toothpaste or maybe the gum she was chewing earlier.

And then I press my lips to hers.

We sit there for a second, warm breaths from our noses

exhaling against each other. Her lips taste sweet, and I wonder if she's wearing candy lip balm or something. They're soft. Pillowy compared to mine. I like how she smells when I'm this close, like sugar icing or something else sweet.

My heart ricochets into my throat as I realize what I'm doing.

I'm kissing my best friend.

I move my mouth, and then she moves hers. We do that another time, then a third. We keep doing it, and my body is brimming with energy. I turn my head to the side because it's easier to kiss her that way, and she does the same. I hear her legs squeak against the seat as she scoots closer to me. Her knees hit mine. A shaking hand lands on my arm, gripping the sleeve of my T-shirt.

My stomach is churning and flipping and twisting every which way imaginable. My legs are like blocks of cement, stuck to the floor. I'm too afraid to move. But at some point, Ruby purses her lips more than usual—*usual,* as if it were so normal for us to kiss now—and I can tell it will be our last.

We pull apart at the same time, and both of us look away. The energy of Honeywood comes rushing back into the tunnel. The rickety clatter of a roller coaster track, the laughter of families, and then the bright sun peering through the exit of the ride. I raise my hand to my forehead to block it out, but my mind is still buzzing.

I just kissed my best friend.

"Was it ... slobbery?" Ruby asks.

I swallow. "No. No. It was good."

"Cool," she says, then adds, "Y'know, I think I like kissing."

I like kissing you.

We unload from the boat. I place my hand on her lower

83

back to guide her through the park, but this time, her back is ramrod straight, and everything feels ... *different*. I look down at my wrist with the pink bracelet twine. At our promise.

And when I glance back up, we're somehow in front of The Bee-fast Stop, and Quinn and Lorelei are talking about the last Grizzly ride. But all I notice are Ruby's lips, which are no longer pink, but red—from kissing me.

Me.

My body tenses.

It was just a first kiss. No big deal. People kiss all the time, right?

I reach out to hold her hand, but I pull back instead because it doesn't feel okay anymore.

People kiss all the time.

This meant nothing at all.

We were just two friends, helping each other out. Hell, I could kiss anyone I want now, right?

I mean, Ruby's gonna go off and kiss Michael now, isn't she?

But just the thought has my insides twisting, and it knots even more when we see Michael inside The Bee-fast Stop, staring at my best friend with a sly grin and greedy eyes. And she smiles back.

Ruby can do whatever she wants.

It's not a big deal at all.

Not a big deal one bit.

In fact, it's the smallest of deals.

Like, miniscule.

That afternoon, when Sarah shyly smiles over at me before we hop on Bumblebee's Flight, I finally smile back.

9

Ruby

Thirteen Years Before
Ruby & Bennett are Seventeen Years Old

"One ... two ... three ..."

We bolt, and I'm already stumbling past pushing limbs. Lorelei's house is busy, filled with too many teenagers whipping around corners, scrambling to find a hiding spot.

"Seven ... eight ... nine ..."

Bennett's head is tucked into his arms in the corner. He's counting to twenty.

I've never been great at hide-and-seek, and I don't like playing that much either. But Lorelei seemed really excited about the idea of hosting, and I love when she gets into her party-planning mode, so I didn't want to spoil her fun.

I'm almost positive Bennett would have read my mind and said it wasn't an ideal birthday party for either of us, but Bennett wasn't at the party-planning night to back me up.

He was with Sadie.

"Thirteen ... fourteen ..."

I run up the stairs, pass Lorelei's closed bedroom door, and open the hall bathroom door. The shower is already filled with three people I barely know, sardined together and waving at me to move on.

"Sixteen ... seventeen ..."

I twist the knob into another bedroom. It's empty, and it has none of the large balloons or streamers throughout the rest of the house. There's a vase of flowers on the polished mahogany bedside table, and the bedsheets are meticulously tucked in.

It's Lorelei's parents' room. I'm definitely not supposed to be in here.

But then I hear a whisper from the closet. "Psst. Red."

The door is open by a sliver. I can't see who's inside, but hearing that nickname, I know who it is.

"Eighteen ... nineteen ..."

"Come on," he hisses.

I don't have any options, and it's not like I can pretend I didn't hear him at this point because I've been lingering too long. Plus, I have no reasons to give him other than, *Hey, two of my best friends* really *don't like you.*

"Twenty!"

I run to the closet and shut the door behind me.

Illuminated by the small hanging bulb is the beautiful face of Michael Waters. It's only a month away from his senior year of high school, and he's already got the look of a college boy. Hardened, lined jaw, larger biceps, the tiniest bit of stubble starting to grow under his nose and on his chin. And those reliably searing blue eyes.

The corner of his mouth tilts up in a smirk.

"You almost ran," he whispers.

"Well, you had the closet," I say. "I didn't wanna steal your hiding space."

It's a lie, and he knows it.

He averts his eyes with a chuckle, tonguing the inside of his cheek. God, I've never met another boy who knows he's this attractive. But when his eyes snap back to mine, I think he enjoys how one simple look can make me squirm.

I hate how much I like Michael. I hate that there's something oddly appealing about him. Dangerous almost. I would never tell Quinn that I still like him. I feel bad enough as it is. But I guess we can't pick our crushes in life.

Michael stretches his legs out, moving one foot on either side of my hips.

He totally knows what he's doing.

"Studying for the SATs yet?" he asks. I nod, and he gives a teasing smirk. "And where do you want to go to college, Red?"

"There's an engineering university in Atlanta."

He sticks out his bottom lip, as if impressed. "Very cool. Always figured you were smart. Robotics Club, right?"

Of course he remembers that fact about me.

"Yeah," I say through a breathy laugh. "I mean, it's kinda lame."

"Nah. It's different."

"What about you? Where are you going to college?"

He heaves out a breathy laugh. "Wherever will take me, I guess. My old man says I'd better get a football scholarship or else I'm done for." He squints at me playfully. "I'm not as smart as you, Red."

"Don't say that."

"No, it's cool." He holds up his hands. "We all have our place in life."

If I didn't know him well enough, I'd say he was self-

87

conscious. It's well known that Michael is very good at teasing, and maybe that's what he's doing to me now. Or maybe he's not the type of person rumors claim he is.

"I tutor most subjects," I offer. "I could always—"

He shakes his head. "I'm not gonna waste your precious time. Don't worry about me."

He toys with a loose string on his ripped jeans, and I watch the twiddling of his deft fingers and defined wrists. I'm mesmerized by the motion.

"So, what are you gonna do without Bennett?" he asks. "When you go to college."

My head juts back. "What do you mean?"

He laughs. "People drift apart all the time."

I blow out a laugh through my nose. "We'll still talk."

"Come on. You know he's not gonna keep in touch with you after high school."

I don't like that my face contorts on instinct, but I can feel the shot of adrenaline course through my veins, furrowing my brow.

"Yes, he will," I counter.

"I don't know," Michael singsongs. "Who's he locking lips with this week? Sarah? Susie?"

My body heats.

"Sadie," I answer.

I don't like imagining Bennett kissing someone else even though it happens literally all the time.

Just not with me.

Bennett and I don't talk about our kiss last summer. It happened, and then it just ... didn't. I think about it a lot though. I think about our kiss when he's concentrating really hard on a test and he bites the tip of his pencil, or when he stretches out on the couch with his bicep tucked under a pillow and his shirt rides up, or when he scratches the back of his neck with an embarrassed laugh when I ask him who the *new girl* is. Because there's always a new girl.

I've kissed two other boys. Earlier this summer, I was a camp counselor, and the bonfire was warm, and this boy smelled good, and we'd been joking around all week, so we just leaned in and tried it. The kiss was fine, I guess. Not great.

The other boy was some kid in our grade, who copied my homework. He said I was pretty, and that day, Bennett had been kissing Sarah a lot, so I kissed this boy. It was too wet.

Bennett's asked me before why I haven't tried dating anyone, but the truth is, aside from stealing kisses, I'm too busy. It's either study and date someone, or study and hang out with Bennett. I'll choose Bennett every time.

"Right," Michael says, bringing me back to his pumping eyebrows as he hisses out the name, "Sadie."

My stomach clenches tight.

"You're being mean," I accuse.

"Am I?"

"Yes."

"I like when you're like this."

"Like what?"

"Not putting up with my shit."

I snort, which only makes him smile more.

Footsteps pound up the stairs, and someone starts laughing outside the room.

"Sometimes, I feel like Bennett is missing out," he says.

"On what?"

"Well, he's going after all these girls, but you're right in front of him."

I can't help the uncomfortable giggle that leaves my

mouth. Michael laughs with me, but I don't think he realizes I'm only laughing because I can't do anything else.

"I don't want to date my best friend though," I say because it's the automatic response I've practiced for over a year. Because, if I don't, I'll picture myself kissing him instead, and then he'd probably get freaked out, and I'd lose him.

And that's the worst-case scenario—losing Bennett.

After my mom left and since my dad has been head-over-business-shoes obsessed with Miranda ... Bennett is all I have. I cannot lose my best friend over something as simple as wanting to kiss him again.

"If I were your best friend, would you want to date me?" Michael asks.

I blink at him, shifting my knees closer to my chin. "What?"

"I'm just saying ... you're really pretty, Red."

He's disarming me, and he knows it.

"You're blushing."

I shake my head. "I'm not blushing."

"Yeah, you are. Bet I can make you blush more."

Footsteps come closer. Echoing laughter comes from the hall bathroom. The sardines must have been found.

Empowered by his smirk, I counter, "Try me."

Michael's smile creeps up his lips, and he whispers, "I think about you sometimes. When I ... you know."

"When you what?"

"Come on." Michael's voice is husky and low as he tilts his head to the side.

This closet is suddenly so stifling and uncomfortable. He gets that look in his eyes—that lustful, smoldering look when his eyelids lower and his blues get hazy.

Footsteps grow closer.

"Red," he growls, "you know what."

Without thinking, my eyes dart down to his buckle and back up.

I *do* know.

My heart pounds at the thought of his hand over himself, pumping up and down to the thought of *me*. Blood rushes to my head, and my stomach flips in a position I'm not sure it ever has before.

Something in me feels wrong. But another part feels empowered.

The closet door rips open.

"Found ... you." Bennett stands in the doorway, his beautiful white smile fading instantly as he takes in the tight closet scene.

Shame trickles down my spine. His brown eyes whip over to Michael, who gives an exaggerated shrug.

Coming up behind Bennett is Sadie, her chin now resting on his shoulder with a teasing smile. My fists curl by my sides.

"Oh, hi, Ben," Michael says, tipping his chin down. "And Sadie."

"Mikey," Bennett counters.

"Are we gonna cut the cake soon?" I ask quickly, scrambling to my feet, flashing Bennett an innocent smile.

I'm trying to keep the optimism up, but his eyes are roaming over my untouched body and then back to Michael.

"You all right?" Bennett asks.

"Christ, we were just sharing a hiding spot," Michael says with a laugh. "Playing around."

Both of Bennett's eyebrows rise to his hairline.

God, *why* did Michael have to say it like that?

I look over my shoulder at Michael, and his blue eyes dart to Bennett, then me.

He smirks, and all I can think about is what he said about Bennett. *"You know he's not gonna keep in touch with you."*

10

Bennett

"What did Michael say?"

"Nothing."

"So, he did say something."

Ruby gives my hair the smallest of tugs.

"Ow!"

She giggles, threading her fingers through my long hair once more and grabbing another section to braid.

"Mmm," she hums. "Your hair always smells like strawberries."

"You're changing the subject."

"Yes, I am."

I lean my head back, resting it in her lap. Ruby is sitting on the mattress in my bedroom, and I'm stretched out on the floor in front of her. This might normally be relaxing because I like her hands playing in my hair, but all I can think about is our birthday party last night. And I haven't been able to shake the image of her in that closet with freaking Michael Waters.

"Just tell me one thing," I say. "Did he say something bad?"

"Bennett."

"Why won't you tell me this?"

"It's just ... weird. I don't know."

I grumble out an incoherent noise, and Ruby giggles again.

"I just don't like how he looks at you."

"How does he look at me?" Ruby asks.

My blood pumps at the thought of seeing his dumb face looking at her. If it were anyone—literally *anyone* else—I wouldn't care. But it's him.

"He looks at you with ... greed. Or something like that."

"Greed?" Her hands stop mid-twist, and she laughs out loud.

"I'm serious."

"What, is he gonna steal me, like Bowser?"

"Maybe, Princess Peach," I tease back. "From me."

"He won't though. You're my only best friend."

Sure. My best friend who I think about kissing a lot.

I've kissed more girls now—Shannon, Sadie, Sarah—but none of them were like that kiss in The Canoodler. The only one that came close was the kiss with Sarah after wrestling practice late last year. She'd met me in the locker room once cheer practice ended, and her hands drifted below my belt.

Of course I told Ruby after because I tell her everything.

"Did it hurt?" Ruby had asked.

"No," I said. "It felt good. I think."

Ruby laughed. "You *think*?"

"The teeth hurt a little."

"There were teeth involved?"

"Yeah."

"Huh."

"Yeah ..."

We reminisced on it—me more than her, I'm sure—but I couldn't bring myself to tell Ruby that, even with Sarah's lips on a very enjoyable part of my body, it still didn't compare to kissing Ruby on The Canoodler. Nothing could compare to kissing my best friend.

Which is so unbelievably messed up—and I know that. I felt so guilty about thinking about the freaking Canoodler kiss that I broke up with Sarah the next day. It didn't feel fair to compare her to the girl now braiding my hair in my bedroom.

However, even though I thought I was being a gentleman, breaking up with Sarah was apparently the wrong move because Sarah said I used her, which was not at all what I'd intended.

I told my mom about it, and she made me write Sarah an apology letter, which was very publicly ripped up in my face to a chorus of, "Ooh," in the high school lunchroom.

Relationships are weird.

"So," Ruby says, loosening the braid to start a new one, "I was thinking about the first thing I want you to build me in your apprenticeship program."

I smile. "Oh, yeah?"

"Yeah. A little treasure chest. For all the maps we have. That's the first thing they teach you, right? Building pirate chests?"

"You're right. I looked at the curriculum and everything."

Honeywood's general manager, Fred, approached me last week about joining an apprenticeship program after high school. He said he could see me moving up at the park once I had some certifications and experience under my belt. I couldn't believe it. Building things is all I've ever wanted to do. He said I was a natural leader and he wanted to keep me on for the long-term. It felt good to hear.

"Or you can build me a pirate ship," Ruby continues. "I'll take that too."

"I'll have to save for the materials. Or I guess I have the money already."

I glance over at my computer desk with the envelope—a gift from my dad for my seventeenth birthday. The most communication I've ever gotten from him. My mom almost passed out at the sight of all the cash. She laughed and joked that I should write him back and ask if it's drug money. I almost did.

"Isn't that for college?" Ruby asks.

"Sure," I say. "Or ... I could build a pirate ship."

"Spoken like a true buccaneer."

"What else do you do with *sorry I've been a shit dad* money? Maybe I'll get a house. Or a motorcycle. Or tons of tattoos."

"You want tattoos?"

"I think so, yeah." I trace a thumb over her freckled knee, watching goose bumps slowly shiver over her thigh. "I like the look."

Ruby grabs another strand of hair and starts a new braid. "I think you'd look great with tattoos. God, I'm gonna miss you in college."

"Hey," I say. "You're gonna do great in college without me."

"Whose hair am I gonna braid?"

"You'll make friends with hair."

She pushes my arm, and I laugh.

"Really though, when have I *ever* been great at making friends?"

"You're friends with me."

She blows out a raspberry. "That was all your doing."

"But you still have me."

"Yeah, and I wanna keep you."

I laugh, leaning my cheek on her thigh.

"You'll keep me," I say. "I'm yours." I lift my wrist, tilting it side to side, putting the pink bracelet on display. "See?"

"Very convincing argument."

"You know what I think? I think you should get a tattoo with me. Let's tattoo our bracelets on our wrists."

"Are you kidding? My dad would kill me."

I blow out a breath and wave my hand. "Tell him to screw off."

She gasps and pushes my arm again.

I hate the way Ruby idolizes her dad. She'll trash-talk her mom all day long, but the second he's brought up, it's no longer fair game. Mr. Sullivan has cast Ruby aside just as much as her mom has; he just compensates for the absence by putting a roof over her head. Just because he stuck around and her mom didn't doesn't make him a hero.

"I can't talk back to my *dad*," she says.

"You talk back to me."

"Yeah, because it's fun," she says with a sneaky smile.

"And I love it when you talk back to me," I say. "Move over, Parrot."

Ruby scoots back onto my mattress as I crawl up next to her. I lie on my side, holding my head up in the palm of my hand. Ruby stays on her back, looking up at my ceiling with her hands resting over her chest.

"All my hard work on the braids!" she says, tracing a

hand over my hair. It tickles my scalp and sends shivers down my neck. "They're gonna fall out."

"Eh, even what's left will look better than my usual do."

"I like your hair."

I blow out air that sends a few strands flying up, then flopping back down. "It needs a trim."

"No," she says. "Never cut it."

I love moments like this—moments when we're just lying next to each other, talking. It's calming.

But then I think about seeing Michael and Ruby in the closet. If I found them a bit later, what would have happened? Would he have finally kissed her? Would she have run her fingers through his hair as well?

Why *him*?

"What did Michael say to you, Ruby?" I ask, bringing it back.

Ruby rolls her eyes with a smile. "It doesn't matter."

"It does if he was a jerk to you."

"Yeah," she agrees, which she never does when it comes to Michael. "He is sort of a jerk sometimes."

"What if I pissed him off just a little bit?" I suggest.

"Bennett ..." she warns.

"Now, hold on. I have an idea I've been toying with," I say with a hand up. "A prank."

"A prank? Seriously?"

"I've been thinking ... what if I streak across the football field during his championship game?"

She freezes, blinking at me once, then twice.

"You're kidding," she breathes.

"It'd be funny," I say. "The whole day is supposed to be about him, and I'm just gonna ruin the hell out of it."

"You'd get in so much trouble."

I lift a single eyebrow, and I swear her body tenses.

"Maybe I like a little trouble," I tease.

Her green eyes dart between mine, her breathing erratic and quick.

I swallow. "Seriously, what did Michael say to you, Ruby?"

She sits up, tucking her legs underneath her.

"Okay," she concedes. "Fine. You *did* tell me about Teethie Girl."

My blood rushes to my head. "Wait, is this a teethie story?"

Ruby's face grows red. "Oh my God, *no*. I mean ... I don't know. Sort of? Don't freak out."

"I won't freak out," I say, but my body is tense because the thought of Ruby and a blow job and Michael's stupid, pint-sized prick ...

She squints. "You look like you are already freaking out."

I probably do, but I shake my head. "Not freaking out. Go on."

"Well, he said ... he thinks about me."

I narrow my eyes. "What's that supposed to mean?"

"Like, when he ..." Ruby waves her palms around.

"I'm confused."

Then, she squeaks out in a hissy whisper, "When he masturbates, Bennett."

My whole body gets hot. My chest feels like it's in a tightened grasp—no, in a fist. Just like, well, when I'm masturbating, I guess.

"Okay, well, you don't have to yell it," I say with a playful laugh. But I don't feel playful.

Because Michael told her he *masturbates* to her?

"That's a weird thing for him to say."

Ruby rests back on her feet. "I thought so too. I mean, like, people actually do that?"

"What do you mean?"

"Masturbation. Like, do you ... do that?"

My face flushes with heat.

"Uh... ha." I scratch the back of my neck.

She blinks. "Wait, do you?"

I swallow and nod because, "Yeah. I do."

"And what do you think about?"

"People. Girls. Boobs mostly."

"Right," she says quickly. She plays with the pink string on her wrist, twisting it around and back. "God, apparently, *everyone* does it."

"Apparently?"

"I don't."

Somehow, this is more uncomfortable than my *blow job* conversation. This is more personal. Because the thought of my best friend touching herself ...

"You don't?" I ask.

"No," she says quickly. "God, I mean, we don't have to talk about this. It's whatever. That's fine. The whole thing is ridiculous anyway." The words stumble out of her in a mess of vowels and consonants that don't feel like words at all. "He was probably lying to me. I'm not ..." Then, she laughs out the next word. "Hot. At least not hot enough to imagine ... y'know."

"Ruby?"

"Hmm?"

"I'm almost positive he's not the only one who thinks of you."

And I can't believe I said it out loud, but I always tell her everything on my mind, and maybe this is weird, but ... it's the truth.

Sometimes, it's not Sadie kissing me in my dreams. It's Ruby. And when I'm finished, I always have to stare at the ceiling for a few seconds after to contemplate what that means because it feels wrong, but then I just fist my cock and jerk it all over again because ... it's *Ruby*.

Her wide green eyes stare into my face, and we're so close, only inches from each other. I can smell her sugary-sweet scent. I try to look away—at the floor, at the blankets, at the walls, then back to her. She hasn't stopped staring.

"Do you?" she whispers. "Think about me, I mean?"

"Rubes ... that's ..."

"You don't." She says it like it's a fact.

"Um ..."

Her eyes drift south, then back up. My zipper is strained. Hell, *I* probably look strained.

She looks at my lips, and I look at hers. They're so perfect and so pink, and I just want to turn them red again.

Can we do that again? Should we?

But then I hear the creak in the far-right ceiling tile—the one that indicates Mom is near the stairwell—and suddenly, the basement door is ripped open, and she's descending each step.

Ruby and I rip apart as fast as we can, but the sound of the mattress is too loud, and we're not quick enough.

"Hey, kiddos, I was thinking we could make some popcorn and ..."

Mom turns the corner onto the last step, halting in place. Her eyes dart between us. Our knees still touching. The blankets messy around us. The undeniable look of guilt on my face. There's no way I don't look like I've been caught with an internet browser I need to clear the history from. Or like I've been making out with my best friend, which I haven't.

We always hang out on the bed like this. It's innocent. At least when we weren't talking about choking the chicken.

"What's up, Mom?" I say, my voice cracking before I clear my throat. Damn, I sound *so* guilty.

"I figured we could watch a movie soon," she says, throwing a thumb over her shoulder toward the upstairs.

Her eyes are squinting at me, and the pull in my gut is screaming bloody murder.

"Yep," I say. "That'd be great."

"Right." She looks between us. "Great." She opens her mouth, closes it. "Listen ... uh, this isn't gonna be a fun thing to talk about, but ..."

"Mom."

"I know y'all are getting ... older."

Oh God, I want to die. Please let me crawl into the ground right here.

"Mom."

"You're seventeen now," she continues. "I was seventeen before, and if you remember, I had you at that age."

Kill me now. I want to die. Oh my God.

"Oh. This isn't ... no, it's not like that," Ruby chimes in.

"I didn't want to have to have"—Mom makes quotation marks—" 'the talk' with you two, but ..."

"Then, don't." My voice is a groan. A plea. "Please, Mom. *Please.*"

Her eyes swivel over to Ruby, who looks like she's transformed into stone, locked on by Medusa herself.

"Rubes?"

"We were just hanging out. Plus, I've got the talk from my dad. Thanks."

This is mortifying.

"Okay then," Mom says. "Well, I think we should at

least have a new rule. As long as you're under my roof, please do not lie under the covers together anymore."

"Yes, ma'am," Ruby replies quickly.

Mom's eyes narrow. I don't think Ruby has called my mom ma'am since we were ten years old, when she insisted Ruby call her Brittney.

"Uh-huh," Mom says, tonguing the inside of her cheek. "Right. Well, let's go, kiddos," she says, knocking on the doorway. "And make your bed, Bennett."

"Got it."

"Good."

She walks back upstairs, but she leaves the basement door open.

I look at Ruby, who has a thousand-yard stare. My heart is pounding, and guilt is like a hot blanket over my burning skin.

"Rubes? You all right?"

"Hmm?"

Then, I burst into a laugh. It's hysterical the way it bubbles out. And I think I might be—hysterical, that is. Ruby laughs with me.

"Awkward," she says.

"*So* awkward," I echo.

The tension is thankfully broken. I look down at the blankets like they're the reason I feel so uncomfortable. The traitors.

"So, how about that championship prank?" I ask, changing the subject. "You all right with me humiliating Mikey?"

I feel myself smile, especially when I see her own smile returning. It's so pretty. Everything about her is. Her freckles. Her ginger hair that she politely tucks behind her ears. *Her.* The face that I have, admittedly, thought about in the privacy of my bedroom without her here.

"Whatever you wanna do," she says.

And for a second, I think she has that hazy look in her eyes—the kind she gets whenever she looks at Michael. Except it's directed toward me.

11

Ruby

Bennett's in a thick white bathrobe right outside the stadium locker rooms. I stand beside him, holding a towel, looking here and there beside the brick building, like some bodyguard. As if I could ever be. I'm practically half his size.

"Are you nervous?" I ask.

"No."

"I would be."

"I know you would be," Bennett says with a low chuckle.

"So, are you?"

"Okay, sure, a little."

He gives me a side smile. I give him one back.

We can hear cheers from the bleachers, a distant whistle from the field. The band bursts into a pithy fight song. It's all the typical energy of a Friday night football game at Cedar Cliff High, heightened by our final championship game. And Bennett is about to ruin all of it.

The thing is, our football team is good, and Bennett

knew going into this year that we would continue to be as talented. Michael and Landon did not disappoint.

Bennett inhales and exhales. I place a hand on his arm to steady him.

"Quinn's got the car running," I say. "And I have the swim cap."

"Oh. Thanks. I forgot it."

"I knew you would."

I dig in my pocket and pull the floppy cap out. It's the only thing we could think of to hide Bennett's mane. If he came out with his rocker hair waving about, everyone in the stadium would know who he was. Plus, it looks hilarious.

The first time Bennett tried on the swim cap, Quinn couldn't stop laughing for five solid minutes. Even Lorelei had to excuse herself from the room with her hand covering her mouth after she spit out her soda.

And when he puts it on now and it catches on his chin, then his nose, I burst into full-on belly laughs.

It smacks into place. He reaches out and cups a hand over my mouth.

"Shh, shh," he says through his own muffled laughter.

Bennett's arm winds around my waist, and he tugs me under the awning of the building, into the shadows and out of sight from people who might get suspicious of a giggling girl standing next to a bulky guy in a bath robe.

He twists me around, pushing my back against the brick wall. The hand not covering my mouth rests beside my head, caging me in. I can't focus on anything but Bennett towering over me, his hand over my mouth, the twin of my own pink bracelet tickling against my chin.

His eyes dart between mine, the blacks of them so blown out that I can barely make out the brown. He slowly removes his hand. My breaths are heavy. So are his.

A few months ago, when Michael said he thought of me in a sexy way, it made me uncomfortable. It felt invasive and, without a doubt, *weird*. But, for some reason, when Bennett couldn't tell me whether he thought about me too, it made me feel good.

A walkie-talkie buzzes at my hip, and I jump.

"Queen Bee for Gemstone," the voice buzzes. "Queen Bee for Gemstone."

I glance down at it, and Bennett smiles, leaning away from me.

I unclip the walkie from my jeans and click the side button. "Uh, Gemstone here."

Bennett chuckles, reaching into my other pocket, his hand sliding over my ass. My breath hitches in my throat, but he comes back with my pack of gum.

"I've got the car ready to go," Quinn says. "Does Viking know where to go?"

"I know where to go," Bennett chimes in. "Side fence. Between the hedges."

I click the side of the walkie. "He says he knows."

"Ten-four," Quinn replies. "See you on the other side. Queen Bee out!"

The final buzzer echoes through the stadium, and there's an earthquake of cheers. Cedar Cliff High must have just won the state championship.

I swallow and look at Bennett, whose eyes are wide. His hands wind together.

I grin. "Here we go! Nervous, Pirate?"

Out of nowhere, Bennett pulls me in for a hug, tugging me closer and resting his chin on my forehead. His heart is beating wildly. I wrap my arms around that tapered waist of his and tug him closer. I hold him tight, and I don't pull away until he does first.

"I'll see you in the car, okay? We'll zip right outta here. Promise."

He nods and raises his hand, and we high five. Then, I take off down the dirt path and toward the bleachers.

The steel clangs beneath my feet as I jog, sidestepping all the cheering students hanging near the railing, shimmying through the boys with their chests painted in the letters CCHS and the girls with cheeks slashed in the paint of our school colors. I reach the far end of the bleachers right next to the parking lot and spot Quinn and Lorelei idling in Bennett's truck. I anxiously wait too.

A giant trophy is getting carried onto the field. Lorelei's brother, Landon, has his helmet off, punching the air. I feel bad his victory will be ruined by this, too, but he doesn't seem too bothered by it.

He walked in on our planning session one night, and all he could say was, "Neat. Give him hell."

Turns out, Bennett's not the only person with an axe to grind.

Michael runs down the center of the field, hitting the helmet of every other player, and staring up at the championship trophy with lust.

Right as they hand him a microphone, when the cheering dies down and he speaks half a sentence, it's cut off by a collective gasp.

Across the field, leaving the safety of the brick building, is a bald, naked man. Arms pumping at his sides. Legs extended. And freaking booking it across the field. I swallow, my jaw clenching at the sight, at the sudden burst of laughter and cheering and excitement as my best friend streaks in front of the entire town of Cedar Cliff.

But as he gets closer, I see more of him. The way his tight stomach ripples with each pump of his arms. The muscled thighs that tighten and release. And between them, the thick, veiny, heavy thing I've only imagined in the darkness of my bedroom.

I see my best friend's penis.

I'm having a hard time registering it. I knew I would see it today, but I didn't realize it would be so ... big?

I keep staring, the blood rushing to my cheeks with every running step he takes, every time it hits against his strong thighs. I wonder how those thighs would look, pumping between my legs. I wonder how he would feel.

I *want* to know.

I inhale a shaky breath.

The crowd is yelling. The marching band is lifting their gold and silver instruments with hollers even though the director is trying to calm them down. The cheerleaders down front wave their pom-poms. One girl in particular is near the edge of the field with her bright red hair pinned in a bow. She looks entranced at the sight of Bennett.

My Bennett.

I look out at the football team and freeze when I find icy-blue eyes staring right back at me. How Michael spots me in the crowded bleachers, I don't know. Regardless, his face is red. He tosses down his helmet and runs to the coaches down front.

Oh no.

A car honks. It's Quinn. Bennett is nearing the far gate. I bolt and clunk down the bleacher stairs and into the parking lot.

He's rounding the corner of the hedges, and I toss him the towel. He takes it, wrapping it around himself, but not before my AP teacher is running after him too.

I don't know what makes me do it—Courage? Stupidity? That energy of feeling like a badass, like my best friend?

—but I step in front. "Wait, Mr. Murphy! I had a question about—"

"Ruby, now is not the—"

I shift my position so he can't pass, right as Bennett leaps into the back of Quinn's truck.

"Well, the exam, there was a—"

"Miss Sullivan, if you don't move ..."

Bennett watches me stall, standing to run back to me, but I wave my hand at Quinn, and with a nod, she finally squeals off. The last thing I see before they turn the corner is Bennett's cinched-in eyebrows and his worried gaze.

I might get in trouble, but I can't help the smile that rises onto my cheeks.

What a rush.

More footsteps come from around the corner—the football coaches, teachers, and most of the home football team. Landon appears, and so does Michael. They're both out of breath, watching the truck drive off.

"Who was that?" a coach asks.

Michael and I immediately exchange a glance. His eyes dart between mine. I shouldn't be surprised, even though I am a little, that he instantly says, "It was Bennett."

"Bennett?" Landon says quickly. "No, I'd recognize Bennett. He's my sister's friend."

Michael shoots him a glare, and Landon shrugs.

"You kidding me right now, Arden? That was Bennett. He *ruined* our game."

I've never seen his face so red.

I curl my bottom lip in to hold back my laughter. "I mean, you still won."

"I swear it was Bennett Shaw," Michael argues, ignoring me. He's almost the color of a cherry now.

"Definitely not Bennett," Landon replies as if his team

captain isn't losing his mind in front of him. "He has tons of hair. That dude was bald. Right, Rubes?"

I waltz up to Michael, feeling more confident than I ever have in my life, and grin my biggest, winningest grin. "Right."

Michael tongues the inside of his cheek and tilts his head to the side. "One day."

"One day what?" I ask, teasing because I can.

He lets out a breath of air through his nose. "One day, your loyalty will bite you in the ass, Red."

I laugh, but it comes out weaker than I'd like. "Well, let's hope you're wrong."

He rolls his eyes. "Yeah. You keep hoping."

12

Bennett

Twelve Years Before
Ruby & Bennett are Eighteen Years Old

"You're too James Bond."

"How can one be *too* James Bond, Mom?"

She observes my outfit—from my thick boot up to the one leg of my black slacks slung over the seat of my motorcycle, followed by the cummerbund and bow tie.

"You just look like it." I grin, and she rolls her eyes, adding, "Well, no, you look more like your dad actually."

My good mood is wiped clean at the mention of him.

"I'm nothing like him."

Mom holds out her palm. "Uh, motorcycle?"

"I can own a motorcycle and *not* be him."

She crosses her arms. "Well, just stay out of trouble tonight, okay?"

I chuckle. "When do I ever get in trouble?"

"Do we really need to talk about the championship game?"

I curl my lips in and nod. "Fair point."

While Cedar Cliff High never found the bald streaker, my mom was the person sitting on our front porch with her nightly cup of tea, watching as the three of us parked in the driveway with me naked in the back, wearing only a towel.

Ruby only got one detention. I tried to turn myself in to prevent it, but Ruby kept blocking my attempts. She said she was very proud of her badassery.

"In that case," I told her, "we should get the date tattooed on you as a keepsake."

I firmly believe she was two seconds away from doing it before I carried her over my shoulder back into the house and away from her car.

"I'll be safe," I say as my mom walks into my arms and nods against my shoulder. She's a foot shorter than me now, just tall enough for me to place my chin on the top of her head.

"Be safe in more ways than one," she murmurs.

I laugh. "What does that mean?"

"Your best friend is your prom date."

"Oh boy ..."

"Well, I know you and Ruby are close."

"It's not like that," I insist, giving an additional grin of reassurance. But my heart beats faster, and I can feel my face burn red.

Technically, it *isn't* like that. But ever since I streaked across the football field, I catch Ruby staring at me constantly, biting those pink lips when she thinks I don't see her, lingering on every part of me. But specifically, the area below my belt.

I wonder if she has the same thoughts I do from time to time. Thoughts like, *How soft would she feel?* And, *Wouldn't it be nice if we kissed again?* It's been years. We're older. More experienced. I've kissed people, but so has she. Would it be better? Am I romanticizing my first kiss, or was it really that good?

Between school, Ruby's college prep, my busy schedule at Honeywood, and our parents demanding we keep doors open, the mystery of kissing my best friend again is turning into a Schrödinger's cat situation. Or Schrödinger's pussy, so to speak.

"Just don't follow the crowd," Mom says, rubbing my shoulders. "Prom doesn't have to be the time that you experiment with sex, okay?"

"Christ." I tug my hand through my long hair and let it fall. "Ruby and I are not gonna have sex, Mom. She's my friend."

She sighs. "I'm just checking. You've never brought home anyone else. Even though I *know* you dated that sweet girl, Sarah."

"Sadie," I correct.

She squints. "You sure?"

"You're a menace," I say, pulling her in for another hug. "I gotta go. Love you."

Her words are muffled against my chest as she says, "Love you too, kiddo."

I let out an exaggerated, "*Blegh*," just to make her laugh.

"I'll meet y'all at the gazebo for pictures!" she calls as I rev up.

"I'll make sure to lose my virginity before then!" I yell back over the engine.

"Bennett, so help me—"

I cackle before kicking off and zooming out of the driveway.

I feel justified that I spent part of my dad's graduation gift on this beast. It seemed poetic—he left my mom to live on his motorcycle, and I used his stupid money on the same useless junk. I do like the thing though. When I admitted that to Ruby for the first time, she couldn't stop laughing for five minutes, but then she hugged me for another five. Seemed like the appropriate reaction for a complicated father relationship. She understands all too well.

When the front yards start to change from chain-link fences to the white paint and freshly mowed grass of Ruby's neighborhood, I slow down and rumble into her driveway. I hop off my bike, and my new steel-toed boots clunk onto her porch.

I ring the doorbell. There's far less barking than there used to be. Moose is older these days, and the fight in him is relegated to a simple, huffing *woof*. His wet nose presses against the glass, and I tap against it.

When nobody answers, I creak open the door, squeezing through the crack so as not to let out Moose, petting him the whole time.

"Rubes?" My voice echoes through the house.

I forgot Miranda and Richard are gone for their monthly date night. It was coincidence that it fell on prom night, but Ruby insisted she didn't want any pictures taken. They didn't put up a fight.

"Coming down!"

I look at the curling stairs right as Ruby appears on the top step.

Damn.

The dress is tighter than it looked in the store when I saw her try it on. It was beautiful then, but it's breathtaking now, hugging her thin waist, the neckline dipping just low enough to show the area between her breasts. My best friend doesn't have cleavage, but I don't care. I focus more on her collarbone. How delicate it is.

A slow smile rises on her face.

"What?" she asks.

"Nothing," I say. "You just look gorgeous, Parrot."

Her face flushes red, and she looks down at herself.

"Good enough for the Queen?"

"Did we have that planned?" I snap my fingers. "Darn, I got tickets to prom."

"Oh well. I guess we can go to that instead," she says. "But we *must* send her an apology letter."

"We absolutely must," I respond, playing along.

A slow, beautiful smile grows on her lips.

Our friendship may only be that—friendship—but I do love how she looks in a blue dress.

I savor everything about prom.

I savor how my hand rests on Ruby's lower back, where her dress dips down. The way she smells especially sweet in some new perfume. Her sunbeam smile and smattering of freckles.

We go to Honeywood after taking photos in Cedar Cliff's square. Glowing lights and streamers are strewn up on every railing and around Buzzy the Bear's fountain. We dance for one song, then two, then ten. Even when the slow dances start, I pull my best friend into my arms.

"Bennett," she says with a laugh, but I rock back and forth with her, burying myself into the crook of her neck, "don't you want to dance with one of the S's?"

I chuckle. "You're my date."

"Yeah, but ..."

"Shh."

And somewhere between the dancing and the dessert, it hits me that this will be one of our last nights together before she goes off to college. Ruby is going to leave, and I'll be in my apprenticeship program through Honeywood. I'll have to learn to be okay with my best friend's absence for the first time in my life.

But I don't want to give her up just yet. Not yet.

When the night dies down and we walk through Honeywood's parking lot, seeing my motorcycle gleaming in the corner, it feels like the end. And, sure, we have all summer, but not really. Not when I'm working six days a week. Not when she's going back and forth to her mom's, who decided to move back to the city. There's really no time at all.

We stand next to my bike for a solid minute before Ruby reads my mind, like she always does.

"Does this feel like the end of an era?" she asks.

I heave out a breath. "I was weirdly thinking the same thing."

"Not that weird," she replies with a smile. "We think a lot of the same things."

I wonder if she's thinking what I'm thinking right now.

I'd kiss you if you asked me to.

"We do," is all I say instead.

"Bennett, I don't want to go." The words come out with a weak laugh.

I walk closer, moving my palms around her waist and tucking her into my chest.

"Hey, me neither," I say, placing the smallest of kisses on the top of her head. I glance down at my wrist—the pink string we both still share.

"Bennett?"

117

"Hmm?"

"If you could do anything tonight, what would you do?"

Kiss you.

"I don't know," I say. "Something daring."

Kiss you.

She smiles, the pull of her beautiful pink lips so slow and devious.

"Something daring, you say?" she echoes.

"Yeah." I drag out the word. "Why? What's on your mind?"

"I have an idea for you."

13

Ruby

The glow of the lit-up neon sign makes Bennett's inky locks shine blue as he flicks through the binder.

"You're getting one too, right?"

I cross my arms with a grin. "Bennett, do you even know me?"

He closes the book of tattoo templates with a small *fwip*. His playful smirk teases its way onto his cheeks, forming a little line beside his mouth. It's a new one, the kind I've only seen on people like my dad or even Michael. Bennett is becoming one of them—less of a boy, more of a man. The close fit of his tux with the loosely hanging bow tie only accentuates the look.

"I know everything about you," he says. Even his voice carries that low cadence of confidence that comes with maturity. "And I know you'd get one if it meant something to you, you rebel."

I shake my head and poke his chest. "Well, not today."

"But this was your idea."

"Yeah," I say slowly, taking a step forward. "Because you've always talked about getting a tattoo and you wanted to do something daring. So, here we are. I'm making dreams come true."

He tips his head to the side and peers over at the tattoo artist tapping on his phone, patiently waiting.

"Okay, fine, you *can* read my mind," Bennett admits.

I bounce on my toes as if I won, and he chuckles.

"So, what are you getting?" I ask.

"Wouldn't you like to know?"

I narrow my eyes. "So mysterious."

"I'm a mysterious kinda guy, Rubes."

"How mysterious?"

Then, Bennett does something he hasn't done since we were kids. He takes my chin between his thumb and forefinger and says, "Very."

My heart skyrockets. Eighteen-year-old chin-lifting Bennett is very different from twelve-year-old Bennett. We've been like this all night. Little touches. Hands ghosting over each other's skin. I wish I could say it's just Bennett, but I'm not innocent either. We rode his motorcycle to the tattoo parlor, and my arms were tied tight around his waist—tighter than I normally would, splaying my hand over his hard stomach with my cheek pressed to his back. The only things separating our skin were his tuxedo and the helmet he'd bought just for me with a little cursive *R* vinyl decal.

Bennett walks over to the tattoo artist, who lifts his eyebrows and pockets his phone.

"Found somethin' you like?"

"I have an idea in mind, but I don't see it in your book."

"Tell me. I can probably draw it."

"I'd like a parrot."

My heart drops.

"A parrot?" I ask.

"A parrot?" the tattoo artist echoes.

We all sound ridiculous.

Bennett chuckles. "In black and white? Maybe in that classic-type style? You know what I mean?"

The artist's lips draw into a half-smile. "I've got you covered, man. Give me a sec."

He walks off to do who knows what, but I'm still staring at my best friend. Stunned.

"You're really getting a parrot?" I breathe.

Bennett shrugs. "Of course I am."

I can't help the stuttering blinks. "But why?"

"Because I wouldn't want my first tattoo to be of anyone else."

Not anything—any*one*.

For the next two hours, I watch my best friend get inked with the very animal he's called me since we were seven years old. My best friend's first tattoo is of me.

Well, sort of.

Bennett's free hand reaches out to me halfway through, and I take it without question, rolling our fingers together, entwining and releasing and joining together again. Strokes and rolls of thumbs over palms and something that is wholly different from our usual touches.

He winces a couple times from the pain, but he keeps eye contact with me throughout every painful second. I can feel my blood pumping in my throat and to the back of my head. I'm about six seconds away from passing out if I'm not careful. I've never been much of a needle person. Though, whether my nerves are from the tattoo or Bennett's hand, I'm not sure.

"You gettin' one too?" the artist asks once he's close to wrapping up Bennett's piece.

I shake my hand. "Oh, no. Absolutely not."

He chortles but continues on, no sign of offense on his face.

The pièce de résistance—or parrot de résistance—is finally finished hours later, and when his eyes rove over it in the mirror, he won't stop smiling. And it's his best smile—the one that reaches so far up his cheeks that it squints his eyes.

The tattoo honestly looks fantastic. Ink suits Bennett well. But then again, my best friend has always been the coolest.

"What are you gonna tell people it means?" I ask.

"That I'm a pirate," he says casually.

"Nice."

"And that pirates keep their parrots forever. Even if in spirit."

My chest tugs, and without hesitation, I walk into Bennett's arms. He wraps me up in them, placing a hand behind my head and tucking me into his chest.

Forever. I'm inked on my best friend forever.

The smell of his silly little strawberry shampoo hits me hard, and I think my eyes sting a little at the thought of him, but instead of letting myself cry, I look at the tattoo artist and declare, "You know what? I've changed my mind."

When we arrive back to my empty house, I immediately kick off my heels in the foyer. It's loud and clunky, but I am feeling alive and rebellious.

Bennett chuckles beside me, tucking his hands in his slacks pockets. "Wow. Tell 'em how you really feel."

I'm willing to bet our local bar, The Honeycomb, is packed, especially since they opened it up for underage kids on prom, serving Honeywood's hot honey tea and other nonalcoholic libations.

But we aren't there. We're here. Alone in an empty house together. For probably the first time in a year.

I take the stairs two at a time to my bedroom. "Want to watch a movie?"

Bennett clears his throat, a small grunt leaving his chest as his heavy footsteps follow behind me.

"You sure we should be alone? Your dad'll be here eventually."

"Yeah, but he's not now," I tease, plopping onto my bed and clicking on the square TV. The vocals of Celine Dion greet us. It's an infomercial for a new romance compilation CD.

"I didn't know they still made those," Bennett says, the bed creaking beneath the weight of him as he takes a seat next to me.

My body heats at the thought of sharing a bed with him. I mean, we're not technically, but ... we're close enough, aren't we?

I glance at him, at the cut of his jaw, the way the TV illuminates his messy hair falling by his shoulders, the deep browns of his eyes.

I lie in this very bed and imagine a lot of things happening with Bennett. Some nights, I twirl my pink bracelet around my wrist before succumbing to my wandering hand, slipping under my sleep shorts, closing my eyes to the thought of another kiss on my lips, to his potential exhale of, *Christ, Ruby,* as his head disappears between my legs.

I know it's wrong to think of my best friend like that. Plus, what could I offer him that someone else already hasn't? Another virgin kiss? Sure, The Canoodler was his first kiss, too, but since then, he's had loads more practice than me. I've been too busy studying and getting subpar kisses from boys that never extend beyond the first.

I wouldn't have the guts to make a move on my best friend even if I thought he wanted me to. And if I did have the gumption, would I? Would I really want to ruin the only good thing in my life? My dad is out with Miranda on my prom night, my mom is in a different city, and I'm just here —with the one person who has never left my side.

I couldn't ruin that.

Bennett runs his large hand through his hair, looks at the bedspread, then chokes out a laugh. "Uh, y'know what? Maybe we shouldn't hang out in here."

"I've always wanted to sit on the roof," I offer. Anything to stay with him. "And Dad's not around so ... thoughts, matey?"

He grins. "Wow. Look at you. You might be a pirate yet."

"Yarr! Walk the plank!"

We exchange a smile as I run over and pop up my window. His hand goes to my lower back as I crawl onto the roof. He follows behind.

It's a cool night, right on the cusp of summer. The days aren't yet warm enough to keep the nights warm, too, so the small breeze sends a shiver over my skin. I bring my knees to my chest. Bennett takes off his tux jacket and folds it over my shoulders. His jacket engulfs me whole. I love when his clothes do that.

I rest my head on Bennett's shoulder. Bennett's hand slides around my waist and down to the side of my hip. He strokes the tip of his index finger right over my panty line, where the crinkle of thin plastic covers my new tattoo. I was proud of what I came up with. It's a tiny outline of a strawberry. My rebellious ode to my best friend.

"Does your strawberry hurt?" he whispers.

"Why does that sound dirty?"

His laugh is strained as he asks, "Do you want it to be?"

I nudge him with my elbow. "Shh."

I do want it to. But I don't know what that would mean, so I change the subject.

"How's your parrot?"

"She's fine. I'll miss her next year."

I snort. "All right, let's not get mushy."

He chuckles. "No, let's. I'm in a mushy mood." His fingers poke into my side, and it tickles. I grin at him. "Are you nervous?" he continues. "About college?"

"Yeah," I admit. "I think I am nervous."

"You shouldn't be."

"I'll be somewhere new, where I'll know nobody." *And you won't be there.*

"You'll always have me."

"Two hours away."

"Nope. Only one call away," he corrects.

"You're so optimistic."

He chuckles. That sweet chuckle of his that's low and rumbling. I can feel it in my chest, running down my spine, goose bumps exploding over my skin.

I find myself swiveling my head, rubbing my cold nose against his warm neck, exhaling against his skin. Bennett turns, too, placing his lips against the top of my head, holding it there for a moment. I wonder if he's closed his eyes, like I have, cherishing this time we have.

And then we're both shifting. I feel his large hand moving, slowly snaking up the jacket and over my shoulder, splaying over my spine. I pull in a breath, roaming my own hand up to his broad shoulders, over his biceps, moving over each crest and dipping down to his forearms.

He traces a finger over my bony wrist, turning the pink bracelet over my skin. I run a thumb over the veins that twist up his forearm until I reach the thin plastic that covers his new tattoo. A tattoo that is, undeniably, of me. And then I trail back down and give a small tug to the pink string on his wrist as well.

With a low groan, Bennett presses his palm into my lower back, scooting me closer. I inhale sharply, arching myself into him, my chest hitting against his. We're so close. My breathing is drastically turning erratic. I can feel his breath against my cheek, then on my neck, where I feel him purse his lips against my skin.

One single kiss.

Then another.

And another.

Kiss after kiss down to my shoulder.

My breath catches in my throat as he wraps his palm over my ribs, trailing the tip of his thumb just below my breast. His hand is close—dangerously close—to the one line we've never crossed. And I'm shaking under the possibilities. Literally shaking like a leaf at the thought of Bennett's hand running over me, at even the idea of his lips kissing down the center of my dress, leaving heat in his wake.

And I want it. I want it. I want it.

I want *him*.

I shouldn't. I can't. But I do.

I shift closer, and Bennett's palm leaves my ribs in an exhaling groan as he grabs the back of my thigh, hooking my leg over his. In a second, I'm in his lap, grinding down on him right as he slowly thrusts his hips up. I feel the hard length of him—of my best friend—rubbing against me. Nothing but two layers of clothes between us.

"This okay?" he murmurs.

I nod with a very small, "Mmhmm."

We move against each other, little shifting motions that rub clothes against clothes—his hardness against my center. He grunts beneath me, and every long, languid stroke sends waves of energy coursing through me.

"You're so beautiful," he whispers.

I let out a small something—maybe a moan? A whine? A desperate, unspoken plea for him not to stop. His hands land on my waist, pulling me down as he grinds against me harder.

A small grunt leaves him, and I find my voice enough to sigh out a, "*Yes*," which has his throat grumbling again in approval.

Our bodies shift up and down, rubbing over and over until my heart is pounding and my once-cold body no longer needs to keep his tux jacket on my shoulders. I feel like I'm burning from the inside out.

But right as the nerves shoot up my arms and I feel like I can't handle the sensation between my legs anymore, there's the sound of tires coming down the road and then car lights shining onto the driveway.

Bennett clutches my hips, holding me in place as we lean over, peering over the edge of the roof. Miranda exits the car first, her heels loudly clacking over the concrete with deliberate footfalls. She walks toward the house without waiting for my dad to turn off the car.

"Shit," I whisper.

Bennett chuckles in response, patting my butt, ushering me back in the window. I crawl in first, and he shuts the window behind us.

The front door slams open from downstairs, hitting the opposite wall. It's then calmly shut back.

"Who is she?" Miranda sneers.

"Miranda." My dad's voice is exhausted.

"Who is she, Dick?"

Dick?

I'm getting a weird sense of déjà vu. Maybe Bennett is, too, because he reaches out for my hand and holds it tight.

"There's nobody," Dad says. "I adore you."

"Then, who has been calling you?"

"A new client. Come on, baby—"

"Don't *baby* me."

"I'm not cheating on you, Miranda."

I almost laugh at the thought. It's ridiculous. Dad loves Miranda. He worships the ground she walks on more than he ever did my mother. He would never cheat.

"Please," Miranda says, dragging out the sarcastic word. "I know the saying. The way they get with you is the way they leave you, right?"

The way they—

The way—

I blink. I think I might have tunnel vision. The edges are blurred, and nothing is here, but so is everything, and suddenly, all the noises are loud.

"Ruby?" Bennett whispers, but it's muffled.

"He cheated on Mom," I whisper.

"Ruby."

"He *cheated* on Mom with Miranda."

And I feel so ridiculous as I say it out loud because *of course* he did. I just didn't want to believe it. It's like my brain blocked out the possibility of him doing something so horrible. But he did.

"Hey, it's all right," Bennett says. "Everything is okay."

But it doesn't feel okay because I *trusted him*. In their divorce, I always sided with Dad. Mom was the negligent one who traveled too much and wasn't there. I *defended* him.

Bennett rushes over to close my bedroom door, and the moment he does, the voices quiet down to nothing. They know I'm home now, and they probably know I'm with Bennett, but I don't care. Neither does he because he locks the door.

"He cheated on her," I whisper again.

Bennett gathers me in his arms, holding me tightly. I can see his jaw grinding.

"He's a piece of shit, Rubes." The words hiss out of him.

"I can't believe ... and he's ..."

There's a knock on the door.

"Honey?" My dad's tired voice sounds close, like he's leaning on the door.

"Go away," I say, and it's loud and venomous and so unlike me.

"We should talk."

I throw a pillow at the door. It feels good when it *thumps* against the wood. There's a sigh on the other side, and footsteps walk away. He's too tired to even deal with me. But Dad's just that kind of coward, I guess.

"Want to throw another?" Bennett asks, holding out my spare pillow.

I want to laugh, but I collapse back into his arms instead.

"I'm sorry," I say.

"For what?"

"For tonight. I think I ruined prom."

Bennett grabs my face in his palms, tilting my head up and staring me in the eyes. Those deep browns bore right to the heart of me—a tether to something real. To my best friend.

"Hey, look at me. I'm right here, okay? And I'm not going anywhere."

And those simple words—the words I would die to hear every day for the rest of my life—are the ones that have me hugging him. But only hugging. Nothing more.

I could see myself going further with Bennett tonight. I could see us exploring each other in ways we never have. Him kissing my new tattoo. Me kissing his, along with other parts of him I've only imagined. I picture all the fun things that we could try, the things that make my heart race in the mystery of nighttime dreams. And I want to do it all with Bennett. I trust him, and I could.

But I won't.

Maybe if I were a different person in a different life. But I'm not. I'm the person who doesn't want to lose my Bennett. Not when everyone else in my life has let me down up to this point.

Michael's words of, *"You know he's not gonna keep in touch with you,"* echo through my mind again.

"I'm sorry," I whimper out.

He shakes his head and lets out a breathy laugh. "Stop saying that."

"I'm sorry that we almost ... I don't want to do this, Bennett."

"Rubes." And he's smiling, and I don't know how because that's the last thing I want to do right now, but he is.

His hand is on my lower back, but it's our usual level of comfort. The hand he places to hear me, to truly listen. The only person who ever has.

"It's okay if we don't do that," he whispers. "Maybe that's not us, y'know?"

But I *want* it to be us. Touching. Breathing. Sighing.

I want to be that person so bad—the person who takes risks and falls in love with their best friend and lives happily ever after. But the words can't leave my mouth, no matter how hard I try. I can't push them to the surface without feeling like my head is swimming.

So, instead, I lean on his shoulder, just like my mom used to do with my dad when they were happy, regardless of how fake that might have actually been. But I know one thing for sure: This, right here? Me and Bennett? This is far from fake.

14

Ruby & Bennett

Eleven through Seven Years Before

Ruby & Bennett are Nineteen through Twenty-Three Years Old

Bennett: How ya holding up?
Ruby: I don't want to go to orientation.
Bennett: Maybe it's best you're getting out of town. Have you talked to him yet?
Ruby: Sort of. Dad swears he didn't cheat on Miranda.
Bennett: Do you believe him?
Ruby: I don't know what to believe.
Bennett: Just try to have fun at orientation. Maybe you'll have a cool roommate.
Ruby: I should take up smoking.
Bennett: How about no?
Ruby: But then my roommate will think I'm cool.
Bennett: Just talk about your robots. They'll love that.
Ruby: [side-eye emoji]

Bennett: You're gonna do great, R2-B2.

Ruby: I hope so.

Bennett: I know so. Have fun at college.

Ruby: I was late to class, and I'm blaming you.

Bennett: LOL. Sure, why not?

Ruby: We talked on the phone too late!

Bennett: Oh, yeah, that's definitely my fault, Miss Please Don't Hang Up.

Ruby: It was dark.

Bennett: You aren't allowed to watch scary movies alone anymore.

Ruby: I thought my roommate was coming home!

Bennett: I'm telling you, you should have watched old cartoons instead. It'll help you sleep after scary movies.

Ruby: Oh, fun fact: did you know the dorm's internet will send you a warning if you're caught watching something bad on their Wi-Fi?

Bennett: And how do you know that?

Ruby: I plead the Fifth.

Bennett: Watching the ol' porn again?

Ruby: Ye olde porn.

Bennett: You rebel, you.

Ruby: Dad and Miranda are hosting some big holiday party.

Bennett: How are you feeling about it?

Ruby: I told my mom. She offered to let me stay with her over Christmas break instead.

Bennett: Are you going to?

Ruby: Yeah.

Bennett: Oof. Has their fighting gotten that bad?

Ruby: I don't know why they're still married when he's a serial cheater.

Bennett: You don't believe him?

Ruby: No. Would you believe your dad?

Bennett: I don't know.

Ruby: Come on. Where's my daddy-issues solidarity?

Bennett: Mom actually gave me Dad's address. I think I'm gonna write him.

Ruby: What?! How old school of you. And how exciting!

Bennett: I didn't want his cell number. Feels too weird. I'm okay with letters.

Ruby: Proud of you. :)

Bennett: Hey, look at you, sending smiley faces!

Ruby: College is growing on me.

Bennett: You've been sounding happier on our calls.

Ruby: I think I might be.

Bennett: So, I won't see you over Christmas?

Ruby: No. :(

Bennett: No, not the frowning face again!

Ruby: I keep imagining Miranda's fake happy smile at their ridiculous holiday party. Blegh.

Bennett: Yikes.

Ruby: I'd rather have lasers in my eyeballs.

Bennett: Lasers? Wow.

Ruby: A tiger gnawing off my leg.

Bennett: Not a lion?

Ruby: A lion too. All the big cats.

Bennett: How about seaweed between your toes?

Ruby: I draw the line there.

Bennett: I'll start stocking up on seaweed then.

Ruby: Why?

Bennett: Isn't their anniversary coming up?

Ruby: I like where your head is at.

Bennett: Seaweed gift it is.

Ruby: You're the best.

Bennett: Tattoo number three complete.

Ruby: Ooh, let me see!

Bennett: [picture message]

Ruby: You didn't tell me you were getting a tattoo of Moose!

Bennett: I needed something to fill in the arm, and he's the perfect bear-shaped dog.

Ruby: I miss him.

Bennett: Me too.

Ruby: [picture message]

Bennett: LOL.

Ruby: Professional artist over here. Don't be jealous.

Bennett: It's the scribble for the tail that really completes it.

Ruby: It's the way my pen ran out of ink.

Bennett: I wondered why he wasn't as fluffy.

Ruby: Well, now, we match.

Bennett: I love it.

Ruby: You ever heard of Emory Dawson?

Bennett: Should I?

Ruby: He designed The Grizzly. At sixteen.

Bennett: Damn! I feel super dumb now.

Ruby: Right?! What am I doing over here?

Bennett: I bet your coasters will be better.

Ruby: Yeah, but I wasn't designing them at sixteen.

Bennett: You sort of were.

Ruby: Not ones that actually worked! He's a prodigy. I'm not.

Bennett: Can't get hung up on the past.

Ruby: Says the man who started woodworking before he was twelve. How's the apprenticeship going?

Bennett: It's really awesome, Rubes. Fred's lining me up for a manager role at the park.

Ruby: Get out! That's amazing! So, this means I get free Honeywood entry for life, right?

Bennett: You read my mind.

Ruby: Tell me something I don't know.

Bennett: I like the attitude.

Ruby: It's new.

Bennett: Nah, you were always feisty. You just needed somewhere to spread your wings.

Ruby: My flames.

Bennett: Exactly.

Bennett: Come back. Summer break wasn't nearly long enough.

Ruby: You worked half the time!

Bennett: But wasn't hanging out at Honeywood all day a thrill?

Ruby: If I had to ride The Grizzly one more time, I was gonna vomit.

Bennett: There were other coasters.

Ruby: Yeah, but that's the best one.

Bennett: Because Emory Dawson made it?

Ruby: Aw, you listened!

Bennett: I always listen to you, Parrot.

Ruby: Okay, fine, yes, I'll miss Honeywood.

Bennett: You'll miss the pancakes the most, right?

Ruby: Caught me.

Ruby: hello benny

Bennett: Hello, Amy.

Ruby: i'm a wizard

Bennett: I agree, but why today?

Ruby: i'm a tequila wizard

Bennett: Amelia Ruby, you're drunk, aren't you?

Ruby: i'm a drunk wizard.

Bennett: Can I go to your magic show?

Ruby: five dollars please

Bennett: I'll pay ten.

Ruby: thank u for the tip

Bennett: What type of magic do you do?

Ruby: anything you want

Bennett: Can you pull a rabbit out of your hat?

Ruby: only skunks

Bennett: What a weird skill.

Ruby: ask me about another trick

Bennett: So demanding.

Ruby: next

Bennett: Can you saw a person in half?

Ruby: no

Bennett: Can you guess the card I'm holding?

Ruby: you're holding cards?

Bennett: Hypothetically.

Ruby: no

Bennett: I'd like my money back.

Ruby: guess what else

Bennett: You can bend spoons?

Ruby: i'm gonna be a sister

Bennett: WHAT?

Ruby: Miranda is pregant.

Ruby: *present

Ruby: **pregent

Ruby: ****PREGNANT

Bennett: Oh. Wow.

Ruby: yeah ho

Ruby: *OH

Bennett: You okay?

Ruby: i think so

Bennett: Mind if I call you?

Ruby: i haven't showered in a week.

Bennett: So?

Ruby: i stink

Bennett: Nah, bet it's just the magic skunks.

Ruby: true.

Bennett: I promise not to gag on video.

Ruby: only if you promise

Ruby: I have bad news.

Bennett: Is this "I'm flunking out" bad news or "I'm a drunk wizard" bad news?

Ruby: I like to think being a wizard was good news.

Bennett: True. You're a funny drunk.

Ruby: Well, I'm sober now.

Bennett: So, you're flunking out?

Ruby: Worse. I won't be coming home this summer.

Bennett: Oh. That's the worst news.

Ruby: Tell me about it. I think my dad is upset the most. No free babysitter for Lucas.

Bennett: Rude. You're more than that to your brother.

Ruby: [cringe GIF]

Bennett: You are.

Ruby: Anyway, guess why I'm not coming home!

Bennett: You're joining the circus.

Ruby: I got an internship at Dominion!

Bennett: Ruby! That's great! That's not bad news at all!

Ruby: It's not?

Bennett: You're achieving your dream! An internship at a top roller coaster construction company? I wouldn't want anything less for you.

Ruby: But I won't see you.

Bennett: Then, I'll come to you.

Ruby: You would?

Bennett: Just say the magic word.

Ruby: Alakazam.

Bennett: That is, in fact, the magic word. How'd you guess?

Ruby: Wizard, remember?

Ruby: [video of Lucas]

Bennett: He's crawling already?

Ruby: Crazy, right?

Bennett: How often does he stay with you?

Ruby: Miranda and Dad like their vacations.

Bennett: So, a lot. Next time, let me know. I'll come over and help.

Ruby: Last time you helped, we played 52-card pickup all night.

Bennett: Kid's a gambler. What can I say?

Ruby: You're a terrible influence.

Bennett: The best, you mean.

Bennett: [link to an article announcing a new roller coaster build]

Bennett: Is this your doing?

Ruby: Yeah. :)

Bennett: Hell yeah. My best friend is killing it in the industry.

Ruby: Your best friend who misses you terribly.

Bennett: Same, Parrot. It's been too long.

Ruby: Such a softy.

Bennett: Only with you.

Part II

15

Ruby

Six Years Before
Ruby & Bennett are Twenty-Four Years Old

Something about crossing the county line into Cedar Cliff always feels welcoming. I think it's how the pine trees part like theater curtains or how the four-lane highway narrows to two lanes while you climb the mountainside. Or maybe it's that the world slows down a bit. Fewer honking cars. Fewer city lights. More telephone poles with loose hanging lines and perched birds.

For the first time in years, I feel a calm quiet.

I pull into The Honeycomb's lot, put my car in park, and sit there. Just sit, winding my hands over the steering wheel. My passenger seat is occupied by a buckled-in laundry bag. My backseat has four boxes and a suitcase. My trunk is an even messier affair.

I have a text waiting for me from my dad, but I don't answer it. Instead, I thumb through the slew of texts from a new group chat I've been added to—one with Lorelei, Quinn, and Bennett. Each text is more excited about my homecoming than the last.

My whole body is shaking. My hands. My knees. My feet have been vibrating, causing the gas pedal to be very confused during the last leg of the drive.

I haven't seen my best friend in nearly a year. Sure, we still text every day, but it's different to see jokes on a screen than watch those words leave his mouth with his beaming grin—the playful one that reaches his eyes.

What does Bennett look like after one year? Does he still smile like that?

I close my eyes, lowering my head to the steering wheel. I should be driving directly to my dad's house, dropping off my stuff, and playing with my brother. But Bennett texted me, saying that Trivia Night was on Wednesdays, and I will be joining in as a permanent member, considering I'm a Cedar Cliff resident once more.

I'm here. I'm back in my hometown for good.

I cut off my engine and climb out, walking up the two rickety steps out front and then opening the creaking door. There's a low hum of voices, the familiar sound of classic rock flowing through the speakers. It smells like hoppy beer and fried food. Long picnic tables adorn the wood plank floor, and frames on the wall feature vintage Honeywood promotional posters or visiting celebrities.

Then, with one look toward the bar, I see that familiar face I know all too well.

Bennett spots me instantly. He blinks once, twice, and then, slowly, a smile grows on his face. That beautiful smile that reaches his eyes.

His inky-black hair is still long and still wild—more rugged than any man I've seen in the city in the past six years. The veins along his tattooed forearms—*so many new pieces of art*—roll down to his wrist. Peeking just below is a small, frayed pink string.

He leans his head to the side and gives a small wave of his fingers. I raise my hand in response, and even from here, I hear his chuckle, just by watching his chest move.

I walk toward him at first, but then my steps get faster, and suddenly, I'm jogging across the bar. I barrel into Bennett's arms, landing against his hard chest—*dang, he really works out now*—which hurts on impact. I don't care.

Bennett stands from his stool with his large arms wrapped around my waist, and he picks me up off the ground, swinging me side to side. I bury my nose into the soft strands of his hair. He still smells like strawberries.

"Hey, Parrot," he murmurs against my skin. His voice is rumbly and gruff.

"Hi, Pirate."

We hug for a few seconds, then maybe a minute—I don't know how long. All I know is, we must be playing some game of hug chicken because neither of us pulls away.

Not until I hear, "Hey, who's that foxy lady?"

I'd recognize that sarcastic tone anywhere. I twist my head to see Quinn at a long table, hand wrapped around a beer. Lorelei is next to her, giving an eager wave. I haven't seen either of them in probably two years, and they look remarkably the same. Though Quinn is wearing far less black than in high school. And Lorelei, well ... she's still wearing some variety of a Honeywood-themed T-shirt, and I love her for it.

"Stop hogging her!" Lorelei says to Bennett with cupped hands over her mouth.

Laughing, always low and gravelly, Bennett lowers me down, my front skimming over his body the entire way. I feel every new hard edge to his body, all the bulky hills of his chest, down to the thick ridges of his abs. My feet hit the ground, but his hand stays on my lower back, his palm spread over me to hold me close.

Just like he always has.

The more I stare at him, the more I realize what's changed. The sides of his eyes have a fan of lines now, like check marks confirming adulthood. A new wash of dark stubble dips into his cheeks and around his hard jaw, a harsh angle that looks carved with a professional's knife. He has a new scar above his lip.

But his eyes are still the same—those gorgeous dark brown pools that say everything without having to. *I've missed you.*

So, I think back, *I've missed you too*, and he smiles wider.

I jump onto my toes, then back down to loosen the energy inside me—the tiny glimmers of light floating back now that Bennett is around. The world has been a little less beautiful without him while I was in college.

He orders me a beer and grabs both his and mine off the counter, and I follow him to their table. Lorelei pulls me to her the moment I sit down.

"This is where all the Honeywood staff hangs out," Bennett says, sliding in next to me. "Well, and everyone else too, I guess."

I look around and see the old football coach, Bill, with Mrs. Stanley chatting to him and the mechanic, Frank, chewing on peanuts at the bar ... all three still in work clothes of varying degrees. There's a slew of other people I recognize from high school or maybe the grocery store, and every single person is smiling behind sips of beer and laughter. It's easygoing—a nice change from the hustle of city life.

"You're here to stay, right?" Lorelei pleads. "Tell me you're here to stay."

"Yeah," I say through an exhale. "I got a job in the city, so I'll still be commuting, but yeah."

Lorelei pulls me into another hug. "Ahh, yes! I heard about the job! And at Dominion too! You're living the dream! Everything you worked for!"

Everything I worked for.

I went to college for engineering and landed a job at one of the best roller coaster construction companies in the South. On paper, it's wonderful. In reality, my boss has an email response rate of five business days, but expects less than one hour for his own requests.

But there's no need to mention that and ruin the good mood.

"Yeah, it's fantastic," is all I say. Because I can't complain when I got exactly what I wanted, right?

I change the subject and offer to be the notetaker for our trivia team. It's easier to have an assigned task when I'm the quieter one in our group. I listen to their conversations—their gossip about Honeywood, or Lorelei's boyfriend in the Rides department, or Quinn's mom showing up and then disappearing all over again. Conversations that feel familiar and yet different, all at once.

Eventually, the bartender comes and sits down with us, which I assume is normal, considering how casually he slides in. They introduce him as Orson, and when I ask how long he's been working here, he laughs and says he owns the place. He's got a backward cap and a playful smile, and I decide I'll probably like him over time. Before he leaves, he claps Bennett on the back and asks if he's coming over to watch football.

I blink at that because I didn't even know Bennett liked

football. It feels like everyone has moved on, that there are events I've missed out on for years.

How long will it take to be fully comfortable again?

I pull in a deep inhale to steady my growing nerves, but then I feel a large hand on my lower back. It's Bennett, and he's smiling at me.

"You okay?" he whispers because he just *knows*.

I might be a stranger in this town, but not to Bennett. Never to Bennett. And that thought alone has my nerves dissipating on the spot.

"Yeah," I say. "Yeah, I'm fine."

"Good."

"You're very smiley," I observe.

He chuckles. "Well, I'm very happy."

Quinn snorts. "He would not stop talking about you coming home."

Bennett's smile fades to a comical frown. "That's not true."

"Is it?" I ask.

"No," he grunts, giving a pointed look toward Quinn.

Then, Quinn's voice rises to a high pitch as she says, " 'Let's wait to name the trivia team until Ruby comes home.' "

"Quinn. I never said that."

" 'Do you think Ruby will like The Honeycomb?' " Lorelei chimes in with a giggle.

" 'I bet Ruby will really like Orson,' " Quinn jokes.

From the bar, Orson barks out a laugh, twisting his baseball cap forward.

" 'Let's all watch *The Bachelor* together when she gets back. She'll love that,' " Lorelei mimics.

I clear my throat and raise the pitch of my voice to mock, " 'Do you think Ruby will like beer?' "

Quinn raises her drink. "There we go! Rubes is back!"

The three of us girls laugh, and finally, so does Bennett —a laugh that starts slow and reluctant and then it's full-bellied and loud. All four of us leaning forward on the long table, giggling and drinking and settling into the night.

We don't win trivia, but Quinn says our team never does, so not to worry about it. I wasn't worrying though. I'm just thrilled to be spending time with people I love. And as I'm paying my tab at the bar, I spot Bennett leaning against the wall near the exit.

Bennett is so much bigger than he used to be. Bulky. No longer a boy, but a *man* in every sense of the word. Even his thighs stretch his jeans, and I wonder if they're as hard as his arms are. Well, maybe I shouldn't be thinking the word *hard* when I'm around him ...

I shake the thought away as Bennett raises an eyebrow, gives a devastating smile, and curls his finger toward himself.

Come here, it says.

My stomach twists.

Well, okay, sir.

"Do you want to come over?" Bennett asks once I approach. "Mom would love to see you. Plus, I think she's making late-night wings."

"I love late-night wings."

A slow, knowing smile grows as he says, "I know you do."

Christ, my face heats under his gaze. When did my best friend get so charming? He's always been able to flirt, but this feels ... different. Like he's trying.

But then it hits me.

Is Bennett trying to flirt with me?

I blink through the thought as Bennett walks me to my car.

But we can't do that.

"You know what? I should go to my dad's instead," I say. "Drop my stuff off. I'm sure he's waiting up for me."

Probably not because he hasn't in years, but I don't say that.

Bennett slowly nods, putting his hands in his pockets. His demeanor adjusts, pressing the brakes on some of the charm, like my change of plans cemented my thoughts into his.

Please don't flirt with me because I can't lose you.

"Hey, Rubes?" he asks.

"Hmm?"

"Why didn't you stay?"

"What do you mean?"

"In the city," he says. "Why are you living here and commuting?"

"It's expensive in the city."

"Sure, but why move all the way back here?"

"You don't want me here?"

He barks out a laugh. "You know that's not true. Did you not hear Quinn and Lorelei?"

"Aha! So, they were telling the truth," I say, poking his chest. His very hard chest.

Bennett's eyes dart down at my finger, then back up. "I like life better when you're around."

If I didn't think he'd clock it, I might have gulped hearing those words because I like the way he said them far too much.

"Same here, bucko," I respond. Because that'll totally lighten this weird, new tension between us, right?

A laughing breath of air breezes through his nose. "Bucko?"

I shrug. "I'm trying it out. Thoughts?"

"I'm good."

"Fine. How about *buddy*?"

"Thin ice, Rubes."

We exchange grins before my shoulders drop. "If I'm being honest, I moved back because Dad and Miranda wanted help with the baby."

Bennett clicks his tongue. "Ah."

He narrows his eyes and gets that tick in his jaw that drifts back and forth, just like my dad used to.

"What?" I ask.

"You're gonna be their live-in babysitter?"

I let out a breathy exhale of disbelief even though *yeah, I guess I am.*

Defensively, I add, "It's not exactly like that."

He bites the inside of his cheek and shakes his head, looking away toward the tree line to murmur, "God, he's such a piece of work."

"Bennett," I warn.

"You deserve better."

"Better? What does that mean?"

"It means you moved out and moved on from him and his bullshit. And now that *he* wants help raising his child, he's taking all that away."

I let out a teasing yet disbelieving scoff. "He's not taking anything away. This is letting me save money too. I'm not entirely getting the raw end of this. Now hush your mouth and hug me."

His eyebrows raised, Bennett shakes his head with a grin and wraps his arms around me. All of it is consuming—the scent

153

of strawberry hair and his large biceps and hard chest. And then he kisses the top of my head, and I close my eyes to savor it. To enjoy the affection from him that I've longed for so much.

"I'm glad you're home," he says. "I am."

We stand for a second more before he opens my door for me. I climb in and he places a hand above the window.

"Hey, bring Lucas to the park anytime," he says. "I'll make sure he gets in free."

"Ooh, I love free stuff."

"Anything for you, Rubes."

"Anything? I'll have to think about that."

Then Bennett smiles, slow and sure. "I'm really happy you're back."

"Me too."

"So, what are we doing tomorrow?"

"Whatever you want."

"That's a lot of pressure."

"With great pressure comes great responsibility, Bennett."

"Darn. I gotta be responsible? Let me guess, we can't vandalize things in town?" he jokingly suggests.

"Oh, I never said that."

Bennett sighs wistfully, so beautiful and pure. His eyes flick from my freckled cheeks, down to my chin, and then back up. But there isn't flirting behind it now. I wonder if we can keep it that way.

He closes my car door, and I roll down the window.

"See you tomorrow."

"See you tomorrow," he echoes, then slaps the top of my car.

It's good to be home.

16

Bennett

**Four Years Before
Ruby & Bennett are Twenty-Six Years Old**

"Again, again!"

"Wow, that was quick!" I take the playing cards from Lucas, who, still out of breath, shakes his head.

"I bet I can do it in *one* minute," he says.

"I don't believe you," I tease. "That sounds really fast."

His face scrunches in concentration. "I can!"

"All right then, superkid, you ready?"

Lucas's fists clench by his sides as he bites his lip, nodding fast.

I squeeze my hand, bending the cards just enough to send the whole deck flying into the air. They rain over the little kid's head, like in some dollar-bill cyclone chamber.

Squeals of laughter ensue.

"Hurry, hurry, hurry," I rush as Lucas falls to his knees,

starting to gather each individual playing card off the concrete workshop floor, his giggles echoing off the walls.

Ruby walks in and halts at the scene before us—her brother on the ground, scrambling to gather playing cards, while I lean against the workshop table, arms crossed with a timer in my palm.

"Fifty-two-card pickup?" she asks.

"It's his favorite."

"I'm gonna do it in under a minute," Lucas says.

Ruby shakes her head, handing me one of the two honey iced teas in her hand before sitting on the spare stool I keep empty just for her. I pop off the drink lid and sip from the cup. Ruby slurps through her straw.

It's a slow weekend at Honeywood, so I'm taking time to update the signage around the park. Normally, it's just me and Ruby, but her dad and Miranda planned a last-minute cruise that prohibited children, so Ruby took on her usual role of babysitter to Lucas. The boy has more energy than a power plant.

As if on cue, Lucas trips over a crack in the concrete and falls.

"Oh boy." I hold out my hand for Ruby's drink.

She hands it to me, stepping off the stool and picking up her brother as his wails pierce the workshop.

She looks at me with wide eyes and a cringe before saying, "Shh, you're fine, kiddo. You're fine."

Lucas sniffs into Ruby's arms, and she kisses the top of his head. She'd be a natural mom, which almost stirs some sort of internal need-to-hunt-for-food, He-Man sex brain in me.

Almost.

There's a moment in life, I think, when a biological clock

156

starts to tick for most people. When you feel that overwhelming sense of desire to spread your seed and carry on your genetics or whatever it is people feel. But I've never heard that timer ding. I've never seen a family pushing a stroller in Honeywood and felt my soul pull toward that future. I've never felt left out because I don't have a mini me.

It's not that I don't like kids. I love Lucas. That boy is my favorite person below the age of twenty-six. He's hilarious, smart, and kind. Heck, he even scatters crumbs on the sidewalk because *the ants need food too.*

But being a dad of my own? I don't know if I'd even be good at it. Though maybe it's my issues with my own father leading that conversation. Kind of a chicken and egg thing, I suppose. Do I not want kids because I don't have the urge, or do I not have the urge because my own dad was a piece of crap? Is it genetic? Or is it learned?

All I know is, the selfish part of me would prefer to spend all my time and money on someone else instead. And I'm looking right at her.

"Think you'd ever want kids?" I ask out loud.

Ruby laughs. "Oh God, no. I have no idea what I'm doing."

"Sure you do."

"No. I'm terrible at it. I have to raise my voice."

"True. You hate that," I tease.

She sticks out her tongue.

She sets down Lucas, who is already *so* over his breakdown. I swear kids have the memory of a goldfish. That, or they're just psychos. I'm not sure which yet.

He runs over to tug on my sleeve. "Bennett, piggyback ride!"

I do as he asked because he's too cute not to, loping side

157

to side in exaggerated motions as he giggles. Lucas really is the cutest kid.

He starts to squirm, so I let him down, and then he runs off again to find more cards.

Goldfish memory, I'm telling you.

"What about you?" Ruby asks.

"Do I want kids?"

"Mmhmm."

I inhale and exhale.

She laughs. "Well, there's my answer."

"No, I just ... well, I like this more."

"What?"

"Just hanging out with you," I answer. Ruby blinks at me for a moment, and I scratch the back of my neck before adding, "I mean, I'd be a terrible father."

"Why do you say that?"

"My dad was."

Her face falls. "You're nothing like him. You'd be great."

She takes another sip from her straw, almost in a defiant way, like the drink insulted her mother or something. Though not that it would matter to her. But then her tongue whips out to lick the excess off her lips, and I have to look away because best friends don't look at their best friends in that way.

"So, your dad," she says. "Still writing him?"

My chest clenches at the question, but I answer anyway. "Yep."

I dig into my pocket and pull out the most recent letter. Ruby takes it, unfolding and reading over the first few lines.

"It sounds so cordial."

"Eh, it is what it is. I haven't forgiven him though."

"Should you?"

It's a good question. I've been writing him for years

now, and we've still never crossed the line into exchanging phone numbers or seeing each other in person. But part of me wonders if I should. If maybe I'm old enough to ask questions like, *Why didn't you ever see me?* Or, *Do we have a family history of literally anything?*

That's the more important question because I'm not sure I want to know the answer to the former.

When I raise my eyebrows, she shrugs. "I'm genuinely asking. I don't know. You know what's best for you."

"You normally do too."

"It's a talent."

I smirk. "I wonder if maybe it's time," I admit. "Time to forgive him. Or meet him. Or whatever you do with a long-lost dad."

"Not really a handbook for all this, huh?"

"No. And why does part of me think that seeing him is just giving in?"

"It's not."

I sigh. "See? But how would I know?" I jab my chest with my thumb. "Not father material."

Ruby walks closer, settling in beside me, nudging me with her elbow. "It's okay to be unsure. Some pirate once told me it's even okay to cry."

I blow out air. "You're ridiculous."

"Is that a tear?"

"No."

"I think I see a little wetness."

"I'm fine."

"Yeah, your lip is definitely wobbling. Hang on ..."

She wipes her thumb under my eye, and I laugh, placing a hand on her lower back to keep her close as she giggles through our bit. My hand on her is a safety net of sorts—it's where my palm feels most comfortable.

We're laughing together until, from the corner of my eye, I spot a familiar curly-haired woman popping her face around the corner.

"Is the gremlin here?" she asks, her big eyes peering around.

Ruby laughs. "I should have known you would find him."

"I sniff him out like a bloodhound."

Theodora Poulos, Honeywood's Rides supervisor, moved to Cedar Cliff last year. Honestly, I'm not sure which day she started sitting at our trivia table or when it became habit, but suddenly, she was just *there*. She has this palpable energy around her, somehow captured in tight yoga pants, crop tops, and an infectious smile.

Our friend group chat grew from four to five quicker than I could ask, *Who are you again?*

Theo's just compelling like that.

Lucas's eyes widen, and he bolts, already giggling up a storm as Theo chases after him.

"C'mere, you," she growls.

"Hey, no running in here!" I say. "There're tools."

"Oh no, not the *tools*," Theo mocks, capturing Lucas and hiking him up onto her hip.

"I heard little-kid screams," Quinn says, walking around the corner, wiggling her fingertips in Lucas's direction, which has him yelling with a smile once more.

I cross my arms. "Is the whole gang gonna intrude on my work today?"

Then, Lorelei appears with an, "Oops, yes."

And so there are five.

Lucas holds out his arms, and Lorelei swoops in to grab him.

The three of our friends are such naturals with kids.

Ruby and I, on the other hand, sit to the side with our hands winding together like two uncomfortable kindergarteners who weren't picked for the dodgeball team. I wonder if my dad was like that too. Maybe he was just a guy who hadn't been made for kids, but had one anyway. Honestly, that makes me dislike him more.

I'm not sure if our letters have helped me reconcile the past or just made me more bitter. And with one look at Lucas bouncing between the arms of my closest friends, I wonder if he'll ever get the male role model he deserves. Lucas's dad is technically present, but I swear Ruby spends more time with Lucas than he does. It took growing up and seeing a range of different personalities to finally view Mr. Sullivan as the man that he is—selfish and ego-driven.

Would my dad have been the same? Would I be in limbo with him, like Ruby is with hers? Hell, am I in limbo now?

That—*that*—gives me pause.

An elbow nudges my arm, and staring up at me are the reliably curious eyes of my best friend.

"What are you thinking about?"

I sigh. "You're never gonna believe me."

"Try me."

I suck on the inside of my cheek and shrug. "I think I wanna visit my dad."

Those beautiful green eyes widen. "You're right. I don't believe you."

I laugh in response.

"Do you really want to?" she asks.

"Maybe," I answer. "Is it weird if I do?"

"What are y'all whispering about over there?" Quinn asks.

"Uh, nothing," I say. But when Quinn lifts an eyebrow,

I shrug. "Just maybe visiting my dad?" I admit, and it feels weird to say it out loud, but maybe it shouldn't. "Is that normal?"

I get a collective response of, "Nope," and, "Totally fine," and, "Ah, the ever-present daddy issues."

Thanks, Quinn.

"Where's he at now?" Lorelei asks.

"Florida," Ruby and I say at the same time.

Theo gasps. "I *love* Florida. I mean, aside from the alligators and the humidity. I look like a poodle real quick."

"Why do you want to see him?" Lorelei asks me with a wince.

"I don't know. Closure?"

"You wanna see him just long enough to give him a punch in the face?" Quinn asks.

There's another collective response of, "Quinn!" and, "Rude," and, "I'd pay to see that."

I snort. "I'm not punching my dad in the face."

Quinn shrugs with her bottom lip out. "Just a thought."

"Y'know, I think I heard about a cool pirate festival down in Florida," Theo suggests. "Could be fun."

Ruby looks at me the same time I glance at her. And like with most things, somehow, we're on the same page.

"How do you feel about a festival, Pirate?" Ruby asks with a grin.

"I could do a pirate festival."

"Oh, I love little festivals," Lorelei says.

Quinn shrugs. "Lots of debauchery? I'm in."

And then it hits me that they're seeing this as a road trip of sorts.

"Oh, y'all don't have to come with me."

"We know," Lorelei says. "But we want to."

"For support," Theo adds.

"Yeah, we stick together, Benny boy," Quinn says.

I swallow, appreciating my friends for not the first time.

"I mean, I'd like to visit him alone, honestly," I say.

All four women shrug, as if on cue. I swear we all spend too much time together.

"I want to go to the pirate festival anyway," Theo says.

"Heck yes!" Lorelei raises a fist in the air. "So, we're actually going?"

Ruby grins. "Oh, definitely."

"Well, if Ruby is saying yes, then who are we to argue?" Quinn says with a mirroring sly smile.

"Ooh." Theo bounces on her toes. "Bennett, you'll fit right in too."

I run a hand through my long hair and chuckle.

True.

By the end of the hour, Lorelei has a pen in hand and a schedule plotted out, all with Lucas in her lap. We plan it for next spring, and I try to imagine how I'll phrase that particular letter in my head—how I can possibly propose this to my dad.

Hey, old man, want to finally meet your love child?

Maybe not like that.

The other girls get back to their jobs at Honeywood, but I tug on Ruby's arm before she and Lucas can head out too. I pull harder than intended, and she lands into my chest. Sometimes, I forget she's a lot smaller than me.

"Hey."

She giggles. "Hi."

"Thanks for that."

"For what?"

"For making that decision seem easy."

"I just let you do you," Ruby says with a shrug. "Like you always do."

No, she read my mind like *she* always does.

I trace my thumb over her shoulder. A rush of relief falls over me, like stepping into old shoes. Or like smelling the familiar scent of your home when you come back from vacation. Mine smells like sugar and sweetness. Like Ruby.

"I want you to see him with me," I say.

Her lips—still so pink after all these years—part. "Really?"

"I can't do it without you."

Her hand reaches out to take mine. Our fingers entwine, our pink strings kissing at the seams.

"Well then, you know I've got you," she replies.

I shake my head. "What did I do to deserve you?"

Her face flushes red. The freckles on her nose practically disappear.

"We just happened to have birthdays close together."

"So, you're telling me it's fate then?"

That has her blushing more. I like it too much.

"Maybe."

All I can think to say is, "Lucky me."

The stars must have aligned when they made her my best friend.

But friends don't make other friends blush and love it as much as I do.

17

Ruby

Three Years Before
Ruby & Bennett are Twenty-Seven Years Old

"Bennett?"

"Hmm?"

"I feel ridiculous."

"It's a pirate festival. I think you're supposed to."

"Not *this* ridiculous."

Bennett chuckles from outside the dressing room, but I'm not enjoying this nearly as much.

I stand in front of the mirror, running my hands over the flowing off-the-shoulder white dress. On its own, it might be fine, but the tied corset overtop, along with my very padded bra, accentuates the small breasts I do have. I'm a busty pirate wench through and through.

When Theo suggested the pirate festival, I figured we'd just be drinking.

I was wrong.

She said we were going all out, and after I saw the outfit she'd already bought, I had a better idea of what *all out* meant. It meant having my very tiny, barely there girls *all out*. I swear they're practically reaching my chin, knocking against my face.

"I need another corset," I say.

"Rubes, I'm sure you look fantastic."

"How do you know? You can't even see me."

"I don't need to see you to know that."

"Ha. Your mom taught you well."

He snorts.

Bennett's the worst shopping partner because he claims to like everything I wear, and he keeps hitting on the mannequins, thinking he's being funny. Admittedly, it is hilarious. But that's beside the point.

I've been working and babysitting so much that I waited until the last minute to shop for clothes, and none of my friends who have decent fashion opinions could come with me. So, now, I'm here with my best friend who wouldn't know the difference between an A-line dress or a drop waist. Actually, now that I think about it, I don't know the difference either.

"What are *you* wearing to this thing?" I ask through the door, still cringing at my chest. "Can I wear that instead?"

"Well, I'm not wearing a corset—I can tell you that much."

"Why not? Join the fun."

He laughs. "I don't hate myself nearly enough."

I reach around my back and feel for the strings.

"I'd like a little less self-hatred right about now," I say, waving my hand around, hoping to snag just one knot apart. "Just the teensiest amount."

The attendant tied me up before going to help another

customer. I didn't realize I'd be locked in a pseudo-prison for ten minutes until she came back. I try to tug at one string, fumble, then tug again. I groan.

"You all right in there?" Bennett asks.

"Your dad had better be worth all this."

Bennett barks out a laugh. "You're not dressing up for him, are you?"

"Hilarious," I deadpan.

"Can I help at all?"

I let out a laugh that fades into a whine, flailing at the strings more. My face heats. It's so tight.

Oh God, I'm trapped.

"Rubes?"

"Yes," I say, my voice cracking under the rising panic. "I need a favor."

"Anything."

I wince. "Help me out of my corset?"

I wait a couple seconds. He doesn't respond.

Wait, did that jerk leave me here?

"Bennett?" I whine.

His knuckles rap on the door, making me jump. "Open up."

I catch one final look at my ridiculous chest leaping for freedom, then pull back the lock.

Bennett, biting the inside of his cheek, swivels his eyes over to me. You would think someone just told him it's November 39 or that Buzzy the Bear could fly because his eyes are wide and they're staring—right at my chest. And they linger—like, *really* linger—before snapping back up.

Bennett was totally checking me out.

I wince. "It's super booby, isn't it?"

He swallows. "No. Uh, I like it."

"Really?" I turn around to look in the mirror.

At first glance, I guess it isn't as bad as I thought it was. My boobs *feel* higher than they actually are. I don't see the person I once saw, but she still looks like someone my mom might call a hussy.

Then, from behind me, I see Bennett staring too. His whole body is stiff, like a beautiful statue frozen in time—a tortured one. The hand by his side is clenched tight. His jaw shifts imperceptibly. And there's a small line between his eyebrows as he concentrates on every bit of my figure.

I feel like I'm on fire.

I don't know *this* Bennett. This Bennett that looks at me like he looked at Sarah or Sadie or whatever other S-named girl he dated in high school. The Bennett that looks in pain at the sight of me.

"Maybe I'll keep the corset," I blurt out.

He raises his eyebrows, shaking his head from whatever dazed state he was in.

I made my best friend dazed?

"Really?" he asks.

"Yeah, I think so. It's more comfortable than I thought."

Bennett's jaw tics at the motion.

"Well, comfort *is* key," he finally says, chuckling, low and rumbly and so delicious, scratching behind his head.

Interesting.

"Well, I'm gonna—"

"Wait!" I hold out my hands, slamming the door shut before he can step out.

His eyes, deep brown and intense, slowly move back to me, lingering on my freckles more than he normally might.

"Untie me first. Please? It's a little tight."

Okay, sure, I'm pushing my limits, and the heat slowly covering my cheeks tells me as much. But nobody—and I mean, *nobody*—has looked at me like that. I was with a few men in college, but they didn't have the narrowed eyes that Bennett gets. The small whip of his tongue running over his bottom lip. And it's intoxicating to see that type of look pointed in my direction.

I turn on my heel before I know whether he's giving me that same heated stare he secretly gave in the mirror.

I feel his fingers start to untie my corset. String by string. Loop through loop. The heat of his palms radiates through the fabric. My hair rustles under his low, uneven breathing that exhales onto my neck. I can feel the wispy hairs on the nape of my neck rise.

Then, he growls out a low, "Got it."

Some of my breath comes back when the corset falls, but then his palm splays over my back as he lowers it slowly down my waist. We're in such a tight space, and every movement is like a sting against my skin. Every breath sends goose bumps rolling over my flesh.

"Thanks," I whisper.

"Um, so ..." I feel him take a step back and hear his hand run through his hair. "I'll be back with a ..."

"I could use a belt."

"A belt?"

"Mmhmm. Big pirate belt buckle."

"Cool."

"Mmhmm," I say, still having my lip tucked in. When he doesn't move, I ask, "Bennett?"

"Yep. Yeah. I'm gonna go look for that."

When he finally shimmies out the door and shuts it behind him, I lock it back, lean against it, and shut my eyes.

This weekend is going to be the end of me.

No, my super-hot best friend with his sex-filled gaze will be the end of me.

18

Ruby

I think I can hear pirate music. Or maybe it's a bass line to a popular song. Or a sea shanty.

Someone *yarr*s.

Someone else *woo*s for no reason.

Then, right in my face, there're bouncing boobs with red, white, and blue tassels.

"This place rules," Theo says from beside me, a wide, sloppy grin on her face. "You know, one time, I ..."

But I don't hear the rest.

"What?" I ask, but I know my voice isn't loud enough for her to hear my confusion.

I can barely pick out anything through the crowd, even people who are usually loud enough to cut through the haze. The interior of the musty, packed bar is only a loud hum of conversations I'm getting bits and pieces of that form nothing more than just a cacophony of sound.

A familiar hand lands on my lower back.

"Say something, Parrot?" Bennett asks.

That's better.

My best friend, leaning in to hear me, is a mix of good

smells. There's his usual strawberry scent, but it's combined in a cocktail of rum and sweat, but the pleasant kind of sweat that lingers on Bennett and Bennett alone.

"Yarr," I answer.

Bennett throws his head back and laughs. He has a louder, booming laugh when he's full of alcohol, and I adore it. He's not entirely drunk yet. I've seen Bennett drunk before, and this is the type of tipsy that keeps him merry and happy. He only gets sad drunk when he's had too much, and the last time I saw that version of Bennett was when we were watching the *Honeywood* movie, which, for all intents and purposes, is not a great movie.

But his bottom lip was wobbling because, and I quote, "Queen Bee is *such* a good leader of Honeywood Forest."

Bennett is the cutest drunk.

"Soda water with lime?" he offers.

I nod because, of course, he knows my order by heart.

Bennett squeezes my side before heading toward the bar. I shamelessly—well, maybe with a tiny bit of shame— watch him walk away. I'd be stupid not to. Not when he's dressed the way he is with the loose, swashbuckling white shirt, exposing his chest hair—Christ, my best friend has *chest hair*—the thick belts slung every which way, the heavy boots that kick beneath him, hiked over those tight leather pants that curve over his toned butt.

I tilt my head to the side.

I didn't think I was a leather kind of girl, but you learn something new about yourself every day, I suppose. Plus, it's *Bennett* in leather. It's the fact that he's a teddy bear inside that makes the badass leather all the more alluring.

I wish I could commit this version of Bennett to memory forever. The mysterious kohl eyeliner around his eyes, the coarseness of his dark hair—how I made sure to fluff it up and hair-spray it into a messy position.

I made my best friend look like sex.

And, boy, does he.

Bennett knocks his knuckles on the bar, leaning his weight on his tattooed forearm, peering out to the crowd like he owns the whole dang place. Drawn to whatever pheromones he's putting out in the world, a redheaded woman in a low-cut flowing white dress touches his arm. She just shimmies on in there with some type of confidence and grace I could never have.

She slides next to *my* Bennett.

My heart hammers in my chest, and I know what that feeling is. The gut clench, the way my nerves light on fire, and how, for two seconds, I feel like I should go over there and shimmy between them.

It's jealousy. Raging hot.

But Bennett is my best friend, not my boyfriend, so what do I have to be jealous of? She's gorgeous and probably very sweet. And I'm just an evil, green-eyed monster.

"Whatcha looking at, lady?"

Quinn's breath smells like rum as she slings an arm over my shoulders. She's not normally a cuddly person, but alcohol seems to sway her. Quinn's eyes follow mine to the bar, where the beautiful woman is now arching her chest into Bennett.

God, they look like the most perfect little pirate couple.

Crap, crap, crap.

Quinn sips her drink. "Ooh, Benny boy's getting some."

I curl my bottom lip in. "Mmhmm. Good for him."

It comes off so disingenuous that I instantly feel guilty.

Quinn side-eyes me. "What about you? Want me to play wingman?"

I laugh and shake my head, shifting my boot across the wood plank floor. "I'm not a one-night-stand kinda person."

"Fair. You're probably into super-weird stuff anyway."

"Quinn!"

"What's Quinn doing now?" Lorelei asks, also slinging an arm around the other side of me.

It's too hot in here for touching, but when you've got one friend who's a hugger and the other who's too drunk to care that she normally isn't, I guess I have no choice.

A third arm wraps around my waist, and it's Theo. Now, we're in some form of a group hug, and I've ended up in the middle.

"Love y'all," Lorelei mumbles, her chin resting on the top of my head.

"Love youuu," Quinn murmurs back.

"Let's never stop hugging," Theo says, nuzzling her head deeper into my neck.

It's starting to feel too stuffy, and I'm tangled in too many limbs.

"Um, guys ..." I say, but my protest is drowned out by the sea shanty music.

Bennett comes up with a drink in each hand. "Oh, are we group hugging?"

"Get in here, big dog!" Theo calls, and Bennett wraps his large arms around the four of us, gathering us close.

I think I feel a small drip from one of the drinks. But then I can smell his breath, full of rum. Feel his large chest breathing. His warm air rushing against my ear, like a whisper of heat.

It's suddenly unbearable.

Stifling.

I might pass out.

"I'm gonna get some fresh air real quick," I say, pushing as light as I can against Lorelei's arms.

I'm released, immediately rushing out to the side patio and leaning against the brick wall.

I close my eyes, breathing in the not-so-fresh night air that's muddled with smoke. I'm not sure if it's from cigarettes, vapes, or cannonball fire from off the pier.

I'm surrounded by pirates, but none as hot as Bennett. And that's a problem. A real big problem. Because I'm not supposed to be imagining how to discreetly pinch my best friend's leather-clad ass, am I?

But suddenly, in the midst of thinking about Bennett's tush, I hear a loud call of, "Red?"

Wait a second.

I know that nickname.

Crap on a freaking stick.

My eyes pop open, and I'm greeted by the demanding gaze of icy-blue eyes. The same ones that haunted me as a teen.

"Michael?" I breathe.

Michael Waters's arm is already wrapping around me, holding my waist, dipping around to the spot that Bennett normally touches. He's laughing as he gathers me into a hug, and I can smell the booze on his breath.

I think he kisses the side of my head, but I'm not sure because he's already pulling apart with a, "Hey, you!"

What the heck is happening?

His palms clutch my shoulders as he scans me up and down. I feel like I've been put on display in front of him, and my silly little wench dress with the off-the-shoulder sleeves and very busty corset now feels very inappropriate.

Though, on the flip side, it's also weirdly empowering.

Michael looks at me different. *He's* different. Happier

174

maybe with less of the sly smile he used to offer. His black hair is trimmed shorter on the sides. The length up top looks like it was once gelled, but is now flopped over from the Florida heat and a night of carousing. He has a beard with bits of gray scattered within. It works on him. *Really* works on him.

"You look great," he says.

"I'm fine."

He squints with a crooked smile.

Right. He didn't ask how I was.

"I mean, thanks," I correct.

He laughs, and it's light and pure and ... very, *very* attractive. How can this man pull off everything from broody teen to happy man? He's aged like a fine wine. Or rum, I suppose, considering our location.

"Do you live down here now?" I ask.

"No. Just here for the festival."

"Same."

"Cool."

"Yeah." The word fades off, and he swallows. "Really, you do look great," he repeats.

"You already said that."

A slow smile trails onto his cheeks. "I did, didn't I?"

My face is on fire.

Michael is telling me I look great, and I feel like I've been transported back in time. Back to that closet. Back to teenage insecurities that I thought I'd left behind—though I am still wearing a padded bra, aren't I? I suppose they've never truly left me.

Michael is looking at me with icy eyes, and I'm still melting underneath their gaze, just like I did at fifteen. And just like I did back then, I've still got the thought of Bennett lingering in the back of my mind.

He'd be so angry if he saw Michael.

But who cares?

Michael clicks his tongue against his teeth. "So, you here with anyone or ..."

Bennett has that one girl at the bar, doesn't he? The redhead who isn't me?

I give a slow smile toward Michael, but before I can open my mouth, a large hand with a pink string on its veiny wrist falls over my shoulder. That same hand trails down my spine, all the way to its rightful place on my lower back.

19

Bennett

Please explain to me how Michael "Potato Face" Waters is back in my life.

And touching *my* Ruby.

Michael gives a little smile, and it doesn't look as slimy as it might have nearly ten years ago, but I don't entirely buy it.

His cheeks dent into little dimples, like caverns of deception. God, his face is still so punchable, and I don't know if that makes my jealousy feel justified or if I just feel like a jerk.

"Hey, Michael," I say by way of a greeting.

I hold out my hand. To his credit, he doesn't hesitate before shaking it.

"Bennett. Still with the long hair." He gives a backfiring engine of a laugh. "Well, dang, you fit right in here, don't you?"

"So I've been told."

Michael tongues his cheek. "Still hate me, huh?"

"I wouldn't say that."

"Good to see you with clothes on for once."

I smirk. "Still proud of that prank."

"Guys." Ruby places a palm on my chest.

I realize we're both still shaking each other's hands, like two businessmen stuck in a deal. I pull away at the same time he does.

"Sorry."

"Sorry," Michael echoes, still glancing at her a little bit too long for my taste.

His eyes linger at the small bit of cleavage she now has. At the corset she picked out that tests my limits every time I glance at it myself. At the freckles on her cheeks.

Screw this guy.

Guilt slices through me at the vitriol dripping through my head. I'm not a hateful guy. I don't get all "Macho Man" Randy Savage around dudes just because they look at my friends with lust in their eyes.

So, how is this different? Is it because it's Ruby?

I shake the thought from my head as Michael's eyes swivel to me. Something must show on my face because his eyebrows rise.

"Well, I should get back to my friends. It was really nice to see you again, Red."

"It was nice to see you," Ruby replies.

"Nice to see you, Michael," I add.

"You too, man," he says, giving a wide-eyed pump of his eyebrows, and snorts.

He doesn't mean it. Though I didn't either.

With a final nod, Michael shoves through the crowd, back to whatever hole he crawled from.

Ruby whirls around, a rush of ginger hair falling from her braided bun. She levels a look at me with fire in her eyes. If I didn't know she was such a sweet girl, I might actually be terrified.

She raises a single eyebrow.

Okay, so I'm still a little intimidated.

"What?"

Her eyes widen, and she blinks with purpose. "What was that?"

"What was what?"

"That alpha ... thing."

I laugh. "There was no alpha thing."

"Bennett."

"Ruby."

She shakes her head and grins. "You—"

But her words are interrupted as some new sea shanty starts blasting through the speakers. The whole crowd erupts into cheers.

I reach down, twisting my free hand into hers, and lead her over to a far corner of the outdoor courtyard. I don't like how loud this place is or how I can barely hear myself think, let alone hear my best friend talk.

I rest my other hand on the brick wall next to her head. Her breathing instantly hitches.

Oh.

I didn't realize I'd caged her in. I lean back so as not to crowd her.

I exhale. "I'm sorry if that was weird. I didn't mean it to be."

She nods, more to herself than me.

"Okay. I believe that apology."

She looks off to the side, to my hand on the wall, to some poster in the distance ... anywhere but at me. But even so, she looks so elegant in her search. Her slender neck. Her beautiful freckles.

I sigh. "He's just ..." I bite my bottom lip to think of words, but nothing elegant comes to mind, so I finish with, "He's just always had a weird thing for you."

Ruby finally meets my gaze, her brow furrowing inward. "So?"

"*So?*"

"Yeah. Why does it matter?"

I let out a breathy laugh. "It just *matters*."

"Don't you have someone waiting for you?" she murmurs.

"Do I?"

"The woman. At the bar. The redhead."

Oh.

Sure, she was pretty. Except her hands weren't soft, like Ruby's. Her face wasn't filled with freckles. Her laugh wasn't as light. And when I saw three of my best friends hugging my greatest friend of all, I knew there wasn't going to be another person on my mind tonight anyway.

It's impossible not to notice Ruby in this crowd. Not when she's as beautiful as she is with her exposed shoulders, dotted with pretty freckles. Not when that outfit of hers gives her a winning smile, like she knows the effect it's having on the men around her—no, on *me*. And that confidence is intoxicating.

I reach out, taking Ruby's chin between my thumb and forefinger. I'm being bold. But I've got a little rum in me and a whole lot of nerve, so I do it anyway.

Her green eyes dart to mine.

"You're the only redhead for me," I whisper. "You're my anchor, Rubes."

I gently release her chin, running my palm over her shoulder and slowly up her neck. Touch has never been foreign to us, but this time, I can feel her pulse under my thumb. Her heart is racing just as much as mine. I wonder if it's the alcohol coursing through her. Except, no, she hasn't had a drop all day.

I feel her swallow under my palm and instantly pull back.

Maybe I went too far. Maybe I made it weird.

"Let's get back inside."

"Yeah," she says with a swallow. "Good call."

20

Ruby

By the time I'm back in our hotel room, curled under a blanket that is as thin as a napkin while the air-conditioning moans and Quinn's chain-saw snores keep me awake, I'm still thinking about Bennett.

But when am I *not* thinking about Bennett?

I close my eyes and there he is. Wild hair. Clenched jaw. The heat in his brown eyes, blown out by the rum coursing through his veins. Suddenly, all those old clinch covers on romance novels make sense. I could see me getting swept away by a pirate like Bennett.

"You're the only redhead for me."

No, not a man *like* Bennett.

Bennett himself.

I shake my head.

No, it meant nothing when he said that, and that's what I want. That's how we stay best friends—by not complicating a good thing.

I look down at my wrist and the pink string on it. Frayed, just like our years of friendship with the push and pull of college and laughter. Our promise means nothing but happiness. Trust. Friendship.

I have everything I could ever want. I'm happy. Truly happy.

I've spent a weekend surrounded by my very best, very drunk friends. Quinn's leg is hanging over the side of the bed she shares with Lorelei. Theo is on the ground, halfway in the bathroom. And my best friend of all is sleeping on the other side of this wall.

My anchor.

My phone buzzes, and I smile at the name staring back. I swear he just knows when I'm thinking of him.

Bennett: I can hear Quinn's snores through the walls.

Ruby: She's in the walls!

Bennett: Oh good. So, you are awake.

Ruby: I wonder if her snores are a mating call.

Bennett: You might be right. I could have sworn I heard male snoring down the hall.

Ruby: They must find each other.

Bennett: How's Theo's stomach?

I glance at Theo with her open mouth drooling on the bathroom's tiled floor. Holding back her curls while she leaned over the toilet was a job I wrapped up one hour ago.

Ruby: Empty. :(

Bennett: Poor girl.

Ruby: I hope she doesn't remember dancing on the bar top.

Bennett: I hope she doesn't remember getting us kicked out because of it.

Ruby: Ah, good times. Good night, Pirate.
Bennett: Night, Parrot.

I close my eyes and hold my phone to my chest, feeling good about my decision to end the conversation. I can go to bed now. I can stop fantasizing about my best friend. It's all gravy.

Except I toss and turn under the thin blanket that does nothing to keep me warm.

Left.

Right.

Left again.

One minute passes, or maybe ten, and I'm freezing cold, and I can't stop picturing that hand on the brick wall, the way he caged me in ...

I text him again.

Ruby: Still awake?
Bennett: Sure am.
Ruby: I'm coming over. This room is frigid.
Bennett: Fair warning: mine isn't much better.
Ruby: But you're there. Nothing puts me to sleep faster than our late-night conversations.
Bennett: LOL. Rude.
Ruby: Your voice is nice, I mean!
Bennett: Not as rude.
Ruby: Is your door unlocked?
Bennett: It will be.

I step over Theo and sneak out. When I enter the hallway, the door next to ours creaks open.

Bennett stands in the doorway. He's removed the heavy

pirate eyeliner, and his hair is tied up in a wet bun. He's wearing a Honeywood shirt that pulls across his chest in the most gorgeous way, tightening over every hill and valley of his muscles. He looks more tired than he let on through text, but he's still smiling that smile of his. Lazy with the small line next to his lips.

He smells like strawberries and toothpaste. He must have taken a shower.

"Still drunk?" I ask.

"Nah," he says, shaking his head and rubbing a palm over his face. "Just regretting that last shot."

I smile, patting his bulky shoulder as he clears the way for me to enter his room. It's a mirror image of ours. Though notably less destroyed from the presence of four girls and our collective makeup bags and outfit changes.

I fall backward on the bed, hands stretched above my head, closing my eyes and exhaling into the comfy mattress. But when I open my eyes again, Bennett's gaze is stuck to me. I look down and realize my shirt has ridden up, leaving part of my stomach exposed. His hands are in the pockets of his gym shorts, and I think I see him swallow.

I sit up and pull my knees to my chest. He walks over to the armchair in the corner, stretching out, resting an ankle on the other knee. Bennett's figure overflows in the chair, looking like a king on a throne. His tattooed arm has fresh plastic, encasing his newest ink—an anchor.

Quinn said it was an homage to this wonderful weekend.

I know better.

"Does it itch yet?" I ask, tipping my chin to the tattoo.

He looks down at it and shakes his head. "Not yet."

"I've never really asked. Why do you get tattoos?" I ask. "What's the appeal?"

185

He shrugs. "I like the memories."

"Yeah, okay ..." I say with a laugh. "But all your tattoos are basically things from our childhood."

"My favorite memories are of you."

My heart slams on the brakes, and for a moment, I can't breathe. His barreling laugh breaks the tension.

"You're my best friend, Rubes. Of course I have great memories with you."

"Right," I agree. "Uh-huh."

I don't know why I'm so flustered. Maybe it's the way he's sitting with his wide, muscular thighs spread or how his slightly scruffy chin rests casually on his fist. Or maybe it's because he's looking at me in a way that makes me feel like he's the predator and I'm prey.

I like it. Too much.

"Well, and you're mine too," I admit. "My best friend."

"That's right. I'm yours."

He accepts it like the truth is as simple as breathing. Everything he does is with confidence. I've always admired that about Bennett—his capacity for being in charge of any room he walks in.

"Do you ever get scared?" I ask.

"Of what?"

"Anything. Life. The world. Getting tattoos on a whim."

The sureness slides off his face, and his lips twitch into a sad smile.

"I'm scared of seeing my dad tomorrow."

My heart sinks.

"Oh, yeah?" I ask.

"Yeah."

His eyes trail to the floor, jaw grinding.

"What do you think will happen?" I ask.

He shrugs. "I don't know. I really don't. But it kind of feels ..." He pauses, tipping his head to the side, twisting a thumb through the string on his wrist, running it up and down. "It feels like I'm finally meeting the boogeyman or something, y'know? The unknown entity haunting my life for so long." He blows out air and meets my gaze. His eyebrows are pulled in. His lips tip into a half-smile that doesn't seem happy at all. "It's like I'm standing outside the gates of hell, knocking on the door. Who does that?"

"Someone brave," I answer.

Bennett's half-smile turns into a full one, and this time, it does look genuine.

I don't know what makes me do it, but I reach out and take his hand in mine. He freezes for only a moment before running his rough fingers along mine, tucking themselves beneath my string.

"I'll be there the whole time," I whisper.

"I know you will be."

"Good."

There's a second between us, a moment where his thumb is tracing over my blue veins, up to my palm. I watch the motion, how slow it is, how big and rough his hand is in comparison to mine.

There's a loud pop, I jump, and the air-conditioning starts to whir.

"Great." I give a nervous laugh, pulling my hand away from his. "Cold again."

He chuckles with me, scratching behind his head. "Want me to turn it down?"

"No. We should go to sleep anyway," I say. "I'll power through."

"Extra blankets are in the closet if you need them."

I slide open the closet doors, grab all the blankets and

sheets I can find, and lower down to sit cross-legged on the carpet.

Bennett blinks down at me. "What are you doing?"

"Going to sleep?"

"Are you kidding, Ruby?"

"What?"

He laughs. "You're not sleeping on the floor."

"It's your room that you paid good money for. I won't take the bed."

"You're getting the bed," he says, standing from the recliner, grabbing the pile of blankets from my arms, and tossing them onto the comforter. "Hop up."

"Let's rock, paper, scissors for it."

"No, because it's not up for discussion."

"It's your room."

"Right. And I choose the floor."

"Bennett—"

"Get on the bed, Ruby."

And the sentence—the demand—halts me in my tracks. It feels like a hammer against my chest, pounding on the anvil inside me. Just as I'm told, I stand up and plop my butt right down on that mattress, as if forced by his words.

I think I see his jaw twitching back and forth as his eyes scour over me. A few strands have fallen from the leather cord holding his hair up.

"Okay," I say. It comes out quieter than I would have liked.

"Okay," he echoes. His voice is also hushed.

But then I see him getting to the floor and the coolness of the room rushes in and I don't like it.

Maybe I'm a little high from tonight, from his little whisper of *yours*, or maybe I just don't want my friend sleeping on the floor. Either way, I close my eyes, inhale, and say, "Let's just share the bed?"

I didn't mean for it to be a question, but it is what it is.

I peek one eye open, and Bennett stares at me. His chest is rising and falling.

He quickly shakes his head. "No, I don't think—"

"I'd feel horrible if you were on the floor."

"It's just the floor, Rubes."

"Please?"

There's a beat of silence.

He narrows his eyes.

"Come on," I say, a laugh bubbling out of me. "It wouldn't be the first time we've slept in the same bed."

What I don't say is that the last time we had a sleepover was probably when we both wore matching sheep pajamas and definitely before we were conscious of our adult limbs and didn't have sexual tension you could slice with Bennett's fake pirate sword.

But it's not a big deal.

We're simply two friends who have known each other forever.

Sleeping in the same bed.

Next to each other.

Alone.

Easy-peasy.

21

Ruby

"Right," Bennett agrees, then laughs. "No, you're right."

A hand runs through his hair. It falls from the leather cord in tiny little strands until he pulls it back up. I can't help but watch his biceps shift as he does.

"Well, scoot over then."

And I do. But it's not as simple as *scooting*.

Bennett's eyes lock on to me as I run my palms over the sheets, gripping the edges, pulling myself backward as I slide up the bed. He watches my legs as I push against the sheets. He stares as my back hits the headboard.

I pull one knee up to my chest, and with an almost imperceptible twitch of his eyes downward, I wonder if my sleep shorts are too short. I wonder if my panties are showing through the leg holes. I really hope they're my cute lacy ones but I can't remember.

No, I really hope he didn't see them at all.

That's what a sane person would hope, right?

I meet one knee with the next and finally dip my legs underneath the covers.

Bennett walks to the other side of the bed. The floor

creaks beneath him. It's not even a rickety hotel; he's just such a large guy that the world bends around him. The bed squeaks as he lowers onto it. The cool air follows him under the covers. Goose bumps skitter across my skin. Then, he clicks off the lamp, and we lie there in the dark.

It's silent as we pretend to fall asleep. Well, I do. I don't know if he's pretending. But all I hear is the whir of the air-conditioning as I stare at the ceiling.

He shifts in place. His leg hits mine.

Fire. Pure fire.

"Sorry," I apologize even though it wasn't my fault.

"No, it was me. Sorry."

More silence.

I can feel him beside me, the rising and falling of his chest as he breathes. I can't remember the last time I took a breath at all.

"Do you still wear sheep pajamas?" I ask at the same time he says, "Remember that time we built a pillow fort?"

We both clear our throats and laugh.

"This isn't weird," I say out loud.

"Definitely not," he agrees. "And, no, I don't wear sheep pajamas."

"Bummer."

"I wear dragon ones."

"You're so cool."

He chuckles. "And you? Pink sheep?"

"Clowns."

Bennett bursts out laughing. "Clowns?"

"I have to scare away the monsters under the bed."

"Good call. Clowns are definitely scarier."

"I know. And honestly, if I'd known how cold it was, I might have worn pants."

"Those shorts are short."

191

My face heats, and all I can think to say is, "So, you noticed."

He clears his throat. "I notice things."

"Oh, yeah?"

"Yeah. That's why you're cold, Rubes."

I don't know what makes me say it—the cold making my heart race to keep me warm, the memory of his gaze after he saw me with Michael, or maybe it's the fact that he got an anchor tattoo for me just two hours ago—but I answer, "And what would you have me wear?"

Bennett chokes on a low laugh, followed by a low hum and another rumbling chuckle.

My body tenses at the sound. I haven't heard a jumble of noises sound so sensual in a while.

I hear him swallow. "We should just go to bed. It's late."

"Oh. Okay."

I am so embarrassed. I don't know what I was trying to do, but this, making our shared bed awkward, wasn't it. I think I just wanted more innocent flirting after the fun of tonight, but I should have known not to push our limits.

"Night, Rubes."

"Night, Bennett."

He rolls over.

It only takes a couple more seconds before he murmurs, "Do you ever think about prom night?"

My pulse stops. Absolutely careens to a halt, leaving tire tracks on the road of my heart.

"Prom night?" I ask, as if I have zero idea what he's talking about. "Like ... ten years ago?"

"Was it that long ago?" Disbelief.

I agree. Prom night still feels like yesterday. The way his hands roamed over my skin, down to my ribs, over my tattoo still resting beneath my underwear. The heavy breaths and rushed movements of our bodies together. A permanent mark of *him* that will forever be stamped into me.

"I was shaking," I recall. "At prom."

"I remember. Why?"

"Nervous."

"About the tattoo?" he asks.

I laugh nervously. "Yeah. The tattoo."

Then, Bennett turns over and stares at me. Even in the dark, I can still see the curiosity in his gaze. Maybe it's because I see him every night in my dreams, every line of his face, every small scar etched on the outside. Every little twitch of his mouth that I wish were pressed against mine.

"Have you gotten any other tattoos?" he asks.

Something tells me we're not actually talking about tattoos, which is why I obviously ask, "Have you?"

Sensing what I'm getting at, he lets out a low, rumbling chuckle.

"I tell you everything," he hoarsely whispers.

"Everything?"

"Yeah."

"Well, remind me."

He clears his throat. "Well, since high school, there's been Juliet. And Lily. And ..." He gives a sardonic laugh. "You sure you want to hear this?"

"I do. I'll go next if you want."

"Well, you've told me about ... Sam. And Jacob," he recites slowly, as if expecting more. But there isn't anyone.

Sam. My first college hookup. The first person who ever touched me, outside of Bennett. What he lacked in knowledge, he made up for in enthusiasm. But then again, I was just as inexperienced and just as excited.

Then, there was Jacob with definitely more notches in his belt and who was far more daring. But even though he had a tongue that could spell the whole alphabet and make me finish before he got halfway through, I remember wondering if this was what I'd missed experiencing with Bennett. His fingers weren't Bennett's fingers, and his hair didn't smell like strawberries. I felt too guilty about my thoughts, so we broke up shortly after.

But despite all that, I've never crossed that final line. I couldn't.

Under the covers, I reach out at the same time I feel the back of Bennett's fingers ghosting over my arm, a trail left in their wake as they rise to my shoulder. My breathing hitches in my chest.

"Have you ... are you still ..." I feel so ridiculous even asking. And I don't know why it would even matter. "Because I've never ..." I swallow, and I can't believe I'm even admitting this, but, "I've still never ..."

And in the darkness, I hear Bennett exhale a low borderline growl.

"Me neither," he responds.

"You haven't?"

"No." He laughs, and his voice feels so boyish in the moment. "I don't know why. Couldn't bring myself to do it, I guess."

Bennett's hand runs along my arm again, up to my collarbone, then into the dip below.

And just like with prom night, I'm suddenly shaking. Shaking like a sad little leaf.

His hand retracts when he feels it, as if allowing me space. But I follow the absence, rolling onto my side to face him.

"Rubes ..." The raspy way he says my nickname is now so ... different. "You're shaking."

"Okay," I admit.

"Okay?"

"Yeah."

And in some unspoken exchange, Bennett reaches for me again. His hand lands on my waist, gripping my hip, dragging me even closer. My body is flush with his, and I can feel how quickly his heart is beating. And it only seems fitting that it's beating just as fast as my own.

His lips touch my forehead first, then the space beside my eye, down to my cheek, the corner of my mouth ...

"Can I kiss you?" he asks.

"Yes."

Then, they press against my lips.

And it is *bliss*.

We kiss slow at first. Calm. Gentle. Like Bennett is taking me in, absorbing the feel of me for the first time since we were fifteen. Since our first kiss in Honeywood. But this one already feels different. We're both more practiced. We both know how to move our mouths and sink our tongues. Even though I've kissed a few guys over the years, it was nothing like this. It wasn't the ebb and flow of two people who knew each other in every way but this.

His hand starts to roam up from my hip to my side, along my ribs, resting just below the curve of my breast. The same spot it was in after prom. Like he's waiting. But for what, I don't know.

I let my own hands journey. He feels so different from back then. Now, he's hard everywhere—on his arms, shoulders, chest, stomach. He's made of hills and valleys I've never explored before.

I pause just above his waistline, my heart pounding against my chest like a warning.

Can we go back after this?

His thumb runs a path along the U above my ribs and

below my breast. A barely there line, but he doesn't seem to care. Bennett exhales against my mouth, leaning into a long, unmoving kiss. And then he pulls back.

Our mouths are just inches away, little exhalations in the darkness. Hints of minty toothpaste.

I wonder if he's thinking the same thing I am.

Where do we go after this? Can we still be best friends?

I lean in and place a small kiss against his exposed neck.

I can, the kiss says.

That one little kiss is what causes his thumb to finally rise, trailing under my bra and over the peak of my breast. His thumb rubs over my hardened nipple. A moan escapes my mouth.

His lips collide with mine again, and suddenly, it's frenzied, but so am I. Inhales and exhales that are no longer sweet but needy.

His fingers move along my bra to the back where he unhooks it with two fingers. I feel it fall down my shoulders, caught under the loose sleeves of my shirt. His hand finds my breast again, kneading it in his palm. I can feel my face heating.

"Bennett."

He halts in place. "Sorry, too much?"

"No, just ... I'm sorry."

"For what?"

"They're ... small." And I feel so ridiculous even admitting it, but what if he expected more? What if I'm just a letdown? So, the words flow out in a garbled mess of, "I wear a push-up bra. Which I know is so ridiculous because I'm twenty-seven, but ..."

"I love them," he growls against my lips. He palms the one breast again, the roughness of him making my nipples harder, sending zips of nerves down to my stomach. "They're a perfect handful."

With another swipe of his thumb, I let out the smallest of whining exhales.

"So perfect," he repeats, tugging up the hem of my shirt and dipping his head under the covers to capture my nipple between his lips. He flicks his tongue. "So, so perfect."

I lift a leg to wrap around his hip, and he presses against me. And he's so hard. I've known since forever that Bennett isn't lacking in size, but feeling him grind into me makes me almost light-headed.

With every ounce of courage I have in me, I reach out between us and palm the length of him.

Bennett lets out a heady sigh, biting my nipple and taking it between his lips again, licking and sucking and groaning as I glide my hand up and down his cock.

He places a single kiss on my breast before crawling up to lean his forehead against mine.

"Want to know a secret?" he whispers. I push my palm down the outline of his cock, and he grunts against me. "Christ, Ruby."

"Yes, I want to hear a secret."

He chuckles as I keep stroking. "I've wanted to kiss you for a while," he admits. "And I should have kissed you again immediately after our first one."

"Why didn't you?"

His hand slides down between my legs, pushing my sleep shorts and panties to the side. He traces a long line along my slit.

"Because I was very, *very* stupid."

A single finger dips inside me. My back arches as a second finger joins the first, curling and pumping. I've never felt so nervous, so wild, so filled with energy in my life.

"Bennett," I whisper against his lips because it feels right and because I like that he grinds against my palm even harder when I say it.

"God, I need you," he insists in a rumbling tone, pulling away and ripping the covers off of us.

The cool air hits my sleep shorts, and I can tell just how wet I've gotten.

He's pulling the hem of my shirt over my head, then sliding my bra straps down my shoulders as he kisses across my chest.

"These pretty freckles," he murmurs so quietly that I'm not sure I'm even meant to hear it.

He tosses my bra and shirt to the floor, kissing over to my stomach and licking a small line down the center. I suck in a breath.

"Not shaking now, are you, Rubes?" he says, and he's right.

I'm so relaxed, falling into him as he kisses his way down my torso, hooking his thumbs into both my sleep shorts and underwear and tugging them down. And then his lips meet my hip bone, right where my only tattoo is normally hidden by layers of fabric.

"Hello, old friend," he says to the strawberry.

And I'm smiling. I'm smiling so big that it hurts. At his words, his touch, his familiarity that only he can achieve ... everything.

His warm breath hits between my bare legs. His palms part my knees, and my instinct is to tug them back together, to hide from my best friend. But I don't. Because there's no hiding from Bennett tonight.

He must sense my hesitation because he pauses.

"Talk to me, Ruby. You all right?"

"Mmhmm," is all I can get out.

"Is this okay?"

"It's better than okay."

"Perfect," he says. Then, his head disappears between my legs, and a single kiss lands on the inside of my thigh. "My sweet, sweet girl," he murmurs, and the sound of it has my heart skyrocketing into my throat. The care behind it. The way he cherishes the words with his tongue. He kisses up, up, up, until his smooth tongue finally laps over my wet center.

A breath catches in my throat, the start of a word that never finishes.

"My sweet girl tastes just as sweet," he says, and then his tongue rolls over me again. It's warm and wonderful and unreal.

And when I chance a look, I'm amazed by the sight—the come-to-life vision of so many fantasies. The broad shoulders of my best friend. The tattooed arm curled up onto my stomach. And that pink string tied just below a hand holding me down.

I watch as he feasts, licking and sucking and moaning. It's lewd but somehow also beautiful and intoxicating—how my best friend devours me. Nerves spark through me with every lashing of his tongue. My chest heats when he slides two fingers inside once more. I buck against him.

Have sex with me, Bennett, I think.

No, I moan it.

The words echo in the room, but they don't feel like my own. His licking slows and gently turns to soft kisses against my thigh.

He places his chin on my pubic bone, as if we were just sitting here, hanging out. Just two pals.

And then he laughs and kisses my tattoo again.

"I ..." A choked-out chuckle. "Ruby ..."

My face heats. "Sorry, it just came out. If you don't want to—"

"Please," he says. Then, he starts to crawl over me, large arms caging me against the bed, his hair wild around us both, eyebrows turned in, like the words physically pain him to say. "Please say that again."

I reach out to run my hand over his cheek, against his jaw. The light stubble tickles my palm, and he turns his head to kiss the center of it.

"Would you want to ..." My confidence is a little lost now—lost in the sudden softness of his demeanor and the heaviness of his stare.

And Bennett, being Bennett, he just knows. He closes his eyes and nuzzles against my hand.

"Whatever you want," he whispers against my palm.

Say it, say it, say it.

Have courage, Ruby.

"Please have sex with me, Bennett."

Our eyes meet, and he nods.

"Anything you want, Ruby. Anything at all."

22

Bennett

I tried to not do this. But did I try as hard as I could have?

Probably not.

If I had, I wouldn't be greeted with the image before me right now—my beautiful best friend with ginger hair splayed out around her head like a fiery halo. Her freckles, like constellations over her cheeks and nose. And her plush pink lips, slightly parted, as if anticipating what's to come.

"Condoms?" she asks at the same time I say, "Protection?"

We laugh, a skittering sound of nerves floating between us.

I've had partners through the years. I like everything about the female body—too much to not explore. But sex? No. I've never had sex. And the way my chest hurts when I look at Ruby tells me why I could never go that extra mile. I was waiting for this—for her.

"Miranda put me on birth control at sixteen," Ruby answers.

"I remember," I respond, leaning my head in, placing a kiss on her neck. "You were sick for a week."

"You dropped off Gatorade," she says with a laugh, and then I laugh, too, because that seems so ridiculous in retrospect.

"I had no idea what to do. I just didn't like to see you in pain."

"I know."

Her palm runs along my chin. I lean into it.

"What about you?" she asks. "Condoms?"

"Well, as a virgin with zero expectations of having sex this weekend, no. No condoms."

My best friend simply shrugs. "I'm fine with that."

I snort. "Rubes."

"Well, we've ..." She stops before adding, "We've never been with anyone else. And I trust you."

I trace my thumb over the curve of her cheek, up to the fine ginger eyebrows, to the array of freckles across her nose. It feels greedy, being this close, being able to observe her in such detail without her hiding behind strands of hair or averted gazes.

"I trust you too. More than anyone else in my life."

"I trust you more than a bungee cord," she adds. "Or a plane. Or even a roller coaster brake system."

"That's a helluva lot of trust."

She pumps her eyebrows. "I know."

"So, we're doing this?"

Ruby nods eagerly without saying words, but her movements are answer enough. She snakes her hands down my chest, over my abs, and to my gym shorts, where I'm as hard as a rock, waiting for her. The feel of her hand sliding over the length of me is so surreal.

How many times have I imagined this?

She dips her palm underneath my waistband and tugs my gym shorts down, along with my boxer briefs. And then

I'm hovering over her, forearms on either side of her head, my cock bobbing down and throbbing from want.

I slide a hand between her thighs, dipping a finger in. She's soaked. She was before my lips even touched her.

"Bennett ..."

I love the way she says my name. The way it lingers on her tongue in a way it never has before. I can feel my cock jump forward.

"So wet for me," I groan.

"Please," she begs, and, God, if that doesn't almost make me come on its own.

Taking myself in my hand, I center in front of her, teasing the head between her legs. And after a moment or two of her squirming beneath me, trying to scoot closer—the greedy girl—I start to dip in. One inch in, out, then back in, watching Ruby's beautiful face with her tilted-in eyebrows and small exhalations.

"How's that feel?" I ask.

"Keep going."

I push in more, but she's so tight. I slide my palm up between her breasts, splaying my fingers out to capture both nipples with my thumb and pinkie. Her chest is so narrow, and my hands are so large. She's perfect for me. How she could ever be embarrassed about her breasts is baffling.

My fingers trace over her nipples, and it has her relaxing enough for me to give a final push, sliding enough so that our hips touch. And it's otherworldly. It's heaven. And the angel beneath me, with her soft skin and parted pink lips, looks like a gift from above.

I work my way out and back in slowly, trying to move in a way that makes sense. Ruby starts shifting against me too, pushing down as I push in. After a couple seconds, we find some form of a rhythm, and I don't know why I'm surprised. *Of course* we were going to be good at this.

I start to move fast, and, *Christ*, she feels so good. Her body is bobbing up and down with each thrust, her fists gripping the sheets.

My hand goes up to her neck, trying to steady her more. I can feel her pulse under my thumb, just like I did at the bar, and it's racing.

Maybe that's too much.

But when I pull away, her hand jerks up to grasp my wrist and place it back. I follow her lead, placing my palm around her neck. Her hand applies pressure to my own, tightening my grip.

Well, isn't she full of surprises?

"Like that?" I whisper.

"Please."

I tighten my grip more, and she moans.

"My girl's so polite."

My sweet, not-so-innocent girl.

I hold her there as I thrust in harder, and what a gorgeous sight it is. My best friend under my palm, the pink string of our promised forever adorning my wrist, and the tattoos trailing up my arm, all dedicated to her.

There are so many things unsaid, but I don't need to say them.

She's *my* Ruby.

I pump faster, breathing heavier, and she feels *so* good. Everything about her is intoxicating. Her red hair. Her freckles. How small she is beneath me, clutching at my arm, pushing her neck into my palm.

"Ruby, I'm not sure I'm gonna last much longer."

"I don't care," she says through rasping breaths. "Please."

She's gonna end me on her niceties alone.

But my real undoing is when I watch—actually watch—us *fuck*. I steal a glance below at my cock sliding in and out of her, her body squirming beneath me.

"Bennett—"

She doesn't need to finish her sentence before I can feel her clenching around me, letting out a soft moan that sends my own orgasm barreling through me. Both our moans muffle into each other as I bite into her shoulder, and she grips my hair into a fist.

I laugh a little—at how long it took us to get here—and then she's laughing, too, and I'm kissing her freckled shoulder all over again.

This is what relationships are supposed to feel like. This is what true companionship is.

"Why does it feel like I've been saving myself for you all this time?" she whispers against my skin.

I chuckle. "I think I've been doing the same."

And I wonder if I have, if I just knew this was my future.

I've worked for so many things, but this? True love and companionship—a type of commitment that my mom never knew—is the final puzzle piece to make me feel whole. And to think I found it at seven years old and kept it.

I pull the covers over us and hold her against my chest. She runs a palm over my cheek. I peek at the string adorning her wrist. The promise of our future wedding. But I'm not waiting any longer.

I plan to wife up my best friend as soon as possible.

23

Ruby

Bennett's hair is wilder in the mornings. I can't help but reach out my finger to trace through the mess of it. The inky-black of each strand is highlighted by the sun's morning rays, granting them a burnt-copper tint. I never knew it could look like that.

I start shaking again.

I should be overjoyed that I woke up next to this gorgeous man with his barrel chest pressed against my back and thick arm thrown over my waist. But instead, my gut feels like it's filled with lead, heavy, and dragging me deeper and deeper into the depths of my drowning mind.

Too many questions.

Where do we go from here? Do we date now? Do we know how to date?

And do we know how to break up too?

I haven't met a single couple that's made a lifetime of love work. My dad. My mom. Bennett's mom. Heck, all of my friends are nearing thirty, and none of us have encountered a successful anything. Valentine's Days and first dates and anniversaries ... it's all just performative love. The type of emotions I have for Bennett are beyond holidays. We aren't boyfriend-girlfriend material.

Sometimes, I hear the phrase, "This is my person," thrown around by the youth at Honeywood, but they don't get it. Not really.

People who haven't experienced this type of friendship will never understand. A *person* is not your college drinking buddy or your nine-to-five lunch pal or your makeshift therapist roommate.

A *person* is when everyone else in your life—siblings, parents, close friends—are a third, fourth, or fifth wheel, no matter the circumstances. When the larger group or party or town is just ancillary noise around the bubble encapsulating the two of you. You will always feel ostracized from society, but the other odd bird is *your person*, so who cares that nobody else *truly* gets you? There's a tether between your heart and theirs.

If you don't have a person, you'll never understand.

And Bennett is my *person*.

What if this crashes and burns, and I'm left with the scraps of a best friendship that once was? What will happen to the boy who spoke up for me in Honeywood? Where will my voice be once he's gone?

There's also the embarrassing fact that I begged my person to wrap his large hand around my neck and squeeze.

Yikes.

Honestly, how do you come back from that kind of truth?

The worst part is, I know we'll laugh about it.

I know Bennett will run his large hand through my hair, tuck a strand behind my ear, and kiss right where the freckles meet between my nose and eyes before murmuring something like, *Sweet girl*, with a smirk on his face and a rumbling chuckle in his throat.

But then what?

Then what?

I do think we were meant to be each other's firsts. I was waiting for him, just as he was waiting for me—even though it's not like we ever shook on it or anything. And maybe we're just both waiting for the hammer to drop on our thirtieth birthday. Another bit that we'll laugh our way through because that's what we always do.

Ha-ha, you bought a gown, right?

And, *Ha-ha, here are my vows!*

Everything is a joke.

But a real—big R—relationship?

Who survives that?

Marriage isn't truly my destiny, and it never will be. So, where do we go from here?

I close my eyes and run a hand down my face.

I feel so ridiculous, like a little girl trying to reconcile teenage promises to reality, but what is there to reconcile? The fact is, I had amazing, nasty, wonderful, movie-production-level sex with my best friend.

And now?

I don't know what.

I slowly slide a leg out from under the sheets and place a toe onto the carpet. Bennett doesn't move.

I take step after step, walking silently backward toward the door, watching my best friend's adorable, sleepy face fade away as I sneak into the hall and back to my own room.

My back lands against the closing door, and the moment the door snicks shut, a voice whimpers, "Ruby?"

I look at the floor. Theo squints up at me, still curled

into a tight ball, covered in kicked-around blankets and hugging a pillow to her head.

"Hey," I coo. "How ya feeling?"

Her eyes dart to my waist and back up. "Why are you coming in from the hall, not wearing any pants?"

Oh my God.

I fist the hem of my shirt and pull it down.

I left my freaking panties in Bennett's room.

"I ... it's ..." I can't find the words. My face is red hot. My nerves are incinerating.

"Are you okay?" she croaks.

"I'm fine."

"Where were you?"

"Just ... getting ... um ..."

My brain cannot compute any response.

"Your eyes are red."

They are?

From the bed, I hear a muffled voice ask, "What are we talking about? Is Ruby on drugs?"

I tug down the hem of my T-shirt again, making sure my ass is fully covered, and walk from the entryway to see Quinn, face-down in a pillow. Lorelei is next to her, squinting at me through the beam of sunlight filtering through the window.

I slowly nod and joke, "Yep. Sure am."

Quinn's fist pops in the air. "Hell yeah, Florida!" But then she immediately groans, flopping her face back into the pillow.

I wince. "You okay?"

She shakes her head side to side with a muffled moan. "No. Too much movement. Need. Coffee."

"I can get us coffee."

There's a zombie-like chorus of agreement with words that sound like *puhhh*, but might actually be *please*.

I let out a weak laugh, tiptoe to my bag with my tee held in my fist, and dig out underwear and some pants. I'm not even gonna worry about a bra because who would notice anyway?

"Perfect," he called them.

My small breasts were perfect.

I smile to myself, but wipe it clean just as quickly.

I don't want anyone to know—not until I touch base with Bennett. I'm not worried about him telling. He knows how to keep a secret from anyone but me.

I'm shaking again, trying to maneuver my wobbly legs into the holes of my pants.

Theo, now cocooned in blankets, scrunches from the bathroom like a worm.

"I wanna come back here next year," she mumbles. "Even Ruby parties hard."

Ha. Yay me.

I'm trying not to look at Bennett, even though I love how my best friend looks when he drives. I love the way the Florida sun highlights those copper tones I only just noticed this morning. I love how he squints because he forgot his sunglasses, and I especially love the way his large arm looks bigger in his crowded truck as he lowers the visor.

But I focus on other things, like palm trees, or tiny strip malls with peeling paint, or cracked sidewalks, or the rev of a sporty engine as a red car races past us. I focus on anything, except discussing last night because I don't even know where to start.

I startle when Bennett's hand suddenly lands on my knee.

"Hey there," he observes with a chuckle. "You're jumpy."

"Just nervous." I try to smile. "We *are* meeting your scary old man after all."

"Oh. Yeah ... well ..." He clears his throat. "I'm not entirely focused on that right now, to be honest." The side of his lip twitches, but the smile won't come out to play, no matter how hard he wants it to.

I curl my lips in. "Hey, today is about you, okay?"

Bennett's palm tightens on my thigh before pulling away, greeting his other hand on the wheel. His jaw cuts back and forth. He winds his fists over the leather, causing it to whine under his grasp.

"Rubes?"

"Hmm?"

"Do you regret last night?"

"What?" I swivel my head to him quickly, watching as his stoic face stays on the road ahead.

The line between his brows cuts deep.

"No," I argue. "I would never regret sleeping with you." And I mean it. But the problem is more complicated than regret, isn't it?

He lengthens his arms, stretching out before exhaling.

"You just seem off. And that's fine," he adds quickly. "That *is* fine. We did things we'd never done before. But I just wanna make sure that it was okay."

I hate how easily he can read me. My thoughts are circling fast, and for thoughts that are unsaid, they sure are loud. I might as well have subtitles flashing over my head: [*internally screaming*]

When I don't respond, Bennett sucks in, expanding his

large chest, and lets more words rush out. "Listen, I know you better than I know myself sometimes." He gives a choked laugh and raises an eyebrow. "I mean, yikes, that sounds kinda cocky."

"Super cocky," I agree with a grin.

"Right. But I know every twist of your beautiful lips, Rubes. I can call you beautiful now, right?"

"Sure."

He chuckles. "Well, I know what it means when you speak less than usual. I know that you're nervous when you pick at your fingernail. Like you're doing right now."

I gasp and jerk my hand away from my thumb.

He smirks. "So, what's wrong?"

I open my mouth to joke, *Well, I had your wiener inside me*, but that doesn't sound right. And neither does the truth of, *I cannot live without you, so let's pretend your wiener was never inside me.*

Thankfully, the GPS cuts me off before I can speak, and reality sets in. We're driving to his dad's house. Today isn't about us or me or whatever our complicated friendship might become. It needs to be about Bennett.

I point out the window. "Looks like a left up here."

Bennett turns the truck into the gravel lot, mumbling in a singsong cadence, "Changing the subject ..."

His truck rumbles under a peeling wooden sign, past rows of trailers with varying forms of wooden porches, concrete slabs, colorful doors, and plastic armchairs.

"Lot seven, right?" I ask, rolling down the window, as if that will help me search better.

It's like when my mom would drive and say, "Turn down the radio! I gotta see where we're going!"

But it's honestly just something to occupy my mind.

"Oh, there it is!"

Bennett takes an empty parking space in front of an off-white trailer. There's a rusted gold plate nailed to the side that reads 7. A silver and black motorcycle is parked out front. Deflated plants sit single file in terra-cotta pots. A tinkling wind chime hangs beside the screen door.

I reach for the door handle, but the lock clicks into place.

Bennett stares at me from the driver's seat. The divot between his eyebrows is deeper. He looks in pain. When his hand reaches out, I take it without question because I can't stand sad Bennett. I wrap his large mitt in both of my smaller palms, and he slides me across the bench seat to him.

"Don't you want to go in?" I ask.

"I don't care about him right now. Only you. So, talk to me."

"But your dad—"

"Screw my dad."

"I'd rather not."

He grins as his free palm spreads over my leg, hooking behind my knee to pull me even closer. I'm partially in his lap now. My butt honks the horn, and I jump, causing the deep lines in his forehead to lessen as his face eases into a smile.

Bennett tilts his head to the side, running a hand up to my shoulder, over the strap of my tank top, then to my neck, where he gives a small squeeze. He quirks up a single eyebrow. My body erupts in goose bumps.

"Ha-ha," I say sarcastically, sticking out my tongue and tugging his hand away. "Very funny."

He lets out a breath of air through his nose, tonguing his cheek.

"Listen." Bennett's fingers fumble into mine. "We tell each other everything, right?"

"Right."

"Well, what if I said I've kept something from you?"

I give a mock gasp. "For shame."

He chuckles. "It's just about one thing though. A very small thing."

"Okay. What size of small are we talkin' here?"

His lips twitch. "Mouse-sized."

"Mouse? Not ant?"

"I'm pulling out the big stops. Is mouse-sized okay?"

"I can handle mouse."

"Good." He grips my hand tighter, and I give a quick squeeze back. "Ruby, I ... Christ, this is hard." His eyes dart up to mine, and slowly, a breath deflates out of him. "I want you."

There it is.

My heart races. I imagine it skipping rope in my chest—doing all the fancy whips and double-Dutch gymnastics—and it's all to the triple-word beat of *I want you.*

Bennett Shaw wants *me*, Ruby Sullivan.

His hand pulses against mine. "Penny for your thoughts?"

"That's not mouse-sized," I murmur.

"No," he says with a chuckle. "I guess not."

My mind isn't fast enough to consider a snarky response or a silly bit or, worse than that, the truth—that I don't know where we go from here because Bennett Shaw is my lifeline. I won't brandish the scissors to snap our taut thread.

But what if it worked? my mind thinks.

What if it doesn't though?

"This weekend was perfect." I twist my hand in his,

playing with the string on his wrist. "Why do we have to mess with something so perfect?"

It was a terribly wrong thing to say.

The energy is sucked out through the cracks of the truck, vacuumed away by my words. Every little line on my best friend's face is smoothed out. But he's not relaxed. He's a corpse of himself. I wish I could rewind time just to never see his face look like this ever again.

"It's just ... I've seen so many relationships end horribly," I add. "I haven't seen a single one go right. Have you?"

He shakes his head. "No. You're right. But it's us, isn't it?"

"And what makes us so immune?" I ask.

He opens his mouth and closes it. "Because it's us."

"And a gut feeling is gonna be enough?"

"Vows might be."

My head jerks back. "Vows? Vows don't work, Bennett. We know that."

"Okay, but ..." He blinks, as if my sentence just hit him. "Wait, don't you want to get married one day?"

"To you?"

"In general."

It's a tricky question. If I were to marry anyone, it would be Bennett. But even then, it'd be a risky move.

Marriage feels so superficial. I don't want a participation trophy for love. Commitment like that hasn't been on my radar since my parents told me they were breaking up at twelve years old. I saw the ups and downs of it all and its inevitable end.

"No," I answer. "No, I don't really want marriage."

Bennett stares at me with slightly parted lips, a slash of a line between his eyebrows once more. I look down at our joined hands, feeling every scratch and callous and rough, wonderful edge of his fingers. But his hand is limp in mine.

"I didn't know that," he says softly. "I mean, I did. Sure, after your parents divorced, I knew you didn't like marriage, but ... I didn't exactly know it was a never kind of thing."

I sit there, winding my finger through his bracelet as he does the same to mine. My heart is pounding. I wonder if he can hear it. We don't speak, but I know I should.

"I mean, a piece of paper guarantees nothing. What if I lose you?" I ask, voicing the biggest fear of all. "Then, we're just two people stuck in an unhappy marriage."

"All I'm asking is to be your best friend forever," he counters. A beautiful twitch at the edge of his mouth. A gracious smile. "That's it."

I want to mirror him, but I can't.

He doesn't get it.

"That's all I'm asking for too," I argue.

"But not really," he says. "Not in the same way."

I try to look away, but he gently places his forefinger below my chin. He tilts my head up. His eyes dart between mine.

And then my best friend repeats with all the confidence in the world, "I want you. And marriage, to be honest."

"Bennett ..." But the word fades away, lost in the cloud of his confession. And I want to agree, but, "I can't?"

It comes out as a question, as if my brain wants to say yes.

I understand where he's coming from. I do. We've always had a need to be together, like two halves of a soul clutching on to their matching piece. But he's not understanding that our friendship transcends something as trivial and ephemeral as *I want you.*

When I don't respond, he sighs. "I mean, not believing

in marriage ... it's not like saying, *I don't believe in ghosts.*"

"Well, I don't believe in ghosts either."

"Do I even know you?" he jokes. To his credit, he is smiling, and it does seem genuine even if there is a crack—a small wink of unease.

He tucks a piece of hair behind my ear—a nervous move to stay close while still uncomfortable. I get it. I do. "I'm sorry. I just ... how could I have not known this was a deal-breaker for you?"

"I didn't know it was a deal-breaker for you," I counter.

"It's not. I mean ... it shouldn't be. It ... I don't know. Maybe it is."

"I *have* thought about it before."

"You have?"

"Yeah. When we made these bracelets. But after everything I've seen since then ... the real world and all these failed relationships around us ... I just ... I don't know."

"But you've considered it?"

"At one point."

Bennett is sitting there, playing with my hand, but blinking to himself. Partly here. Partly not.

I open my mouth, then shut it. I don't know how to respond. He must know that, marriage or not, he's the only thing in my life that matters.

"How about we talk about us after we meet your dad, okay?" I suggest.

After a second, a quick dash of his eyes to mine, he nods. "Okay. I can wait."

"Yeah?"

"Yeah."

Then, he tugs on my pink bracelet, as if cementing the agreement. But it doesn't matter how we slice the differences; I'm not sure what else can be said.

24

Bennett

This isn't how I imagined today going.

I fell asleep with my arms around my best friend, hearing her small puppy-like snores, and now, I'm sitting outside my deadbeat dad's house with that same woman of my dreams halfway in my lap, but pulling away with every passing second.

I turn off the engine. "All right. Let's do this."

I get out of the truck and walk-jog around to open Ruby's door for her. She takes my hand and hops down to the crunching gravel. But when I place a hand on the small of her back, she jumps.

Ruby's acting weird now, and it's my fault. All because I mentioned marriage.

But I had no idea that wasn't on her life map. I know her feelings toward matrimony are uneasy at best, given her parents, sure, but I figured, based on our promise at twelve years old, it'd be different with us.

It's always different with us.

Maybe I'm just being romantic—the voice of a boy who watched his mom long for something concrete. At the end of the day, my promise with Ruby was between naive teenagers, wasn't it? What did I expect? A legal contract?

When I look at Ruby, she seems fine. She's just taking everything in, blinking at the sunny morning sky and feeling the breeze coming in from the far-off ocean. She looks so out of place here with her pristine floral T-shirt and ginger hair, tied back in a demure braid. My quiet, shy girl.

"So, we're here," she says as way of conversation, looking around.

There's a small stump, tabling an ashtray and old cigarette butts. A weathered foldout chair is by the stairs. A rusted picnic table is between his house and the neighbor's. Wind chimes tinkle in the breeze.

We walk across the gravel and up the stairs, each wooden board creaking beneath my boots and slapped with Ruby's sandals.

I ring the doorbell.

Meeting my dad should have been the hardest part of this weekend, and now, I don't even care. I just want Ruby to look at me with her little smile and dotted freckles and everything in between. I want our friendship.

Not *this*—this awkwardness.

I need my best friend. Not a distant one-night stand.

Nobody answers the door. I can feel the frustration bubbling up. I jab my finger on the doorbell again.

"Bennett," Ruby chastises.

"Well, if he's not gonna answer, what's even the point?"

What was the point of coming down here—of partying and ruining the best thing in my life—if the guy we're here to see isn't even going to answer his damn door? I've waited more than twenty years to meet the man who carelessly brought me into this world and he's not even ready for us?

Finally, the door swings open, my heart rises in my

chest, and I take a step back. Because staring back at me is ... *me*. Sort of.

Ben Shaw has my chin, my brown eyes, and he's the same height as me. But while I inherited my mom's black hair, Ben's is an ashy blond with little streaks of gray, cut short on the sides and rough up top. He's wearing a gray shirt with a few stains—maybe motor oil—but it cinches tight against his large arms that hang limply by his sides.

I'm staring at a distorted time machine.

His eyes are wide as he says, "Ben."

"I go by Bennett actually," I correct, holding out my palm.

"Bennett," he echoes, shaking my hand.

There's a twitch at the edge of his mouth. It should be nice, but I can't help but feel put off by it. If he's so happy to see me now, why hasn't he seen me before?

I try to shake the thoughts off.

Christ, I'm on edge.

"Was making breakfast. You like blueberry pancakes?" He throws a thumb over his shoulder before glancing between us on his front porch.

"Sure," Ruby answers.

I nod in agreement, but say nothing.

He steps aside, and Ruby and I walk past him in silence. Ruby's fingers gingerly entwine in mine and give a small squeeze. My heart settles into the familiar comfort, of my best friend doing what she does best—being my anchor.

Ben Shaw's house is, dare I say, a little cozy. A well-worn couch sits in the corner. A stack of old magazines lies beside it. A coffee cup sizzles on the low table, resting on top of a coaster that resembles a tiny vinyl record. The walls are covered in frames, housing memorabilia, ranging from vintage concert posters, photos of him in a leather jacket

220

beside the motorcycle outside, and group pictures with similar bikers in varying degrees of leather garb.

"Smells good," Ruby says, nodding to the small kitchenette, where bacon sizzles on the stove.

Ben shuts the door. He's watching me closely, maybe trying to find pieces of himself in me, like I did to him.

He wipes his hand on his dark denim with rips and holes that don't look manufactured. "Didn't even introduce myself. I'm Ben. What's your name, little lady?"

I don't like how he approaches Ruby. I hate even more how casual it seems, like I'm back in high school, introducing a girlfriend to my parents—something he and I should have done in a perfect life, but we never did it in mine.

"I'm Ruby." She takes his hand with a smile that lights me up from the inside out. Those freckles could power the world. "I'm Bennett's friend." And they could destroy it too.

Friend.

Ben's eyes dart between us, skepticism in his look. I know because it's the same expression I have.

"So, y'all went to the pirate festival?" Ben starts, and I'm happy he drifts past the awkwardness.

"Yes, sir," Ruby says.

"I used to steer that ship, y'know. The one in the harbor?"

Her face brightens. "No way."

Ben grabs a spatula, flipping it around in his palm. "Yeah. Me and a few buddies with our big hats and earrings."

Ruby's shoulders rise to her ears in excitement, like she's sitting in a library story time. I chuckle because it's adorable.

I could marry her.

221

But, no, that's a dangerous thought, isn't it?

"Why don't you do it anymore?" I ask him.

"Requires a lot of partying. Day drinking ourselves to death." He winks at her. "I'm old now."

The wink has my smile dropping. "You're only in your mid-forties. You're not that old."

He looks to me and clears his throat. "Yeah, well, you party too much when you're younger—"

"And you knock up your girlfriend?"

"Bennett," Ruby hisses.

My dad's jaw clenches, but he stands still. "Yeah. Something like that."

I'm being rude, and I know it. I need to calm down.

I turn and stare at the frames. "You in a motorcycle club or something?"

Ben's face breaks into a nostalgic type of smile, one you only get when the memories are especially good. "Just a crew I like to ride with."

"Bennett has a bike too," Ruby chimes in.

"Yeah?"

Ruby nudges me. "Oh, yeah." She leans onto her elbows, ghosting a finger over my figure. "Fits his bad-boy look, huh?"

This is the Ruby I know. Supportive. Comforting. The Ruby that only comes out when it's just us. And right now, even though we're in the presence of my personal demons, she's the one wearing chain mail and wielding the sword for me when I can't.

"I had hair like that, too, when I was your age," Ben says. "Drove the women crazy. Though it was the bike mostly."

My jaw grinds. I don't like the insinuation of *women* who aren't my mom. I also don't like that there's more we might have in common. The motorcycle was enough.

"Neat," I answer because I can't think of anything else that wouldn't be some semblance of rude.

Silence again.

Ben flips the pancakes in the skillet. They look like they don't need to be touched at all.

"So ..." He clears his throat, and it comes out almost like a cough. "You ride. That's cool. Where do you work then?"

"Honeywood."

"That ol' theme park? No kidding."

"He's actually head of maintenance," Ruby says.

I glance to her, and she's beaming like she can't hold in the pride she feels. God, I want to bottle it up and save it for a rainy day.

"Wow," Ben says. "Look at you. Big man on campus. Well, big man on theme park?"

Ruby giggles at his attempted joke. I blow air through my nose. A sort of laugh.

They're both trying. Just try.

"I like it there," I offer. "The people are good. The pay is good. I love Cedar Cliff."

"I've always said you gotta love it to live there. It's a lot warmer down here. Not like those mountains. Your mom always loved the breeze."

"You didn't?"

"No," he says, kicking out his boot to hit the cabinet below. He looks like a shy kid in that moment. "Not for me."

"Not enough to visit?"

"Eh, you wouldn't have wanted me there, kid."

I run a hand through my hair. "I don't know. Would have been nice to have a dad."

"Bennett," Ruby whispers again. Her eyes are wide, as

if saying, *Cool it.*

Cool it. Sure. *Let's cool it.*

Ben shuffles from foot to foot, slapping the pancakes with the spatula. They must be black by now.

My irritation has been arriving in waves, but this time, the tide isn't going down. Everything about this home screams, *Home*, even though there are no pictures of me, of Mom, of anything other than the life he built far away from us.

"She waited for you," I blurt out. "I waited for you."

Ben tilts his head to the side, smacking his lips. He doesn't look so friendly anymore. His cheeks are so red; they're almost blotchy. I don't know him well enough to know if he's pissed off, but he sure looks it.

"I did everything I was required to do," he says sharply. "I paid my child support even though it put me in bad positions. I lived in debt for years to get by. I gave you graduation money to pay for whatever you wanted to do. I regret the decisions I made as a kid, but I did right by you."

"You gave me money out of guilt. How'd you even get that money?"

"Does it matter?"

"Yes."

He grunts, "No, it doesn't, Ben."

"Bennett," I correct.

He lets out another irritated scoff.

What did I expect to find here? The reason why he'd never visited? To see if I'm similar to him? To figure out why I had been abandoned and why it feels like it's only going to happen again?

Ben shifts to his other foot, crossing his arms, biting his cheek, and he looks all too like the picture Mom stowed away when I was a kid. She looked at that picture so often—

too often. Waiting. Always waiting for him to be the same boy she'd met.

Ruby reaches across the table to stroke my hand. And it hits me—am I doing the same thing? My best friend doesn't want to get married, and I'm just here. Holding her hand. And waiting. Just like my mom did for my dad.

Shit.

Ben Shaw looks me up and down before placing a hand on his hip and asking, "Why are you here, kiddo?"

Kiddo.

The nickname my mom uses for me and Ruby. It feels unfair to have that leave his mouth, like the wholesome word is tainted under his tongue. I open my mouth to talk, then close it.

Why am *I here?*

I swallow. "I wanted you to be different, I guess. I hoped you were a guy worth waiting for."

He sucks on his cheek and nods to himself. It's quiet, just the sound of the cuckoo clock ticking in the corner and the low vent over the stove. I hear a click and see him turning the dial down to Off.

"I think I'd like y'all to leave."

It hurts, like a punch to the gut. We traveled all this way, and he still wants nothing to do with me. Can I blame him? Have I been nice at all? But is it my responsibility to be nice? Shouldn't the parent want to be present? Why does it fall on me?

I glance at the bowl of blueberries he never mixed into the pancakes and nod. "I prefer strawberries anyway."

I stand. Ruby is only seconds behind me. Her face is red —so red that her freckles are barely visible. I feel bad, putting her in the middle of this. I run a hand up her spine. She shivers and walks a step away.

This sucks.

"It was nice to meet you," Ruby says to Ben because she's nice and that's one of her best qualities. She's nice. Always so nice.

I allow her room to cross the threshold first, and before I can step out, Ben grabs my wrist.

"Hey."

My jaw tics as I see his palm snag on the frayed pink string. He pulls away, sensing the wounded animal in front of him.

"Girl seems like a keeper."

That might be the worst thing he's said so far.

"Enjoy breakfast," I reply, nodding toward his kitchen before shutting the door behind us.

Ruby lets out a deep exhale the moment we're off the porch. Then, she walks toward me, pulls her arms up and around my shoulders, rising to her toes to let me bury my face in her neck.

This really, really sucks.

I refuse to be like my dad. I won't abandon people I love, and I refuse to desert Ruby. If all she ever wants is this —just this—then that's what I'll be for her. Because if it's between the two options of Ruby and me meeting up every so often with conciliatory blueberry pancakes and awkward small talk or enduring life as only friends, I'd pick the latter every time.

Maybe I am too much like my mom, waiting for the impossible. And I wonder if it would slowly drain me the same way it did her.

How do you pine after a woman who doesn't want the same future as you?

If Ruby told me to wait, I know I would. But I've never considered whether I should.

25

Ruby

The drive back to Cedar Cliff is quiet. The girls left earlier that morning, so Bennett and I ride alone, walking on eggshells together.

We don't talk about how Bennett's own father kicked us out, and we don't talk about us either. Not when we stop for snacks—Bennett getting the salty one, me getting the sweet —trading gummy worms for chips, like we used to do as kids, and not when we cross the Florida-Georgia line to pause and stretch our legs.

Instead, we talk about work. His recent promotion. My boring job. How, even after years of employment, I'm still not confident I fit in. Bennett says I'm a project lead because I'm awesome, but of course, Bennett thinks I'm awesome because he's Bennett.

We put on a true crime podcast, talking over it and rewinding, then discussing again until we're forced to pause it, then go on tangents before we're talking about something else entirely.

We do everything but bring up the subject of us again.

Until we pull into my driveway.

Until we can't avoid it anymore.

Because Cedar Cliff and reality were only going to wait for so long. The last time we were here, it felt more innocent. More alive with possibility—the colors more saturated, the birds more in tune.

Bennett puts the car in park. The truck rumbles beneath us and our unsaid words. The sounds of the radio fade out as his fingers twist the dial down.

Calmly, Bennett asks, "Can we talk now?"

"Sure. Loved your dad," I joke.

He chokes out a laugh. "Best part of the trip if you ask me."

I join in on the weak, barely there laughs, but there's no real humor behind it. Our voices slowly fade, and then we're left, just sitting there.

"So," Bennett finally says, "us."

I nod. "Yep. Us."

Bennett's face is stoic as he takes my hand in his. Our eyes snap together, and we're stuck in this little universe with just us—the private island that's always existed with our population of two.

"Ruby?"

"Hmm?"

"I want to get married one day," Bennett says.

My stomach clenches.

"I know."

"And if you don't, I'm not sure how I feel about that."

A knife runs through.

"I know."

"And I don't think I can wait for you, like my mom did. I can't go through that same limbo."

The knife twists.

I nod. "I know that too."

I know, I know, I know.

Because I do. And I'd never want to hold Bennett back from his dreams. And he'd never want me to do something I didn't believe in either.

Would I marry Bennett? Could I see myself committing to someone, trusting that it wouldn't fall apart?

He takes my wrist and brings my hand to his chest. He pulls my knuckles up to his lips, giving them a long kiss before lowering them back down.

Maybe.

But *maybe* isn't good enough for my best friend. I need to be able to tell him yes or no because he deserves that.

"I think I need some time to think," I say.

"Me too," he agrees.

All of this, this weirdness, our impulse decision to sleep together ... I think we just need some time to simmer. And I need time to consider whether I can sacrifice our friendship for the potential of something more.

In our silence, I hop out of the truck, and Bennett does too. He grabs my duffel bag from the bed and carries it to my porch. He sets it down before squinting up at the tall pine trees that loom over Cedar Cliff. I wonder if they're giving him an answer I don't have.

Then, he says, "I'll text you later?"

I nod even though that seems too vague for my comfort level. But both of us need this time.

"Sure," I say.

Bennett takes a step off the porch, then back on, like he can't decide if he wants to leave or stay.

"Rubes, this is ... complicated. But I want you to know that as long as I have you as my best friend at the end of the day, that's all that matters to me."

"Yes. And that's all I want too."

"Okay?"

"Okay."

"Yes."

"Yes."

"Perfect."

It's just a jumble of words to fill the space, and somewhere in there, we start hugging. I breathe him in as deep as I can—the strawberries in his hair, the faint minty breath—and he holds me closer, planting a kiss on my forehead.

Then, Bennett backs up, gives a weak smile, gets in his truck, and drives away.

26

Bennett

It's been one month since Ruby and I got back from Florida. Almost four weeks of awkward Trivia Nights and tiptoeing around each other. Thirty-one days of surface-level texts. Lots of gym therapy.

Heavier weights aren't making me feel stronger. Running faster on the treadmill isn't making me feel lighter. Squatting lower isn't making me feel more confident. Honestly, it's probably just hurting my knees. But it's better than my heart, I guess.

I re-rack the weight because that thought was far too dramatic, even for me.

I shake out my arms and sigh, falling down to the mat, leaning my head between my knees.

That whole confession thing was supposed to go differently. She was supposed to say, *Yes, let's do that crazy thing called love!* and it should have turned into mind-blowing sex in her kitchen, living room, and maybe her bedroom if we made it that far. We were supposed to laugh and hold hands and all the super-cute stuff we always did but with the new veneer of having figured *it* out.

I scratch my head.

That's the problem. I *did* figure it out. I figured it out at twelve years old. Ruby was destined to be my future wife. Sure, it was mixed with a cocktail of flighty hormones and weird boners, but I mostly knew what I wanted, and that hasn't changed.

I want Ruby.

I bury my head in my hands. I wish it were Ruby's hands running through my hair again. I wish it were us together and our only stress was how to tell all our friends we'd be upping our levels of affection to the point of making them feel awkward—not how to come to terms with the fact that my best friend and I no longer wanted the same things.

"You look sad," a voice says from above.

I jerk my head up, and for a second, my heart leaps because I think Ruby is talking to me.

But, no, this woman is different. And the more I look, the more I notice just *how* different. Her hair—on the spectrum of orange and red, like Ruby's—is a darker, more dramatic auburn. She's curvier than Ruby, but only in the way lifting heavy weights does. Strong. She has one eyebrow raised in defiance—no, in disappointment. Like my crouched position is insulting to her.

She's nothing like Ruby.

"I'm fine."

"You don't look fine," she says. "You slammed that weight down. I heard it all the way across the gym."

I look at the barbell with narrowed eyes. *The snitch.* Then, I swivel my eyes back to her.

Her arms are crossed under her breasts. A leg is stuck out. If I didn't know better, I would think she manages this gym. Her attitude screams ownership.

But she's right. It's a jerk move to toss around weights.

"I'll be careful next time."

I expect her to walk away, but she doesn't. Her green eyes—more intense than Ruby's softer color—trail from my wild hair, tied in its bun, down to my sweat-soaked shirt. I'm a mess.

I don't know what she's waiting for. A better apology?

"Okay, well—"

"I need a spotter," she interrupts. "Want to help a girl out?"

She holds out her hand, and I stare at it for probably too long because she shakes it in my face.

Who is this woman?

I finally take her hand, and she pulls me up with next to no effort at all.

Whoever she is, she's strong.

I follow her wordlessly to the bench she's already racked up. She lies down, and silently, I hover my hands under the weight. She brings the barbell down, then back up. Over. And over and over. Until I realize the barbell is loaded with heavy weights. Until I realize she's doing a ton of reps. Until I notice just how low-cut her sports bra is.

I clear my throat and turn my attention back to her face, where she's grinning back at me. Her teeth are impossibly white. There's some sparkle in her eyes that screams mischief.

She looks like she's going to re-rack, so I say what I'd say to anyone else I'm spotting, "Give me one more."

With a single raised eyebrow, she does as she was told, lowering it back to her chest with a strained, "You always say that to women?"

My mouth opens and closes like a fish on land, breathing in the sudden words.

Is she flirting with me?

233

Julie Olivia

By the time she's placed the barbell back on the rack with barely any help from me and thrown me a wink in the process, I decide that, yes, she probably is.

The woman twists on the bench. Her cheeks are red enough to match her hair. And there's even a small dimple poking into them, like a little secret beneath her hard exterior.

"I like that look on you a bit better," she says, out of breath. "Your smile."

"I didn't realize I was smiling," I admit, but I guess I am after that wink of hers.

She lets out a laugh, and it's nice. Purposeful. She doesn't strike me as the type of woman who laughs when it's inconvenient or unwarranted. The honesty of it has me joining in. It's the first good laugh I've had in weeks.

I'll take it.

She extends her hand. "I'm Jolene, by the way."

"Bennett."

Even her handshake has a grip to it, a sureness.

"Oh, I know who you are, Bennett."

"You do?"

She barks out a laugh. "Bennett Shaw. Cedar Cliff High. Wrestling team. Streaked across the football field after the championship game."

My face burns red. "Oh. You saw that, huh?"

"I was on the cheer squad that year. You were my first crush, you know."

"I'm flattered."

"Should be."

And I think, for a split second, her eyes might flash down to my gym shorts and back up, one eyebrow raised.

I realize then that we're still shaking our hands, so I let go, but not before she gives my palm an extra squeeze.

234

"So, you gonna ask me on a date or what, Bennett?"

I choke on my laugh. "What?"

"Fine," she says, pulling a tank top strap up her arm that at some point fell. Her shoulders are littered with beautiful freckles. "I'll do the honors then. Want to go out to dinner?"

"You're asking me out?"

"Sounds like it, huh? Come on, big dog. I'm already off the clock and everything."

And that's when I notice her shirt with the logo of the Bear Arms on it.

"You manage this place?" I ask.

"I do, and I've been trying to talk to you for months," she says.

I don't know how I haven't noticed her. Then again, I don't notice anyone here. I'm here to work out, not pick up women. To clear my mind of my best friend, not make new ones.

"Wait, *trying* to talk to me?" I put my hands on my hips. "You don't strike me as a woman who simply tries."

"You're right. I don't. But you seemed sad today."

"Vulnerable, you mean."

She flashes another winning grin. "I call it perfect timing."

"Funny."

"I know, right?"

I shake my head in disbelief. I've never met someone like her before. She's bold, almost too much, but I kind of like it. Maybe I need that kind of brashness right now. A distraction from other things in life—from my best friend and my broken heart.

Ruby.

I reach up to my hair, letting it fall before retying it

tighter. She watches every movement, eyes clinging to my arms.

"I'm gonna be honest with you," I say. "Because you seem nice."

"I can be *very* nice."

I struggle to get through another laugh. *Christ, the confidence of this woman.*

"All right, well, Very Nice Jolene, I'm kinda hung up on someone else right now. And I might be for a while. A very long while."

"Is that why you're sad?"

"Yeah," I admit. "That's why I'm sad. And I'm probably gonna be a real bummer to eat dinner with."

Her eyebrows slam together, and she points to me, then herself.

"Oh, you thought I was wanting dinner to hang out with *you*?" she says. "No, it's the free food I'm after."

I squint, and she mirrors me.

"You're pulling my leg?" I ask.

"I sure am."

And then I do laugh, loud and so happy that even I can't believe it.

"Listen," she continues, "I'm happy to be a distraction, Bennett Shaw. You can be a total bummer around me all you like. We can even just talk for a while."

I chew the inside of my cheek. "You're persistent."

"It's one of my better traits." She slaps her thighs. "But, I'm not the waiting kind. And I'm not a second-chances kinda girl either, so it's now or never to get this ball rolling. Even if we do just talk for a bit."

"Not the waiting kind."

I feel the edge of my mouth tug into a smile. "You also seem to like ultimatums."

Jolene rises to her feet, takes one step forward with the poise of a boxer entering the ring, and pokes me in the chest. "I know what I want."

And for the first time in years, my stomach flips for someone who isn't my best friend.

"So, dinner at seven?" she asks. "Pick me up at six thirty?"

"Okay," I concede. "Just one date though."

"You say that now. But I'm an excellent date."

"I don't doubt that."

She pumps her eyebrows, juts her chin to the bench behind her, and says, "I spot you this time?"

So, she does. And then I return the favor after that. Except, this time, when I glance down her tight shirt, she gives me a very obvious, open-mouthed wink.

27

Ruby

I've barely talked to Bennett in the two months since we arrived home from Florida. Everything feels wrong, and nothing makes sense. It's like my dominant hand has been ripped from me, and I've been left to write messy, illegible scribbles instead.

I should be enjoying Honeywood's Employee Night, even as a non-employee. Normally, I prefer Honeywood Fun Park at night. It's the only time there are beautiful, bright lights on the roller coasters as they roar by, screams from employees who haven't lost the thrill, and the smell of popcorn and booze in the air.

But tonight, I'm the buzzkill friend.

I'm just as much to blame for my and Bennett's silence. I haven't sent any meaningful texts from my end. It didn't seem fair. It'd be rude to coordinate a conversation with someone who ripped out their heart for you when you still have no clue on how to mend it back together.

Some days, I wake up and think, *Let's take the risk.* Those days, I start to clear a place in my closet for Bennett. I complete a workout video. I buy doughnuts for my office of curmudgeonly engineers who don't say thank you, but *who cares? It's a good day!* One morning, I even ordered a large case of his strawberry-scented shampoo with overnight delivery because *he'd be moving in soon, right?* I was determined this was the start of our forever.

But then there are other days. On the bad days, I practice *I'm sorry* in the mirror. I work from home and don't shower. I zone out during meetings, and then my boss emails me things like, *I'm gonna need you to speak up more.* I take those bottles of strawberry shampoo I impulsively ordered and inhale their scent like a drug, and then I take over-the-counter pain meds because I accidentally gave myself a headache from basically snorting hair products.

The days mix and match in a messy arrangement until I'm still dressed in a tacky attire of indecision.

I glance up at Bumblebee's Flight, the first roller coaster I ever laid eyes on. I was once scared of this beast, too, but I took a risk and rode it, hand in hand, with my best friend. Why can't I take that same hand-in-hand risk with my best friend once more?

Maybe it's a good day. Maybe we can do this.

But then I remember the design of these beasts. There are precautions, fail-safes ... there is nothing else more dependable than a roller coaster, as long as it's operated correctly. Maybe that's why I like them so much. I've never been good with gambles, and choosing to date my best friend is the biggest gamble of all.

Okay, so maybe today is a bad day instead.

I inhale sharply as someone else's arms wrap around my waist, and a chin rests on my head. I'd recognize those long limbs anywhere.

"Hi, Lorelei."

"You've been grumpy lately." She pouts. "You're never

239

grumpy."

"I'm not grumpy." I laugh, and it's definitely too forced.

Lorelei's hum vibrates from her chin to my head.

"Something is up with you. And where's Bennett, by the way?"

I shrug. "I don't know."

"You don't know?"

I would laugh at her clear confusion if it didn't also make my heart snag too.

"No, I don't know where Bennett is," I admit.

"Huh."

I get it. I always know Bennett's location, like I'm some Bennett-Only GPS. Heck, if it were any other week, we would have driven here together. But I had to find a parking spot by myself for the first time, and some teenage girl asked for my employee ID at least five times before Quinn walked by to save me.

"Well, you know what will make you feel not so grumpy?" Lorelei asks.

"I'm not grumpy," I counter.

"Riding on The Grizzly."

Lorelei and her obsession with that roller coaster is one of my favorite things about her. But right now, the thought of getting slung around that first harsh turn makes my already-nauseous brain more sensitive.

I lean into her arms. "How about I watch you ride it?"

She hums again. "That seems less fun."

"I'll hold my hands up at the same time you do," I say. "I can already *imagine* my stomach flipping."

But then my stomach suddenly *is* flip-flopping, and it isn't because of an imagined roller coaster; it's due to the very real emotional ride my body takes when my best friend walks through Honeywood's iron gates.

Bennett takes one step at a time, feet turned out in his usual world-owning stance, large hands tucked in the pockets of his black jeans. He's searching the crowd and looking for me, just as he always does, and when our eyes find each other, my heart skips a million beats, just like *it* always does.

He slowly raises a hand in the air. I mirror the motion with my own.

An olive branch.

"Bennett!" Lorelei calls. "Ride The Grizzly with me!"

He bends his head to the ground with a chuckle. "I just got here. At least let me grab some whiskey first."

This is all too casual and familiar, but maybe it should be. At least until we can get time alone to talk. Until I can tell him what's been haunting me—that the way he walks, talks, and simply *exists* is both my poison and my antidote.

It's a good day.

Today is one of the good days.

Okay, so, if we do this, there have to be rules. We'll take this process slowly. Maybe we'll even keep it a secret for a bit, so we can navigate the nuances of being a best friend couple rather than just a couple of best friends. We can stay in our safe bubble before the world has the potential to pop it.

Yes. That could work.

"You're late, mister!" Theo says, leaving The Bee-fast Stop with an iced tea in her hand.

She jabs her finger into Bennett's chest, and the gesture has my heart twisting. Theo always touches Bennett—heck, she touches everyone in that casual way of hers—but it bothers me tonight. It bothers me because it should be me touching him.

I open my mouth to say something equally snarky, but

the group is already walking past me, so I follow behind. Our group of five walks to the back of the park in the direction of The Grizzly, chatting about nothing and everything. I hear maybe five percent of it because I'm close to my best friend and I have no idea how to react.

We file through the queue, jumping over ropes and hopping over the track. If all my friends weren't some form of management or senior leader at the park, I might feel weird about our delinquency. But, as it is, we're the same five people we've always been—doing whatever we like in this small-town theme park of ours.

But we're different now, aren't we?

I steal a glance at Bennett as he leans against the railing. He's flashing a bright white grin at Quinn as she shuffles into the operator's booth with Theo. Then, for a second, his eyes flash to me before darting away, his smile fading with it.

No. Please no.

"Ooh, let's turn the lights off!" Quinn says, pressing a button that, with a *click*, turns off the ride's floodlights and floor illumination.

Lorelei, thrilled, hops into the front row of the train.

Her hands fly in the air. "Go, go, go!"

Theo and Quinn each mash a button, and Lorelei is flying down the track, whipping around the corner toward the lift hill.

I could spend all night soaking in my friends' laughter, the carefree way we all exist, like puzzle pieces joined perfectly together. But I have other things to do.

It's going to be a good day.

I stare at Bennett until he finally looks at me, peering over through hooded brown eyes. This time, he doesn't look away. But he doesn't seem happy either.

I pretend to kick a rock to exaggerate the awkwardness between us, to lighten the mood. A low, rumbling chuckle leaves his throat, like the rev of his motorbike. I miss his bike.

I take steps forward until I'm close enough to smell the strawberries I love so much—so much better than from the bottle—then pause in front of him.

"Hey." My voice is quieter than it should be, given all the loud roller coasters around us.

I expect him to lean in to hear me better, but he doesn't. A sliver of disappointment cracks through my confidence.

"Hi," is all he replies.

"How've you been?"

"Good. You?"

"Yep. Been good."

Nope. Been bad. I've been horrible.

And now, we're having small talk. I don't know how to have small talk without wearing a blazer. Bennett and I have always turned everything, including the mundane weather, into a funny gag. But here we are, using the same boring sentences I use at work with colleagues I only vaguely like.

We're quiet for a couple more seconds, and then he pulls in a breath and says, "Listen, I have something to tell you."

Bennett swallows, then levels a look at me.

Oh no. Bad day. It's a bad day, isn't it?

I don't like it. My heart doesn't either. It's beating wildly and then—

CRACK!

At first, I think it's the sound of my heart shattering.

But then I hear a separate scream coming from The Grizzly.

28

Ruby

"He sent flowers."

"Gross." Quinn snatches the note off the side of the vase, skims the words with a nasty sneer, then tosses it on the table. "Throw them out."

Lorelei looks at the bouquet in my hand. Her exhale is instantly tied to the heart monitor's increase.

"It's fine," she mumbles.

It's almost all she says nowadays after the accident.

Almost one month ago, The Grizzly's train wheel disconnected from the track with Lorelei still in the seat, causing her hip to collide with the car's interior. Thankfully, she's alive. Unthankfully, she's been stuck in hospital limbo. Out one day, back in the next week due to pain, and finally, she got surgery on her hip. Now, all we do is wait to see if it's better, I suppose.

We're still not sure why it happened. The Grizzly passed all appropriate inspections over the years. But a bouquet of flowers from the ride's manufacturer doesn't exactly make the situation better.

I look at the label. *Wishing you all the best.* Signed, *Emory Dawson.*

I cringe. My hero in the roller coaster industry is now nothing better than a slur among my friend group.

Taking the bouquet from me, Bennett gives a little smile. I don't resist smiling back.

We haven't had time to talk since the accident. I didn't feel comfortable hashing it out as our friend languishes in a hospital bed. But I'll take every small smile he throws my way.

After this accident, I realized that all days were *good days* with Bennett. That it doesn't matter when we discuss it because the discussion will be the same.

I think I want to try this with you.

I don't want to marry anyone else but *you.*

"Okay, Mr. Roller Coaster got you stupid flowers," Quinn says with an eye roll toward Emory Dawson's note. "But I got you the real present."

Lorelei's eyebrows rise while Quinn digs into her tote bag. She pulls out a T-shirt and hands it to Lorelei, who unfolds it.

She blinks at the design. Once. Twice. Then, slowly, she lets out a weak laugh that quickly grows louder and happier until she finally turns the shirt around to us. I've seen this shirt before in The Grizzly's gift shop, and I wish it didn't have me clamping my hand over my mouth to hold in my own bubbling laughter.

Stamped over an illustration of a roller coaster track are the words *I SURVIVED THE GRIZZLY.*

"That's horrible," I breathe.

But Lorelei is still cackling, and Theo is in the corner, trying to mask the snorting laughter leaving her mouth.

"Fred took these out of inventory after your accident," Quinn says. "But I figured you deserved one."

"It's terrible," Lorelei says through wet laughs. "But amazing."

After a second, she hugs the shirt closer to her chest and sighs.

It's funny how life happens, how even the special things you love still hurt you. I don't think Lorelei will ever forget the accident, but she will forgive it. Because she's kind like that.

I laugh a little because it seems so ridiculous now.

All of this.

My indecision with Bennett is such a ridiculous risk when things like *this* happen. Accidents that are close to ending lives.

My parents are who they are. They loved and lost, but weren't they happy they'd tried it at all? Nothing is perfect. *We* aren't perfect. But I've never seen my mom joke with my dad like I do with Bennett.

I've practiced so many words so many times. And once I got to the point where I could say them without cringing at myself in the mirror, I knew it was time.

Bennett, you're my favorite person.

Bennett, I'd only marry you.

Bennett, your butt is cute.

I'll start with that one.

Bennett's phone buzzes.

Maybe the time is now.

"Food's here," he says. "I'll go grab it."

"I'll come with you," I offer, shooting to my feet.

Now is the time.

This is it.

How romantic will this be? Telling Bennett that I love

him in a hospital. How perfect. It's a story we can tell our kids one day, assuming we have them. Maybe we won't. Maybe life will be wonderful with just us. If I had my best friend, I don't think I'd want anyone else.

Maybe it's selfish. Or maybe I just love him.

Love.

I've never thought it in those exact words. I've considered that I want him. That I need him. That he's my soul mate. But the word *love* seems so small compared to what we are. But of course I love him.

It's Bennett.

We walk past the nurses' station, saying hi to the same two women we've seen for the past month, and my hand twitches to reach out for his, but I hold back. I'll wait until after we talk. Just a bit farther, when I can catch my breath.

We turn the corner to a small hall, where it echoes with each step we take. We walk together, left and then right, and when he notices, he purposefully changes up his step order with a grin. I mirror it, making us both laugh.

It's time. This is it.

I spout out, "We should talk," at the same time he says, "I gotta tell you something."

"Oh, you go," I say when he says, "You first."

He smiles. I hold my palm out.

I glide my eyes over his sleeve of tattoos. Every single one dedicated to me in some way. A parrot, my beloved Moose, our anchor, everything that is just *us*. Because he's mine. He always has been, and I've just never been brave enough to claim him as my own. I've always been quiet and said nothing. But no more. No more unsaid thoughts.

Then, I hear a voice behind us say, "Hello?"

I twist to see a woman. She's gorgeous. Bright red hair.

247

An even brighter white smile. She's holding bags that smell like teriyaki chicken and steamed rice.

She must be our food delivery driver.

"Sorry," I apologize even though I'm not sure why I say that.

But then she slides an arm through the crook of Bennett's bicep, right where I was just looking and absorbing every ounce of *mine* in my brain that no longer seems so *mine-like*.

But, wait, why is the delivery driver touching Bennett?

My Bennett.

The energy in the hallway shifts on the spot, like the opposite end of a magnet, shoving me away from my best friend.

Bennett takes the crinkling grocery bags from her.

"Ruby," he starts slowly, making me flick my eyes up to his, "I want you to meet someone."

And my heart plummets, just absolutely barrels into my stomach like a boulder. No, like a lot of boulders. A whole landslide into my gut.

"Hi." The woman's hand juts out before Bennett's mouth can open to explain. It doesn't matter though. She says all that needs to be said. "I'm Jolene. I'm his girlfriend."

And I think I get tunnel vision. Everything around me starts to fade to nothing, the edges of my vision blurring.

I shake her hand without thinking, without considering any other option, like maybe running away or melting into the floor or simply dying right on the spot.

Her handshake is hard and fast and confident. So unlike mine, which is weak and slow and barely catching a grip.

Dazed, I watch my best friend's arm slide around her waist and land down to her lower back.

His favorite spot.

"You're the only redhead for me," pings through my brain.

The lie. My gut wants to counter with *he tells lies like my dad,* but I know that's not true. Bennett's not like that.

Jolene smiles at me, and finally, I can process her more. Her curves I don't have. Her perfect fire-engine-red hair that isn't like the flat ginger mess I don't bother to style. Her little dimples, like thumbprints into her cheeks, which are full and not hollow like mine.

God, I didn't stand a chance.

So, I smile and nod and say nothing.

Because that's all I'm good at.

Being quiet once more.

Part III

Part II.

29

Bennett

Sixteen Months Before
Ruby & Bennett are Twenty-Eight Years Old

"All right, I'm heading out!"

I twirl my keys over my finger. Jolene, still facing the screen of her exercise bike, throws her hand in the air to wave.

"You sure you don't wanna come?" I ask.

She swivels her head to me, red hair a sticky mess around her sweaty face, and she gives me a laughing grin with a look that's like, *Are you kidding me?*

I chuckle. "Figured. Always gonna ask though."

"And I love that you do," she replies, out of breath as her shoulders shift side to side, pedaling toward the virtual track in front of her.

It's Wednesday Night Trivia, and I'm off to meet the girls for beers at The Honeycomb. Jolene never joins us.

She attended once, simply to meet everyone. But after that, she's kept to herself.

I've invited her time and time again—heck, I know the girls have invited her to their get-togethers too—and I asked why she won't come. Jolene insists it's simply not her friend group. The five of us are too close, and there's no room for one extra, she says. I don't think that's true, and I wish she'd join us. But Jolene does what Jolene wants, and I've always loved her gumption—even if I don't agree.

I look down at my phone as it buzzes for the fiftieth time this evening.

Quinn: Remember y'all: today was Mr. Roller Coaster Day.
Lorelei: Guys, we really don't have to talk about it.
Theo: Is it bad if I say Emory is hot?
Ruby: You're kidding.
Lorelei: He's really not hot.
Theo: Blind. You are blind.
Quinn: Wait, how did you see him and I haven't yet?
Theo: Lucky you, I'm a super spy.
Theo: [picture message]
Theo: Look at the eyebrows! THE EYEBROWS.
Quinn: They say so much.
Theo: Universes of thought are in those eyebrows.
Lorelei: Did you seriously take a sneaky stalker picture at the park?
Theo: Maybe.

Then, my phone buzzes with a separate text from Ruby, away from the group chat.

Ruby: The man I idolized as a kid is apparently a hunk?

I smile, my fingers flying across the screen.

Bennett: Is that gonna be your opening line?
Ruby: No! Maybe "I like your brain"?
Bennett: Creepy.
Ruby: Is it though?
Bennett: You sound like a mad scientist.
Ruby: But is that creepy?
Bennett: One hundred percent.
Ruby: I bet I could steal his brain. For science, of course.
Bennett: You're not improving your case here.
Ruby: This requires more brainstorming.
Bennett: Brainstealing.
Ruby: Nice.
Bennett: Brainstorming/stealing dinner?
Ruby: Always.

I smile to myself. When I glance back up, Jolene's sweaty gaze is leveled on me. She's cute when she's like that with a raised eyebrow and a mischievous smile growing by the second. It's my favorite version of Jolene.

I pocket my phone and chuckle. "What?"

"You're gonna ask."

I tease a hand through my hair. "Ask what?"

She shakes her head and turns back to pedaling. "Just ask."

"Can we have dinner with Ruby next week?"

"Yes."

I give a small smile, which she returns with a wink.

I didn't think I'd find someone who can read my mind

like Ruby does. But after our first date, I knew there was something different about Jolene. She's bold, but not rude. Intense, but still empathetic. Since the day she told me I looked sad in the gym, she's been capable of reading my emotions like pages from a book, written all over my face.

There's something to be said about that.

Her hand releases the handlebar to stroke my cheek. The workout glove scratches over my skin. I don't mind it because the glove reminds me how tough she is—how resilient—and I love that about her.

"You know, our two-year anniversary is coming up," I say.

"Yes," she answers slowly. "In five months, Bennett. And?"

I tease my face closer to her, tucking a strand of her fire-red hair behind her ear. "And I have something special planned."

"Oh, yeah? You think that far ahead?"

"Yes. And you'll be so surprised."

She huffs out an exhausted laugh. "Well, not now that you've told me."

I kiss her forehead. "Then, it'll just have to be that much more special." I glance down at my phone that buzzes once more. "I'm running late," I say, planting another small kiss. "Be back later, okay?"

There's a twitch in her jaw—so small that I might have almost missed it—before she nods and twists away from me.

"Sounds good," she says brightly. "Have fun."

Jolene starts the bike again, and the whirring sounds of the pedals follow me all the way down to the basement.

My childhood bedroom is far from what it used to be. After my mom left Cedar Cliff to explore a new life now that "my child has left the nest"—her tearful words, not mine—I bought the house from her. I'd be lying if I said it didn't sting my soul, watching my mom's beat-up Hyundai putter down Cedar Cliff's mountainside.

Jolene moved in shortly after. Her apartment lease was up at the time, and we were at the crossroads of *is this relationship serious*, which we both decided yes. Plus, I like having her sass in the house. Helps ground me.

It's been a little over a year since then, and the basement is still littered with boxes and remnants of childhood. My old boxy computer collects dust in the corner. There are rough spots on the wall, where my old posters used to hang. A few storage cases are stacked in the corner. It's a sitting time capsule—a project I have yet to get to.

By the time I reach Ruby's house, she's already waiting on her porch. I pause at the end of the driveway. I can't get past the car parked at the end. Her new neighbors like to party, and their guests always park on her property.

Unable to leave the street, I give a little honk that makes her jump. She sticks out her tongue as she runs down the driveway and hops in.

"Another rager, huh?" I ask, leaning out to see the house next door, filled with cars.

She buckles her seat belt. "I honestly admire their stamina."

"You know, I don't mind telling them to park elsewhere."

"Oh, ho-ho, big, bad Bennett here to save the day."

I chuckle, picking up an old bubblegum wrapper from the center console and tossing it over to her. She bends down to the floorboard to get it, but instead comes back with a letter with an all-too-familiar address.

She holds it up, her lips curled in, eyebrows pulled together. "Is this one new?"

257

I clear my throat, wheeling us back onto the main road.

"No," I say. "It's from two weeks ago."

"Has he written since then?"

"No."

The regular correspondence between me and my dad slowed significantly after our visit to Florida. Whereas he used to write me monthly—regardless of my response rate—he now only replies to my sent mail. I penned my last letter one month ago. I've only gotten the one reply since. I didn't think it was worth it to attempt further communication.

She hums to herself. "Anything of note?"

"He says he's moving this year."

"Oh," she says slowly. "So, you don't know if your letters will get to him now?"

"Yeah."

She puts the envelope down and looks out the window.

"Our daddy issues really do show up at inconvenient times, don't they?"

I have the urge to reach out and touch her knee in solidarity, but I ignore the impulse.

I turn the wheel into The Honeycomb's gravel lot, parking beside all the cars I recognize week after week—Theo's sedan, Bill's pickup, Mrs. Stanley's little Bug.

Ruby claps her hands once we park, leveling a look at me with a small smirk.

"Okay, so Mr. Roller Coaster Day. What's the game plan here?"

I laugh. "We discuss how awful he is?"

"Right. Yeah. I can totally do that."

I curl my lips in. "Can you?"

"I mean, he's a master in the field and—"

"Probably things we shouldn't tell our friend."

Ruby gives a sheepish smile. My best friend is pulled in

two directions. One where Emory Dawson—or Mr. Roller Coaster, as our group calls him—is in fact a leader in the roller coaster design industry and Ruby's personal hero since college. But then there's the other side of the coin, where he's also the villain who designed The Grizzly—the same attraction that sent Lorelei into the hospital. After two years of legal battles, he's finally in town for a few weeks to repair the ride. Lorelei is less than enthused to be working with him.

"Supportive," Ruby concedes with a stern nod. "We are supportive of her."

I put the car in park. "I won't mention how much you want his brain for science." She buries her face in her hands, and I wrap an arm around her shoulders, pulling her in and whispering, "Sociopath."

She pushes me. "You're the worst."

"The best, you mean. But that's okay."

"I'm sure some delusional people think so," she says, hopping out and crunching over the gravel to my side of the truck.

We walk into The Honeycomb, creaking open the wooden door before it slams shut behind us. Cedar Cliff's main watering hole is filled with the loud hum of conversation and classic rock playing over the speakers. Chairs squeak, the wooden floor whines, and pints clunk after being picked up and placed back down again.

Our friend crew is gathered around the same table we've had for years on Wednesday Trivia Night, and I can already tell the conversation is circling the subject of a certain Mr. Roller Coaster. Lorelei's face is in her palms. Theo is leaning across the table. Quinn has her arms crossed with a smirk, probably enjoying the drama of it all.

I nudge Ruby, and she nods.

"Oh, hey, happy Mr. Roller Coaster Day!" she says as loud as she can, receiving a whimper from Lorelei.

Off to a good start.

The night is filled with talk of how frustrating Emory Dawson is, how he claims to only be in town to *fix* The Grizzly, but every comment is laden with snark and disdain. But every time Lorelei comments on his unsavory demeanor, I shift my focus to Ruby—the way she tilts her head to the side, how she smiles with each new inkling of information she receives.

She's formed some parasocial mentor relationship with Emory Dawson through textbooks and news articles that have shaped him into an image very different from the man who designed Lorelei's borderline death trap.

But she's not the only one intrigued.

The more Lorelei talks about Emory, the more her face twists with indecisive words of, "Well," and, "Oh, but ..."

I'm not sure what's happening, but once she and Quinn go to the bar to get refills, Theo leans over to me and Ruby.

"So, can we have a pool on how quickly she falls for him?"

I bark out a laugh. "Who? Lorelei and Emory? Seriously?"

Theo rolls her eyes. "Of course! Don't you see the way she talks about him?"

"She hates him."

"I don't know," Ruby muses slowly, her eyes swiveling over to Lorelei at the bar. "I could see it."

"Jealous?"

"Ha-ha. No," Ruby says, extending the word out and leaning her head in closer to mine. "But maybe that'll mean I'll get to meet him."

Theo sniffs. "Traitor."

Ruby gasps. "I am not!"

"So are," I tease.

She shoots me a look. "Well, I can't help if he's—"

"Yeah, yeah, youngest designer ever. Youngest CEO. I get it."

She tilts her head to the side with a pointed look.

I hold my hands up. "I do. I get it. I get it."

She sticks out her tongue. I stick out mine in return.

Then, I take another swig of my beer.

And another.

And another.

I lose track of the amount of beers Orson brings to our table. I lose track of how many times Ruby and I stumble to the bar, asking for more. I lose track of how many times my hand hovers over my best friend's lower back as I try to lean in to hear her.

Even after our friends clear out, I'm still blinking over and over and leaning on my fist as Ruby motions through a new roller coaster design she's thinking about, mimicking the movements and speed to both me and Orson. When she gets drunk, she discusses theme parks.

"Sounds great," I say. My words aren't as clear as I wish they were.

"I think so too." Hers aren't either.

Orson rests his hands on the bar top with a squint. "Y'all need a ride?"

I glance at my watch, realize I can't tell the big hand from the little hand, then look at the digital numbers flashing over The Honeycomb's exit door. It's nearly one in the morning.

"Oh God," I say, burying my face in my palms.

Ruby leans back on the bar with a sigh. "Walkin' time."

"Yeah, let's go," I answer, quickly rapping my knuckles

on the bar but missing the wood top. I pretend it didn't happen even though Ruby lets out a snicker.

I drop I have no idea how much cash into the tip jar, but enough for Orson to hand it back. I shrug, shoving the money back into the cup and pushing away from the bar before he can return it again.

I stumble because the floor is too damn move-y, and Ruby trips enough for me to reach out and loop my arm in hers.

"Hey-lo, Pirate," she says, swaying beside me.

"Parrot."

"Sounds like carrot sometimes, doesn't it?"

Parrot. Carrot.

A laugh bubbles up. "It does."

We start our adventure back home, walking down the sidewalks in Cedar Cliff, balancing on the edges, kicking rocks like irresponsible teenagers, and tripping over storm drains, where Ruby whispers a hello to the nonexistent clown hiding inside. It's the same Pennywise bit she's done for years, but somehow, it never gets old.

We hop over the broken fence to Miss Lisa's yard and into the woods, lined with summer leaves and a babbling creek.

"Babbling," Ruby whispers, almost to herself.

It's so quiet on these trails. I love how clearly I can hear her in the dead of night without having to lean in.

"I was thinkin' the same thing," I say.

She giggles. Light. Airy. Just like her.

I don't know how much time passes because time isn't really a thing when we stumble through the trails. We're no longer twenty-eight, but ten years old again—traipsing through the backwoods, cackling, leaping over the creek, running until Ruby trips over a stick and I catch her in my arms.

We reach the back gate to my house. Crunching across the yard, I see the warm light still on in the kitchen. A flash of red hair appears, then disappears in the window. By the time we're at the basement door, Jolene is standing in the open doorway with her arms crossed.

Ruby trips ahead of me. She looks like a newly born giraffe, and I'm laughing all over again.

"Fun night?" Jolene asks, looking between us.

"Joleeeeene." I wanted the word to be smoother, but we'll work with what we have, I guess. "Jojo."

"You're totally gone, aren't you?"

"Jojo ..."

Jojo shakes her head with her beautiful lips pulled in a half-smile.

"You're ridiculous," she says, shifting her weight to the side and peering over my shoulder. "You staying the night, Rubes?"

I love it when she calls her Rubes. It's like they're best friends. I would love if my best friend was my other best friend's best friend.

But Jolene's face when she offers for Ruby to stay ... it looks off. I want to say it's irritated, but maybe I'm just too drunk.

I don't hear Rubes respond, so I twist on the spot. Ruby nods to us with her eyes closed, barely clutching on to the railing.

Oh no.

"Got her," I say, wrapping an arm around Ruby's waist right as her palm slides up to my shoulder.

Jojo joins me on the other side, and together, we lug Ruby into the house, up the basement stairs, and to the guest room. We lay her down on the bed in the dark, the moonlight shining in through the window illuminating her ginger locks, cascading over the bedspread.

Jojo looks between me and Ruby before patting me on the chest. "Glad you're home safe."

"You're the best. Really."

With a kiss on the cheek, she says, "I know I am."

She gives Ruby one last look, and it's that same expression from earlier tonight that feels a little off—but then again, I'm very tipsy, so maybe it's a trick of the light. She shuts the guest room door behind her.

Ruby lies on the bed, nuzzling her head against the pillow. Her small legs pull up closer to her chest. She never used to drink like this.

She groans to herself and rolls to her side. I stumble my way to the attached bathroom, grab the trash can, and place it near her head. She immediately cradles it in her arms. I lie down beside her, grab a fistful of her hair, and hold it back while she empties whatever's left of The Honeycomb's beer selection into the can.

"Sorry," she mumbles weakly.

"Don't be," I say. "Never be sorry around me."

I stare at the ceiling. The fan rotates round and round. The bed feels like it's floating on a wave pool rather than on carpet.

"Bennett," Ruby moans, rolling over and curling into my arms.

I keep my arm around her, resting my palm on her lower back and holding her closer.

Her breathing slows against my chest, getting calmer the closer she cuddles in. The tiny pink string, frayed and barely there, hangs loosely on her wrist as she curls a fist close to her eyes, like a child hiding from the light.

I wait until I hear her small, breathy snores before sliding off the bed. I grab a spare pillow and tuck it beside her so she can't roll onto her back in case she gets sick again, and then I spread three blankets over her because I know she gets cold easily. I stumble back toward the guest room door, and with my palm on the handle, I steal a final glance at my best friend sleeping.

If things were different, I would stay next to her all night. If we were teenagers again, I wouldn't have left the bed. But the promises we made then and the bracelets we both still wear are nothing more than a symbol of our ever-lasting friendship.

If I'm being honest with myself, I know I still love my best friend. But I can't stay with her. Because there's a woman I love in a different way on the other side of this door. A beautiful, exciting woman who I have every intention of proposing to on our two-year anniversary.

30

Ruby

Thirteen Months Before
Ruby & Bennett are Twenty-Nine Years Old

The mural painted on the far wall of The Bee-fast Stop is taunting me—I'm sure of it.

I stick my tongue out at the large cartoon painting of Buzzy the Bear, grinning with blushing furry cheeks and giving a hearty thumbs-up. He seems far too happy. Or maybe I'm just projecting.

"Rubes?"

Bennett and Jolene stare at me across the table.

"Sorry. Buzzy's giving me a weird glare. You know how he is."

The side of Bennett's mouth tips up into a smile before he forks more of his pancakes into his mouth.

We're at Honeywood for our Friday night dinner. It's become something of a fun tradition for us to meet Bennett after work some nights—if by *fun tradition*, you mean there's a fifty-fifty chance of having a good time.

I hate our odds tonight.

Most days, we have a great time. The three of us browse the crowds in Honeywood from The Bee-fast Stop's window, spotting all the wacky kids wearing Buzzy the Bear headbands, or older folks walking the park for exercise, or the overly affectionate couples who make out while waiting for their food.

"Get a room," Jolene grumbles.

What I really like about Jolene is that she says all the things everyone else is thinking. It's funny once you get past how uncomfortable it can be when guests overhear her. But I love seeing my best friend happy, and Jolene's sassy words make Bennett chuckle every time.

But some dinners end up like tonight's. Scrapes of forks on plates. The low hum of the jukebox in the corner. The side of our table occasionally getting hit by fanny-pack-clad moms and sticky-handed children. And silence. So much silence.

Dinners like this always occur after Bennett and I get a bit *too* wild on a Wednesday Trivia Night.

"So, Ruby"—Jolene clears her throat—"how's your brother?"

Jolene is aiming for the safest conversation. At least as safe as it can be, given that Jolene doesn't know my dad's sordid history. I don't think it's worth it to share, especially not when Lucas is our lifeline for common ground. Jolene likes children, and having a cute brother who enjoys my company gives her peace. It humanizes me.

I mean, I *am* a human. But I'm also her boyfriend's best girlfriend.

Well, not *girlfriend*.

I ...

You know what I mean.

Jolene does like me. I know she does. She lets me crash in their guest room. She always invites me out to dinner with them. But she also doesn't hang out with our group of friends unless it's me, her, and Bennett. And sometimes— only sometimes—I swear she gives me this look. The look. The smile that's a little too tight, the eyes that are slightly more narrowed, and the dimples that don't exactly depress all the way into her cheeks.

I wonder if I'm just imagining things, if it's similar to the weird feeling I get at these dinners post-rowdy Wednesday nights. It's probably all in my head.

I shovel a tiny piece of pancake into my mouth.

"Lucas is doing good!" I answer. "I have pictures if you want to see them?"

Jolene's eyes brighten. "Oh my God, *please* share."

See?

I'm just imagining it.

I scoot my chair closer, showing her the video of my brother on his new trampoline, squealing with each higher bounce.

"He's so cute," she coos. "Is Lucas a family name? I love family names."

"No, my dad just really likes Star Wars," I say. "But my stepmom wouldn't let him be named Luke, so they settled on Lucas."

Jolene squints. "But isn't the creator named George Lucas?"

I snort. "Yeah, don't tell Miranda that."

"Right," she muses, twisting her lips to the side. After a moment, she says, "Bennett's a family name, right, babe?"

Bennett lets out a small, playful groan, running a hand

over his face, but even that can't bury his knowing grin. "Technically."

"You don't want to continue it down?"

He lets out an awkward laugh. "Ahh, it's just ... dads, y'know?"

"Dads," I echo in solidarity.

Jolene lowers my phone to the table, her green eyes darting between us.

"But I like the name Ben," she says. "I didn't know you hated it that much."

Bennett's arm shifts between them. I wonder if he's holding her hand underneath the table. I look at the grinning mural of Buzzy again.

What do you *want?*

"You know how I feel about him, Jo."

"He's the worst," I add.

"Sure," Bennett says with an eyebrow raise and a grin. "But you two totally hit it off."

Like a dart finding its board, Jolene's eyes swivel to me. "You've met his dad?"

And there it is again—that look. For half a second. If that.

"Oh," I say with a small laugh. *Thanks a lot, Bennett.* "Well ... yeah. It was just ... a small trip. Very brief."

But the memories of Florida come rushing back— touches and breathy moans and a tattooed hand around my neck and "sweet girl" ...

I slide my plate away from me. I don't have an appetite anymore.

Jolene straightens her back, rolling her shoulders back with tiny cracks.

"You should see him," she declares.

Bennett's forkful of pancake pauses halfway to his

mouth. "What?"

"Your dad. I think everyone should have a good relationship with their parents."

A response is on the tip of my tongue, but I bite it back. That type of statement is only made by someone who clearly has an excellent relationship with their own family. Some people can't comprehend strained parental dynamics, and that's fine. Honestly, good for them. But sometimes, it seems like, when Jolene doesn't understand a dynamic, it's simply one that should not exist.

Bennett adjusts in his seat, giving a small, grunting response of, "That's not exactly how we work."

His *we* probably means *me and Ben*. But when his eyes flash to me, a part of me wonders if he actually means *me and Ruby*. That's not how *we* handle our dads.

"You can do it," Jolene continues. "I bet you could."

In the space between them, I see Jolene's arm shift, just like Bennett's did earlier. I wonder if she's doing something reassuring, like squeezing his hand, like I used to. Or rubbing his leg under the table. Or something else that I can't think about.

I turn away, and Buzzy is still grinning.

Can you not *right now, man?*

"You're right," Bennett agrees. "Maybe I should try."

My eyes shoot over to him.

What the ... how did she change his opinion so quickly?

Jolene has some type of magic that I'll never understand. It only takes a couple of sentences before Bennett is convinced to do something by her encouragement. I wonder if she makes him feel empowered. Or maybe she simply runs her nails up his leg to his inner thigh—

No, that's what my best friend needs. Someone to push him.

Good for him.

Good. For. Him.

"Oh, don't look now, Rubes." Bennett's lips tip up into a grin. "But Emory Dawson is right outside."

"What?!" I peer through the curtain behind me, and sure enough, there he is.

Emory Dawson always looks so out of place from the rest of Honeywood Fun Park. Not because he's so tall, which he is, or because he has broad shoulders that barely fit through doorways properly, which he does, but it's because he's simply unhappy.

Like, all the time.

Emory's thick eyebrows pull together into the deepest of frowns that looks permanently sculpted into his face. He's undeniably handsome, but his energy runs at a very low frequency, like a vampire attracting with beauty but deterring with its threat of danger.

"Who is Emory?" Jolene asks loudly.

Bennett chuckles out a, "*Shh.*" Then, he whispers, "He's her hero."

"Maybe when I was in college," I mumble back with a shake of my head.

"She's underplaying it." Bennett leans into Jolene. "Ruby would kill to work for him."

Okay, so that part is true.

Emory might be an intimidating man, but he's a competent man. Lorelei's legal team has spent two years researching what possibly caused The Grizzly to malfunction, but no results have come up to blame either Honeywood or Emory. The accident is still a mystery, and while I'm a good friend to Lorelei and I agreed to hate the guy, I can't help but admire his efforts at making things right again.

"I applied to a leadership role at my company one month ago," I respond. "Even if Emory had open positions, I don't think I should leave now."

"You haven't heard back?" Jolene asks.

"No, not yet."

"Why not? Don't you want to know?"

"Sure, but I don't want to be pushy."

Outside the window, I spot a tug at the edge of Emory's mouth, almost as if he's denying himself a smile. I follow his line of sight, and across the midway is our friend Lorelei.

Odd.

Lorelei is paying no attention to Emory at first, but the moment he looks away, her head swivels over to watch him back, and she gives a little smile too.

Theo was onto something.

She does *like him.*

"You should apply to Emory's company then."

"Hmm?" I blink back to see Jolene giving me a pointed stare.

"You should apply to Emory's company," she says.

"Oh. I don't know ..."

"Where's he based?"

"Midwest somewhere maybe? But his company is so small and rarely hiring. Plus, he's really, really smart."

"You're smart," Jolene counters with a shrug, casually cutting into her pancakes. "Don't count yourself out, Rubes. You never know if you don't apply. Right, Bennett?"

Bennett's eyebrows are tugged together, looking between me and Jolene.

"Of course," he says, pulling his hair up into a bun. He ties it off with a rough tug. "Yeah. You know you could do it, Rubes."

Jolene smiles at this, forking pancakes into her mouth.

Jolene is motivated, and I admire that about her. She's finished two marathons in the two years I've known her. She's the best personal trainer at our local gym because she knows how to balance compassion with testing your limits. Heck, she's even convinced Bennett to use a better conditioner for his hair. It took away his familiar strawberry smell, but his long hair *is* noticeably shinier, and I think I like the new smell of Pacific Breeze Coconut just as much.

Sort of.

She's never steered my best friend, or most people who trust her, wrong. But sometimes, I wonder if the pushiness toward me is as genuine. For the tiniest of moments, I wonder if she's asking me to apply so I'll move away.

God, I feel terrible, even thinking that.

"You should see if he's hiring," Jolene says.

My phone buzzes. I dig it out of my purse.

Saved by the babysitting job.

"I should go," I say. "Dad and Miranda are going out tonight. They need me to watch Lucas."

Bennett's eyebrows sink down. "Again? Third time this week."

I laugh. "Bennett, c'mon."

"Go have fun with your brother," Jolene says.

Her smile is sweet, but I'm not sure if it's the type of sweet that's good, like honey, or the bad kind that leads to tooth decay.

I think I'd want her to move away too if she got the opportunity.

But the moment I think it, I grab my purse and stand.

"I'll see y'all later."

I need to leave before I start to feel like a really, really bad friend.

273

31

Bennett

As we rumble down the road after dinner, Jolene is quieter than usual. Even when I put on her favorite artist, she doesn't sing along.

"All right, I give up," I say with a chuckle, shaking her hand in mine. "What's on your mind, Jo?"

Her mouth is a solid line as she responds, "Nothing."

"Uh-huh," I continue. "And what's the real answer?"

I try to give my most winning smile when her eyes swivel to me once again. It doesn't change the energy in the truck though. Her back is still ramrod straight, and her lips are pursed as tight as can be.

"C'mon," I coax, trailing my thumb over her palm.

Finally, after a moment's silence, she says, "Why haven't I met your dad?"

Surprised, I accidentally jerk the truck a bit. Her eyes widen. I squeeze the wheel tighter, and the leather whines under my knuckles. I try to release the tightening in my chest by shrugging and rolling my shoulders. It doesn't help much.

My dad is the divide between my new, wonderful life

and younger Bennett. The complicated thoughts of younger Bennett that were left behind the moment I met this redheaded bulldozer I adore.

"My relationship with my dad isn't great," I answer. "You know that."

"This mysterious dad you rarely talk to me about."

I chuckle. "Well, what do you want to know?"

"Anything."

"Okay," I say, nodding my chin to the floorboard. "That letter down there is the last one I got from him."

"You don't write him anymore?"

"Haven't in a while."

She releases my hand, bending down to pick up the letter before placing her palm back on my thigh, fire-engine-red nail polish gripping my muscle.

"You know what? I think reaching out could be good for you," she says.

I bark out a laugh at her confidence. "The thought of trying to forge a relationship with Ben Shaw sounds like torture."

Her face falls, and she releases a mix between a groan and a sigh before tossing the letter back on the floor.

"Well, I hate that I feel in the dark about all this. I don't know your dad. Is this why ..."

I can feel my eyebrows furrow in the center.

"Why what?"

"You don't even like to look at videos of Lucas."

I laugh. "Okay ... well, because I see him all the time."

"Do you not like kids because you think you'll be like your dad?"

I stiffen. This is very new territory. My fingers flex again. I swear her eyes dart to the motion.

I try to laugh it off. "Wow. Digging deep."

She smiles. "Maybe."

"First off, I do like kids."

She sticks out her tongue.

"But I'm not sure if I want kids, to be honest."

Her face falls.

Quickly, I add, "I'm not sold either way though." And it's true. I've never wanted them before, but if Jolene did, I wouldn't exactly be opposed. "Why? Do *you* want kids?"

She doesn't hesitate before responding, "Yes, I do." She's very quick to answer, which only makes it worse when my gut clenches tight at her answer.

"Well, what else do you want, Jolene?"

"A lot of things," she replies with a slow, beautiful smile. "Specifically, with you."

I can't help but smile back as I turn the wheel into the driveway, winding around the house to park in the backyard.

"Me too, baby."

But when I cut the engine and catch her gaze again, she's staring at me with a very different expression. She reaches out for my hand, the one littered with tattoos and my small pink string.

"I'm nearing my late twenties, Bennett. My parents were married young, and so were my sisters. I just always thought I'd have the same timeline. We've been together for two years, but we've never talked about a future. Is there something I'm missing?"

"You're not missing anything," I say with a grin. The secret engagement ring sitting in our bedroom upstairs agrees.

I bought it a couple of months ago. I have every intention of proposing on our two-year anniversary. She's unlike any woman I've ever met. But not that I'd tell her that just yet.

She sucks in a breath and releases it. It's like she wants to say something, but won't. But I know Jolene better than that. And it's only a matter of seconds before—

"Ruby wants the job at Emory's company," she says matter-of-factly. "And I think she'd be great at that job."

My head jerks back. "Okay ..."

I try to laugh, but the energy in the truck has shifted too much to ignore.

She pulls in a sharp inhale and releases it. "Don't you want Ruby to be successful?"

I laugh. "Of course. I'm a little confused why this is being brought up though."

"You just seemed weird at the idea of her moving."

"Well, yeah. I've been around her since I was seven years old. It'd be weird if she wasn't here."

"But you'd want her to move, right? Like, she could do the job?"

"She could," I agree. "Ruby's one of the smartest people I know."

Jolene squeezes my hand with a playful smile. "I'm the smartest though."

I kiss the tip of her nose. "Of course, Jo."

The fact is, Jolene is very intelligent. She's a quick learner. She has a unique way with words, where she can convince literally anyone to sign gym paperwork within ten minutes of meeting them. She picks up on subtle emotions quickly and has a deeper understanding of body language than I ever will.

That type of quick wit makes me wonder why she brought up Ruby and if that's something I should be concerned about.

Which is probably why Jolene, master of understanding body language, gives a small laugh and says, "Hey, forget I said anything. Want to watch something tonight? I'm even fine with watching wrestling."

I nod, giving her the best smile I can manage. "Sure. Definitely."

But even as Jolene and I walk up the stairs and turn on the TV, even as she cuddles into my arms and says nothing sarcastic about the silly dialogue between the wrestlers that is over-the-top but still fun, I can't decide what Jolene meant by that conversation. And even worse, I suddenly wonder how she feels about the woman wearing the other half of my pink string.

32

Ruby

There are a lot of powerful women in my life who take what they want. There's Bennett's mom, Brittney, who raised a stellar son who makes sure to raise his fist in solidarity every time our friend group discusses the oppressive patriarchy. There's Quinn, Lorelei, and Theo—all confident in their own skin and ready to tackle said patriarchy. There's my mom, who saw a losing battle with a cheating man and cut town to start anew. And there's Miranda, who has that same man in a tight grip.

"Is Alice gonna be there tonight?" she asks. Her tone is calm, but I feel the tension, even from the living room. "The accountant?"

After a second of processing the venom in that woman's job title, Dad answers, "Yes."

Richard Sullivan can pretend he's calm, but I swear I hear his molars grinding. I stroke a hand through Lucas's hair as he stares, transfixed, at the TV.

"Oh good," Miranda says. "I figured she'd be there. But I'll be sure to let her know receptionists are your type, not accountants."

I can hear his grunt from here.

It's hard to feel bad for my dad. And if Lucas wasn't involved, I might even applaud Miranda for being a bulldog about it all. But I feel for the kid in front of me, who is probably out of his selective hearing phase, understanding the banter between them at a much younger age than I did.

It's like, one day, kids only hear the word *Robotron*, and then the next day, they're asking you, "What does *douche* mean?"

That wasn't a fun one to explain.

I don't get why Miranda and my dad are still together after all this time. Maybe it's because of Lucas. Or maybe she really does like my dad despite his flaws. Or maybe, just maybe, she simply enjoys busting his balls.

Dad's shoes snap on the hardwood as he enters the living room, shifting his tie back and forth. "Amelia, we've also got a work thing tomorrow," he says to me. "I have an extra pizza in the fridge."

He didn't even ask if I'd be available.

I force a flat smile. Dad doesn't look me in the eyes, but I guess neither do I. We're two sides of the same coin.

I nod because Lucas needs me, and saying anything other than, "I'll be here," would cause a raised eyebrow, and even at almost thirty, that eyebrow makes me feel like I'm headed for time-out.

I'm pathetic.

I'm twenty-nine. I pay my own bills. I own a freaking house. I don't need my dad's approval anymore. But God if it doesn't hurt to see the downturn of his lips when I tell him no.

After they leave, I spend the evening watching whatever Lucas likes, eventually coaxing him to build Legos with me when I feel like his eyeballs start to melt from too much screen time.

I check my phone throughout the night. I haven't heard from my boss about the position I applied to within our company. No confirmation he received it. Nothing.

"Don't you want to know?"

Jolene's words hit my gut.

Of course I want to know where I stand. But the idea of following up feels pushy. Though I bet Jolene already would have were she in my position.

But I'm not Jolene.

I tuck Lucas in a little past his bedtime because neither of us could settle on a book to read, and then I bag up the leftover pizza for Dad and Miranda's lunch tomorrow.

I check my work phone once more.

Nothing.

Nada.

Zip.

Sometimes, when I stare at my work phone for too long, I get weird impulses. It's like there's a tiny devil on my shoulder, coaxing me to open a new email to my boss and type, *Excuse you, fucker, but did you even see my application?*

It's probably best that I don't listen to the demon.

Instead, I place my work phone to the side and grab my personal device, shooting a text to Bennett.

Ruby: I miss being a kid sometimes.

Even though it's late, he only takes a minute to respond.

Bennett: I miss eating wings every night.

Ruby: We ate too many wings.

Bennett: Not enough, if you ask me.

Ruby: We should have had more variety. More mac and cheese or something.

Bennett: Absolutely not. You always added food coloring to it, like a weirdo.

Ruby: I like green mac and cheese. Sue me.

Bennett: Someone should. That's a crime on macaroni. But what's with the nostalgia?

Ruby: I was thinking that life was easier when I was Lucas's age. All I worried about were roller coasters.

Bennett: You still worry about roller coasters.

Ruby: Yeah, but now, I worry about promotions in tandem with roller coasters. Very different.

Bennett: Did you ever hear back from your boss?

Ruby: No.

Bennett: Let's burn his house down.

My lips tip up into a familiar smile.

Ruby: Arson? So soon?

Bennett: It's either that or poison.

Ruby: Extreme.

Bennett: I like to think I narrowed our options down to the best ones.

I pause my fingers over the keyboard. My heart itches. I take a chance and scratch it.

Ruby: Want to brainstorm my company's destruction at The Honeycomb after Dad and Miranda get back?

There's a delay. Dots forming and then disappearing. For it to take this long, I already know the answer. But the text still hurts to see.

Bennett: Not really a good night.

I close my eyes, holding my phone to my chest, remembering where my best friend is. Who his arms are wrapped around. Who is tracing over his tattoos, breathing into his ear, and wrapping her legs around his waist.

I want to scream every curse word that comes to mind, but instead, I type back.

Ruby: Totally get it! No problem! Have a great night! :)
Bennett: You too, Parrot.

Instead of throwing my phone through a window, I gently place it next to me and blink up at the ceiling.

It's like I'm right back where I was at thirteen. Running through the woods with only my nerves and a flashlight. But this time, I can't run to my best friend.

33

Bennett

Eleven Months Before
Ruby & Bennett are Twenty-Nine Years Old

Theo was right. It only took three months for Lorelei to fall in love with Emory Dawson.

I've actually come to like Emory. He's quiet, and when he speaks, it's only because he has something important to say. It's a nice addition to our group dynamic.

After we found out it was Emory's dad who meddled with The Grizzly's construction, resulting in Lorelei's accident, the group welcomed him with open arms. Quinn was seconds away from ordering me, herself, Emory, and Ruby a *Daddy Issues Club* T-shirt, but Lorelei talked her out of it. I think I saw a twitching smile from Emory at the thought though, which was a big win for Quinn.

One thing about Emory Dawson is that he doesn't generally smile unless he's looking at Lorelei. He stares with those big eyebrows of his pulled to the middle, like she's the brightest sun. Which she is, especially when she smiles like he's the next best roller coaster she's gonna ride.

I'm happy for her. I'm happy for him. But I'm happiest for Ruby, who now gets unlimited access to Emory's engineering brain.

It's wild, watching him work, seeing the way his eyes dart between the tracks, as if he were a surgeon, studying an open heart. My best friend stands right next to him, nodding with every word and occasionally glancing up at me with wide eyes, as if to say, *Ohmigod, ohmigod, ohmigod.*

I chuckle and give her a thumbs-up, which she anxiously returns.

It's a beautiful evening at Honeywood. The sun is setting, painting the sky in pinks and purples. All of my best friends and I are hanging out near The Grizzly while Lorelei, Emory, and Ruby analyze the track. Honeywood is rebuilding the roller coaster, and considering Ruby's expertise, she's contributing to the brainstorming process.

I can tell Emory is impressed by her. But she's too busy freaking out to notice Emory's little glances when she explains something complicated or solves a problem he's been mulling over.

From my place leaning on the railing, I hear Emory try to make small talk with her, and I have to turn and bite the inside of my cheek to stop myself from laughing. Ruby is horrible at small talk. It'd be cringey if it wasn't so cute.

"So, you're still at Dominion?" he asks.

"Oh. The job? My job? Yes. Dominion. Mmhmm."

Oh, sweet Ruby.

Emory nods slowly, squinting in the setting sun. "Why there?"

"It was my first job out of college."

"Most people job-hop, you know."

Emory is similar to Jolene in that he doesn't sugarcoat anything, which I like, but also know it sets Ruby on edge, which I like a little less. I don't know how to tell him that Ruby's not a job-hopping kind of person. She found a roller coaster construction company and rolled with it—no pun intended.

Okay, maybe a little bit intended.

"They're a really good employer," Ruby responds, which has me frowning.

It's a lie, and the worst part is, I don't know if she knows it's a lie.

Dominion sucks. It's been months, and the leadership position Ruby applied for is still wide open. They've sent a *we're still interviewing* type of email, but that's bullshit, and we all know it. Ruby is still holding out hope though.

I love that about her.

"Dominion is fine," Emory says, his eyebrows pushed together, as if even he doesn't believe his own words. "Competent, I guess."

"Weren't you thinking of leaving?" Lorelei chimes in.

There we go.

And with one word from Lorelei, Emory perks up as well. Anything coming from Lorelei gets his attention.

"Were you?" he asks.

"Oh." Ruby's fumbling. "I mean, sort of. Yeah."

"Sort of?"

"Yes, she is," I call over.

Ruby's eyes dart to me, wide as saucers. I give another thumbs-up. She doesn't return this one, but oh well.

"Our Ruby is very risk-averse," Quinn inserts in a fake hushed tone, as if it were some secret.

Theo is beside her, nodding, her legs swinging over the railing.

Ruby's face heats, but it's only because she knows it's the truth.

"It's just ... I've been there for a few years, you know?" she says.

"Very loyal," Theo adds with a nodding wink toward Emory.

Emory grunts, "No company deserves your loyalty—I can tell you that."

"Emory!" Lorelei says, lightly pushing his shoulder. "I've been with Honeywood for years."

"Same," Quinn says.

"Ditto," Theo chimes in.

And just because it's true, I add, "Yep."

"Okay, well ..." Emory's words fade. "You guys are anomalies."

"Or we just love this park," Lorelei says, taking a seat in his lap, which has the whole gang yelling variations of, "Boo," and, "Gross," and, "Get a room."

Lorelei sticks her tongue out at us.

"Well," Emory says, shamelessly running a large palm over Lorelei's thigh, as if he owns it, "considering I'm starting a new business, if you ever want to hop away, I'd need someone like you."

My eyes dart to Ruby's. They're wider than saucers now—they're freaking plates.

Take it! I want to yell. *Take the offer!*

After The Grizzly fiasco, Emory left his dad's company and started his own. It's in town and everything. Ruby wouldn't even have to move. But I can sense the hesitation in her. The way her lips twist to the side and her subsequent nod of agreement aren't agreeable at all.

"I'll think about it," she answers.

The energy rushes from me, and I have to look away again. It'd be too hard to hide my disappointment.

Ruby is probably internally screaming at this opportunity, and yet ... it's a risk. And she hates risks.

I exhale, and Ruby catches me in the process. She looks panicky, so I toss her a smile. As if on cue, Ruby nods, I nod back, and two seconds later, we both send similar texts.

Ruby: Wanna meet at the ship?
Bennett: Meet at the pirate ship?

34

Ruby

The fall air is eerie tonight, and it's not even Halloween yet. Not that Halloween is needed for a creepy night, but the air is *off* in a way that feels particularly foreboding.

I left Honeywood shortly after Bennett, both of us using our usual excuse of being tired or having work early in the morning. It wasn't the first time we'd snuck away from our friend group to hang out just the two of us, but normally, it's to watch wrestling or drive to the edge of town and watch the sunset. But tonight, I already know what we are going to discuss, and I feel like I'm walking into the principal's office.

We're meeting at our tree in the woods tonight. He's already there when I arrive, hands in his front sweater pocket with the hood pulled up and his long hair spilling from the collar. He leans on the tree trunk and smiles when he sees me—the special kind with the lines at the edges.

I crunch through the leaves and twigs on the ground. "Yarr, it's an angsty teen."

Bennett rolls his eyes before tugging his hood down. "Yarr, it's my jerk friend."

I giggle and walk past him, nudging his hips to the side

so I can climb up the tree. He holds out his palm, and I place my foot in it. He boosts me up to sit, letting me settle in the junction between the branch and trunk.

Our tree is a good marker of just how large Bennett has grown over the years. He couldn't sit with me in these branches anymore even if he tried.

"So," he starts, kicking a rock like a little kid, "Emory offered you a job, huh?"

"Oh, we're gonna start there?"

"Oh, we're starting there. It's your dream job, and you just brushed it off like it was nothing."

I shake my head. "Nah, he was just being nice."

People tend to use kid gloves around me, and I get it. I'm quiet, and I rarely say anything offensive. Even when I receive criticism sandwiches, I tend to get more bread than meat. I'm used to it. And Emory Dawson, a man who only gives criticism with meat, would not want me at his company, where he feels he has to tiptoe around my sensitive soul.

I get it. I do.

Bennett blinks at me. "Rubes, you're serious?" He shakes his head. "He wasn't being nice. Do you think that guy is capable of being nice?"

I laugh. "Lorelei was there. He's always nicer around her."

"No, I saw the way he looked at you," Bennett continues, his eyebrows pinching in, looking a lot like Emory's at this moment. "You were schooling him on that coaster, and he'd built the damn thing."

I laugh. "That's not true."

"It is."

I let out a skeptical, "Hmm," to add humor value, but Bennett just tilts his head to the side, his smile fading.

Oh, he's being serious right now.

"Okay, fine, let's just say he is then," I say. "What do I do? Quit tomorrow?"

Bennett does that barking laugh where his head leans back. "Yes! You do."

"No. I couldn't. It's so ... I don't know."

"Risky?"

"Yes!" I answer with a laugh. "Emory is starting a brand-new company. That's so unstable!"

"Okay, but the opportunity—"

"Is great," I finish for him. "Yes, it is. But what am I gonna do about insurance, huh? Or ... pay? He can't exactly guarantee a salary, can he? I need to pay my mortgage."

Bennett tongues the inside of his cheek. "Okay. You make a good point."

I roll my hand around and bow. "Thank you."

"But just think about the position. That's all I ask."

"Fine. I will think about it, I promise."

He shakes his head with a smile. "You are lying through your teeth."

I gasp. "Am not!" *I am.*

And as if on cue, my work phone rings.

"Nope, hand it to me," Bennett says, holding out the palm of his hand.

"No."

"Rubes, hand me the phone. It's pirate ship time. Not work time."

"Bennett—"

"Ruby."

I let out a frustrated exhale that has him chuckling. I plop the phone into his palm. He pockets it.

"You get this back when you leave."

"Rude."

"*They're* rude."

I hmph.

"Hey, do whatever you want, Ruby," Bennett says, his hands in the air. "If you want to stay at Dominion, stay at Dominion. But you could work for Emory and be so much happier and fulfilled. You're talented. And he'd be lucky to have you."

"I'm not that talented. They don't even promote me where I'm at."

"Yeah, because your company just sucks."

"Well—"

"No. It's true," he interrupts. "Take a risk. For once."

I suck in a breath and look away. He grabs a leaf and absentmindedly starts ripping it into tinier pieces, like little dots of confetti sticking to his large fingers. He's more upset than he should be over this, and I remember his own look of concern back at Honeywood.

"So, what's all this about?" I ask.

He grunts, "What's what?"

"The sulkiness."

"I'm not sulky."

"Bennett, that poor leaf is crying for its life."

Bennett's eyes widen, and he gingerly places the remaining pieces on the branch beside me. "Well, thanks. Now, I feel bad for the thing."

I giggle and nudge him with my dangling foot. "Seriously, what's up? I come here, and you're in full teenage angst mode."

He sighs. "I don't know. It's just ... don't you think about what you want in the future?"

"I don't know. Will there be flying cars?" I joke.

Bennett huffs out a half-laugh. "Yes. I definitely think there will be flying cars in the future."

"Oh, definitely. Me too," I agree. "I'd want that or the little transportation thingies, like in *The Jetsons*."

"You'd wanna materialize somewhere else?"

"Absolutely. As long as someone else had a transporter thingy in their house, I'd be there in no time at all."

Bennett's smile tips up at the edges. "I gotta keep that in mind."

"Oh, don't worry your pretty little head. I'd figure out how to transport all over your house."

"Would that be considered illegal transporting?"

I twist my lips to the side, as if thinking. "Could be. I don't know the future laws yet."

"Y'know, you're assuming I'd have tons of transports just randomly in my house."

"You wouldn't?"

He shrugs. "Seems kind of excessive. I don't know what the future currency would be like."

"Touché."

Bennett laughs, and so do I. I lean my head against the trunk of the tree to breathe in the cool air of the forest.

Then, Bennett murmurs, "I'd always have a transport for you though, Rubes."

It's weird how nerves spark in my stomach, like a light switch getting clicked on after so long, the fluorescent inside my soul flickering to life.

"Same," I agree. "And I'd make sure it had little welcome signs and pictures of you."

He barks out a laugh. "You'd make a shrine for me?"

"Well, it wouldn't exactly be a *shrine*."

"It'd be a shrine."

"You're so full of yourself."

"I'm not the one with a shrine of me."

"Oh, look at me," I mock. "I'm Bennett, and I think the world revolves around me."

"No, just your transport," he counters with a laugh.

I push his shoulder, but I reach too far and have a bit more confidence than I should, so my foot gets caught in the divot in the tree trunk. I windmill my arms as I fall forward, and Bennett grabs me by the waist. I land in his arms.

We stand there, chest to chest, breathing in and out. And slowly, I slide down the front of him, running over every ridge of him with my own body until my sneakers touch the leafy forest floor.

My eyes dart between his, just as his are doing to mine. It's been so long since his large hands have gripped my waist like this, since we've been this close. My breath is caught in my throat as I watch his large chest pick up and fall over and over. His jaw tenses, grinding back and forth, tightening and loosening and accentuating every little line and scar and dip in his beautiful face.

I forgot how brown his eyes are, how they have layers and tints and depths. And for the first time in two years, I see a very specific look in them. It's the same look he gave me in that dressing room mirror when he thought I wasn't looking—the stare through glassy eyes and a furrowed brow. The look of *want*.

No. That can't be right. Can it?

I open my mouth, but I don't know what I'd even say, so he speaks first and quick.

"I should go," he says.

"Yep. Me too."

"Yeah," he agrees. "I'll walk you to your car."

"I can go myself."

"No, let me walk you."

I don't argue further because it only means we'd spend

more time in this forest, which we shouldn't be doing at all. So, we walk. And I feel every movement. Every shuddering crunch of leaves, every whipping blow of wind, and even the too-loud whine of Miss Lisa's back gates as we take her path back to my car parked on the street.

I unlock my door and step inside. Bennett's large palm lands with a *thump* on the roof of my car as he leans in. I roll down the window.

"Thanks for the talk, Pirate."

"Anytime."

He chews the inside of his cheek.

Finally, he nods for the both of us. "G'night, Rubes."

"Night, Bennett."

He pushes off my car and walks back toward the woods and his home. Back to the woman who isn't me.

35

Bennett

I wasn't thinking. I caught her when she was falling, and then the world shifted. Her waist was in my palms, just as it had been two years ago, and she was looking at me, just like she had in the sheets of that hotel room.

I pulled away as fast as I could, making sure Ruby got back to her car safely before cutting back through the woods.

Weakness is what it was. It was a moment with Ruby that I'd never thought we'd share again. I didn't think we were still capable of heat and longing because I can't—no, I *don't*—long for Ruby.

I *long* for Jolene.

I *want* Jolene.

I'm excited to *marry* Jolene.

I unlock the basement door and shut it behind me, exhaling as I do.

I should not have been out there alone with Ruby. It's never been a problem before, but now ... now, it just feels inappropriate.

I love Ruby. I know I do, but it transformed into friendship love again. Something very different from the love I have with Jolene.

So, why did it feel weird tonight?

I ascend the stairwell, and I'm not even halfway in the kitchen before Jolene is asking, "That you, Bennett?"

I glance at the pasta bubbling on the stove, inhaling the smell of onions and garlic in the air.

"Yeah, just me," I answer. "Smells good, Jo."

But when she comes forward to kiss me, I feel guilty. Guilty for the nothingness that just happened between me and my best friend.

I return Jolene's kiss, then place my hand on her waist, keeping her close. She beams up at me, such a beautiful smile with those bright red lips and shimmering hair.

"What?" she asks.

The odd pull in my stomach doesn't want to be quiet.

"I hung out with Ruby," I admit. "She got a job offer from Emory and was freaking out. I talked her through it."

The moment I say it, even though it's the truth, I know it wasn't what she wanted to hear.

"Okay ..." she says slowly.

"We were on that trail behind our house. You know, the tree we used to hang out at as kids?"

Jolene blinks. "Okay ..."

And my gut clenches. Nothing happened. Not a single thing. But how do you explain a look, a glance, or a pulling feeling in your chest? How do you dissect that? Was that considered something?

"And I feel like I should tell you ... something weird happened. I don't really know what it was or why."

Her jaw tightens. "What happened?"

And there's the shimmer of something behind her eye once more. The rare one that suddenly doesn't seem so rare now. I wonder how often she looks at me this way and I've never noticed. Or maybe I've ignored it. I wonder how many times it's been because of Ruby.

"Nothing," I say, holding my hands out. "Nothing at all. It was just a moment. I don't know. She fell off the tree, and I caught her. It's stupid, but I'd have felt uncomfortable if I didn't tell you. Which I know sounds weird, but ... yeah."

She grinds her jaw and nods, shifting to stir the pot on the stove. She can no longer meet my eyes.

"But you felt the need to tell me, so ..."

"I did."

"Thanks for telling me. I guess." Then, she rolls her eyes and huffs out a breath.

"What's that?" I ask, nodding toward the invisible exhale between us.

She tongues her cheek. "I don't really like that. That a 'moment' happened. Ruby's nice, but ... only if you break past her shell. And that's kinda the problem. Only you can." She snaps the wooden spoon on the side of the pot. "You're her lifeline."

I find myself crossing my own arms, so I uncross them. I don't want to appear angry or upset because I'm not. Jolene is in the right here. It doesn't matter if Ruby is my best friend; I was out in the woods alone with another woman because she needed my help. It looks terrible because it is terrible.

"I'm sorry," I apologize.

Her jaw shifts. "Yeah, I really don't like this," she continues. "How you vent to each other. How she knows so much about you. All the experiences, the nostalgia wrapped up in it ... God, like, how she's met your dad and I haven't."

My stomach clenches. That hasn't been brought up since dinner a couple of months ago, and now, I know it must have been lingering ever since. Why hasn't she brought it up again? Why now?

"She has," I agree. "But that was a different time. A lifetime ago really. My dad and I don't talk anymore."

"But why?"

"It's complicated."

Her shoulders drop. "Maybe it's not though. Maybe you need to—"

But I don't know what she was close to saying because we both pause when wheels rumble down the driveway and crumble over the backyard gravel. Bright car lights shine through the window.

Jolene leans back, pulling the kitchen curtains to the side.

It's Ruby's car. My heart drops.

Bad timing, Rubes.

Jolene's head whips over to me. "Why is she here?"

Something about the way she says it has my back stiffening. The vitriol spouting from her lips at just the sight of my best friend shouldn't make me defensive, but it does.

Ruby closes her car door, and the autumn leaves crackle beneath pink Converse. They aren't the same ones from high school, but she keeps buying similar styles because Ruby doesn't veer from what she likes. She never has. She's not a risk-taker.

The basement door clicks with the sound of her key.

"I'm tired of this," Jolene says, holding her hands in the air. "I am."

"Tired of what?"

"You know what, *Ben*." The name is like a spit of venom. A shot to the chest.

"What the—why—" I rub the bridge of my nose between my thumb and forefinger.

I've never heard Jolene's voice switch like this—from something so sweet to something harsh, bordering on mean.

I try to find the words, but all I have is, "Don't call me that."

"Ben is the name of a man," she barrels on. "Not some boy, still in love with his best friend."

Heat rises from my stomach up to my neck and face.

A boy, still in love with his best friend.

I feel stuck to the spot, like I just stepped in quicksand. I can tell from the pointed glare on Jolene's face that it doesn't matter what I say next. I'll still be steadily sinking into the floor inch by inch.

"Jolene, you're crossing a line," I say, my tone even and low.

I want to disagree with her so bad. But she's right. I do still love Ruby. It's different though. Doesn't she know that? It's friendship. I love Jolene in a relationship way.

It's different.

It's different.

"I call bullshit. And you're being irrational if you think otherwise."

"Irrational?" I ask with a disbelieving laugh.

"Yeah. Do you remember what I said the first day we met? I'm not the waiting kind."

My eyes dart between hers. The realization that, even though I don't know what's coming next, it sounds all too familiar.

"What's that supposed to mean?" I ask.

She shrugs. "It means you either love me or you don't."

"You know I do."

Jolene leans all her weight toward me and pokes me in the chest. "Then, *prove* it."

A small chink in her strong armor finally peeks through as she shakes her head side to side.

I could crumble to the ground right there.

This tough woman stands before me, putting her heart on the line, thinking I'm making her wait. I am no better than my dad.

But I have the engagement ring upstairs. I have every intention of proposing. If only she knew.

She leans back and parts the curtains again, looking at Ruby's car and sniffing out, "She's still here."

I take a step forward, running a hand through her soft hair. "I'll go talk to her, okay?"

Jolene doesn't respond, shifting away from me before turning back to the stove. Her wooden spoon harshly breaks apart the hardened pasta in the water.

Every stab is filled with force—the same force that accused me of being in love with another woman.

But the idea of still being in love with my best friend tugs at my chest, like a long-lost secret. A tap on the shoulder. A wink. A whisper.

I do though.

That little whisper doesn't sit right with me.

But it's not the same love I have for Jolene. Jolene isn't just my other option simply because my best friend doesn't want marriage. Jolene is feisty and fun and headstrong.

But she's also right.

I do love Ruby. And I can't anymore, no matter how different it is.

36

Ruby

"Ben is the name of a man. Not some boy, still in love with his best friend."

Jolene thinks Bennett is in love with me.

The basement stairs creak, and I turn as if I might run, but what the heck kind of decision is that? He clearly sees my car. I'm like a rabbit in a trap.

My best friend might still love me?

Bennett appears around the corner, hands in his pockets, head tilted to the side. I only saw him thirty minutes ago, but he looks more ragged now. His hair is messier, as if he's been running his hands through it.

I wonder if it's because of me.

"Did you hear all of that?" he asks.

I swallow, looking to the side, as if some guardian angel will pop out of the wall and help me out here. But that doesn't happen. It never happens in real life.

I pull my shoulders up and let them drop. "Tried not to," I admit. "But yes."

At first, I wonder if he's going to be upset.

But all he does is take one step forward and say, "I am so sorry."

"No," I respond quickly, waving my hands. "No, don't apologize. I'm the one who's intruding."

"You're never intruding, Rubes."

The nervous energy fades from the room, leaving me with that sentence and Jolene's accusation.

Does Bennett still love me?

"Why are you here?" he asks.

"You still have my work phone," I say with a weak laugh.

"Oh." He digs in his hoodie pocket and pulls it out. "Ha. Right. Sorry."

He takes one step toward me. I take it, my finger sliding over his rough ones.

Bennett loves me?

"Thanks," I say.

We stand there, me tossing my phone hand to hand and him nodding.

"So." I break the silence, leaning on the desk beside me, "Ben, huh?"

Bennett swallows, pacing away from me, walking the length of the room. He twists on his sneaker heel, slaps his palms on his thick thighs, and shrugs.

"Maybe," he says. His voice is filled with heavy breaths and exhaustion. "I don't know." He scratches behind his ear, ruffling the long locks of beautiful hair hanging on his shoulder. "Maybe it's time I embrace my legal name."

My face falls. I wonder if he means it.

He exhales. "Can I ask you a question?"

"Of course."

"You like Jolene, don't you?"

It trips me up, to the point where my palm slips from

303

the desk and I stumble in place. Bennett's posture falters, his hands reaching out, as if to catch me, but I shake my head and stand up.

"Um ... yeah," I answer. "Of course I do. I've always said that. *You* know that."

I hold out my palm to him, as if providing a peace offering. But peace for what, I don't know.

He squints at me, head tilted to the side. "I don't know if you've ever said it."

I give a laugh that I wish were more genuine. "Well, how often do we even talk about Jolene?"

"It's weird that we don't."

This moment feels so different from when we were in the woods. The longing glances and hands on my waist are gone. We aren't hanging out as pals anymore; we're entering the unknown. It's a reality where Bennett talks about his relationship while the unspoken accusation of *you're in love with your best friend* floats in the air. But those words are fading faster by the minute.

"I've just been thinking about the future," he says.

"Not about transporters, I'm assuming."

"No." A twitch at the edge of his mouth. "Not exactly."

"That's ... good." I force myself to say it.

I look around at the room—the boxes, the mattress, the old computer. This room isn't what it used to be. We aren't what we used to be either.

"I do like her." I blow out a breath, nodding more to myself than him. "I do."

Silence and then, "I like her too."

"I hope so," I say with a snort.

"Yeah. I love her, you know?"

"Oh." The silly, useless little words catch in my throat until all I have is, "That's great, Bennett."

He loves her. I don't know if I've ever heard him admit it before. It's like a fist is wrapped around my heart, squeezing as tight as possible.

His eyes stare at me, then through me, like he's trying to see past the here and now.

Something buzzes in my pocket. I pocket my work phone and pull out my personal. It's my dad.

I wince. "I gotta run."

Bennett's jaw tenses. "Is that your dad?"

"Yeah. I'm sure he just needs a last-minute babysitter for Lucas or something."

"It's nine o'clock, Rubes. You don't even live there anymore."

Bennett seems irritated, and I wish I could tell myself I didn't know why he was angry, but I do. I hate that I'm like this. But Lucas needs me. He needs the mother figure I didn't have even if it's in the form of a sister.

I glance down at my phone, then back up. And when I do, he's exhaling.

"I should go," I say.

"Sure."

"Okay."

I turn to walk out, but his voice follows.

"Hey, Rubes?"

"Hmm?"

That little smile of his returns for half a second. A sliver of light through the door.

"Call me Bennett," he says. "Not Ben."

I return his grin. "Only if you never call me Amelia."

"Never."

"Good."

"Night, Ruby."

"Night, Bennett."

37

Ruby

Love.

The word cycles through my head for one solid week as we do our usual Trivia Night, as I toil away on my work computer, as I text Bennett with our usual smiley faces and GIFs.

Does my best friend still love me?

Rationally, I want to say he doesn't. Bennett is with Jolene. He loves Jolene. He told me so, and he was confident too.

But it still invades my brain.

Even when they announce my coworker getting the promotion I wanted, I congratulate him with a smile because my best friend might still love me, and that is so much better than the silly celebration cake at my job with icing that paints my teeth and tongue blue.

Bennett plans a dinner for the group at Chicken and the Egg on Friday. We don't normally stray from The Honeycomb, but I'm too nervous to care. I want to talk. I want to ask him if it's true.

Do you still love me?

Should I ask that though?

I walk into Chicken and the Egg on Friday, feeling off. Normally, I love the restaurant's kitschy theme. There are chickens upon chickens upon chickens. Little glass cases are built into the walls with windup toy chickens, chipped plastic plates with a chicken mascot from this fast-food chain or that corporation, and faded Polaroids of chicken suits from various sports teams.

It's all fun and happy and weird, but when I see Bennett standing under the curtain to the private room, when he flashes me a playful grin with the fan of lines beside his eyes, I wonder where the chicken-y optimism disappeared because the weirdness in me is unsettling.

Bennett looks great tonight, as he always does. He's wearing that one band T-shirt that fits tight around his chest and hugs his biceps. His jeans flex around his muscular thighs with each step. His hair is down by his shoulders, which I love because it's wild and messy and so *him*.

After I take him in, I also finally notice Jolene on his arm.

Oh.

Jolene never hangs out with our group. Not that we haven't invited her to a million things, but she prefers to stay at home, doing whatever it is she does. But she's here. Tonight.

Any remaining chicken-y good feeling seeps out of me, like a chicken-shaped balloon squealing out air.

That's okay. Not a big deal.

I nudge Bennett, my arm hitting his bulky biceps. I look around the private room with its hanging curtains and framed chicken prints and whisper, "Swanky."

He chuckles at me. Jolene gives me a side-glance. I tug my arm away.

I take a seat at the long table in the private room we rented, next to Emory, who looks bored out of his noggin, staring at the chicken clock on the wall, like maybe the feathery big hand will be farther along in the night than it is.

He grunts in greeting, raising his eyebrows with a sigh.

I look around the table at the rest of my friends, watching as Theo fiddles with the free bowl of cherries, eyeing Lorelei, who looks just as weird about tonight as I feel. Quinn is next to Lorelei's brother, Landon, and they sit just a little too close. Weird. I thought they hated each other. Ever since he moved back in town, they've been fighting. What's changed?

Orson finally arrives late, waving his hand in the air and standing next to Theo. They've been secretive lately, too, now that I think about it. A few weeks ago, I could have sworn she was flirting with him at the bar, and now, they're laughing, and I think I see Orson pinch her side under the table.

Bennett grins over at me, but it's nervous. He's off too.

Seriously, is *everyone* strange tonight, or is it just in my head?

Then, Bennett orders champagne, which is also super unusual. He stands with a single flute of bubbly, knocking a spoon against the glass.

His eyebrows are pulled in as he looks from us to the glass, then back again. He's a mess of nerves, but then again, he's never been one to present in front of people—whatever he's presenting.

Maybe this is something big. Maybe he got a promotion. I wish he'd told me about it beforehand. That's not normal for him. But we haven't been entirely *normal* for a week now, have we? Not after the woods. Not after I heard the *still in love with his best friend*.

Maybe he is.

Maybe.

"Um, hi," Bennett says awkwardly, cringing at himself as he holds the flute of champagne.

"Hi," we all chorus together.

I giggle. I like us.

He laughs and continues, "Well, I wanted to thank everyone for coming."

"Speech!" Orson yells.

Theo nudges him in the stomach.

"Getting there." Bennett grins that gorgeous grin of his with the halfway smile and the little lines. "Um, well, I like to have my close friends around for all the big things in my life. For all the moments that mean the most to me. And today is a big moment. Tonight, I mean. Right now. Uh ..."

Something in me turns like a key. A hidden lock in my soul, a clicking in my brain.

Bennett reaches out his palm toward Jolene. Blinking, she rises out of her chair.

My stomach drops right down to my lap.

No, further down.

To my feet, which are stuck like anvils to the floor.

Wait.

"Jolene," he starts, but I blink because I swear I'm seeing spots across my vision.

Wait, wait, wait.

Bennett lowers down to one knee.

Stop. No.

I want the Earth to stop turning. I want time to freeze. I

want to disappear back to our tree time and our treasure maps and ...

And then my best friend pops open a ring box with a ring that is not meant for me and asks, "Will you marry me?"

38

Ruby

"Yes."

The word leaves her mouth so easily.

Yes.

Of course it does. Who wouldn't say yes to Bennett Shaw?

There's a loud clatter. I realize it's my fork hitting my plate.

Lorelei chokes on her water with an, "Oh my God."

Landon starts clapping slowly, then faster with wide eyes. Orson joins in.

Jolene is crying, but I barely register it because my own eyes sting.

No. Don't you dare cry.

But I think I might cry, and maybe I already am.

I'm the worst best friend.

I watch them hug, blinking over and over until my mascara feels damp.

No. No, no, no.

Pull it together. Be happy for your best friend.

Be happy.

I stand, my chair squeaking back. Nobody notices; they're too excited for Bennett. And so am I.

Right?

I walk over to hug my best friend, but when his eyes meet mine, the eyebrows tugged inward, I have to turn my head. I hug him, my nose getting buried in his hair. His hair that doesn't smell like strawberries anymore. Only that damn coconut-scented conditioner.

I squeeze part of his bicep to wordlessly say, *Congratulations*, because I can't voice it myself.

And then I think I might add, "I have something in my eye," and maybe Bennett says, "It's the spices they use in the scrambled eggs," but I don't know.

My feet carry me on their own until I'm turning a corner, jogging down the restaurant's hallway, and pushing open the restroom door.

And then I cry.

No, maybe I wail.

I'm so ashamed of myself, so embarrassed because the sound is louder than I could ever think to be, and I'm whipping open the door to the handicap stall because it's the biggest—feeling bad for taking yet another thing that doesn't belong to me—clicking it shut, and sinking to the floor.

My face is so wet, and my chest hurts, and everything is awful.

He's going to marry her.

He's going to marry Jolene.

I take a breath, and then I can't, and then I can again. My face is so *wet*, and my hands won't stop shaking.

The restroom door squeaks open. I try to hold my breath, the tears choked in my throat, blocking everything, including sense because, even though I don't want to take a breath, I'll have to breathe eventually.

But if I do, people will know I'm in here.

They'll know that I'm a coward.

"Rubes?" It's Quinn's voice that finds me, and the softness of it—so unlike her—is what releases my breath, my choked cough and half-sniff that is a mess of snot and phlegm. "Shit. Ruby?" Then, I see her feet under the bottom of the stall—the black nail polish poking through her open-toed heels. "You in there?"

"I'm fine," I garble out.

"I'm coming in."

"It's locked."

Apparently, that doesn't matter because her knees appear in the space between the grimy tiled floor and the off-white stall, and then she's crawling underneath. I cringe. She cringes. But neither of us comments on how gross that is because she quickly pulls me into her chest and more tears spill out of me again.

I cry so hard that my chest hurts and my body feels empty. I cry until it feels like I'm drained of tears, but somehow, they keep falling like an open faucet, and all I can think is, *How is there still more?*

"I know," is all Quinn says, patting my back. Probably because she can't get anything else in over my loud, blubbering mess. "I know."

But she doesn't know. None of them do. Bennett and I have been so good at hiding everything. This pivotal moment in my life, a moment where my world is wildly spinning on its axis with no stopping in sight, probably seems so random to them.

I've lost him though.

And even as one of my best friends hugs me—the one person in our group who hates hugging altogether—I suddenly feel the crushing weight of loneliness.

I did this to myself.

I did this.

Her palm rubs over my back until I can finally take a breath and mumble, "I can't go out there."

God, I hate the words when they're said out loud. I hate how selfish, how silly, how absolutely *dramatic* they sound.

To Quinn's credit, she hesitates for a moment before saying, "You love Bennett."

It's not a question. It's a statement.

"No," I answer because, "Love can't even begin to describe how I feel."

She rubs my back.

"Why don't you just ..." she starts, but then stops.

It's probably for the best. We both know anything else she could say would be blasphemy toward our friend. What do we do? Tell him not to marry the woman of his dreams? The redheaded bombshell who is confident and exciting and *me*, but also *not me* at all?

I lean back, pressing my head against the wall, and blink over at Quinn through my mess of tears. She cringes, which means I must look god-awful. Her thumb swipes over my cheek, and I sniff.

"It's complicated," I answer.

She gives a weak laugh. "No kidding."

Leave it to Quinn to tell a joke. Lorelei would cry with me. Theo would tell me men were stupid. Quinn doesn't beat around the bush though.

"So, how long?" she asks.

I sniff. "A while. Twenty-something years."

"Twenty *years*?"

I laugh wetly. "Yep."

Turns out, my relationship with Bennett is exactly what I didn't want it to be. A *crush*, just like Miranda had said.

What a cruel joke.

God, Miranda and her glorious life lesson from so many years ago were correct. And I hate her for it. Mostly, I hate myself though because I see Miranda's side of things now. I feel how much she craved my dad, a man already captured in love. I know she must have felt entitled to him because I feel entitled to Bennett.

I'm just as bad as her.

"Why'd you never do anything about it?" Quinn asks.

"We did. Sort of."

"You *did*?"

"Sort of."

"Wait a sec. Did you ... y'know ... with Bennett?"

"No," I lie because, instinctually, I don't want to share what we had. That night was special, and I want it for myself. God, but why? Why does it matter? What significance does it have now? So, I instantly close my eyes and admit, "Sorry, that's a lie. Yes. We've had sex."

Quinn, to her credit, only gasps a little—more like a *I poked my thumb with a sewing needle* type of gasp rather than a pearl-clutching gasp.

"Oh," she says.

"On our Florida trip," I finish.

She gasps louder. "No!" Pearls are now clutched.

"Yep."

"Why did you never get together?"

"It's complicated."

"Always is. Try to explain."

"Well," I sigh, "if I'd met him yesterday or last week or five years ago ... maybe I would have. Maybe." But even I know that is yet another lie. Because I don't have that type of gumption, do I? I'm not a Jolene. I'm only a Ruby. "Or maybe I wouldn't have," I admit. "I don't know."

Quinn's hand strokes over my arm.

"But I met him when I was seven," I continue. "I couldn't lose him. He's my soul mate, I think, if that's even a thing. And I couldn't bear to lose part of my soul. I didn't think I'd ever get it back."

After a moment, Quinn just says, "Damn."

Damn.

Damn, damn, damn. The curse word reverberates through my body like an echo in the hollowness of my chest.

"It hurts," I finally admit. "But it's all my fault for doing nothing."

Quinn intertwines her fingers with mine and leans her head on my shoulder. "Life's unfair sometimes, lady."

I look down at my wrist—my shaking wrist—and the pink string hanging there.

"Um," I choke out, "this bracelet was actually our promise to marry at thirty." I want to bury my face in my hands. "God, that's so dumb."

"No, it's not."

"Two twelve-year-olds made that promise. And who actually remembers the things they said as a teen?"

Quinn nods more to herself than me. "I don't know. I've been thinking that a lot lately too. Did you know Landon and I were friends?"

I laugh. "You hate him."

"Sort of. Maybe. I don't know anymore." She sighs and pulls me closer. I curl in. "Nobody is perfect, Rubes. Maybe we both need a little more courage in our lives."

And then I say the one thing I've kept inside for years.

"I just wish I'd found mine two years ago. Before my best friend fell in love with someone else."

I'm drinking again. At least it's acceptable at an engagement party. I take another sip—no, swig—from my champagne flute right as Landon cracks another joke about Bennett's big hands holding his own teeny-tiny drink.

I like Bennett's hands though, so *glug, glug, glug* for me.

I tilt my head to the side, watching as those big bear paws grip Jolene's waist. He's grinning ear to ear. So is she. It's the happiest I've ever seen them, and part of me wonders if it's fake.

No, maybe I'm just going through the stages of grief.

Hello, denial.

"I'm gonna get us another bottle," I murmur.

Quinn rests her palm on my shoulder, as she has all night, but the hand drifts away as I stand and walk off.

The room is a bit spinny, but not as much as it could be, I guess. I swear the kitschy little chickens on the wall are laughing at me. Or ba-gawking.

That makes me giggle to myself until I realize I'm too sad to be smiling.

Oh well. Bennett would have found that joke funny.

I lean on the bar top, but when the bartender asks for my order, I've already forgotten why I'm here. It's just a nice bar, and the air is clear, and I can no longer see my best friend's beautiful inky hair clutched in another redhead's hands that are not my own.

My forehead starts to lean forward, then down, down, down until I hit the counter with a groan.

A low voice beside me chuckles. "You look sad."

I turn my head so my cheek rests on the bar. I look at the man beside me. Gosh, he's cute. Bearded with a sly little

317

smirk. Some speckled gray across his temples and ... icy-blue eyes.

"Michael?" I murmur with a squint.

There's that laugh again. "Hey, Red."

"Christ, he looks great now."

Michael gives the prettiest grin. "Do I?"

"Did I say that out loud?"

"You did."

"Oh God."

His beautiful blue eyes travel down my face and to my lips before trailing back up.

"What are you doing here?" I ask, my lips still clinging to the wooden countertop with each word. I don't have the strength to pull my head back up.

"Visiting my kid."

My mouth opens in surprise. "You have a kid?"

"Yeah. Daddy Michael here."

Oof.

That, plus the gray streaks in his hair? I've gotta pull myself together.

He leans an elbow on the bar and grins. He's always had a stellar smile, fit with dimples and white teeth. But he no longer looks like the teen heartthrob I used to know. Now, he looks a little more refined. Debonair. Fancy almost.

"Congratulations on getting married," I mumble because, apparently, *everyone* is happy.

He chokes out a half-laughing grin. "Ah. No. I'm not. Just a dad. His mom and I never worked out."

I wince. "I'm sorry."

"It's fine. It's in the past. So, you still living here?" he asks.

I nod and slur out, "I'm at Bennett's engagement party."

His lips part. "Whoa. That so?"

He leans back on the heels of his shoes to peek over to the party room. I don't know what he sees, but the click of his tongue tells me he likely sees just how happy my best friend is. Just the memory of his arm around Jolene has me rolling my forehead on the counter again.

Michael sighs. "His loss then."

"No, no, no," I say, lifting my head—*oops, that's not fun*—and waving my hand around. "No, it's good. It's perfect. He's happy. This is what I wanted."

Michael's expression shifts, his mouth tilting down, his knuckles rapping on the bar top. And, weirdly, he replies, "Y'all sure have changed."

"Not really," I reply with a sniff. "Not that much."

If I had changed, maybe I would have taken a chance. Maybe I would have been less of a pushover. Or maybe I would have just stood up for myself for one second in my life and let myself be happy. I would have said, *Choose me.*

Michael lifts a single eyebrow. Is that a thing they teach you at handsome-man school or something? Though, while it's gorgeous, it's still not as wonderful as Bennett's single eyebrow lift.

"I've never seen you like this, Red."

I close my eyes.

"I've never *felt* like this," I reply.

"Too many drinks?"

"Yes," I say because that's not entirely why I feel like crap, but I don't want to get into it again. Not when I probably have more tears to offer.

He scans me for a moment before asking, "Do you need a ride home?"

I shake my head side to side. "No. I'm parked—"

"Not what I asked," he interrupts. "Can you drive?"

"I have keys."

"Christ, Red. Hand them to me."

"No."

"C'mon."

"Stop."

"You're not leaving like this."

"God, *screw off*," I snap.

Michael's head jolts back. Mine does too.

"I'm sorry ... I ..."

But a smile spreads over his face. He nudges my shoulder. "Well, look at you, having some fire."

Do I? I don't know what that was. I've rarely had fire in my entire life. But something beneath my bones hurts a little. My soul aches, like the burning of an ember. Doesn't it know I'm the wrong person? I don't get angry. I don't get emotional. I'm Ruby.

God, I'm not ready for the anger stage of grief, thanks. I'll stay in denial just fine. It's where I'm best suited.

"What are you doing for the rest of tonight?" Michael asks.

I gesture to the bar top. He barks out another charming, silver-streaked-demon-type laugh.

"Okay, well, how about this? You give me your keys. You keep partying on, but with *water* only. And then we'll meet back here, and I'll assess whether you can drive home. How's that?"

"Sounds like a shit night for you."

He chuckles. "I don't know. Sounds like a blast with a beautiful woman."

My eyes widen, and my heart goes into panic mode. "Oh, I don't want to sleep with you."

He blows out a massive rush of air. "Good Lord. You've been drinking, Red. Who do you think I am?"

I blink up at him, narrowing my eyes. "Michael Waters?"

He chews his cheek before letting out a small snort and shaking his head side to side. "I'm just Michael, all right? The whole double-name thing makes me seem—"

"Like a dick?" I finish.

"Yeah," he responds with a chuckle. "Yeah, like a dick. I'm not gonna take advantage of a drunk woman. I promise I'm nicer than that."

I smile. "I always thought you were a little nice."

"Well then, just you wait. I'm practically ... I don't know. Who's a nice person?"

"Gandhi?"

"There we go," he says with a snap of his fingers. "You were always the smart one."

I find myself laughing, and it feels good. I love laughing. I miss laughing.

Michael grabs my hand and places a small kiss on the back of it. "Keys?"

I dig in my pocket, place them in his palm, and nod.

"Good. Now, wait for me before you leave," he orders.

And I follow his direction.

39

Bennett

When I pull up to Ruby's house, the night is still. I always thought that was a weird thing to see written in books, but tonight, I finally understand what it means. I can't hear crickets. I can't hear the hum of streetlamps. Even the wind feels elusive.

It's much too late to be at her house—I know that—but Ruby left her purse at the restaurant. When I plucked it from the back of her chair, Jolene suggested we drop it off. She said it with a smile, too, which I can't imagine she would have done a week ago. But then again, she's thrilled about everything since I placed that ring on her fourth finger three hours ago.

I love seeing Jolene happy. I like the way her dimples press into her cheeks and how giggly she gets when she's not much of a giggly person at all.

Ruby's driveway only has one car—a bright red Camaro. I see no sign of her clunker.

"Who's that?" Jolene asks.

"Probably just her neighbors, using her driveway again."

I've been telling Ruby for years she should talk to them

when they have parties because they always block her in or out, but she won't have the tough conversation.

I look at Jolene running her thumb over her ring again. She looks over at me and grins. I can't help but return the smile.

"Hi, fiancé."

"Hello there, fiancée."

Jolene is a woman who deserves to be given everything in life, and I cannot wait to give it to her. Marriage. A life. A future.

But then my mind drifts back to Ruby and how she looked tonight with red eyes and a stumble in her step. How every time I caught sight of her, she was downing another flute of champagne. I was assured that Quinn and Landon were watching over her, but my hands itched to reach out to her and keep her from falling.

I was stuck in conversation for too long at one point, then couldn't find them again. One—most likely panicked-looking—glance at Emory, and he quickly explained that the three of them had left a minute or two ago. With her purse left behind, phone and all, I knew she'd grabbed a ride with them.

At least, I hoped so. But I can't text her to be sure.

I fist her purse in my hands, hoping to God she's inside.

I exit the still-running truck and knock on Ruby's door. The living room blinds are drawn, so I can't see if she's on the couch, watching sitcom reruns or eating late-night cookie dough. Normally, when she's a little tipsy, that's her favorite thing to do.

Nobody answers after a second ring, so I pull out my own key to her house, turn the door handle, and step inside.

"Rubes?"

Her TV is on in her bedroom. The hall light is on too.

There's a squeak of a mattress, and then Ruby's ginger hair pokes out from the hallway.

"Oh, thank God," I breathe.

Her green eyes are as wide as I've ever seen them, like a teenager caught in the act. It almost makes me want to laugh if it didn't strike me as weird.

"Bennett?"

She quickly glances behind her in the hallway before walking out into the living room. She's wearing a loose Buzzy the Bear T-shirt with ratty blue sleep shorts she's had since we were teens. Her face is flushed.

"You left your purse," I say, walking forward to place it on the counter.

Her eyes drift behind her once more.

Then, cold sluices over my skin when I'm hit with a realization. A daunting one.

Does she have someone over?

I want to laugh it off, but the smile won't cross my face. Not even for a second.

The question barrels out of me before I can stop it. "Is someone here?"

I know it's a mistake the moment I say it.

With each passing second, Ruby's face transforms. Tilted eyebrows start to furrow in the middle. Her parted lips purse and downturn to something new. Her green eyes narrow.

"Why?" she says slowly. "Why would it matter if someone was here?"

Unease rolls over me, quickly followed by guilt.

Why *does* it matter?

It shouldn't. It can't. If she wants to have someone here, that's not my business. Except part of me feels like it is. And

324

just like always, I know Ruby can read my mind. I hate our little parlor trick for the first time ever.

"It doesn't," I answer quickly.

"Then, why'd you ask?"

"Forget I did."

I've never seen her like this—with suspicion in her eyes and anger twinkling behind it.

Ruby is never angry.

Her foot taps on the carpet. She's crossed her arms, her fingers twitching against them. "Why did you ask, Bennett?"

The world tilts just the slightest bit, and my heart slides with it.

Why did I?

And why is my heart rate rising? Why are all my nerves shooting like sparks? Why do I want to scream?

"Shit," I hear myself say before I can stop it. My palm runs over my face, pulling down, trying to massage away the question. Trying to take it back.

And slowly, step by step, with the sound of creaking wood under her carpet, Ruby walks closer, then stares in my face.

"You're engaged."

I nod, my jaw twisting. "I am."

"But you're here. Asking if someone else is in my bedroom. Even though I'm not with you."

I freeze. Everything feels like it's moving forward, but the room is moving back. It's tunnel vision. It's nausea. It's everything in between.

"It's not like that—"

"I won't be your Miranda."

"Wait, do I make you feel like Miranda?"

325

And with a grind of her jaw, blinking as she looks away, she just shrugs.

I rush toward her, faster than I can think to stop, and I pull her into me. I hug her tight, burying my palms into her back, sinking my nose into her soft hair. She doesn't hug me back. Her arms hang limply by her sides. And they stay that way until, finally, I feel them wrap around me.

We hold each other for a second or two before both pulling away. And I'm happy it's at the same time because I don't know what would be worse—her pulling away first or me.

Ruby and I stare at each other, just the sound of music coming from her room and the thought of *someone else in there* lingering in my mind.

"I'm sorry," I choke out. "I am so, so sorry."

Her lips pull in, and she shrugs. Her mouth opens and closes. She looks away and sighs.

"I'm happy for you," is all she says. "It's gonna be a beautiful wedding."

She's lying through her teeth, but I don't think now is the right time to call her out about it. I don't know when the correct moment would be, if ever.

"I'm your best man, right?" she asks, and it breaks part of the tension, but not all of it.

A sliver of a smile twitches at my lips. "Of course."

"Best maiden?"

"Groom of honor even."

"Good."

She smiles back, but I don't know how. Our banter is somehow the same, yet not.

I glance over the little freckles on her cheeks, her small chin, her twitching eyes. But Ruby stares back at me very differently. Her eyebrows are flat. Full lips as thin as possible. Arms crossed tight over her chest once more.

"I should go to bed," she announces.

I nod with her. "Okay. I'll see you later then?"

"Mmhmm."

I walk to the door. She doesn't walk with me.

I twist on my heel, tilting my head to the side. I feel like I should ask more questions and say more things, but nothing comes to mind. Instead, my eyes flick to the hallway light, the television in her bedroom, and the thought that there might be someone in there who owns a red Camaro.

"Congratulations," Ruby says, drawing me back. "Really."

But she doesn't mean it.

I do the socially responsible thing and smile anyway. "Thanks."

There's something behind my best friend's eyes. And it sure isn't happiness.

I walk out the door, and the *thump* of it closing behind me feels like getting kicked out of my own home.

40

Ruby

My best friend—*my* best friend, *my* Bennett—smells like stupid freaking coconuts.

I was sad. I was so sad, and now, I'm just ... God, I'm so ...

I've crossed into the next stage of grief.

Anger.

It bubbles in me, so hot and irritating and wild that I can't stop it. For once in my life, I might boil over.

I'm so *fucking* angry.

"Well, that was a soap opera."

I twist on my heel, staring at Michael in the hallway. He leans against the threshold in a white T-shirt that fits him too well, running a hand through his beautiful, gray-streaked hair. Only ten minutes ago, I was cuddling close to him as he gave me a glass of water and turned on the TV to some random sitcom. I remember being disappointed that his hair wasn't longer and messier, like my best friend's. And I hated that it didn't smell like strawberries.

But I guess Bennett's hair doesn't smell like that anymore either.

Michael tilts his head to the side. "You love him."

"Shut up, Mikey."

He chuckles. "I knew it."

Michael is grinning, and it's cocky and kinda cute, but, God, I also wish I could just punch the smile right off his face. Bennett was right. Michael truly does have a punchable smirk.

And then I laugh. I laugh at the absurdity of it all. How Michael freaking Waters is here, in my house, being the perfect gentleman even though I'm a sloppy mess. Younger me would be in heaven, especially when he's as gorgeous now as he was then. My eyes sting because I think I might cry again, but I laugh through that too.

I cannot believe I've liked Michael for so long. He's always been a prick, hasn't he? But I've been so wrapped up in his coolness and the idea that someone—anyone—might like me, even as an awkward teen.

I've spent so much of my life in naivety.

With Michael.

With Bennett.

"Why not tell him you love him?" he says.

"Well, right now, I hate him."

"Because you love him so much."

"Seriously, screw off."

"Y'know I think *I* might love you when you're angry like this, Red."

"I need more water."

I rush into my kitchen. Michael's eyes follow me. He looks like ever the cool guy in the doorway with his gorgeous crossed arms and charming smile. But not as charming as Bennett. Nothing about him could ever be as tantalizing as Bennett.

And I hate that. I hate it so much.

I turn on the faucet. I don't have time for the slow-pouring fridge water with a filter that is probably way past needing changed. My hands are shaking.

"I'm so ..." The water sloshes over the lip as I shake.

"Pissed?" Michael offers.

"Pissed," I say out loud. And it feels *good* to say.

I am. I'm pissed. The man I was supposed to marry, who I had given everything to—my first kiss, my virginity, my soul—just proposed to another woman, and it wasn't freaking *me*. And it's all my fault.

It's like all my emotions from years and months and minutes and seconds are catching up, and, God, did I always feel this *angry*? Have I ever felt this pissed in my life? My heart hurts, and the twist in my gut keeps knotting tighter and tighter. And before I know it, my glass of water is crashing to the ground.

I threw it.

There are little shards of glass all over my tiled floor, and my arms shake by my sides.

After a few seconds, Michael lets out a low whistle.

"Want to throw another?"

And that sentence alone reminds me of prom night—of Bennett asking if I wanted to throw another pillow at the door.

I thought there were more stages to grief, but leave it to Bennett to get them all jumbled in my head. I linger on anger for a bit because I've never felt it and it feels good. It feels empowering, and I *like it*.

So, I do what maybe I should have done when I was eighteen, and I grab another pint from my cabinet and hurl it to the ground.

Smash!

Michael grins, but to his credit, he does take a cautious step back.

"Feel better?" he asks.

"Sorta."

"Relieved at least?"

Looking at the messy and honestly dangerous floor, it feels less like *relief* and more like *control*. Like change. One second, that glass was fully functioning, and now, it's ... nothing. And I did that.

"Yes," I finally answer with a gulp. "Yes. I feel great."

"Okay then, what's next? Wanna go for the plates?"

"No," I say with a laugh. "No. But thanks."

Michael smiles back at me, head leaning on the doorway, just like Bennett does. But it's not as cute, and maybe nobody will ever be as cute as Bennett is or was or will be.

I look down at my pink string and suck in a breath.

If *Ben Shaw* can grow up, so can I.

It's about time I get some courage in my life.

I dig through my purse, pulling out my phone to see a few texts from my dad and from my own employer, who lacks the decency to text my work number. I have a text from everyone but Bennett, and that just angers me more.

I shoot a text to my boss. A simple *I quit.*

I send one to my dad. Another *I quit* because he'll know what it means. I'm nothing more than a stupid babysitter. Me. His daughter.

I throw my phone across the counter.

God, I'm tired of being a pushover. I'm sick of being a rug for people to walk on. I'm over craving approval and people-pleasing and trying to solve every problem in the world for everyone but myself.

I snatch my phone again and dial up Emory. It's two in

the morning, but he instantly answers. The man has insomnia because what great creative doesn't?

"Ruby?"

"Hey, Emory. You know what? I'd really like that interview."

I think I've officially entered the acceptance stage of grief.

That, or it's my villain era.

We'll see.

All I know is, it's time to make some changes around here.

Part IV

41

Bennett

Three Months Before
Ruby & Bennett are Twenty-Nine Years Old

"My little gemstone! Ahh! Look at you! Oh my God, put away those weapons!"

Ruby giggles as my mom pinches her biceps.

My best friend has biceps.

If she twists them certain ways, you can see the little bulges poking out from her former twig-like arms. She's got some meat to her now. She looks strong.

"I pick up heavy things and put them back down," Ruby says proudly. "I'm basically a gym rat, Brittney."

I snort with a grin. "We've had to tell her to get out of the trash cans actually."

My mom's head falls back in laughter right as Ruby crosses her arms with a grin.

"That would make me a gym raccoon," she jokes.

"A gym possum."

"I'm fine with that. Possums are cute."

It's been almost one year since the engagement party. Things feel normal again.

They're great.

No, they're perfect.

"Oh," Ruby says, bouncing on her toes. "We're having wings for dinner, by the way!"

My mom fans her face, still looking not a day over thirty-five.

"Wow. And she cooks too? Woman after my own heart."

Ruby tips an invisible cowboy hat. "I intend to treat you right, ma'am."

"Much better than my son. Refusing to house his poor ol' mother? Tsk-tsk."

"Mom ..." I say, wrapping a hand around her shoulder right as she leans into me, swatting at my arm with a laugh.

She's joking. My mom can work anywhere with her new job, so she decided to come into town for the last two months of wedding planning; said she missed Cedar Cliff badly. I insisted she stay with me and Jolene. But even though I had a bed cleared for her, our house has been so overwhelmed with Jolene's handcrafted reception decor that Jolene said it would make the house too crowded with one extra body.

Thankfully, Ruby, my best maiden, offered up her house instead.

"So, how's the project going?" Mom raises her eyes at Ruby with a small smile.

"What?" I ask. "What project?"

"Oh"—Ruby waves me off—"it's nothing. A work thing."

I laugh. "Okay, well, what work thing?"

"We just made some headway in the project, is all."

"Emory is finally giving her the reins on a few things," my mom tosses in, knocking Ruby on the shoulder. "She's killin' it."

I'm still blinking through the new information. "You're spearheading stuff?"

Ruby squints. "Yeah. Didn't I tell you that?"

Did she?

There are too many things I no longer know about my best friend. I didn't know she'd hit a personal best at the gym until Theo told me. I didn't know she'd had a verbal altercation with her neighbors about parking in her driveway until Quinn and Landon baked her a celebratory cake and brought it to Trivia Night. I didn't know she had been saving up for a better house until Lorelei showed up with the research she and Emory had done earlier this year for their own house. Even her wins at her dream job seem to be discussed with everyone *but* me.

"You need to step up your game," Mom says, elbowing me. "Little Rubes has it all together."

"Little?" My eyebrows rise. "Not so little anymore. She's like a bull now."

"Dragon," Ruby corrects, absentmindedly handing my mom her glass of pinot.

"Bison."

"Pegasus."

"Why are you only choosing mythical creatures?"

Her green eyes dart to me through hooded ginger lashes. "Because they're the coolest. And I'm cool." She gives a slow, teasing smile that gives me a pause before snapping her tongs at us, just like Mom did when we were younger. "I'm gonna go check the wings. Stay out of trouble, you two."

I watch after Ruby disappears through the sliding glass

door. She opens the grill—something I couldn't have imagined her doing a few months ago. Hell, she didn't even *own* a grill until recently. But she does now. Ruby has been doing a lot of new things recently. She tried out rock climbing, joined Theo at yoga, and even paid Landon for some cooking classes.

Honestly, Ruby seems happy. I can see it in the way she bops in front of the grill to no music, the way her toned thighs and calves show off the commitment she's given to the gym month after month, and the confidence in which she flips the wings over with the tongs without asking any questions first.

"Bennett," my mom whispers.

I turn to look at her. Her eyes are wide, her eyebrows practically raised to the peak of her forehead.

"What?"

Her eyes float to Ruby and back. My chest tightens.

"What?" I repeat.

Ruby's front door creaks open.

"Bennett?"

Jolene.

"Come on in!" I call back.

Jolene appears in the kitchen, a bag slung over her shoulder and a binder propped in one arm.

"Jojo!" my mom calls over, screeching her barstool back and embracing Jolene.

I bite my tongue to not laugh, but a chuckle still draws out. Jolene throws me a middle finger behind my mom's back.

The sliding glass door whines open, and Ruby steps inside with her arms raised. "Jojo!"

"I swear I'm gonna kill y'all for that nickname," Jolene jokes through gritted teeth.

Ruby's phone lights up on the counter, and when she glances down at the screen, her smile brightens.

My chest feels pulled taut, like a wire.

Maybe she just saw a text from Theo or Quinn or Lorelei. Heck, maybe it's Emory. He is her boss now after all.

Or ...

Maybe it's the mysterious man who stayed over after my engagement party.

Or maybe it's not him. Maybe this imaginary person never even existed. I've never had it confirmed or denied. We've never mentioned that night again.

I look down at my own phone, but there's no buzz even though I've been expecting one.

I started writing my dad again at Jolene's insistence, and just two months ago, we exchanged phone numbers. He hasn't been the best at responding, which is normally okay. But my last text was an invite to my wedding. The thread indicates it's been read. But no reply yet.

Jolene's eyes catch on my phone as I pocket it. I give a small, totally-not-upset shrug. I don't want to worry her, but she frowns anyway.

"Okay," Jolene says loudly, slapping her binder on the counter. "So, your thirtieth is coming up soon."

Ruby and I simultaneously groan.

Mom waves her hand in our direction. "Oh, hush, you're both still so young."

"Thirty is a big birthday," Jolene says. "I feel like it should be a blowout."

I sigh. "We really don't have to."

"I'd look like a terrible fiancée if I didn't plan something."

"And I'd be a pretty bad fiancé if I didn't say how much I hated the idea."

"You can plan my birthday," Ruby offers with a laugh, sipping on her cup of water.

Jolene's face twists, a subtle glance that's there for a moment, then disappears again. It's the same weird look I've noticed more and more over the past year. I know now that I'm not imagining it. But I wish I were.

She shakes it off and smiles.

"Then, maybe I will since Bennett is being a big baby about it all."

"It's just ... thirty is a weird age," I say, running a hand through my hair. "Do my bones start creaking when I turn thirty? Do I wake up with a painful back? Do my hangovers get worse?"

"Yes, yes, and yes," my mom confirms.

I point. "See? What's there to celebrate?"

"Life," Ruby says. "Freedom, I guess? All the clichés?"

Freedom.

Jolene grabs Ruby's bottle of wine and pours herself a glass. "Well, I think your thirties will be the best so far. Y'know, I always thought you'd be married before thirty," Jolene says to Ruby. "We gotta tackle your happy ending next."

Ruby chokes on her water and follows up with a half-laugh. "Nah. Getting married has never been in the plan."

I take the wine passing hand to hand through the kitchen and pour myself a glass.

Everything is absolutely perfect in my life. My best friend is making waves at her dream job, my mom is in town for two months, and my beautiful fiancée is planning the biggest birthday party I'll ever have in my life.

I glance over at Jolene to smile, but her eyes are

lowered. I follow them to the place they're zeroed in—Ruby's wrist. The pink bracelet still sits there, clear as day.

Yep. Everything is absolutely perfect.

"Let's just plan this, okay?" Jolene says sharply, whipping open her binder. "And fix your hair, Ben. Christ."

I tense, but so does everyone else in the kitchen. Jolene's been more whip-quick with her words the closer it gets to the wedding. I think she's just stressed. Wedding planning isn't easy, especially with how particular she is with everything. I've been trying to handle things like flowers or invitations, but she insists on planning it herself.

I wish I knew how to help.

But for now, I laugh to lighten the mood, shoveling my long hair into a bun and tying it with the leather cord around my wrist. And when the hair tie accidentally snags at my pink string, I feel my heart stutter until it lets go.

42

Ruby

Two Months Before
Ruby & Bennett are Twenty-Nine Years Old

"Pass me the marker?"

"Marker," I confirm, handing the Sharpie to Quinn.

"Tape?"

"Tape."

"Elephant?"

"What?" I ask.

"The elephant in the room."

I sigh, swiveling my eyes over to Quinn.

"What elephant?" I ask in as innocent of a voice as I can muster. "There is no elephant."

Quinn hums with a nod. "Sure there's not."

And because I'm entirely too predictable, I glance over at Bennett next to Jolene, sitting on the railing across the midway. Her arms are crossed, but then again, they're always crossed nowadays. And Bennett is smiling that gorgeous smile of his, but then again, his is always gorgeous.

Ugh.

"Uh-huh," Quinn notes, starting to scrawl on the poster board.

"Whatever. You missed a letter."

She pauses to check, sees she didn't miss anything, then clicks her tongue. "Very funny."

I like being at the park with my friends, feeling the late-summer warmth. Cedar Cliff's generous mountain breeze breaks some of the oppressive Southern heat wave.

It's the afternoon of my birthday and the day before the huge celebration Jolene and our friends planned for me and Bennett at Honeywood. They're still decorating, and I'm not sure if the birthday duo is supposed to be here decorating, too, but when all your friends are doing one thing and hanging out only with each other is now awkward, you tag along and decorate for your own party instead.

I guess.

It's been almost a year since the engagement, and I'm still not sure how to navigate our friendship. It was awkward at first, only visiting each other at Trivia Night and barely texting. But then we slowly started sending GIFs and memes, and our friendship blossomed into a semblance of what it once had been.

But not exactly the same.

When we're in a group, we're fine. When we're in a text thread, we're perfect. When it's just the two of us? Well, we don't go there anymore. It's filled with weird looks and stumbling words.

I steal another glance at Bennett, and I find he's already looking at me. He averts his eyes.

I straighten my spine and turn back to Quinn.

"Guilty," she singsongs.

"I can handle a silly birthday," I whisper. "I can do this. I'm confident. Never been more confident in my life."

And I am. I have my dream job, learning every day from my dream mentor. I'm fit for the first time in my life, finally eating more than scraps of bread and cheese, like some medieval mouse. I even ignore texts from my dad, which he's not a huge fan of, but they're finally paying for an actual babysitter, and that's a big step for them. It's big for me too. Now, when Lucas comes over, the dynamic has shifted. I'm his sister, not his caretaker. As I should be.

I'm growing. I've grown.

But then I hear the familiar low call of, "Hey, Rubes! Blue or pink?" and sometimes, I wonder just how far I've actually come.

Bennett holds two streamers in the air, draped over his large fingers, so delicate, unlike him with his sleeve of tattoos and crooked smile. I've always loved when his harshness is juxtaposed with something gentler.

"Pink!" Quinn calls back for me, then leans in to whisper, "Like the massive pink elephant in this whole damn park."

"Shush."

"*It's just a birthday,* she says." Quinn mocks the words I've said too many times to count.

Emory walks across the midway toward us, hands in his pockets, looking at Quinn's handiwork on the poster board, then back to me. His face scrunches up, and those reliably thick eyebrows of his turn in.

"You look awful," he observes.

"Wow. Thanks, boss," I mumble sarcastically.

"It's your birthday. You shouldn't be helping."

"That's what I said," Quinn grunts.

"Boy, am I glad I gathered all the grumps in one place," I say, raising my shoulders to my ears in a faux innocent gesture. "I'm fine. I don't mind helping. It's just a birthday."

"It's just a birthday," Quinn echoes in her mimicking, high-pitched voice.

My pocket buzzes, and I tug out my phone.

Michael: On a scale of one to "I need to fly down there," how nervous are you for tonight?

I immediately lock my phone back.

Okay, so apparently, everyone can read me like a freaking book.

"How's snot face?" Quinn sneers.

"Michael is good." I tap my fingers on the railing.

"And?"

"We're just friends," I answer, and when she tilts her chin down, I laugh. "Promise. Still just friends."

I repeat it because it's true, but also because I have to remind myself and Michael constantly. He's in New York, achieving his finance bro dreams or whatever. We've only messed around once—last New Year's Eve when I flew to New York to watch the celebrations from his fancy apartment right near Times Square. But that one night under fireworks was the furthest we've ever journeyed.

I've tried to date a few people from dating apps, but it's never worked out. A kiss here. A hug there. But ultimately, if I were to date anyone, it would be Michael.

Unfortunately, Michael is only a good friend. He's the one person I've unloaded the whole sordid saga of me and Bennett to, and he didn't judge me one bit. Just a few snarky comments that made me laugh. He's still an ass after all these years.

"You know I'll be fine if you want to invite him," Quinn says even though her tight lips say otherwise.

"I know," I say.

Quinn really is trying to be accommodating when it comes to Michael. The two of them still haven't fully reconciled, even after he came down this past spring to hang out with the two of us and Lorelei. Bennett was out of town, but that wasn't on purpose.

Entirely.

Okay, so it was definitely on purpose.

Bennett still has zero idea I'm talking to Michael, and that's honestly for the best. I hate keeping things from my best friend. Well, from ... my friend. Just friend. Not best friend. Because Bennett and I are ... well ... I can't even form the words to describe what we are. And if I did, I might be calling Michael in tears again, and I'm getting tired of crying to my pseudo-boyfriend and/or pal.

I immediately pocket my phone when Bennett walks up. His hair is tied up in a bun, as it always is nowadays, per Jolene's request. I miss how it hung on his shoulders, wild and free, like he just hopped off his motorcycle. But he doesn't really ride that much anymore.

"Jolene says she wants purple streamers," Bennett says with a heavy sigh. "Please tell me you know where those are."

"Yeah," Quinn chimes in. "I think Lorelei has them in the boxes backstage."

"Figured."

"I know where the box is," I offer. "I'll go with you." And I don't know why I even said a dang word, but I did because it's Bennett.

He smiles. "Are you luring me to my death?"

"God, I was hoping you wouldn't notice."

"Well then, lead the way."

I faintly hear Quinn whisper, "Elephant," as we walk off.

Just the two of us.

43

Ruby

Bennett and I journey down into the outdoor amphitheater, where Honeywood hosts Queen Bee and Ranger Randy shows each day. The set pieces litter the stage, looking less thrilling sans the stage lights. I climb the backstage stairs, and when I almost miss one, Bennett's hands land on my waist, steadying me.

He grunts out something like, "Got ya," and I mumble back an awkward, "Thanks."

It's totally not weird.

But it is.

I step through the stacks of boxes backstage, finally finding the one Lorelei labeled *Birthday Buddies*. Right on top are purple streamers. I dig them out and toss the rolls to Bennett. He tilts his head to the side.

"What?" I ask.

"Nothing," he says. "Just ... does it look *too* purple?"

I smile, seeing the twinkle in his eyes. The start of a bit.

"Oh God, yeah," I say, playing along. "I thought I was gonna be the first to bring it up."

"It's Barney purple, right?"

"I think she said it was a dino-themed party, so maybe that's perfect."

"Did she?"

"Oh, yeah," I joke. "Lorelei got the dino costumes and everything."

"Think we could change it to a fruit party instead?"

"Why?"

He shakes the streamers and grins. "Grape color."

"Oh, right. Dancing grapes. How silly of me to consider anything different," I say, taking the streamers from him. "See, but I was gonna pitch vegetables."

"Vegetables?"

"Yeah, for an onion party. Y'know, so then if I cry, it'd be acceptable."

Bennett's eyes swivel to mine. "Wait, why would you cry?"

"I ... it was a joke," I say with a weak laugh. "Turning thirty and all. The big three-oh."

I wave the streamers around absentmindedly.

This is the worst part about us now. The fact that we can spiral down one of our joke rabbit holes and it feels like the old days, and then somehow, it screeches to a halt with one slightly off-kilter comment. It happens so quick that I can practically smell the rubber burning the road.

Bennett nods to himself, then lets out a small, quick laugh. Almost like he had to work for it.

"Weak bones, and one step closer to a midlife crisis," he says.

"Ooh, I can't wait for a crisis." I crouch down to sit on the edge of the stage. "I'm thinking I'll buy my mom's house and get a motorcycle. Oh, wait ..."

"Hardy-har," Bennett says, sitting down beside me.

"What do you have left on your list?" I ask, counting on my fingers. "You've got the tattoos ..."

"I still have to check off a mental breakdown."

"Ooh, that's always a good one."

"You act like you've checked it off already."

"I've broken a few dishes," I say, and when he laughs, I don't laugh back because, well, it's not a joke. *I have*. "What about you?"

"Well, I'm talking to my dad, so ..."

I blink. "Wait, you are?"

"I thought it was a good idea," he replies, his feet swinging out, the heels kicking the stage. "A good push in the right direction."

"He sucks though," I say with a laugh.

Because Ben Shaw *does* suck and Bennett has no reason to be texting a dad who was absent in his life. I should know.

The ache in my heart immediately wants to accuse, *Is Jolene making him do it?*

I hate that I jump to that, but I know I'm right. Even if I asked though, Bennett would never admit whether it was her idea or not. Because he loves her. And he's going to marry her. And if Bennett is anything, he's loyal.

"So ..." He changes the subject. "Thirty."

"Thirty," I echo, and the word bounces through the empty amphitheater.

We sit there in silence.

He shrugs. "We made it."

"We sure did. I didn't even have to find a new best friend. You really saved me a lifetime of awful friendships."

"Oh, me too," he says. "Can you imagine?"

"Would have been too much work."

"Absolutely."

"I would have had to open up and be vulnerable and stuff." I twist my lips and scrunch my nose. "Yuck."

He chuckles. "Not worth it."

"Definitely not."

We exchange smiles, and I should look away, but it's hard when Bennett's perfect smile squints back at me.

I *am* thankful he's still in my life.

Life might be weird sometimes, but it is good.

This is good.

My best friend's arm bumps against my shoulder, and the roughness of his string bracelet rubs against mine, like they're two magnets that refuse to part. Just like us.

I melt into the memories, letting my head land on his shoulder. His arm snakes around my waist. It's comfortable for us. Friendly. The same type of cuddling we did as kids that was innocent and meant nothing.

"Ben?"

And like the nothingness it is, I scoot away once I see Jolene standing at the top of the amphitheater.

I snatch the streamers from Bennett and hold them up like a beacon. "Found the purple ones!"

"Oh," she says as her eyes dart between us. "That's good."

I get up to leave, but Jolene sucks on her teeth.

"Oh, hey, Rubes," she says. "I'm looking for some string lights too actually. Do you think there's some back there?"

I clear my throat. "Uh, yeah, we probably have some. I can look for ya."

And I don't know why I feel guilty about her walking in because nothing happened. We were just sitting here.

"I'll meet you at the midway, Ben," she says, giving Bennett a tight smile.

I walk behind the stage again while they exchange a kiss

or something else that couples do that is totally normal and doesn't at all hurt my soul.

I dig in the box, distantly hearing Bennett ascend the steps out of the amphitheater, feeling the creaking of wood under my feet as Jolene walks behind me.

And then, sharp and to the point, she asks, "What are you doing?"

I straighten up with string lights in my palm. Her hands are on her hips. Her lips are tight and pursed.

"Getting ... lights?" I laugh. "What do you mean?"

She throws a thumb over her shoulder. "What was that back there?"

My stomach drops. And because I know I'm not crazy, she has that look. But this time, it's different. It doesn't disappear. I can barely register what's going on because Jolene has never looked at me like this. I see the fire in her eyes, and I don't like it.

"I ... what?"

"Ruby, I like you. But Bennett is marrying me. You know that, right?"

"I ..." I let out a small laugh, and I feel so silly and weak. I'm better than this. I've grown above feeling like this. "Yes," I say confidently. "Yes, I know that."

She squints and takes a step forward. "Do you? Because it seems like every time I turn around for even a second, you're right back in his arms."

I shake my head and let out a disbelieving laugh.

"We weren't doing anything," I insist.

"Sure," she says. "But that back there? I don't want to see that after my wedding."

My wedding.

Not *our*.

I feel like I'm getting reprimanded by a teacher, and the guilt almost swallows me whole, but I shake it off.

"Jolene, nothing is going on."

"Promise me."

"Jolene, I promise. I would never."

"And promise me it never will."

"It won't."

Her jaw grinds.

"It won't," I repeat. "Like you said, he's marrying you. I'm just a girl he's known since he was a kid."

I give a shrug. A shrug that shatters me inside because I know it's true. I'm just the little girl who stuck to him like glue, and I'm still sticking around after all this time. I can't imagine how frustrating it must be for her. How unfair.

She shifts her weight from side to side, her tongue pressing into her cheek. I know I'm not gonna like what she says before she even says it.

"I'd really like it if you weren't at the party."

But I didn't expect that.

It's a knife cut right to the core of me. A sharp twist in my gut.

My best friend's fiancée doesn't want me at my own birthday party.

My thirtieth birthday.

But what do I say? How do I argue when I'm standing here with the promise bracelet I made with him at twelve? When the idea of taking it off feels like a death sentence I don't want to face? When that's the only reason this birthday even matters?

How do you tell a bride you're still in love with her groom?

So, all I reply is, "That's fair."

It's not. Nothing about this is fair. But this is Bennett's life. I won't argue with the woman who makes him happy.

"Okay," I answer, tossing the lights back into the box. "I won't be there."

She blinks for a second, like she doesn't believe me. Like maybe she's surprised her intimidation worked. I'm not scared of her though. I'm scared of losing Bennett. And going against her? I'd lose him for good.

"Good," Jolene finally says, straightening her spine and nodding. "Good. I'm glad we had this talk."

I nod back. "Me too."

"Good."

"Great."

Yep.

Happy birthday to me.

44

Bennett

Our birthday party does look like a grape exploded. But I don't mind. I'm happy. *We're* happy.

And when I pass through the iron gates with Jolene on my arm and everyone jumping out, screaming, "Surprise!" as if I didn't just decorate with them yesterday, I can tell it's going to be a great night.

Orson places a tumbler of my favorite whiskey in my hand.

Theo looks around me and furrows her eyebrows. "Where's Ruby?"

Jolene's hand tightens in the crook of my arm. "She's running late."

I didn't know she was running late, but that's fine. I've come to terms with the fact that I'm not fully in the loop with my best friend anymore. Maybe that's how it should be.

"Actually," I add, "can we do this again in maybe an hour? I'd love for her to get the full effect too."

I can only imagine how excited Ruby will be when they

yell, "Surprise!" mostly because of how ridiculous it is that this isn't a surprise at all. Ruby loves that kind of humor.

We jump on roller coaster after roller coaster while we wait. I hop on Bumblebee's Flight with my hands in the air, Jolene next to me, whooping along. Lorelei sits in front of us with Emory. Quinn is with Landon. I'd bet Theo is somewhere in the park with Orson too. I can't help but grin. This is how I imagined today, side by side with my beautiful partner and our closest friends.

But once I get off the ride, I check my phone for texts. I come up empty. My smile fades.

Where is she?

Jolene and I ride The Romping Meadow, hand in hand, watching the animatronics. I check my phone again, the bright light making me squint in the ride tunnel's darkness. Jolene's hand squeezes around mine. I give her a reassuring squeeze back, but she still eyes my phone until I put it back in my pocket.

We walk through the buffet line set up near the amphitheater picnic tables. Emory and Landon agree to see who can ride Bumblebee's Flight the most times. Quinn is laughing at some joke Orson told her and Lorelei. Everyone is experiencing the night to the fullest, but I'm barely paying attention. My gut feels unsettled.

I look at my phone again. No texts. I check my watch. It's almost an hour past when she should have arrived.

I feel the happiness start to flicker. Once turning bright like a light switch, it's now suddenly clicked off.

She's not here.

Ruby is not at our thirtieth birthday party.

"Ben, what's wrong?"

I'm in line for The Beesting again—*when did I get here?*—and Jolene is beside me. Her hand is still clutching mine, but it's tighter than it's been all night. Almost painful.

"Earth to Ben," she says, but it's not sweet. It's sharp and irritated, and she's looking at me like she's been calling my name for a while now.

"Hmm? Yeah?"

"You all right?"

I nod with a forced smile, but then my chest lurches like it's detecting my lie. And Jolene's eyebrows rise as if she can too.

All I can manage is, "She'd never miss our birthday."

That was apparently the wrong sentiment because Jolene disentangles her hand from mine. I lift an eyebrow as she takes a step back.

"Our?" She crosses her arms. "You know you weren't actually born on the same day, right?"

I can feel the tension coursing through her. There's a twitch in the corner of her mouth. It's an emotion that seems so familiar, but it's also one I don't have a name for.

Jealousy? Resentment?

Hatred?

Why is she being like this?

"Jolene, come on," I say, the words sharper than I'd like them to be. "Ruby's my best friend."

She lets out a bitter, scoffing laugh. "Oh, and what does that make me, Ben?"

"Jolene," I say, repeating her name like it might snap her out of whatever weird mood she's in. But I can feel myself tensing up as well.

"Right," she says, sucking in her cheek. And then she walks off.

"Jo ..."

I swing a leg over the queue line ropes and run after her.

Jolene rushes across the midway with her fists clenched by her sides. I shuffle past Mrs. Stanley, Fred, and then Lorelei, who flashes me a worried expression.

I shake my head, as if to say, *Don't worry about us.*

Lorelei's bottom lip curls in anyway because she's a smart woman and I don't have to say something's wrong for her to know.

I follow Jolene all the way to the front of the park, right near the Buzzy the Bear fountain, where water shoots up in spurts.

"Are you leaving?" I ask. "Don't leave."

She twists on her heel, her jaw grinding. Her eyes scan mine.

She shakes her head side to side. "No. Because you know what? I'd rather talk."

My shoulders drop, and I nod, relief washing over me. I hate it when Jolene gets upset. It's not common, but why does it seem less rare nowadays?

It's just the wedding, I think. *Just the stress.*

I reach out to take her hand. "Okay, good. Let's talk."

My phone buzzes, and finally—*finally*—I see Ruby's name.

But then I read her text.

While the park around us is still enjoying their night with blinking attraction lights and screaming laughter and a carefree pancake buffet, my heart instead slowly breaks.

45
Ruby

It's all too much. My fingers tap over the screen of my phone as I text Michael exactly that.

Michael: Then, run away.
Ruby: To where?
Michael: Anywhere but there. You know you've always got a room at my place.
Ruby: I'm not driving to New York.
Michael: But you could.

It takes exactly two seconds to consider it. Because I'm a new Ruby, one who can just jet off to New York. Ruby, who is now close friends with the old high school football captain with beautiful eyes and a nice beard. Ruby, who can dead lift almost one hundred pounds. Ruby, who cooks meals by herself and has her dream job with her dream mentor.

Ruby, who gets a flat tire on her way out of town.
Crap.
It feels like fate, sitting here on the side of the highway

with my feet dangling over the trunk of my car, all alone on my thirtieth birthday.

I consider calling Bennett for help, but the thought drifts away in the wind. I wave it off.

Good-bye, cruel dreams.

Then, I cycle through everyone else in my phone. I consider calling Quinn first, but I know she'd give me some giant sarcastic speech, and I'm a little worn out from the elephant talk. I could call Lorelei, the most responsible of us all, but being the responsible one, she's playing party host. I can't pull her away from that.

I end up calling Theo. Theo, who almost eight months ago, secretly eloped with Orson in a courthouse marriage of convenience. She trusted me to be their witness and keep things hush-hush. If she can trust me with that, then I can trust her with this.

She answers on the second ring, agrees to pick me up without question, and says she'll bring Orson, too, which is good because I'm trying not to freak out about just how quiet the interstate is when it's just me and the whistling mountains. I try not to think about coyotes—though being ravaged by them doesn't seem too bad about now—and instead try to admire the stars. The stars that failed me so miserably by aligning my fate with Bennett's and making our birthdays so close.

I wish I could go back and rearrange the constellations. I wish I could tell little Amelia to avoid Honeywood's day camp. But, no, I don't actually wish that, do I? Because I would relive this pain again and again in every single lifetime, if only to experience the good memories with Bennett Shaw as well.

The way he spoke up for me when I couldn't. The way his eyes traced over my freckles. The way his hand guarded the small of my back. The way his breath caught at the sight of me when I lay bare before him so many years ago.

I sit up when a Jeep rumbles up and parks behind my car. Orson peers out of the driver's window. I give a wave, and he returns it with a crooked smile. Orson always has the gentlest smiles. He could make anyone feel like a dear friend even if he's meeting you for the first time. And in eager contrast is Theo, who jumps out from the passenger seat, runs over, hops on my car's trunk with me, and collects me in her arms.

"Oh my God, you must have been so scared."

I laugh as she cuddles in closer, like I'm a babe lost in the woods.

"I'm fine. Really."

"You called the tow company?" Orson calls over.

I give a thumbs up.

Theo nuzzles into my neck. "God, you're so late for your party."

"It's fine."

"No, it's a tragedy," she says with dramatic emphasis.

"Really, I'm okay."

Her eyes flicker to the road, and then it's like everything registers with her all at once—particularly what *side* of the road I'm on.

She looks at me and squints. "Wait, were you leaving town?"

"Kinda." I start twiddling my thumbs and passively tug at my pink bracelet, but then I stop because finding comfort from it feels wrong at this point. I'm not that person anymore.

Theo's eyes dart down to my wrist, then back up.

She pulls me in for a hug, pressing our cheeks together.

I've always liked how she smells, like oats and honey. Down-to-earth, just like her.

"Thanks for coming," I murmur.

"Have you told Bennett you're not gonna make it?"

I swallow. "No."

Theo places her hands on my shoulders, looking deep into my eyes. It's so weirdly intense for her that I let out a nervous laugh.

"Seriously, is everything okay?"

A lump catches in my throat, and slowly, I shake my head.

"No," I admit. "No, not really. I don't really wanna talk about it though."

She puts her fingers to her lips and zips them closed. "Say no more. I hear ya loud and clear. We don't have to say anything at all about tonight if you don't want to." Theo twists at the waist, glancing over at Orson, who is pacing in front of his Jeep, hands deep in his pockets. "Right?"

He blinks when he catches her gaze. His eyes dart between us before he gives another wonderful smile.

"Say what?" he agrees, walking closer, acting like our silent guardian against the whispering winds around us.

When Theo turns back around, his gaze still lingers on her. Orson and Theo might have initially married for practical reasons that didn't involve love, but it's so obvious that Orson has fallen for her now. My stomach tugs at the way he leans toward her, like a flower toward the sun.

Maybe that's my reality with Bennett. A push and a pull. A balloon and its eager string, ever in pursuit. That's not the future I want though. I don't want some unspoken longing that slowly guts me from the inside out. I want more. I deserve more. And so does he.

It's time to move on.

So, I text my new friend instead.

Ruby: Want to be my date to a wedding?
Michael: THE wedding? Red, I'm so honored.
Ruby: And so dramatic.
Michael: Well, you're asking me out on a date. A fancy date at that.
Ruby: I'll even wear a fancy dress.
Michael: I love fancy dresses.
Ruby: You're wearing one too?
Michael: Funny.
Ruby: Sorry. Please be my date?
Michael: Of course I will. Wouldn't miss it for the world.

"So," Theo says, pulling me back, "are we headed back to Honeywood for fun birthday times?"

I give a weak smile and shake my head. Her expression falls as she mimics the motion.

"I mean, *duh,* obviously, we're not going back to Honeywood," she corrects. "Yuck. Sounds awful anyway."

She tosses me a playful wink, and I can't hide the smile that follows.

The tow truck finally arrives minutes later—because, of course, I didn't have a spare—with the chains dragging my car by the wheels onto its back.

I pull out my phone and swipe to my messages with Bennett—the jokes and one-liners and shared videos from who knows how far back—and then I send him one single text.

46

Bennett

I stare at the text.

Ruby: I couldn't do it, Pirate.

I couldn't do it.

I want to say I don't know what Ruby means by that, but I do. I really do.

Shoving my phone in my pocket, I run my hand through my hair. It falls from the bun, and Jolene watches the strands cascade over my face. She stands with one leg out and her arms crossed. A power stance.

Honestly, I'm exhausted. I'm sad. I'm disappointed in myself. And when the woman across from me with pain slashed over her features looks like she's having the very same thoughts about me, my disappointment buries itself further.

"Well?" She tilts her chin toward my phone. "What'd she say?"

We don't need to discuss who it is. We both know.

"She's not coming," I answer.

Her shoulders roll back, but she says nothing.

I nod, rocking back on my heels until I lean against the brick wall behind The Bee-fast Stop. We're mostly alone, except for a few familiar faces passing by the alleyway. They raise their hand in a wave.

I shake my head quickly, as if to say, *Definitely not a good time*.

"It's fine," I murmur. "A birthday is a birthday."

We don't talk for a moment, and as the silence continues, I find myself tracing the string on my wrist with my thumb. I thought I'd stopped the habit, but I'm still absent-mindedly fiddling. The string is frayed and barely hanging on. It's been rebuilt, rewound, and retied so many times that I don't know where the original string starts or ends.

Jolene taps her foot on the cobblestone, sucking in a breath. "Bennett, I want to talk. About that."

My eyes dart up to hers, and I follow her stare right back down to my wrist.

"What does the bracelet mean?" she asks. "And why do you both have one?"

I have no idea how to explain our history and what makes us, *us*. How do you shove years of protection and care and reliability into one sentence?

I try because Jolene deserves the truth.

"We made these when we were twelve," I explain. "It was a promise. Just a silly wedding pact."

But the truth isn't what she wanted to hear.

Her green eyes spark like wild flames. Her fists are clenched tight by her sides. The roar of Bumblebee's Flight screams over the track, but the screeching sound of steel can't rival the anger that seems like it's steaming out of her ears.

"A wedding pact?" Jolene asks.

"Jolene—"

"Ben." The word is spit out, landing like splashes of venom against my chest, rising up my neck, radiating into my cheeks. She's fuming, insisting with, "No. Please. Keep going."

"It means nothing past simple nostalgia," I say, reaching out to her.

She steps away.

"So, let me get this straight," she sneers. "You basically had promise rings with your best friend? And I'm just now hearing about this?"

"Jolene, it was just something we did as kids."

"But you still wear it."

My head hurts. My heart hurts—no, everything hurts.

"So, what else did you do with Ruby?" she demands. "I want to know it all."

I sigh, nodding. "Fair enough. Where should I start?"

"I don't care. How about ..." Jolene says slowly, as if trying the words, swashing it like mouthwash between her cheeks, only to spit it back into the sink. "Your tattoos?"

My stomach plunges into ice water. I look down at my arm and back up.

"I'm not stupid. I've noticed," she taunts with narrowed eyes. "What? I assume she has one too?"

Ruby's tiny tattoo—the cute little doodle that I've kissed, soft and sweet against her skin.

I nod stiffly, and Jolene looks away, tonguing her cheek. She begins to pace, like a panther stalking prey.

"Yes. A strawberry," I answer. "On her hip bone."

"On her ..." Jolene stops pacing. "On her hip bone? How do you know that? Have you..."

I lift my chin up and meet her gaze head-on. I don't say anything, but at this point, I'm not sure I need to.

I could say I was with Ruby when she got the tattoo, but that'd only be half the truth.

I clear my throat. "I slept with her once before you and I met."

She blinks so fast that it's unnerving. I can sense her processing, the little cogs and wheels trying to break this down to something more palatable. But I know it can't be easy. And I hate that she's going through this. That I'm the man putting her through this.

Jolene stalks closer, head dipping a little, shoulders arced up, jaw tightening and releasing.

"Are you kidding me, Bennett?" she whispers before shouting, "Are you *fucking kidding me right now*?"

I swear birds scatter from the trees. The music feels more distant. The general ambiance of my very favorite theme park falls dead to her words.

I run a hand through my hair. "Jo—"

"What? You want me quiet, like Ruby?" She lessens her stance. "Demure, like Ruby?"

"I have never once said that."

Then, she huffs out air through her nose, tapping her fingers on her hips.

"Wait. Wait a second." She puts her fingers on her temple, closing her eyes and almost gasping for the next words. "Oh my ... oh my *God,* did you lose your virginities together?"

"Yes."

"Christ, Bennett!" Her exclamation is loud. Too loud, echoing off the brick walls and through the tree line.

I let her fume.

But where there was once fire in her eyes, there is now nothing. Her hands tremble by her thighs.

Then, she croaks out the one thing I would never expect. "You can't see her anymore."

My heart stops mid-beat. I didn't know the world could feel as small as it does, but somehow, what felt so big and wide seconds before now feels too delicate.

"What?"

"You cannot see her," Jolene repeats slowly. She sniffs and clears her throat. "Was I not clear enough?"

The idea of ripping Ruby from me is like stripping me of a limb. An arm. A leg. The very heart right out of me. And Jolene—the woman I love—is asking me to tear myself to pieces. And she knows it.

I can feel the sting behind my eyes. The tickling at my nose. And when my eyes are probably circled in red, I swear she looks at me with this sneer of disgust.

My mom told me men can cry. I now wonder if Jolene was taught differently.

"I'm sure you think I'm being unfair," she murmurs, picking at the underside of her red nails. "But you know what's not fair? What's not fair is being second to the woman your fiancé really wishes he had."

I shake my head. "That's not true."

"Then, don't see her anymore."

I love Jolene. I have spent nearly three wonderful years standing beside her and defending her feisty remarks and tenacious approach to life to everyone around us. I don't mind explaining that she's just headstrong, which she is, and that Jolene is simply a force to be reckoned with. It's why I fell in love with her.

But this?

Demanding something like this?

It's like I'm talking to a stranger.

And the idea of me wanting to be with Ruby instead?

That's not true.

But then a sneaky voice asks, *Is it?*

And Jolene, with her eyes locked on me and a deep line between her eyebrows getting only deeper, makes me wonder if she heard that little whisper too.

I swallow. "You're serious."

With a concluding shrug and crossed arms, my fiancée nods and says, "Yes. And I won't settle for anything less."

47

Ruby

I wake to the sound of my front door opening. My first thought is, *Yikes, Bennett's mom sure knows how to party.* I didn't expect her to get back so late, but she's younger than me in spirit.

But my second thought, as I roll over on the couch, trying to curl closer to the cushions to block out the porch light and bypass Theo's socked feet lying next to my ear, is, *Wow, that's a familiar, salty coconut scent and—*

A hand covers my mouth. I let out a tiny squeal.

"Shh, Rubes, it's me."

I blink up at Bennett and his totally-not-a-serial-killer face. His eyebrows are tilted in. His frown at one hundred percent.

He releases my mouth and puts a finger up to his lips, jerking his chin toward the front door.

I look to Theo, still passed out with one arm hanging off the couch. Easing myself up, I grab my phone and tiptoe across the floor, laden with our blankets, pillows, and DVD cases from the makeshift girls' night. Theo suggested we still celebrate my birthday, so we made do with what we had. It was exciting, but not as much as it could have been with the man I'm following now.

I close the door behind me once we're both on the porch, and together, we walk to the end of the driveway, far from the house where Theo might be able to hear.

"What the hell, Bennett?" I hiss-whisper.

"Sorry. I didn't wanna wake anyone."

"Well, you woke me up."

"Yeah," he says with a chuckle. "That was kinda the point."

I give a nonthreatening eye roll as he crosses his arms, rolls his neck, and starts to pace the driveway.

In that moment, I remember that we're kind of fighting, but also not. I didn't go to our most important birthday, and he never responded to my text.

I cross my arms over my chest, trying to stave off the summer humidity that is eerily cool tonight.

"Why are you here?" I ask. "What time is it?"

He stops, blinks at me, and inhales. "Two. Ish."

"Two?"

"Rubes, you didn't show up."

The night air gets sucked from my lungs as I watch Bennett's shoulders slouch and his eyebrows stitch in.

"No," I state, "I didn't."

He nods, tugging his hair from the leather strap before winding it back into a bun once more. I used to love watching him do that, but now, not so much. It means he's stressed.

He fastens the tie back. "Why didn't you come?"

I curl my lips in. I consider for half a second telling him that Jolene requested my absence, but I don't. That's not fair to anyone involved.

So, I give a small shrug instead and say, "I think we both know what this birthday meant."

Bennett lowers down to the concrete, lifting his knees up and burying his head in his palms. He rubs them down his cheeks, tugging at the skin before letting it go.

"I thought we were doing good, Rubes."

"We were," I argue. "We are." I sit down beside him, crossing my legs, one over the other. "This was just a big milestone. It's thirty, y'know? A bump in the road of life."

He snorts out a laugh through his nose and shakes his head. "A bump?"

"Yeah. A bump." I tug a weed out from between the crack in my driveway. "That's the best analogy I got right now."

Bennett grunts in agreement.

My phone buzzes. I see Michael's name flash in too-big letters. I flip the phone over so that the screen faces the concrete instead. Bennett's eyes snag on the device once it's flipped, and they don't break away.

"Who are you texting this late?" he asks.

"Honestly?" I add with a laugh. "You don't want to know."

He nods again before running palms over his face once more. He lets out a low groan, almost a growl, and then an irritated exhale.

"God, you have a boyfriend, and I don't even know about it. How out of touch am I?"

"Well, he's not exactly a boyfriend," I answer. "He's a ... pseudo-man-thing."

Bennett chuckles, resting his forearms on his knees, his feet spread apart on the concrete. And he's smiling. I missed seeing how happy he could look. I missed the feeling that comes with being alone with my best friend—the little secrecy of inside jokes and twenty-year bits that always seems to wrap its way around us, like a blanket of solitude.

Well, solitude, save for the low music coming from my neighbors' house. I bet they're winding down from a party.

Is that Celine Dion?

"Why are you here?" I ask.

Bennett's eyes dart away from mine. His shoe scrubs against the concrete. And in that moment, he's almost a kid again. The little boy ripping the name tag at Honeywood. Me and my pirate in our little bubble of friendship.

I giggle. "You wake me up in the middle of the night, and you can't even—"

"I'm here because I can't see you anymore."

The bubble of friendship bursts.

I think I have tunnel vision. Or maybe the night gets darker or the pit in my stomach gets deeper and hollower. I'm falling. No, the world is spinning too much.

My thoughts are no longer coherent as I croak out, "What?"

Bennett clears his throat. "We can't hang out anymore."

I can't hang out with Bennett.

My Bennett.

My pirate.

Somehow, I find myself laughing.

Bennett's eyes widen. "Uh, Ruby?"

I laugh because the sentence doesn't feel real. I've got to be living in some goofy fun-house version of my life. Maybe someone with a camera will jump out of the bushes and tell me I'm the star of a new reality show. Honestly, being embarrassed on national television would be better than this.

But the more he looks at me, the more real it becomes.

My brain feels stretched thin. My body too tight, too

uncomfortable, like this skin isn't even my own. My emotions are playing tug-of-war, pulling at the left side of the brain, then the right until I think my head is in pain.

But I can't stop laughing.

"It's not funny," Bennett says.

I laugh more.

"Rubes."

Then, through the laughs, I finally start to cry. I'm Dr. Jekyll and Mr. Hyde. I'm not sure when the change happens or when my eyes started to hurt.

Bennett puts his arm on my lower back, and I lean into it. He wraps his hand tight around my waist and tugs me in, just like he used to. But the second my nose presses against his shoulder, breathing in his stupid coconut scent with not a single hint of strawberry, I choke out another laughing sob.

"I don't know if I should be concerned or not," he jokes.

I laugh harder and sniff. "Very."

Bennett then barks out a laugh, too, but his comes with a sniffle. It's wetter than it should be for his normal laugh. Mine probably is too.

"I'm sorry," he says, burying his head against mine.

"Don't be."

His palm strokes up my side, then back down. The thick mess of his hair hangs down like a curtain between us—the same one I loved as a teen—trapping in our heated breaths and heavy exhales, mixed with choked tears.

"I'm sorry I got us to this point," I murmur.

"What? It's not your fault. What are you talking about?"

"No, it is my fault, isn't it? You offered to love me three years ago. And if I'd said yes, maybe we wouldn't be here."

"We wanted different things."

"We did."

Bennett doesn't answer for a moment, and for a second, I think maybe I stepped into an unspoken hallowed ground. We never speak about that day. I pull back and watch as he chews his shaking lip and shakes his head back and forth.

"And, Rubes ... I wasn't offering to love you. Three years ago, I was simply telling you the inevitable. Because what I felt for you? It was inescapable, Ruby. I loved you more than anyone could ever love another person. And it would have been nice to have it back, sure, but it didn't matter what you told me. It wasn't an offer. It was a confession. And I will never ever take that back. You understand?"

Past tense.

Loved.

I nod. He nods back. And I can't bear to look at him any longer, so I lean into his chest, letting his thick, tattooed arm wrap back around me, looking down at the pink string barely holding on to his wrist.

"So, this is it, huh?" I ask.

"I mean, you're still invited to my wedding."

I laugh. "Oh, thank God. I was really worried about that one."

Bennett lets out a wet chuckle, and I follow with my very own.

"Happy birthday, Pirate," I whisper.

My former best friend nuzzles his head against mine.

"Happy birthday, Parrot."

Distantly, my partying neighbors switch the music to Whitney Houston. Because of course they do.

I sniffle out laughter, and so does he.

"If this were a commercial, what would we call this album?" Bennett asks.

"*Fall of Friendship.*"

"Autumn themed. Nice. But also very dramatic."

"Oh well. I'm feeling a little dramatic today."

"Me too."

We sit there, at the end of my driveway, huddled together, listening to my neighbors blast Michael Bolton. Boyz II Men. Mazzy Star.

And that is how a childhood friendship dies—with a thirtieth birthday under the soundtrack of '90s romance ballads.

48

Bennett

One Week Before
Ruby & Bennett are Thirty Years Old

"Oh my God, I hate it."

"Nope. Leave. Leave right now."

"Jump scare. For real."

Those are pretty much the reactions I expected. However, when I walked into The Honeycomb with my long hair chopped off, I thought the gawking would be kept only at my table. It's not. All around the bar, regulars are staring—even Mrs. Stanley is clutching her heart.

Oh God, did I give the old lady a heart attack?

Emory, who is also blinking like the image of me is still buffering before his eyes, holds out a steady hand. "You look sharp, Bennett."

I place my palm in his hand, giving it a firm shake. "Thanks, man."

But the nice gesture is still accompanied by the befuddlement from everyone else. Lorelei is chewing on her thumb. Quinn's arms are crossed. And Theo's eyes still can't stop roaming up to my head.

In response, I run my hand through my hair—my very short hair.

The girls collectively gasp.

What was once a long mess of hair that touched just below my shoulders is now almost nothing. My head is shaved close on the sides and styled short up top. It's a shock to the system, especially after caring for my long rocker hair my entire life. The first time I looked in the mirror, I thought I should introduce myself as Mr. Shaw, moving forward. I considered buying a briefcase, but the thought had me deflating. It would have been a funny bit if I was able to laugh about it myself. As it is, my neck is cold.

I take my usual seat at our trivia table, pinning my elbows to my sides. It's a tight fit. I'm accustomed to a tiny ginger sitting next to me, but now, the seat has been taken by Landon, who is far taller and broader.

It's uncomfortable, but what isn't nowadays?

I blink at the shocked faces. "You're allowed to say something nice about my haircut."

Quinn squints, waving her hand in the air. "Sure. But, y'know, why lie?"

Landon rests his arm around her shoulders. "It's nice."

Lorelei places a hand on my forearm from across the table. "It does look good, Bennett. It's just ... different."

Theo leans forward, eyeing every inch of my face. "So, why'd you cut it?"

Quinn coughs into her fist something that sounds very obviously like, "Jolene."

I tilt my head to the side. "Quinn."

"What?" she says, holding up her hands. "Am I wrong?"

"No," I say, dragging the word out. "She wanted me to look clean for the wedding. I can't fault her for that."

"Right," Quinn says, rolling her eyes. "Because you totally didn't wash your dirty hair beforehand, you caveman, you."

"Your hair was prettier than mine," Theo muses, now fluffing up her own curls, as if ensuring they haven't disappeared too.

"You know what? You look smart," Lorelei says.

"Soccer-dad style," Theo says.

"Businessman bright," Quinn chimes in.

We all wait for a fourth female voice to chime in, but nothing follows. Because that voice isn't here.

At the same time, we shuffle in our chairs, feeling the absence of *her* too much.

"I like it," I say. "Change is good."

Emory, of all people, grunts in response. But when I cut a glance at him, he's already looking in the other direction.

"What?" I ask.

The whole table is looking elsewhere, either at the floor or at their drinks or at the trivia question posted on the television.

"What, guys?" I repeat.

"Well," Lorelei says, chewing on her bottom lip, "it just kinda seems like you've been changing a lot lately."

"No, I haven't."

"I haven't seen your motorcycle in a while," Theo mumbles.

"Or your band tees," Lorelei notes.

Quinn snorts. "Well, and I don't see our little ginger-headed friend here, do you?"

I freeze on the spot, and when I look at everyone else,

there is a mix of expressions, ranging from Emory's pulled-in eyebrows and Theo's cringe.

"We just miss your banter," Lorelei says, winding her hands together. "That's all."

"Trivia isn't the same without the both of you," Theo throws in. "Plus, I hate this choose-a-side thing. Like, I can't text the original group chat because it's weird, so we've had two separate group chats with either of you, and now, I have to basically text the same thing twice, and I get confused on who's heard what and—"

I exhale. "I know."

"You miss Ruby," Lorelei says matter-of-factly.

"You do, don't you?" Theo asks with a wince.

"I do," I admit. "Of course I do. She is—*was*—my best friend."

Another collective groan.

"Yikes, that hurts," Quinn mutters under her breath, bringing her drink to her lips.

"Hey," I caution, shooting her a look.

"Just know that we're here for you," Lorelei says quickly, "whatever you need."

"Yeah, we'll make sure you don't cut and run on the big day, buddy," Landon says with another pat.

This has the table bursting out in words of, "Landon!" and, "Don't say that!" and a simple, "Nice," from his girlfriend, Quinn.

I point between Landon and Quinn. "Two peas in a pod, I swear."

They got together shortly after my engagement party a year ago, and I'm not sure why they waited so long, not when they egg each other on like they do.

"Is she at least coming to the bachelor party?" Theo asks.

"Oh." My body deflates. "No."

"What?!" Lorelei nearly shrieks. "But it's at Honeywood! I rented out the whole park for us!"

"We do that all the time."

"Yeah, but this time, it's just *us*. The fab, uh ..."

"Well, we're not exactly the fab five anymore," Quinn says with a laugh.

"Yeah, yeah, I'm doing math ..." Lorelei says, pointing to all of us and then at the bar, where Orson is. "Eight of us."

"Seven," Emory corrects.

"Right, because, now, Ruby isn't coming," Quinn adds, shooting me an accusatory glance.

I run a hand over my eyes. When I told them I couldn't see Ruby anymore, they understood. But as we've settled into the reality of what that truly means, how much social juggling it takes, they aren't as agreeable anymore. Even Lorelei, the kindest woman in Cedar Cliff, twists her lips to the side when I bring up Jolene.

"Guys, I'm getting married. I did what I had to do to make my future wife happy. You don't understand. And I don't need your judgments for it."

I'm doing what's right by Jolene. She deserves better than what my mom got—a future of waiting. And I refuse to be Ben Shaw.

The real Ben Shaw still hasn't responded to our wedding invite or anything since. Jolene stopped pushing me to respond after my birthday. Yet, somehow, it's been easier and harder, all at once, to know that he is choosing to opt out of my life for good. Turns out, I've learned Mom's lesson too. There's no amount of waiting that will pay off with Ben Shaw.

"You're right," Emory says. "We don't understand what you're going through. So, we'll drop it." And then, with that look that only Emory can give, he glances around the table. "Right, everyone?"

They sigh in response.

"Fine," Quinn says, jerking her drink up to her lips.

"We'll drop it," Lorelei agrees. "Never mention it again."

But part of me hates the thought of never addressing it again. Because talking about my situation is the only time *she* feels real now. It's the only time I can say her name. It's the only time I get even a glimpse of her.

And I miss her so, so much.

"How was trivia?"

"Good."

"Y'all win?"

I chuckle. "Not a chance. What are you looking at?"

I lean over the couch, peering at her laptop with our wedding's RSVP list. My dad's name is the only one still highlighted in yellow. Jolene gives me a weak smile. It takes everything in me to return it.

"How'd they feel about the hair?" she asks, running her fingers through it.

I'm still getting used to how soon the fingers are gone. There's not much to thread through.

"Ah, not great," I explain, then add, "But they were more concerned about the bachelor party anyway."

"Are you excited about your bachelor party?" she asks.

"Sure."

"Lies," Jolene says, teasing her head toward me.

I chuckle. "You know big parties aren't really my thing."

"True."

We sit in silence, letting the words flow over us. We've been doing that a lot lately. Just existing with the sound of our air-conditioning unit and the random whir of the refrigerator from the kitchen. I know all the insignificant noises of this house due to our lingering quiet.

"Okay." Jolene claps her hands together, turning on the cushion with her knees tucked underneath her. "Well, I have a proposition for you."

"Do I get to bypass the bachelor party altogether?"

Jolene laughs. "No, but ..." Then, she smacks her lips together and exhales. "I think you should invite Ruby to your bachelor party."

Hearing her name leave Jolene's lips feels so incongruous. It's like when the rides at Honeywood make announcements in another language, but keep the one native noun. It throws off the whole sentence.

Mantenga sus manos y pies dentro de The Grizzly *en todo momento.*

"You should invite Ruby *to your bachelor party."*

"What?" I ask. "Invite Ruby?"

"You should."

"No," I say, shaking my head.

She laughs. "I'm asking you to."

"But why?"

"She's your best maiden or whatever," Jolene says, clicking her tongue and looking away. "It wouldn't be right."

It seems nice enough, but something feels off about it. It's how casual she's saying it, compared to the last time when I could have sworn Ruby's name was erased from Jolene's vocabulary indefinitely. But even so, she is in fact smiling at me as she delivers this news.

She hikes her shoulders up to her ears in an exaggerated shrug. "Invite her. Really. I trust you for one night."

One night.

It's like a small itch on my neck I can't scratch. Hell, I don't even try to.

"Plus," she says, winding a piece of string from her sleep pants through her fingers, "she RSVP'd for two."

Bull's-eye.

"She did?" I ask.

"Yes."

I don't know what hurts worse. The fact that Ruby has a boyfriend I haven't met or that Jolene seems happy about it.

I swallow. "Well, good. Good for her."

"That's what I thought too. So"—she pats my arm—"go ahead and invite her, Ben."

"Okay," I say, my voice feeling more distant by the second. "Yeah. Sure."

"Good."

I don't say anything more as Jolene gets up from the couch. I just continue leaning on the back of it, my hand absentmindedly traveling over my wrist, attempting to find its reliable piece of pink string, only to remember that there is nothing to grab anymore.

I removed my pink bracelet two months ago, and I haven't felt the same since.

49

Ruby

Four Days Before
Ruby & Bennett are Thirty Years Old

Emory's dusty workshop is one of my favorite places in Cedar Cliff, right behind Honeywood and the lone tree in the woods. I'm toiling away on my newest work project, tapping my fingers over laptop keys, and trying to drown out any thoughts related to my not-friend best friend. Though thinking about the lone tree probably isn't helping.

Keys clatter on the workbench, and I jump.

"Christ," I say, covering my heart.

Emory gives a small chuckle as he stands behind me, eyes darting to my screen and back up.

"What are you still doing here?" he grunts. "Don't you have a brother-sister day or something?"

"Had to wrap some stuff up."

My dad demanded I pick up Lucas at four o'clock, to which I countered with five thirty instead. I told him that I got off work at five and that was nonnegotiable. I don't bend to my dad's schedule. Not that Emory would have minded —he was at a lunch meeting with new clients. But it's the principle of it all.

"Well, I'm gonna have to dock your pay for using company materials off the clock," Emory says.

I shoot him a look. "Funny."

"I've got some good ones every so often." He sighs, taking a seat on the stool beside me. "So, anyway ..."

I straighten up, pinching my eyebrows together. "Anyway? Did you just say *anyway*?"

I can count on one hand the things Emory likes—Lorelei, roller coasters, running, and silence. Small talk is not and will never be on that list. Over the past year, Emory and I have designed nearly five roller coasters on our own from start to finish. And how do we do that? Long hours. And zero small talk.

Anyway? Not exactly in his vocabulary.

He clears his throat. "I saw Bennett."

I suck in a breath and hold it. It's like a cool, ghostly hand wraps around my heart, giving a small squeeze. Just hearing his name gets me on edge.

"Okay ..." I exhale. "What about him?"

"He seems fine."

"And that's code for ..."

"Fine," Emory grunts.

"So ... you started this conversation just to tell me Bennett seems ... fine?"

"Yeah."

"Okay."

I go back to my laptop, clicking here and there, but solving nothing. He sits on the stool with a wrench, but it's just balancing from one palm to the other.

Almost a full ten seconds later, Emory finally gives a low groan, a kind of whine that leads into a grunting, "He doesn't look the best right now."

I pause my fingers over the keys and look at him. "He doesn't?"

"No. He chopped off his hair."

"Wait, what?"

I grip the edge of the table while my heart slowly breaks. I can't imagine Bennett without his beautiful hair.

"Mmhmm," Emory responds.

"So, you're trying to tell me he *literally* doesn't look good?"

"No." Emory's eyebrows scrunch inward. Sometimes, those caterpillars have a life of their own. But right now, I can sense the real concern. "Well, yes. But he also seems ... sad."

"Oh."

"Yeah." He heaves a breath. "Anyway ..."

"Another *anyway*? We're on a roll today."

He snorts. "I just figured you'd wanna know. An update or whatever."

"Thanks. You really are a softy inside."

Emory gives a wry smile. "Yeah, yeah. Now, get out of here. You have to be back in ten hours or something."

I pack up my bag, slinging it over my shoulder, and walk toward the workshop door. But I turn on my heel before creaking it open. "Do you think he's meant to be with Jolene?"

Emory blinks for a moment before lifting his caterpillars to the sky.

"Ahem, well ..." He heaves out a sigh. "Do you?"

"I think you know my answer."

"And I think you know mine."

I give a weak smile. "Thanks."

"And, hey, if Bennett asks you something soon, say yes."

"What's he gonna ask me?"

"Just do it. You're smart, Ruby. You'll find your way, all right?"

"Promise?" I whisper.

"Yeah. I promise."

"Can I go again?"

"I'm not stopping until you do, kiddo."

"Yes!"

Lucas runs down the exit ramp, takes the first left out of the line, and circles right back into the starting queue for Little Pecker's Joy Ride.

I've lost count of how many times we've ridden this thing today, but if I'm lucky, I'm only molding another roller coaster enthusiast in our family.

I don't babysit Lucas as much as I used to. He's ten now, so it's not like he needs one anyway. But now, when we hang out, it feels more like hanging out with a little brother. There's less pressure to be a disciplinarian. And I much prefer being the older sibling that sends him home with too many pancakes in his stomach and endless vertigo from too many rides.

"This time, I'm gonna hold my hands up *really* high," Lucas says.

"Bet I can hold mine up higher."

"Nuh-uh."

"I don't know. You're gonna have to try really hard then."

Lucas hmphs and rests his chin on the railing.

"You know," I say, leaning in, "I bet they'd go even higher if we rode The Grizzly."

His eyes grow wide, and he swallows. "I don't know ..."

"Oh, come on," I coax, fluffing up his hair. "You've got this. We all need a little courage in our lives, right?"

"Maybe."

"Definitely."

"Okay, cool. You'll sit next to me though, right?"

I smile down at him. "Of course I will, kiddo."

I hope he grows up to be braver than me. More daring. More thrilled by life and unafraid of its consequences. I don't want him to make the same mistakes as me or have similar regrets.

But I am learning. I'm getting better, trying to mitigate future ones.

I've been looking at places to vacation after the wedding. I've never left the country before, but I registered for a passport. I might not know the language of wherever I'm going, but that's okay. For once, I don't want to apologize for existing.

I'm learning to stand up for myself. Because at the end of the day, there is nobody in the world looking out for me other than myself. I don't have a safety net or an anchor. And maybe that's okay.

Maybe.

My phone buzzes in my pocket. I pull it out, expecting another snarky audio message from Michael. He's been giving me a play-by-play of his flight to Atlanta.

But it's not Michael's name I see.

It's Bennett's.

Emory was right.

I grit my jaw and straighten my posture. I tell myself I'm strong. I can do this.

I swipe to open my phone, but one glance tells me, *Nope, I'm not ready for this at all.* But it's happening whether I want it to or not.

Bennett: You are cordially invited to my bachelor party.
Ruby: You're kidding.
Bennett: I'm thinking I need strippers.
Ruby: All Cedar Cliff has are clowns, I hear.
Bennett: Clown strippers then?

I close my eyes, inhaling a breath right as Lucas tugs my shirt forward. I take a step forward, then another metaphorical one through my fingers.

Bennett: It's in two days. We're starting at The Honeycomb around seven.
Ruby: I've got a guest in town. I'm not sure I can make it.

There're a few seconds with no text.

Bennett: Oh, Mr. Not-Boyfriend?
Ruby: The very one.

Dots start, then stop. Start. Then stop.
Christ, Bennett.
And finally—

Bennett: Bring him. The more, the merrier.

I let out a laugh.
"What's so funny?" Lucas asks.

I shake my head. "Trust me, nothing about this is funny."

Ruby: Probably not a great idea.
Bennett: Not taking no for an answer. I'd rather you be there with company than not at all.
Ruby: You're sure?
Bennett: I'm gonna need my parrot for our pirating festivities, aren't I?

I take a giant inhale, tilt my head side to side, then hit Send.

Ruby: I'll tell Michael then.

50

Bennett

One Day Before
Ruby & Bennett are Thirty Years Old

Michael "Potato Face" Waters is the ghoul haunting my very existence. I must be cursed. Or maybe I drunkenly signed a contract with the Devil, and this was the result. Hell, maybe he's Satan himself.

It might be odd to have a bachelor party at my local bar and theme park, but all I wanted was my best friends' company and relaxation after the rehearsal dinner. We're wandering around an empty version of The Honeycomb with drinks in our hands, laughing at memories of me, and devouring the food Landon catered for the event.

"Can we at least hire strippers?" Quinn begs.

"Out in Cedar Cliff? You think someone is gonna make the trek up these mountains?"

"What if they could though?"

"No. Absolutely not."

"Bennett, sex work is a legit business, and they deserve to be compensated."

"Quinn."

"Okay, well, what about fun games after this?" Theo asks. "Go-karts? Axe throwing?"

"We have Honeywood."

"We always have Honeywood."

"Okay, I have Uno stashed in my office too," I say. "Is that good?"

Lorelei grins at me, probably okay with a low-key party herself, but still bemoans, "God, Bennett, you're so boring."

Wedding planning is finally over, the guest list is finished, and all I need to do now is walk down that aisle.

Easy.

Except then the front door creaks open, and my ex–best friend and her new beau, Michael "Potato Face" Waters, waltz in, hand in hand.

I give a polite wave. He returns it.

I meet eyes with Ruby, who clears her throat and gives a small shrug, as if to say, *Sorry, Pirate.*

It's hard not to smile at her, so I mouth back, *He's cool.*

It's not entirely the truth, but I'm just happy that she seems happy. Eventually, I make my way to the bar and hunch over my glass of whiskey. It's there, away from the laughter, that I start to stew.

Since when are they together? How did they even connect again?

And why, out of all people, is it him?

I inhale sharply at the memory of him in Shop class. The way he claimed he'd go after her.

What a long con.

I don't understand it either. Isn't *he* the guy who was

393

always skeevy? Isn't *he* the guy who bullied Quinn? Since when is he the hero?

No. Think positively. You're here. She's here. That's all that matters.

And who knows? Maybe he's changed. Maybe she sees something I don't. The best I can do is trust Ruby.

Orson leans across the bar, twisting his baseball cap around and darting his eyes over to Ruby, then back. "He seems nice."

My eyes swivel to him, and I wonder if my face gives me away because my expression only makes him laugh.

"Have you said more than two words to him?"

"No."

"Well, there's still time to make a good first impression!"

I tip my tumbler to him. "Hilarious."

Theo bops behind the counter, wrapping her arms around Orson's middle and smacking a kiss on his cheek. He tugs her tight, and regardless that I'm still watching, he continues to stare in awe—maybe because she's finally his, after too many months of pining. He's been looking like a puppy dog for the past month since they went official.

I'm happy for them. Truly. I'm happy for all my friends. Theo and Orson, sure, but also Quinn and Landon. They've been together nearly a year now, and he keeps resting his chin on the top of her head like he's her own personal guardian. Even Emory and Lorelei exchange little smirks back and forth. They're more subtle about their love, but, God, you can tell it runs deep.

And there's ... Ruby and Michael, I guess.

I steal another glance at them again. She's full-on laughing at something he said.

Christ, there's no way he's that funny.

"How's Sulky here?" Theo asks.

Orson nods. "Ah, the worst of the seven dwarfs."

"I'm not sulking," I say. "I'm just enjoying the company of friends."

"In a sulky position," she adds.

"Not Sulky. I'm Bennett."

Theo leans her forearms on the bar top. "Are you? Because I thought I was looking at a ghost of our friend."

I shake my head, dragging down more of my whiskey.

"Come on." Theo laughs. "Look! Even Quinn is talking to him."

I watch as Quinn does in fact converse with Michael. Even her sneer is kept at bay through Landon's consistent rubbing of her shoulders. And then, suddenly, they're laughing too.

Okay, he's got to be hiding a joke book or something. This can't be real.

"She looks like she's in pain," I mutter.

"But *friendly* pain," Orson adds.

I watch Michael and Ruby, and the moment I sigh, Ruby makes eye contact with me. Always reading my mind. My lips tip up into a half-smile.

Whispering something in Michael's ear—in a secret way that used to be ours—Ruby breaks apart and walks over to the bar. She lands in the stool next to mine.

My smile grows wider. "Hey, you."

So does hers. "Hi there."

From those few words, I can feel myself settle into the seat—the feeling of our weird tether loosening after being pulled taut for so long.

It's nice to have my friend here.

Theo's eyes dart between us. "I'm gonna go do ... something," she says, gathering Orson's hand in hers as he asks,

"What? Why?" before she tugs him behind her and they both wander off.

Then, there were two.

Ruby and I exchange little smiles and matching exhales, resulting in joint laughter.

"You know, I have those clown strippers on hold," she jokes. "Whenever you want them."

"I'm tempted."

"I figured. Which is why they're already on their way."

"Thank goodness. I wasn't sure I could handle one more hour without them."

"You're gonna get the lap dance of your *life*, Bennett Shaw. I'm talking honking noses and squeaky shoes."

"Do they keep the shoes on?"

"You bet they do."

We both burst into laughter. Our exhales are little puzzle pieces connecting once more.

But then he walks over.

I turn away just a moment too late, so I don't miss the way he smiles at her, how his hand lands on her back. How his gaze lingers on those freckles of hers.

"Congratulations, Bennett," he says. "Love the hair."

I swivel on the barstool, my arm leaning on the counter. "Thanks, man."

"Y'know, I never thought I'd be at your bachelor party."

"Funny how life happens."

"Funny," he echoes.

It's still tense between us after all these years, and part of me wonders if that will ever change.

I take another swig.

Ruby looks between us, nodding slowly.

I didn't register that all three of us stopped talking.

Awkward. I was just reveling in the silence and lack of *Michael-ness* in the air.

Ruby claps her hands together once. "Well, this is so uncomfortable that I could die, so could you two try not to kill each other while I use the restroom?"

Michael chuckles, and I swear he thinks he's so cool when he says, "Don't miss me too much, Red."

I roll my eyes.

"I'll try my best," she teases, leaning in so close that her nose just barely touches his. It's a move she used to do with me, the kind that isn't followed with a kiss, but a genuine smile.

I wonder if I've been replaced.

Good. She deserves a best friend.

Though my foot taps on the barstool faster.

I stare into my whiskey.

"So ..." he says. "Are you excited?"

"Yeah."

"Feeling like a jailed man?"

I laugh. Typical bro talk. I've never been one to buy into it. Those old newspaper cartoons of men shackled at the altar always made me uncomfortable. Where's the punch line?

"No," I correct him. "I love my fiancée."

He nods slowly, as if he doesn't believe me. Which makes my fist clench tighter around my drink.

"Sure," is all he says.

This guy ...

I clear my throat. "So, Ruby seems happy. How long has this"—I motion between him and the spot where Ruby just stood—"been going on?"

He sniffs, straightening his posture and puffing out his chest. "A year maybe? Sort of?"

"Happy for y'all."

There's a pause before Michael says, "No, you're not."

I side-eye him. His head is tilted to the side. Michael swirls his own tumbler, looking into the cup with a half-smile.

"Pardon?"

"You're trying. Which I appreciate. But I'm here," he says, "with your girl."

"She's not my girl."

"Sure. I just find it funny that we're at your bachelor party." He gives an exaggerated shrug. "And, well, you can't stop looking at my date."

My blood pressure beats under my temples.

"She's just my friend."

"Hey, I'm not implying anything, big dog."

"Big dog?"

"Kidding."

His hand collides with my shoulder in a light gesture that might be innocuous if coming from Emory or Landon or Orson. But with Michael? I don't like it.

"Right. Though tell me something. How'd this even happen?" I ask.

Michael's face falls, and for a moment, I think he might feel some form of remorse.

"You got engaged," he admits. "And I was simply there."

"What?"

"I was at the bar that night. And I drove her home. Y'know, you really shouldn't have dropped by after."

My stool screeches out from under me as I stand. We're similar height, but I've got a good bit of bulk on him.

"That was you? She was *drunk*."

Michael's hands shoot up in mock arrest. "Nothing

happened!" And then, with a playful laugh, he adds, "Jeez, why do people keep thinking the worst of me?"

But I don't care if he's joking. My jaw is grinding. The nerves shoot through me like buzzing bees, zipping in and out, unable to be contained.

"Then, why were you there?"

"Because she needed someone," he answers. "Because ..." And then he grins that stupid, cocky grin, as if he's just checkmated me. "Because you shattered her heart and I didn't. And you know what? I'm pretty good at reminding her of that every day."

It all happens in the span of a blink.

A blink.

My barstool is knocked over. My arm rears back. And there's a crunch against my knuckles right as my fist collides with Michael's very punchable face.

And what follows is overwhelming guilt.

Good God. I'm thirty years old, and I just punched a guy in the face. For my best friend. The woman who isn't my future wife.

"Bennett! What the hell?!"

I don't know who yelled that. I'm honestly not sure who's holding my shoulders back either.

Landon runs over to help Michael from where he stumbled onto the floor. Quinn, who I'm pretty sure barks out a laugh, then quickly tamps it down, grabs a paper towel because Michael's nose is gushing blood like a fountain. And then there's Ruby, ginger hair tucked behind her ears, staring at me from the restroom hallway.

She rushes past our small crew, landing by his side. Her hands roam over his face, and her thumb swipes over his swollen cheek.

I feel awful.

Orson hands Michael a bag of ice across the bar, and he takes it.

"Jesus," Ruby hisses. Her head whips to me. "Bennett, are you serious right now?"

I hate how her eyes collide with mine, furious yet concerned and disappointed.

Disappointed.

Yeah, me too.

"No, no," Michael says, wagging a finger while holding the bag of ice to his eye. "I actually deserved that punch. Let's not get angry at the groom."

My eyebrows rise, and shame slides through me again.

Well, points to him for that, I guess.

Ruby, with one arm wrapped around his waist, sighs. "Are we done here? Should we leave?"

Michael glances at my face, eyes darting between mine, then looks back at her with a crooked smile.

"Nah, things were just getting good," he says with a boyish laugh. "I'd love another whiskey actually."

"What happened?"

"You know what? I was being a dick," Michael says. "Couldn't help myself. Old habits and all."

Ruby snorts. "Michael ..."

And, damn it, if I don't like the guy for that.

I snort out a reluctant laugh and cross my arms. "I mean, I actually feel a lot better."

"Honestly, I do too," Quinn says with a laugh.

"Me three," Landon adds.

"Wow. Thanks, everyone. Really feeling welcome here," Michael groans, eyes widening and blowing out a breath.

He leans against the counter, and his lips curl into a smile.

His chin dips toward me. "Sorry. We good, man?"

The thing about punching someone in the face is that it humbles them real quick. And the thing about being the punchee is that your fist rams through the veneer of a man's cockiness, energy gets released through that hit, and you can finally see him for the dude that he is.

He's not my favorite man, but he could be worse.

I hold out my palm, which Michael shakes with a firm grip, and some wordless truce slips between us.

A truce that says, *You'd better take care of her*.

51

Ruby

I spend too much time watching Bennett the night before his wedding. Even after he punches Michael—seriously, he *punched Michael*—I can't help but gaze at my best friend because I wonder if it's the last time I'll ever see him.

Tomorrow, when he's in a tux, that won't be my Bennett anymore. My Bennett wears band shirts and messy sneakers and has long hair that makes him look like Thor. Sure, his new haircut is handsome, but it's no god of thunder. It also makes him look like he's about to get a hard-on from picking out business cards or hosting meetings on a golf course.

Even when our group bursts into The Bee-fast Stop like a bunch of delinquent college kids, jumping over booths, cranking up the volume on the restaurant's jukebox, I still feel the pain of us ending, like we're peeling off the Band-Aid of our friendship.

Slowly. The way everyone tells you *not* to peel off Band-Aids as a kid.

We fall into our comfortable friendship roles like it's just another day—Quinn and Theo leading the conversation, Lorelei and Orson politely laughing, Landon chiming in one-liners from the kitchen, and Emory giving small half-smiles that he tries to hide.

But then there's *us*. Bennett and me, sitting next to each other, playing off each other's words, joke after joke. References that maybe the others get, and maybe they don't. But we do, and that's all that's ever mattered as we descend into our own little spiral of humor.

I miss this. I miss hearing Bennett's amusement when my joke lands perfectly. I miss Bennett's little whisper of, "Nice," and the covert high five he offers like high fives were invented for us.

If I could close my eyes and capture this moment, I would. Regardless that it's his bachelor party and that my heart aches. Regardless that tomorrow will change everything. I want to keep *this*.

And I know—I just know—I'll never find anyone like Bennett again.

Michael swings his arm around my shoulders, trying to wink with his black eye that makes him wince, and I laugh because Michael is funny. But he's not funny like Bennett. It's a different, more obvious humor. He's nothing like my best friend.

I take greedy peeks at Bennett, but I'm not as sneaky as I'd like. Or maybe he's not either. Nine times out of ten, he's already staring at me with that tilt of a smile on the edge of his lips—the gorgeous smile that is inescapable. And my chest hurts from the weight of it all, from the knowledge that this is all ending.

This is our swan song. And it is sad, but, God, it is also so, so good.

I can feel my eyes start to sting, and there's no need for me to ruin his beautiful night, so I rise from the table.

"I'm gonna get some fresh air."

"Need company?" Michael offers.

"Nah, I'm fine. Keep playing. I think you might win this time."

"Funny," he deadpans, slapping his cards on the edge of the table.

Michael has ended every game of Uno with the greatest number of cards. Poor guy doesn't know when to play his Wild cards.

I leave The Bee-fast Stop, closing my eyes and breathing in the Honeywood night air. I revel in the sound my sneakers make, echoing through the park as I take a seat on a bench nearby. I wonder how often it's quiet enough for someone to hear their own footsteps in Honeywood Fun Park.

"Hey."

I jump at the sound of Bennett's voice. He hovers near me, hands in his pockets and shoulders hiked to his ears. For such a big guy, he looks so small.

"Hi," I respond.

His heavy boots thud over the midway's blacktop as he walks over.

"Weird. I can hear my own footsteps," he says. "Normally, it's too loud."

The smile on my face grows so wide, so fast that I wish I could stop it.

"I was actually thinking the same thing," I confess. "Couldn't decide if that was a lonely or happy realization."

He lets out a breathy laugh, but doesn't answer. He sits down on the opposite side of the bench—just enough room between us for Jesus. Or Jolene, I suppose.

Lonely, I conclude. *The park feels lonely.*

"So, you punched Michael, huh?"

Bennett barks out a laugh before raising his arm around the back of the bench. "I did. And to be honest, I feel bad."

"Do you?"

"I actually do."

"What a weird world."

We both let out little laughs that disappear into the night, then exhale at the same time, which only makes us laugh again at the synchronized timing. Bennett kicks a rock nearby with the toe of his boot, sucks on his teeth, and clears his throat. I mimic him in that exact order. He gives me a side-eye. I give him a playful one back.

"I kinda like this," I finally say.

"What?"

"This whole awkwardness between us. It's a new, exciting dynamic. I could totally get used to it."

"Oh, yeah?" he responds, following the joke. "Well, I can't wait to avoid you in a grocery store."

"Oh, same. And ignoring texts."

"That's a good one."

"I might even butt-dial you and pull the whole *oh no, wrong number* bit."

"I can just picture our high school reunion." He points his finger toward me and puts on some fake, nasally accent. "Oh God. Amelia, is it?"

"Ben!" I exclaim, playing along with a high-pitched voice of my own. "From Geometry class!"

"Y'know, I thought that might be you."

"Wild. What are you up to nowadays?"

"Joined a motorcycle gang."

"No kidding! I'm over here with my five children and growing turnips."

Bennett laughs so loud at that, the beautiful kind of laugh, where his head falls back. I take all of it in—the corded neck, the white teeth. Heck, even his new haircut is handsome. It's impossible for Bennett Shaw to be anything but gorgeous.

In his normal voice, he asks, "Why turnips, Rubes?"

I shrug. "I dunno. I figured it would be something interesting."

"You're interesting already though. You design roller coasters for a living."

I open my mouth to retort, but I'm not sure what to even say, so I close it right back. There's a whip of wind that rolls past, the scent of autumn floating with it and then the coconut conditioner that is not Bennett one bit.

I grip the side of the bench. It irritates me more than it should right now. And when I look over at Bennett, he's doing the same.

"So, are you really seeing him?" Bennett asks. "Michael?"

"Not really," I answer. "He's just my friend."

He nods. "That's great. I'm happy for you."

I giggle out, "You don't have to lie."

"Fine. Then, you deserve better. You always deserve better."

I take in every etching of his face, the little lines that have popped up since the last time we were allowed to sit this close. It feels wrong that I've missed any new scar origin stories. But the longer I look, the more I see Bennett's face fall … fading, fading, fading.

"He's your best friend now, isn't he?" he murmurs.

"No," I respond. "That's your job, remember?"

"Nah, that was Bennett's job. I'm Ben."

"But I promised to always call you Bennett."

"That you did."

"And I always will."

And for a split second, I think he leans closer—a habit left over from older days, where he wanted to hear every whispered word I had to say, when he longed to hear me before anyone else would. I miss the curtain of hair that would fall over us, the little canopy we'd talk under to block out the rest of the world. I wish I could relive those moments for even one day. But that pirate ship has sailed.

"Nice haircut, by the way," I say, trying anything to keep the conversation moving because this might be the last time we're ever alone. I need to hear his voice. His happiness. His jokes. I need to savor it all.

I wish I could reach out and run a hand over his new hair, feel what it's like shaved close instead of long. But I won't because that's Jolene's jurisdiction now. And I know better.

"Yeah, it's not the best, is it?" Bennett admits, running a palm over it.

I wonder if it's for me, like he can tell that my hand longs for that motion. I smile at his ability to know exactly what I'm thinking.

But that's when I see it—or the lack of it really.

His bare wrist.

No shock of pink.

He's not wearing our string bracelet anymore.

Sometimes, I wonder how many times my heart can shatter before I've lost all the pieces.

My head pivots away.

I never imagined a day when Bennett wouldn't wear his string. I never imagined a day when we'd be sitting here with nothing more than a nostalgic bond between two warm bodies.

I play with my own bracelet I still wear, running a finger through the strands, picking and picking until a new

407

errant fray sticks out. Another loose thread in the binding that is barely holding on as is.

I can feel it in me—the moment I snap.

The moment my brain realizes exactly what I'm about to do.

The end.

My words erupt into flames so quickly that I wonder when the pilot light even came on. Or maybe it was always lit, just waiting for my spark to set it ablaze.

"I actually really hate your haircut," I blurt out.

Bennett laughs. I don't.

"And you look stupid in a polo shirt."

He laughs again, but it's not as confident as the last one. "Wow. You're feisty tonight."

I'm not feisty. I'm filled with fire. I'm filled with irritation. I'm filled with the *wrongness* bubbling over into my chest and over my shoulders, rippling goose bumps down my spine.

"And I actually don't like being awkward strangers," I finally admit. "Not one bit."

He's frozen now. I wonder if he can sense the danger coming, just like I can.

"Ruby." It's a warning. I don't heed it.

I'm tired of heeding warnings. I'm tired of not having the guts to say something. To speak up for what I want.

This conversation turned so quickly, but my hands are still on the wheel. I'm in the pilot's seat for once in my entire life, and I refuse to be ejected.

I turn toward him, taking in all the parts of him that are still familiar. His high cheekbones. His full lips. And those little lines beside his eyes, the ones that show just how often he's laughed and how most of those laughs have been with me.

I love my best friend. I will always love my best friend. And simply sitting back and watching him be taken away is no longer an option. I must fight. I must at least attempt to scramble up the mountain, scraping my fingernails and bruising my knees, fighting like hell to save my heart even if I fall when I reach the top.

"Don't marry her."

Saying it out loud feels horrible and good and awful and exciting.

I think I might vomit actually.

Bennett blinks. "What?"

"Don't marry her."

It feels worse the second time. But that's okay. I'm done sitting back and watching the world pass me by. A little rudeness is just fine with me.

Bennett keeps staring at me with his mouth opening and closing.

"Ruby," he whispers, "this is the night before my wedding."

"And you punched my boyfriend."

"Thought you were friends."

"Does it matter?"

Bennett lets out an irritated growl, running a hand through hair that I know he wishes were longer. I can tell because he grumbles more when his fingers hit the short ends. Then, he scratches the whole thing, messing up the delicately gelled top.

He stares at me, rising to his feet, pacing away, and then back, blinking through an expression I can't decipher yet. Because even though his eyebrows are pulled in, I also see the slight tug at the edge of his mouth, as if maybe he's proud of me for saying anything at all.

"I know," I continue. "I know this is unfair."

"Damn right it's unfair. This ... I ..."

He doesn't finish.

"You ..." I prompt.

His shoulders slouch, and that's when I know my time is up.

"I love her, Ruby."

My heart stammers in my chest, clanging over my ribs and stomach and shooting into my throat.

"I do." Bennett lowers down to the bench and takes my hands in his. They're warm and rough and everything that makes him Bennett. But they're not mine. "And Jolene is going to be my wife."

I can feel my hands start to shake. It's been so long since they have.

"I know," I answer with a small nod. "No, you're right. I know."

"Rubes ..."

I swallow.

It hurts. More than I thought it would.

"The only thing I know is loving you," I admit with a shrug. "And I don't want to know anything else."

His jaw clenches.

I've never said the word *love* before.

Not once.

But I mean it.

I love my best friend.

I should have taken the risk three years ago. But past Ruby wasn't that type of woman. Past Ruby didn't want marriage, nor did she believe in it. Present Ruby does though. Present Ruby has seen relationships work between friends. And present Ruby knows that marriage with Bennett would be the realest marriage of all. She's a different, more confident woman, but she's also very, very late.

Bennett's shoulders drop, and he lets out a long exhalation. His thumb goes down to my wrist, toying with the strands, gently wrapping it in his large finger until something in it breaks loose. The pink string drops off my wrist to the grass below.

My weak laughter starts first, then his. Then, we're both looking at the flimsy string on the ground.

"The universe sure has a sense of humor," Bennett says.

"Oh, definitely. Fantastic timing."

"Impeccable," he finishes.

Bennett bends down to get my string before holding it out to me in the palm of his hand. It looks like a flimsy craft project. Maybe that's all it ever was.

"No," I say. "Keep it."

"Ouch," he says with a playful smile.

But I'm not joking anymore. All I want to do is hold his hand and wait for the moment when we let go one final time.

"I'm sorry I'm so late," I mumble. "And I'm sorry for mentioning this at literally the last minute."

"No, the last minute would have been tomorrow, I think."

"Well, I'm sorry I didn't do it three years ago then."

"I forgive you."

"Good. I don't know if I could bear the thought of you being mad at me."

He tilts his head to the side, running his thumb over my cheek.

"How about this? I promise to never be mad at you again, Rubes."

I smile. "I'd like that. I promise that too."

"Good."

Bennett scoots closer to me on the bench, wrapping his

arm around my waist and gripping my side. I curl as close as I can, burying my face into his neck. We sit like that for a bit, just like we have so many times before. When my parents got divorced, when we celebrated at prom, when he said we weren't going to be friends anymore ... so many memories we've had, from Honeywood day camp to high school to college to Florida. All just to come back to this.

"Want to go back inside?" I ask.

"Can we have just a couple more minutes?"

"Always."

52

Bennett

When I get home from the bachelor party, I enter through the basement door. There, I move one box to the side and search through the other. It's in this one—the fifth—that I finally find it. My own box of buried treasure.

I flip through everything—the flyer for my first Honeywood summer camp, the treasure map Ruby made for my tenth birthday, her crayon sketches of roller coasters, our prom picture with awkward teenage grins and my hand on the small of her back, like always. There's the blog post I printed, announcing Ruby as Dominion's latest hire; my bulky plastic pirate belt buckle from Florida; the unopened seashell shampoo from the hotel; and the receipt for one soda water with lime and one shot of rum.

I'm sure some people save old baseball gloves their dad gifted them or movie tickets with a first date, but my favorite memories were always with Ruby. It's inked on my soul and in my skin—my parrot, my anchor, her strawberry tattoo's twin that settled along on my ribs. And then there's our birthday constellation, dotted over my ankle in orange, like the freckles that exist on no one else but her.

I dip a hand deeper into the box, and nestled between an elementary school yearbook with Ruby's signature written at least five times and our old PC game disc for RollerCoaster Tycoon is the pink string bracelet I removed two months ago.

I roll it between my fingers, feeling the weak string and roughened edges. And I think. I think and think and think, but the only things I imagine are playing pirates, high fives, bad jokes, climbing trees, and freckled smiles at sunset.

"Hey, Ben?"

Footsteps come down the stairs. I pocket the string and shuffle to close the box, hefting it in the corner before opening another.

"Ben?"

"Here! Sorry. I was looking for tax documents. Orson reminded me we'd have to combine soon."

Jolene steps around the corner, her eyes darting from the discarded box and back to me.

"I'm leaving for the hotel," she says.

"Already?"

"It's almost eleven."

"Oh. Must've lost track of time. Wait, why are you still here?"

"Keeping an eye out in case you got smashed at your bachelor party."

"Ha. No. Very sober." I ruffle my hair.

Jolene's palm runs over my hair too. "God, I love it short. You should keep it this way."

"If you want, sure."

"So, crazy bachelor party, huh? Back before midnight and everything."

I let out a weak laugh. "Crazy."

Crazy in that my best friend essentially told me she

loves me. Crazy in that, as I look at Jolene with her red eyebrows turned in and a slight smile, I know that I do love this woman right here. Crazy in that I don't know what that means anymore.

Jolene sits down beside me, bringing her knees up to her chest and tilting her head to the side. I don't think I've ever seen Jolene this tentative in the three years I've known her.

My face falls.

"You all right?" I ask.

"Yeah," she answers, tracing a line over her own freckles dotting the outside of her knee. "Can I ask you something though?"

"Of course."

She tilts her head to the side. "You would do anything to see me happy, wouldn't you?"

My head rears back in surprise, but I laugh it off. "Yes. Absolutely."

"I know," she says wistfully, tossing her head side to side. "Yeah, I know."

I chuckle. "Where's this coming from?"

Her smile is weak as she rips off a loose strand from her shorts. "I want you to know that I'd do anything to make you happy too."

I place a palm on her knee, leaning in to kiss her cheek. "I know that."

Jolene would, and she has. She's tried so hard to understand me, to do what she thinks is best for me and will make me happy. She tried to mend the relationship with my dad. She tried to get me to move on.

Sometimes, it's worked. Sometimes, it hasn't. Jolene always tries though.

But then my eyes linger on the box in the corner. The limb I was forced to cut off.

I wonder if Jolene will grow me a new one in its place.

I wonder if that's even possible.

"All right." She rises to her feet, slapping off invisible dust with a grin. "I'm gonna head out. Don't stay up too late. You'll oversleep and miss seeing me in a gorgeous dress."

"Five a.m., max," I joke.

Jolene claps me on the shoulder, but doesn't continue the bit, like I'm used to. It's just a one-liner. No high five. Nothing.

But that's because she isn't Ruby.

"I'll see you at the altar, big guy."

I reach out and squeeze her hand. "Yeah. See you then."

53

Ruby

Morning of Bennett's Wedding
Ruby & Bennett are Thirty Years Old

When I wake up on my couch, the birds are chirping a symphony that is loud and beautiful and *obnoxious*.

I shove my face deeper in my pillow—*maybe it will suffocate me?*—and try to forget last night.

My embarrassing confession.

His rejection.

My guilt.

My shame.

And then I remember what today is, and I give a muffled scream into the pillow.

Distant footsteps walk across the living room and toward the couch, where I lie. A hand soothes my hair behind my ears.

"Up, up, best maiden," Bennett's mom coos. "The birds are awake, and you should be too."

I grunt. "Do you think the whole *two birds, one stone* thing is actually possible?"

"Try screaming for real, and maybe we'll scare them off instead."

I peek one eye open, and that's when my face immediately flushes red.

In my kitchen, standing alongside Brittney, are also Theo, Lorelei, and Quinn. They all have varying looks, but the common thread seems to be sadness and worry.

"Oh. Hi," is all I get out.

"Hey, lady," Quinn replies, her mouth twisting to the side. "Feelin' all right?"

"No," I admit.

"That's okay," Lorelei says, but it's followed by silence.

What do we say? It's my best friend's wedding day, and there's probably not a single person in this room who's oblivious to my feelings for him. I've been carrying a lovesick boombox over my head this whole time.

Theo takes a loud slurp of coffee to fill the quiet.

"Well, let's get this day going," Bennett's mom says with a clap of her hands. "We've got a chapel to get to and a reception buffet to eat. Want some coffee, my little gemstone?"

"No thanks." The thought of Bennett's reception—of him walking around with a ring on his finger—makes me sick to my stomach.

Lorelei sets her mug down and rests her chin on the arm of the couch. Her finger tucks my messy hair behind my ear. "Want me to curl your hair for today?"

Theo shakes a clear bag full of makeup. "I've got a smoky-eye look with your name on it."

I glance at Quinn. "You gonna try to make me pretty too?"

She shrugs. "Nope. I'm just a gal with two ears, ready to listen and trash-talk the bride."

The room erupts in calls of, "Quinn!" and, "Rude!" and Brittney's very motherly, "That's my future daughter-in-law!"

My heart sinks at that, but I try not to let it show, especially when she winces at me after.

"I think I'm just gonna get some extra sleep," I moan, rolling over on the couch.

They descend on me like vultures—grabbing my arms, pulling me up, hoisting me in the air. They carry me to the shower, where the cold water shoots out and stings my skin, drenching me through my pajamas.

I squeal at the harsh bite of cold, but then I think I'm laughing. And suddenly, Quinn is jumping in the shower with me, fully clothed, tossing shampoo on my hair as the water slowly warms.

Lorelei takes her phone out, saying, "Ooh, ooh, I have a joke for today."

"Why, how perfect. I love to laugh," Bennett's mom replies, leaning in the doorway with her mug of coffee, tossing me a little wink. "Let's hear it."

"Okay," Lorelei starts with dramatic emphasis, as if she were about to tell a campfire tale. "Did you hear about the two cell phones that got married?"

I blink through the suds running down my face. Everyone stares at me to answer.

"Um ..." I start, Quinn's fingers massaging into my temples more. "No. What about them?"

"I heard the reception was amazing."

The whole room bursts out into laughter. I can't tell if their reaction is real or fake, but it's a cheesy joke, and it's just silly enough to have me laughing too.

A little laughter is better than nothing.

I stare at the little white chapel on Cedar Cliff's Main Street. It's the same chapel my parents got married in and where Dad married Miranda sixteen years later. The maroon double doors are propped open. It's, admittedly, a beautiful autumn day.

I didn't arrive at the church early, like Orson and Landon did for groomsmen festivities. I spent the morning with the girls until Bennett's mom, with her arm looped through mine, decided it was time for us to go. Now, still arm in arm and staring at the building, Brittney nudges me with her elbow.

"Ready, kiddo? Nervous?"

"I'm not the one getting married," I say. "I'm not allowed to be nervous."

"You can feel however you'd like. That's your right, okay?"

It's not a secret, but for some reason, she says it like one.

I can do this. I've done so many brave things in the past year. I quit my crap job. I've set up boundaries with my dad. I've even learned how to do a pull-up, which might have been the hardest task to date.

It's very humbling to hang three feet in the air, begging the entire gym, "Please help. Oh God, I'm going to die."

Not my finest moment.

The point is, I've come so far, and yet today—a day full of laughter and nice food and wedding bells—might be the thing that breaks me.

Brittney and I step through the double doors, and when we reach the threshold with the room full of groomsmen—

when I can hear my friends talking and my little brother's giggles and Bennett's beautiful laughter through the door—I take one step back. Then another.

"You gonna be all right?" Brittney asks.

"I don't think I should see him yet," I admit. "The bride wouldn't like it."

Brittney nods, but doesn't argue my point. "Up to you then. But it's not gonna get easier."

I wince. "Can I pretend it will?"

She smiles with her head tilted to the side. "Sure, kiddo."

Bennett's mom disappears behind the door alone, and there's a roar from all my friends, calling her name simultaneously, as if she were the special guest on a sitcom. Even Lucas, probably looking adorable in his ring bearer getup, says her name like they're old friends.

I walk backward, farther and farther away, until I finally hit the main chapel. It's small and quaint with guests here and there mulling around. Everything is decorated in white —the aisle runner, the sashes thrown over the backs of the pews, and even the roses.

Roses, just like the flowers Bennett got me for my ninth birthday.

I spot Michael in the corner, talking with Fred and Mrs. Stanley, looking gorgeous in his suit.

Oh my God, I can't do this.

I reverse, sucking in a breath as I rush through the emergency side door. It slams shut, and I lean against the brick wall beside it. I close my eyes. New guests arrive around the corner, exchanging greetings like it's just another Sunday morning service—not like it's the day I'll lose my favorite person in the world.

No. I can't think like that. He's my best friend, and he's

421

happy. That's all I've ever wanted for him. Even if I'm not in the picture, I can be at peace, knowing that he's happy.

He's happy.

I don't know how long I stand there, but my chest keeps rising and falling, trying to keep up with my whirling thoughts.

Suddenly, the exit door jams into my back as someone opens from the other side. Orson peers through the crack.

"Oh, sorry, Rubes!"

"Hi. What are you doing out here?"

"What are *you* doing out here?" He holds out his wrist to display his watch. The time reads nearly ten minutes until the ceremony starts.

"Oh no," I say. "I'm so sorry. I was getting fresh air, and I lost track of time."

He places a hand on my shoulder to steady me. He looks worried though, which makes me wonder how worried I must look too.

"You doing all right?" he asks.

"As good as I can be."

"Well, keep that feeling. Because I'm about to bring the mood down just a little bit."

"Why?"

Orson sucks in a breath, lets it out, then bites his bottom lip.

"Because we can't find Bennett."

I choke on nothing. Orson, with wide eyes, places a palm on my arm.

"What?" I hiss, blinking through my thoughts. But I have none. Not a single thought can penetrate my mind past, *What, what, what, what?* I'm basically singing Macklemore over here.

"We left him in the groomsmen room while we ushered

in guests," Orson explains. "And I have no idea where he is now. Checked the restrooms, the classrooms, the preacher's office ..."

"Wait, why there?"

"I don't know."

I let out a laugh, but it's because I can't hold in the anxiety coursing through me. I cope with humor instead. I always have.

"Did you think he was getting some last-minute advice?"

"I don't know!" Orson throws his hands in the air with a laugh. "I'm panicking!"

"Okay," I say quickly, trying to parse through my thoughts. "Okay."

Did he run?

No. Don't think that. He's just somewhere they haven't looked.

I shake off the intrusive thoughts.

"Let's split up and see if we can find him."

I'm sure Bennett's just combing his brand-new, super-swanky hair. Or maybe straightening his tie in a mirror somewhere. Or shining his shoes.

Do people still do that?

Or ... maybe Bennett is thinking about what I said last night.

Maybe I ruined everything for him.

No.

No, please, no.

I need to find him and get him down that aisle.

54

Bennett

I'm in a storage closet, and it's an awkward, claustrophobic fit, but it's my wedding, and if I want to sit next to bottles of window cleaner, I will.

I don't know how I got here. I mean, I do. I ran down the hall and slammed the door behind me. But, *here*, thinking and thinking and thinking ... that's more complicated.

I was fine this morning. When Orson and Emory showed up at my house to hang out, everything was great. When Landon made everyone pancakes, I was fine. When my mom showed up and she and Lucas kicked our asses in a round of Mario Kart, I had no worries.

But the moment they all left me, when I was abandoned to lounge in that groomsmen room alone, I stared at my empty wrist and sank into my thoughts.

Turns out, thinking was not a good idea.

If I'm being honest with myself, it wasn't the first time I'd stared at my wrist today. I'd just been too distracted to discern what it meant. But through every groomsman high five, every forkful of Landon's pancakes, and every flick of the game controller to direct Mario down Rainbow Road, I was glancing at my bare wrist, trying to ignore what was missing—my pink string bracelet and those flimsy little strands that stitched my heart together.

Sitting alone, really staring at the blank space where that piece of string should have been, I felt wrong.

Off.

A stranger wearing a Bennett suit.

I burst out of the holding room and looked at the open chapel doors.

I stopped short of them. Hesitating. Swallowing. Then, I walked right past, journeying deeper into the church, getting farther from the open exit with the breeze and singing birds. I found this door instead, and now, I'm next to a mop bucket and the smell of lemons and bleach.

And for the first time, I think, *Why am I here?*

No. I can't think that. I love Jolene. I love her red hair, her freckles, her smile, and—

The door rips open. I squint into the hall, and illuminated in fluorescent light, is Ruby.

Ruby.

She leans against the doorway, looking at me from head to toe.

"Hey, Pirate. You've got a show in five."

I take all of her in. The ginger hair pulled up into a tight bun. The pink dress with the fabric slung near her delicate collarbone. The freckles dotting her shoulders and arms.

My eyes dart to the hall behind her and back. She nods in understanding, stepping into the tight space and snicking the door shut behind her. I give a weak smile at the fact that she can still read my mind. I wonder if that'll ever fade. But now that we're alone in this tight space, I regret that she did this time.

"I shouldn't be seeing you," I admit.

"Well, the good thing is that it won't be bad luck."

Because she's not the bride.

Even now, she's funny. She's so funny.

"Sit with me?" I ask.

And without hesitation, she lets out an, "Mmhmm."

Ruby plops down across from me, her legs folded to the side, glancing around at the shelves and the narrow space between us.

"So cozy," she says, tracing a pink-painted fingernail over the broom handle beside her. "Really love what you've done with the place."

I stare at her, at her capacity to make jokes, even in a situation like this. My gut twists because I appreciate it. I really do.

She clears her throat, averting her eyes to the floor. "So, did you hear about the two cell phones that got married?"

I shake my head at the conversation change.

"What?" I blurt out stupidly.

"Did you hear about the two cell phones that got married?" she repeats.

I blink at her, still taking in her freckles and gorgeous smile. Her humor. *Her.*

"Psst," she says, holding her hand up to the side of her mouth and lowering her voice to a whisper. "It's a joke. Play along."

Slowly but surely, I smile.

"No," I say with a chuckle. "Tell me, what happened to the cell phones that got married, Rubes?"

She inhales, then says, "I heard the reception was amazing."

The reception *was ...*

A sudden laugh bursts out from my chest, and it's a relief. All the trapped energy releases at once, the nerves sliding over my shoulders and sending goose bumps down my spine.

I reach for a high five, which she returns. It feels just like old times.

Good times.

"So, why the closet?" Ruby asks. "Nervous about all the people out there?"

"Nah," I answer. "Got a stain on my shirt. No stain-remover pens in here though."

Her eyes drift to my shirt that definitely has zero stains. She's got my number. Her smile starts to fade. I don't like it.

"It'll be fine," I reassure her, trying so hard to stop her eyebrows as they begin to tilt in. *No, please don't be sad, Parrot. Not today.* "And this groom right here is gonna be fine too."

There's a twitch at the edge of her pink lips.

"Y'know, 'The Groom Is Fine' could definitely be a song title," she suggests.

I play along. "Oh, it would have to be on a mix CD."

"Called *Songs about Forever?*"

"I can hear the commercial now."

"Airs at midnight or two in the morning, right?"

"Wakes you up from your sleep on the couch."

"Celine Dion is the headliner," she says, then excitedly adds, "Or Etta James!"

I raise a fist to the air and bite my lip in joking exaggeration. "Now, *that's* what I call music."

We both laugh, and my heart flutters like a caged bird. Even when I mentally tell it to stop, it keeps on flapping.

"Yeah," she says. "You're gonna be fine." Then, she jerks her chin toward the door. "Now, let's get back out there, huh?"

I can't believe how supportive she's being—this woman,

who, only yesterday, tried to get a piece of happiness all for herself. And yet, now, she's here, mustering all the courage she can and doing what needs to be done for me to find my happiness.

Thanks, Parrot.

Her lips curl in, and that one simple movement—the subtle little bite of pink lips—is what has my heart beating faster, and its rhythm is to the added beat of, *Mine.*

Mine, mine, mine.

My Ruby.

And right as I think it, I swear I see her eyes start to well up.

"Oh, Rubes ..."

I reach out for her hand, sliding up to her wrist. Bare, just like mine. I shouldn't be touching her, but I can't stop. I press my thumb to feel her pulse, hoping the beating of her heart can jump-start my own.

This is it, isn't it? This is our end.

"Bennett, it's your wedding day."

Ruby tries to smile, but it's so forced and mournful on her beautiful lips. But I did this. I forced her to be this brave.

"You should go out there. Let Jolene see her handsome husband, okay?"

My eyes start to sting, and my nose hurts, too, because, *yes, this* is *it for us,* and maybe I'll see her after, but will she even stay for the reception? Would I if she were here, marrying Michael?

I clench my jaw tighter, willing the tears to not fall, but I still feel the burning and finally the release.

This is it.

Ruby reaches across the small closet space, lifting her

thumb to wipe a tear rolling down my cheek. I lean into her palm before she slides it away.

"Don't worry," she says. "Some nice pirate once told me it's okay to cry if you need to."

And that cements it for me.

I love her.

There's no way around it.

I am currently in love with, have always been in love with, and will continue to be in love with my best friend, Amelia Ruby Sullivan. I don't know when it started, but I know it will never end. Not for me.

I love Jolene, but in a different way.

I love Ruby in a soul mate kind of way.

Ruby from a few years ago didn't want commitment. And maybe she won't now, but I don't care. That's a bridge I'll cross later. The truth is, I can't marry anyone else when the person across from me is the one sacrifice I can't make. When someone like that exists, you make your own sacrifices to keep them. And I'd let go of anything to keep Ruby.

She's been so brave, finding me and pointing me down the aisle toward what she thinks is my perfect future—even though she wants something different. And I need to be brave as well.

If she can have courage, so can I.

Which is why I sniff back my tears, take a deep breath, and say, "I can't get married today."

55

Ruby

I blink at Bennett's dark brown eyes, now rimmed in red, at the way his bottom lip wobbles as he stares with cinched-in eyebrows and a clenched jaw.

"I can't do this."

"Bennett ..."

I watch as he draws in a long inhale before slowly letting it release, his chest deflating with the movement. And like a light switch, his face settles. He clears his throat and then nods.

"I need to find Jolene," he says matter-of-factly.

My head is shaking back and forth, my heart now racing, trying to keep up.

"It's basically two minutes before," is all I can find to reply, but he tongues his cheek. "Bennett ... you want to get married. It's ... what you want. Jolene is ... she's your dream woman. She's wonderful."

But Bennett's head slowly shakes from side to side.

"I can't," he repeats.

"Why?"

He sighs, licking his lips and straightening his posture.

"You just have to trust me on this one, Rubes."

I look at the floor, the ceiling, the spray bottles, and mop bucket. I don't feel here, not really. I'm in some wayward, upside-down dream. An alternate reality. Any second, Brittney will wake me up for Bennett's wedding day, and I'll watch him walk down the aisle.

But I am here. Dream Bennett is never quite as gorgeous as real Bennett. Especially when he looks serious, like he does right now.

Why is this happening? Why now?

Is it because of me?

Does it matter?

He tilts his head to the side. I wonder if he can tell what's going through my head.

"Ruby, I can't do it," he repeats.

I swallow. "But there are ... roses and people and—"

"I'll handle them."

My shoulders drop. "Bennett ..."

He doesn't budge.

I don't know what caused him to change his mind. But the more he looks at me and the more his eyebrows tilt in, I do know one thing: I need to be strong in this moment. For Bennett. Because this is his wedding-day decision, not mine.

I'm not his fiancée. I'm not his future bride.

I'm his best friend.

It doesn't matter why he's doing this. Only that he is. He's made a life-changing decision, and I need to be his rock, just as he's been mine for so very long.

"You're sure?" I whisper.

"Yes."

I run the back of my hand over my nose.

"Okay," I say with a nod. "Okay then. First step: find Jolene."

Bennett lets out a low, shaky exhale. "Thank you."

And I do my best-friend duty and smile. "Of course."

My heels echo in the church's entry. His oxfords snap on tiles.

A low hum of conversation bleeds in from the chapel, but it's distant, practically nothing compared to our heavy breaths as we rush to the other side of the building. With every step, my heart beats faster, but Bennett's steps only get louder, more assured.

"Down this hall," he says.

I don't answer; I simply follow.

We turn the corner toward the bride's room, but pacing at the end of the hall is Bennett's mom. Brittney's eyes dart up, and her head tilts to the side.

"Oh, Bennett ..."

Bennett keeps walking forward. A man on a mission.

"Is she in there?"

"I've been looking for you," she starts, but then pauses.

Brittney curls her lips in, inhales, and then smacks them back open.

"I have to see her," Bennett insists.

His mom's dark brown eyes swivel to mine. I can't decipher what they mean. They don't weave stories in my mind, like Bennett's. But they look troubled. No, they look scared.

"She's ..." Brittney clears her throat, clasps her hands in front of her, and says, "Oh, Jolene's not here, kiddo."

My stomach drops. My legs almost want to give out, but I don't let them. Instead, I do my job now. I cut my eyes to Bennett and reach out for his arm, keep him standing upright. But he hasn't flinched.

"What?" he breathes.

"She's not here," Brittney repeats. She looks at him with her head tilted to the side. "I'm so sorry, baby."

I've never heard her call Bennett that. I wonder if it's saved for moments like this, the ones behind closed doors that I'm not supposed to see. The ones that hurt the most.

"She's ..." Bennett shakes his head. "She left?"

Bennett just stares at her. I can see his jaw ticcing for a few seconds. Maybe he's considering what to say; maybe he's just letting the whole situation process in his mind. And for a single second, for the tiniest of moments, I wonder if he's questioning himself. If knowing she left makes him reconsider whether he should have.

If he's realizing how much he truly loves her.

But then he glances at me, and there's something more behind those eyes.

Brittney slowly nods. "Sort of. She's ... well, she's out back."

Then, she steps to the side and opens the emergency exit door.

On the other side is a woman in a beautiful white dress. Her hair is the color of fire—just like the shade of anger on her face.

56

Bennett

I cross the church's emergency exit threshold alone, giving a final look at Ruby—my sweet Ruby—before shutting the door behind me. My oxfords clack over the stone walkway, and even on a sunny day with birds chirping, it somehow feels like the only noise in the ten-square-foot courtyard.

Jolene blinks at me, eyes darting to the door and back. She turns on the spot, putting her hands on her hips and squinting up into the sunlight as she begins to pace. Her dress is fitted silk, curving around every edge of her and landing in a pool by her feet. It would be perfect, but the hem is nearly destroyed. I wonder how long she's been out here, pacing.

"You were right," I admit. "The dress is gorgeous."

"I know it is."

Her words strike like a whip between us.

"So ... you're out here," I continue, placing my hands in my pockets.

She shrugs. "So are you."

I inhale and exhale.

"I went to find you," I explain.

"I didn't."

Guilt slides through me, and I wonder if she can sense it because, for the first time since coming out here, her shoulders slump.

"I'm sorry," she confesses. "I can't do it."

I give a weak smile. I'm not sure if it's appropriate at all, but at least she returns it.

"If it makes you feel better, I can't either," I admit.

Her smile gets slightly bigger—a little smirk almost.

"You're leaving for her, aren't you?"

Slowly, painfully, I nod. There's no point in denying it. But also, it's not exactly the full story, is it? So, I shake my head as well.

"Yes," I answer. "And no. You and I wouldn't have worked long-term. You know that just as much as I do."

She crosses her arms and looks behind me. I turn and see faces staring back at me through the window—Quinn, Lorelei, Theo, and the rest of the crew. They duck down, disappearing.

So nosy.

But part of me smiles at it anyway.

I don't like that this is how things are ending between Jolene and me—with an audience. But the look of my friends being goofy is such a contrast to the serious situation I'm in that it lightens my heart.

"We wouldn't have worked," Jolene admits. "I don't fit in with your lifestyle."

"It's not you," I say quickly.

"No. Not entirely. But we don't want the same thing. Kids? A family? Bennett, I know what you want." She lets out the biggest sigh. "You just want Ruby. Nobody else will do."

My heart sinks, then buoys back up just as quickly. Guilt, but then peace.

"I'm sorry," I find myself saying because what else do you say to that? I can't deny it. I won't refuse my destiny any longer, and Ruby Sullivan is exactly that—my past, my present, and my future.

"You said you were hung up on someone. That day we met. It was her, wasn't it?"

"Yes."

"I knew I shouldn't have let you see her last night."

I tilt my head to the side, and she grins. Jolene's joking. At least there's that.

"Come on, Bennett," she says. "Say what's on your mind. You know you two were inevitable."

"Yes. We were inevitable," I admit.

"I get it," she says. "You two. I understand. And I think I might hate you for it, but I haven't exactly figured that out yet. Y'know, the worst thing you did was be an excellent friend to the woman you loved. Unfortunately, that woman wasn't me."

I open my mouth, and she shakes her head and holds up her hand. "Hey, no, listen. You tried. But I made the mistake of stepping into the wrong love story. Ruby was never going to be dethroned from your number one spot, and there was no point in fighting for a crown that never belonged to me in the first place."

She lets out a sardonic laugh. "God, I can't believe I tried to come between you two. I was fighting fate. I'm too pushy, aren't I? Too demanding? I even tried to get you to have a relationship with your dad that you didn't even want."

"You couldn't have known how complicated it was."

"But she did."

Her eyes rove over me. "You look amazing in a tux, by the way. But it's so not you."

"No?"

"I'm sorry."

"Why?"

"I tried to make you someone that wasn't Ruby's. Somehow, I assumed short-haired Bennett would be mine. That, once you got rid of the motorcycle and the band tees and that little bracelet, you would finally belong to me."

"I think you were just trying to make me a better man in your own way. And I thank you for that. But you're right."

I do belong to Ruby, is the unspoken sentence lingering in the air.

"I do like her," Jolene admits. Some form of surprise on my face must give me away because she snorts. "Oh, come on. I'm not a monster."

"I know you're not a monster," I respond with a chuckle. "But you are a force to be reckoned with. Unreadable sometimes. But I just know the man who marries you will be able to. He'll be the man that pushes you like you will to him. Steel can only be satisfied with steel."

She tilts her head to the side, and for a moment, I don't see Jolene, but a woman giving up her wedding day. A woman who only wants the world. "Thank you."

A second passes before feisty Jolene is back though. She fluffs her dress, clears her throat, and places her hands on her hips. "Well, if you haven't already, I demand you tell Ruby you love her. And don't take no for an answer this time, all right?"

I open my mouth, but don't argue. Instead, I laugh and shake my head. "You really are something."

She gives a smile, and then her eyes dart to the window and back to me. Her eyebrows cinch in, and she sighs.

"I don't want to go back in there," she admits, her voice almost a whisper.

I turn around, seeing the window is now filled with people who aren't just my friends, but Jolene's family too. It seems her side of the chapel has finally realized what's going on. The worst part is, they're treating it like a sideshow. They don't have the grace to duck out of the way.

I turn back to her, watching her wind her hands together, trying to swallow down bravery that, for the first time, she might not have.

"Don't then," I say. "Don't go back in. Make a run for it, Jo."

She blinks at me, laughing, then stops. "You're serious?"

"Go. You don't owe anyone anything."

I can see the fire in her eyes, the same fire I fell in love with and would have spent the rest of my life enjoying.

My love for Jolene is undeniably real. But there's a different type of fire on the other side of that door behind me. A fire hidden beneath green eyes, right above the freckles I adore. Ruby's fire will always be kindling in my soul, and I'll always carry the match, waiting for when it allows me to set my heart ablaze.

I'm leaving this church with the intent to be with Ruby forever, marriage or not. She essentially told me she loves me last night, and that is good enough.

My heart has been waiting too long for her fire.

Jolene bites the inside of her cheek and grins. "I would look pretty awesome, running away in a wedding dress."

"*So* badass," I agree, leaning back on my heels for emphasis.

She smirks, starting to gather up the hem. I step forward and take some for her, placing the remainder in her fist. She leans in, kissing me on the cheek.

438

"Take care of yourself," I say.

"I always do."

Then, she turns on her heel and runs.

Jolene looks elegant, running away. I would have taken a photo for her if I'd had my phone. Instead, I walk back inside, letting the door snap shut behind me as I peer at my silent mom and Ruby.

Ruby.

My Ruby.

I stare into the face of my destiny, the woman I've loved since we were too young to understand the unease of emotion. I should have known those freckles would be imprinted on my soul forever.

I give her a decisive nod. There's no smile on my face, but there doesn't need to be. I wonder if she can hear my thoughts.

You're my flame.

The side of her lips tips into a smile.

She can hear me loud and clear.

My mom is pacing again, looking down at her hands, then back up. Then down. And back up again. A repeated motion over and over. Finally, she places her hands on her hips and blows out a heavy exhale.

"Okay, so you've paid the caterer, right?"

I finally break eye contact with Ruby and nod to her. "Yes."

She claps her hands together. "Perfect. And the photographer?"

"Of course."

"Fantastic."

"Why?"

My mom ignores me. "I'll tip the pastor for his time."

"Okay—"

439

"And you guys can skedaddle."

Her hands wave us off. Like we're kids, being excused to recess.

I blink at her, swallowing. "What?"

She levels a stare at us, all humor gone, and says, "Leave."

I look at Ruby the same time she looks at me.

"Go," Mom repeats, drawing our gazes back to her. She's determined now. "I'll handle everyone in there."

"No, you're not going to—"

"Son"—she holds out her palm—"you try so hard to protect everyone else, to be what everyone else needs. You tried to be what Jolene needed. What I needed. But we both know what *you* need. So, go. Be your own runaway bride."

"Groom."

She smiles. "Just don't wait any longer."

I feel my lips twitch into a sliver of a smile, and then, slowly, Ruby's grows wider too. It's that secretly mischievous grin I fell in love with at seven years old.

I reach for her hand. She takes it and squeezes.

"Go," my mom says.

So, we do.

We cut and run through the chapel doors right as the bell tolls.

Ruby and I burst out of the chapel's double doors like two bats out of hell. Maybe I will go to hell for this. Maybe I should. But hell with my best friend doesn't sound so bad.

We make it down the steps, me taking less than I normally would as Ruby tries to descend in heels. Eventually, she takes them off, and I place my hand on her lower back—always her lower back—then swing her into my arms.

She bites her bottom lip, and I can tell she is trying not to giggle.

My sweet, sweet Ruby.

"Where are we going?" she asks.

"We'll figure it out," I huff, carrying her down the block. "We always do."

She tightens her arms around my neck as I jog a bit faster.

We go down one street. Then another. Then, we're past Main, and the only things I can see are the pine trees lining the sidewalk and the distant peaks of Honeywood's roller coasters. I finally set her down once we walk slower, after the anxiety from leaving my wedding finally dissipates.

Ruby and I watch as a train rips over The Grizzly's track a few blocks away, shooting past the newly installed launch and barreling through the tunnel to the other side. I smile to myself as a closer roller coaster, the blue zip of Bumblebee's Flight, roars its call.

That was the first roller coaster I rode with Ruby. I remember her scrunched-up freckles, anxiously gritted teeth, and her wide green eyes that transformed into a squinting smile as the wind hit her face on the free fall.

A hook behind my gut tugs at the other memory on that ride though.

Jolene sat next to me on that same attraction after our third month together. I remember how she shrugged afterward and said she couldn't understand the hype. She asked how much longer until we left.

That same dismissive shrug was everywhere—when I told her I didn't want a relationship with my dad, but she insisted I contact him anyway. When I asked her to form a relationship with my best friends, but she said she already had friends. When I told her just how important Ruby was, but she demanded I not talk to her anymore.

I can give up a lot of things, but I refuse to give up Ruby.

We pass by Landon's yard on the edge of downtown, where my black truck is parked in the driveway. I slow my walking, ready to hop in. To go somewhere, anywhere. As long as it's with her.

Ruby pauses beside me.

"Y'know," she muses, "I could go for some pancakes at Honeywood."

I blink at her, then laugh. "Me too."

So, we keep walking and clear another block. Birds chirp an evening song. The grass and pine needles rustle as the wind passes through. The branches creak overhead.

It's silent, but the good kind of quiet. I feel relief. Contentment. Happiness.

We pass the gate into Honeywood's employee lot. Now on the blacktop, Ruby bends to slide one of her heels back on, reaching for the buckle around her ankle. But I lower down to one knee in front of her and pat my thigh.

Smiling, she raises her foot and places it there.

I trail a hand over her calf, smoothing my palm down to the shoe's strap, where I secure it through the buckle. I look back to her and grin.

"Hi," I say.

Ruby beams down at me. "Hey there."

She exchanges one foot for the other. I secure the next shoe, then rise to my own feet.

I forgot how much I tower over her. How small she looks before me. But she's noticeably different now than she has been in the past. Her muscles are stronger. Her posture is straighter, more confident. Her head is tilted to the side in a knowing way, the sly hint of a smile tugging at the edges of those beautiful pink lips.

I want to kiss her. But it somehow feels too soon. I am still in a wedding tux after all.

"Pancakes?" I ask.

"Mmhmm."

"Good," I agree. "Then, let's go."

I key us into the employee entrance, and we shuffle through. Our stroll in Honeywood feels surreal and not just because we're here on a weekend and I'm not working. It's because I'm walking through my favorite park with my favorite person by my side, wishing I were nowhere else in this world. Just like I did when I was a kid. Just like I want to do forever.

We sidestep a costumed Bumble the Bee, both of us giving a small wave to whichever teen is inside the giant bobblehead. They stare. I'm sure we look so inappropriate in our fancy black-tie dress among the guests, clad in fanny packs, matching family T-shirts, and Buzzy the Bear headbands.

We reach The Bee-fast Stop, and I open the door for her as she tries to do the same for me. She sticks out her tongue, and I grab a buffet tray, which she tries to take from me.

"Nope, dinner is on me," she says.

"Absolutely not."

She giggles and gives a playful tug. "Bennett."

"Nope." I pull the buffet tray from her hand with a grin.

She scoffs. "Bennett!"

"You're not getting it back."

"Benny!"

"Nah-ah."

"Benjamin!"

"No."

"Benothy!"

"Never."

She's laughing so hard now that I can hear it over the loud chatter in the restaurant. I've never seen my best friend so happy, smiling so wide, having such over-the-top joy that I can barely contain my own laughter barreling out of me.

This is how my life is supposed to play out.

Messy but fun. Always fun.

57

Ruby

"You can ask what we talked about," Bennett says.

"I don't want to pry."

Bennett has one hand on the wheel as he drives us back to my house. We picked up his truck after walking with a to-go bag full of pancakes from The Bee-fast Stop.

"Is Jolene okay?" I ask.

"She will be."

I watch the streetlamps passing by, the power lines moving up and down like waves in the sky.

"And are you okay too?"

"Yes," he says confidently. "Everything is wonderful." And for the first time in what feels like forever, he seems like he means it.

He turns the wheel onto my street. We pull into my driveway to see Michael's red Camaro, and sitting on the porch in a suit, with his forearms on his knees, is Michael himself.

"Never mind," Bennett mumbles.

Michael looks unsurprised, almost bored, to see us together. His black eye really adds to the broody look, but he gives a half-smile in my direction to compensate. I don't know if that makes me feel better or worse.

I hop out of Bennett's truck. The gentle bird chirps feel so inappropriate. The subsequent hum and yell of cicadas feel more fitting. Funny how a Southern fall day can capture all emotions.

I walk up to where Michael sits. He peers up at me before rolling his eyes with a grin.

"I should have known," he drawls.

I crouch in front of him.

"Don't even try to apologize," he whispers. "I knew what I was getting into with you."

"I'm still gonna say sorry."

"Well, if you insist ..."

I smile. "I'm sorry, Michael."

"For running away at your best friend's wedding with the groom himself?"

"Yeah. For that."

"It's okay, Red."

"You know, you really are an amazing friend."

He laughs. "That's kinda the worst part about me. I'm a fantastic friend, and that's about it, huh?" I giggle as his thumb and forefinger lift my chin. "Not soul mate material, am I?"

"You are."

"Just not yours."

I don't reply because I wouldn't know how. He's right. Bennett is my soul mate. I know that as surely as I know the grass is green.

When I don't say anything, Michael says, "I want to stay friends. For a long time, okay?"

"I'd love that."

He looks past me at Bennett and groans.

"Hey, and if he gives you grief, tell him Mikey can throw a punch too, all right?"

Bennett snorts with a smile. "I'm standing right here."

"Good," Michael states with a tilt of his head. "Then, you can hear the threat."

"Don't provoke him," I joke with a half-smile.

Michael squints one eye. "But it's so fun."

"Still here," Bennett says.

"Always here, huh?"

My heart fills with hope and joy and everything in between. Michael's right. Bennett is here. And he always will be.

Michael slaps his thighs and stands, letting out a strained exhale that's a mix of irritation and amusement.

"Well, I'm gonna get going."

"Tell little Mikey I said hey," I say.

Bennett shakes his head. "Pardon?"

Michael shoots him a wink. "She means my son."

"You named your son after you?"

"I know; I know. I'm a total narcissist," Michael jokes with his hands waving in the air and a small *bleh* to follow. "In my defense, it's a family name."

"Poor kid," Bennett says.

"You're tellin' me."

Michael grabs the suit jacket from the porch and throws it over his shoulder. He pulls me in for a hug, giving a nice extra squeeze for good measure. In the short time we've been friends, we've only embraced a handful of times. But I almost wish we'd hugged more. He's really good at it. He places a small kiss on my temple, his beard tickling my face, before shaking Bennett's hand and lowering into his Camaro.

447

With a final wave, he reverses from my driveway and drives away.

"Okay, I'll give it to him—he has a pretty cool car," Bennett says with a low whistle.

I sigh. "He really does."

"Should I get one?"

"Nah. I like your motorcycle more."

His eyes flash to me. "Good. Me too."

We turn and walk to my house. Bennett uses the key I gave him years ago, and then we're entirely alone.

Bennett sets his keys on the counter, the rattle echoing through my living room.

When I turn on my heel, he's standing there, hands in pockets.

I look him over, the missing tux jacket, the loose bow tie, the haircut that looks disheveled and a little more Bennett than it did before.

I love him. My soul mate. My best friend. And I don't know where we stand with that information, but I don't care. I just need him by my side.

And then, at the same time, we take a step forward and blend into each other's arms.

It feels good.

It feels right.

It's us. Just us.

We stand there together, holding each other for who knows how long. Breathing the same air. Feeling the same skin. Combining our heartbeats. Our souls finally meet in the middle, right where they belong.

"Can I just hold you for a little bit longer?" he asks.

And I smile and nuzzle in closer. "I'm not going anywhere."

His arms grip me tighter. "Me neither."

So, we stay close. Content.

And after a few moments, he finally croaks out a small, "Ruby." His voice echoes in my silent living room. "I feel like I should explain."

"If you want."

Slowly, his hand strokes into my hair, locking his large palm in place. I close my eyes to the feeling. The rightness of it. The surreal excitement of him so close to me.

And then he places his other hand on my lower back.

Where it belongs.

"Ruby," he breathes, "you must know. You must know why I left, don't you?"

I do. I do, I do, I do.

Even as my heart is thumping so hard that I could pass out from the joy of it, it doesn't feel real.

But, God, I know, I know, I know.

I find myself smiling so wide that it almost hurts. It's all the *knowing* bursting at the seams.

He left for me.

"I like your hand on my back again," is all I can think to say, and it comes out in choked laughter.

He echoes the same laugh. "I do too."

Then, he leans forward and kisses my forehead.

"I couldn't marry Jolene. Not when you exist."

"Not when you exist."

I look into his eyes, how they dart between mine. How they linger on my freckles. God, he loves my freckles, doesn't he? I love how much he loves them. How he loves the parts of me I don't.

"I want you," he confesses.

I reach behind my back, entwining my fingers in his.

"I want you too," I respond, just as I should have three years ago.

His eyebrows turn in, and he lets out a shaky exhale. "I've got some things to take care of this week, but—"

"Your life is complicated. I understand. That's okay."

"It is?"

"I don't know if you remember, but we just ran away together on your wedding day."

He grins. "That we did."

"Figure out what you need to. Get your ducks in a row. Then, we'll figure us out."

"I want to give you all my ducks as soon as possible."

"Good. I want you and your ducks. I'll wait for them."

I've spent a long time practicing my ability to read Bennett's mind, so the way his posture falters and how this big man of mine melts back into my arms, it tells me everything I need to know.

After Bennett made the decision to leave that chapel, I know he was prepared to do anything for me. He would make the same sacrifice his mom had made, waiting for me to commit to him even if it meant he would wait forever.

The kicker is, I would do the same. I'll wait for him for as long as he needs.

He is my forever.

"You got something there," I say, reaching up to stroke under his eye, taking a small tear with me.

"Thank you for waiting, but I'm yours, Ruby," he whispers. "I promise I'm yours."

Suddenly, there's a knock at my door. We jump, both our eyes darting to the intruder.

"Bennett Shaw, we know you're in there. I see your truck."

It's Quinn.

"Of course they're here," I whisper with a grin.

Bennett shakes his head and smiles too.

We hear Theo's voice. "The door is locked, and your door is never locked, Ruby," she condemns. "I don't like to use my imagination, but if you two are already doing the nasty—"

"We have leftovers," Emory interrupts loudly.

My face heats red, and I pull away from Bennett's hug. He blinks down at me, but something passes between us. A thought. A hope. A smile.

I open the front door, and our friends' faces stare back. I don't know what I expected. Maybe disappointment? Irritation? But not a one of them is upset. Well, except maybe Emory, whose arms are full of silver tins. But his base level of emotion is vague irritation.

"Where can I put these?" he grumbles.

"Hey, Tweedledum and Tweedledumber," Quinn says, taking a tin from his arms and bumping her hip to walk past me. "About time, right?"

Bennett smiles at me, and I bite my bottom lip.

He nods. So do I.

Another unspoken exchange.

Yes. About time.

"I love this," Lorelei says, looking between us. "Can we do a group hug?"

I blink. "Oh. Well, I guess we—"

But I'm interrupted by her leaping forward. Then Theo. And Quinn. And finally, Bennett, too, with his warmth at my back.

The five of us stand there in each other's arms with me buried in the middle. Eventually, Orson also steps in, tugging Emory by the arm to join. And finally, Landon casts his long arms around all of us.

"This is way too many people," Emory grunts.

"At least we all smell good," Quinn says.

Theo gives a wistful sigh. "All I smell is love in the air."

"On a canceled wedding day too," Orson adds.

"All right, let's not ruin this," Lorelei mumbles.

"It's a good moment though," Landon says.

"It is," I finally add.

Then, Emory clears his throat. "Bennett, are you rubbing my lower back?"

"Sorry, thought you were Ruby."

I couldn't grin wider if I tried.

"Awkward," Quinn whispers.

Lorelei giggles. "No. It's perfect."

And there's a weird collective hum of agreement.

Yes, it's perfect.

58

Bennett

One Week Later
Ruby & Bennett are Thirty Years Old

It's funny how things work out.

Though not really a ha-ha kind of funny.

I'm not laughing at the fact that my bride and I bailed on our wedding. It's far from humorous that we had to pay expensive vendors for an event that never happened.

But it's also kind of funny that the pastor told me he wouldn't bless me to marry in that white chapel again. Once again, not a ha-ha funny. But still funny.

Two days after the not-wedding, I came home to find Jolene had moved her stuff out of the house. There was a note on the coffee table that said, *I sold the engagement ring and kept the money as compensation for playing matchmaker with you and your best friend. You're welcome. Love, Cupid.*

Kind of ha-ha funny.

Now, after I've called every vendor, apologized to every relative, and dotted the last *i* and crossed the last *t* on our apologetic yet sincere thank-you notes with returned gifts, I finally drive over to a different house.

Finally.

To her.

Looking through the kitchen and then the living room, I eventually find her in her backyard, splayed out on the grass. I smile, sliding open the glass back door and shutting it behind me.

I crunch my way across the lawn and lie down beside her.

Ruby is staring up at the stars. The moon illuminates her freckles like constellations in the sky. It's a beautiful sight I can't believe I almost lost forever.

We've texted all week. Little life updates. Little jokes. But this is the first time I'm seeing her again, and it's like seeing a guardian angel in person. It's like being in a dream.

She turns her head to the side, smiling at me with those pink lips.

It's exactly like a dream.

"Hey," I breathe.

"Hi."

I reach for her hand, but our knuckles knock together. She was already reaching for mine.

"What are you doing out here?" I ask.

"Looking at the stars."

"And what do they look like?"

"Psht, I don't know," she responds with a laugh. "Stars."

"Of course. What was I possibly thinking?"

"You thought I was an astronomer."

"You aren't?"

"Amelia might be."

"You know, we dog on Amelia a lot, but she actually sounds kind of cool."

"Does she?"

"I'd date her."

She blinks at me with a slow, growing smile.

One week.

I told her one week, but in reality, it's been six days. I busted my ass this week, trying to tie up every single loose thread I could because I wouldn't make my girl wait any longer.

We've waited long enough.

"Hey, Rubes?"

"Yeah?"

"Did you know I've looked up every single thing about us?"

"Everything?"

"Everything. Every silly little compatibility test I could find, hoping to find how horrible we were for each other. Moon cycles, astrological signs, complimentary eye colors, stupid online quizzes, where you can find your cartoon equivalent—"

"You took personality quizzes?"

"Yeah. And guess what. You and me? We're inescapable, friend."

She blinks, but I see the tug in her heart as clear as day. I nod in confirmation of her unspoken question.

"Yeah, Rubes. You and I are the reason people think soul mates are real. We're that annoying type of perfect—the kind that even the happy couples hate. We're not just cut from the same cloth. We were molded from the same damn clay. Bit by bit. Piece by piece."

The crickets chirp around us, the wind blows, but the warmth between the two of us remains.

"Dang," she finally says, a grin plastered on her face like a beaming sun. "What a speech."

I chuckle. "You like that?"

"A little dramatic, but, y'know ..." Her words fade off.

I'm grinning, and so is she. It doesn't take a compatibility test for me to know just how much I need that smile.

Ruby Sullivan is my destiny.

I trace her freckles with the back of my knuckles.

"I like dramatic though," she whispers.

And there's a clicking in my soul, a locking piece that comes together, like a final cog in the machine of my heart.

I lean down, tucking a strand of her beautiful ginger hair behind her ear, kissing the tops of my best friend's cheeks, the area beside her eyes, over her freckles, and then to the divot where her neck meets her ear. And then, finally —Christ, *finally*—I get to kiss her lips once more.

I draw in a sharp breath at the same time she pulls in a gasp of her own. The heat between us, the sheer magnitude of need, is almost unbearable.

What starts slow goes faster until we're kissing like our lives are at stake, like our very souls fear being ripped apart once more. I wish I knew how to tell my terrified heart that this is permanent—that we can calm down now. We can rest. She's ours.

My Ruby. My Ruby. My Ruby.

Slowly, our kisses get gentler, calmer, happier. I love how her lips leave behind little thank-yous in their wake, like tiny crackles of sparks after the fireworks should have already fizzled out.

We pull apart just long enough for me to whisper, "I love you, Ruby."

She leans over, nuzzling her head closer, and whispers, "I love you too, Bennett. I really, really do."

"Good, Rubes."

She squints at me. "We can do better than that."

"Better than what?"

"I'm thinking *honey*. What do you think?"

I grin and kiss her again.

"You want a better nickname," I murmur against her mouth.

She flushes red and nods.

"Okay then. Sweetheart maybe?" I suggest.

Her face scrunches up. "Ew. Absolutely not. I feel like you should have bowls of Werther's butterscotch to pull that one off."

"I can go out and buy some."

She clicks her tongue. "How about darling?"

I shake my head. "We're not nearly British enough."

"True. Too fancy. Okay then. Bubba?"

"Bubba?" I chuckle. "Am I your fishing buddy?"

"Close enough."

"I don't see how that's close at all."

"Well, you're my best friend, so maybe you should get a best-friend pet name."

Her hand squeezes mine, and I squeeze back. Now that I have her, I never want to let go.

"I like that reasoning, pal."

"Chum," she continues.

"Comrade."

"Commander."

"Colonel."

"Hmm," she muses. "What about ... bumblebee?"

"Peaches?"

She giggles. "I'm a fruit?"

"When you blush, you look like one. See? Like now."

Even under the stars, I see Ruby's face is a beautiful shade of pink.

"You're the worst."

"I'm just spitballing here, *peaches*."

"Ooh. Spitball," she says. "Now, that's a good one."

I laugh. "I swear if I'm called spitball for the rest of my life ..."

The sentence fades off once I realize what I said out loud. But Ruby simply smiles.

"Rest of our lives, huh?" she asks.

I bite my lip and say, "We were always inevitable, spitball."

She leans her head on my chest. I rest my chin on her forehead.

Always inevitable.

"What's going on in that mind of yours, Pirate?"

"Only good things," I confess.

"Filthy things?"

"Amelia Sullivan."

She grins. "No, that was definitely a Ruby thought."

"God, I like you."

"Stay over tonight, Bennett."

"At your house?"

She scoffs, sarcastically replying, "No. In my backyard."

I chuckle. "With thoughts like that? Should we?"

"Apprehensive now, Mr. We're Written In The Stars?"

"I never said that."

"You implied it."

I scoff. "I'm just trying to see what our limits are, you know?"

Ruby laughs. It's so much louder nowadays, more confident. Easy.

"We have no limits."

I run my hand through her hair, little ginger strands, soft and delicate, falling through my rough fingers.

"That's cute and all, but seriously. I want to do this right."

"I'm being serious too," she counters. "I don't know if we have rules."

"Well, when you start dating someone, there're first-date rules, second-date ..."

"I think, at this point, we're on our thousandth."

"Oh, wow. Well, happy thousandth date, Rubes."

She giggles. "Happy thousandth."

"So, what's a thousandth date look like?"

"Well, we've been to all the bases."

"All?" I ask.

"Every single one. And fun fact ..." Ruby turns onto her chest, crawling closer to me. She places a small kiss on my neck and whispers in my ear, "I put out on the thousandth date."

I suck in a breath that is more like a groan. She laughs in response.

Sweet yet persistent.

I let out a strained chuckle. "Is that right?"

"Absolutely."

"Well, lucky for you, so do I."

"What a happy coincidence."

Leaning in, she places a kiss directly on my lips.

She pulls away, tilting her head to the side and into the palm of my hand. I trace my thumb over her cheek and pull her up so I can kiss the top of her nose.

"Well then, you know what I absolutely *love* to do on my thousandth date?" I whisper.

"What's that?"

"I love to eat pussy."

Her face turns a wonderful tint of bright red. I wonder if I've beaten her at her own game. She's never been one for crude words.

"Oh, really?" she stammers out.

"Yeah," I growl out, placing a hand on her hip and running my palm down her side and to the hem of her dress, where I flip part of it up her thigh. "And I like to make it a multicourse kind of meal."

Her eyes dart to my lips and back up. "You like it that much?"

"I really"—I gently roll her over—"really"—rise to my forearms—"*really*"—she's splayed out before me, and she looks too perfect for words—"do."

"On the grass?"

"The grass. The concrete. The back of a car ..." I kiss a line down her stomach, nearing the outside of her thigh. "I don't care as long as it's you I'm eating."

I lift the skirt of her dress up, kissing along the inside, going up, up, up. I slide the edge of her panties down. And there's that beautiful strawberry.

"Hello, old friend."

"I love it when you say that," Ruby whispers with a small laugh.

"I love that you love it."

I look up at her and smile, placing a kiss directly on the tattoo.

"Hey, Bennett?"

"Hmm?"

"You're my very best friend."

I pause, resting my chin on her hip and smiling. The words flow like water through me, giving me a type of relief I didn't know I needed.

"You're mine too."

"Hmm. *Mine*," she muses. "I like that a little bit too much."

"I think I do too."

I crawl up her body and plant a kiss on her lips. We continue savoring each other like that, possibly making up for lost time—I don't know. But the kissing turns from sweet to heated faster than I can keep up. Ruby is insistent against me, and when she finally arches into my chest, I let out a small groan, which she returns.

Her hand travels down to my waist, tugging at my belt. She loosens it through the belt loops, the sound of clinking and the hiss of my zipper echoing through the empty yard. I shuck my pants down, and when I do, she takes me in her hand.

I groan at the feel of her soft hand around me, her palm running over me in long strokes.

I place my forehead against hers, breathing heavy before capturing her mouth again. She tightens her grip, stroking harder and faster. I choke out a laugh.

"Christ, Ruby ..."

Then, I peel her hand from me.

"Wait, what are you doing?" she asks. "I was having fun."

I kiss down to her chest and stomach, finally between her thighs.

"And so am I. Now, spread these legs for me, sweet girl."

She smiles. "I think I like that pet name the most."

59

Ruby

Having my best friend between my legs is the best feeling in the world.

Within seconds, Bennett tosses my knees over his shoulders. Then, one kiss after another, he journeys from my thighs to my center. One swipe of his tongue has my back arching, and another whimper from me has him lapping longer, more languid strokes over me.

I grip his hair, and I cannot wait for the days when it's long again. When I can tug and pull while bucking against his mouth. But even now, with the little I can grasp, I'm desperate to have him closer. After every rough jerk, Bennett moans against me.

"God, you taste so good."

His voice. His tone. *Him.*

Bennett's hand slides up to grip my hip, then my ribs, before running a thumb below my breast. My head falls back when his fingers roll over my peaked nipple, flicking it side to side before pinching it.

"Bennett—"

But I can't finish the sentence. I'm too wound up in how

his fingers dip into me, thrusting and curling and sending another moan from my lips.

I wonder if my neighbors can hear us. Or, heck, I figure they might see us. My yard isn't fenced in. But I laugh when I realize how little I care. Let them hear me. Let Bennett hear me.

"Bennett ..." I repeat his name louder this time, darting my eyes down to find that he's watching me.

Those hooded brown eyes are taking in every bit of my ecstasy. He rolls his tongue, slow and agonizing. His pumping fingers drag in and out.

I'm already so, so close.

"Bennett, please—"

He loops his tattooed arm onto my stomach, splaying his palm out and holding me down. His tongue rolls faster. His fingers disappear inside me.

"You'd better come on my tongue, sweet girl."

Bennett knows exactly the spot to concentrate on because it only takes another second before the sensation starts to rise like a tide around me. And lick by lick, groan by groan, he knocks my orgasm right through me, a hurricane crashing into my chest and out toward my fingers, sizzling and burning and drowning.

I squirm as he keeps licking, and it's too sensitive at first, but then it's better and somehow suddenly perfect, and he grunts out an insistent, "One more for me," which has another wave breaking through my stomach, rolling over the first as I let out a small whine.

"Oh God," I barely make out.

"You like that?"

"Please," I whine.

"Please what?"

"You know what."

"Do I?" he asks with a smirk.

"Yes."

"Well, I like your words better."

My hands bury into his hair, gripping the strands. He grins, crawling over me, his forearms steadied on the grass beside my head.

"Please fuck me," I respond with a smile.

"Yes, ma'am."

I wrap my legs around his center. He holds me in place, and I see his thick cock bobbing between us. I'm not sure I'd ever get sick of seeing it—the veins trailing down the sides and the thick head already dripping with need.

And it's mine.

All mine.

I reach down and tighten my fist around him, twisting my way up and down over the length of him. Bennett's eyes close as he leans forward, balancing himself with a palm on the grass beside my head.

"Is that what you want, Ruby?" he murmurs, the heat from his breath tickling my ear, sending goose bumps across my skin. "You want to make your best friend come apart in your hand?"

I never thought I could enjoy Bennett's company more, but having his filthy words in my ear is a real game changer. We could have been doing this all these years. I wish I could have a serious talk with past me.

Bennett watches me stroke him between our bodies, rubbing my thumb over the head to spread more of his natural wetness over him. He lets out a low groan, making small thrusts to pump himself into my fist harder.

But before I can make another stroke, he removes my hand from him and captures my wrists in his palm, pressing them in the grass over my head.

"Unfair," I whisper.

He plants a taunting kiss on my lips.

"I'm on a mission," he mutters against them. Bennett pushes his cock against me, rubbing the length over my center. "My best friend asks me to fuck her, then I'm going to do as she says."

He drags a thumb over me, rubbing up and down my slit.

"God, you're so pretty," he says. "My girl is so pretty and pink."

He tightens his hold on my captive wrists, grips his cock in his other fist, and pushes between my legs.

"Wider, sweet girl," he says, and I part my knees as he slowly, agonizingly pushes in.

It hurts like it did three years ago, but when he pulls out and pushes back, the pain is replaced by relief. Pleasure.

"More," we chant at the same time.

He chuckles, the sound rumbling through my chest as he thrusts in deeper. Words of insistence catch in my throat as his hips jolt forward to meet mine. My head falls backward against the autumn grass with a moan.

"You like that?"

"Yes," I sigh.

He pulls out, then pushes back in. Harder. Rougher.

"No, I know what you really like."

The hand around my wrists loosens, and he runs it down my arm, across my chest, over my collarbone, and finally around my neck, where his palm gives a little squeeze.

He remembers.

"Oh, yes, do *that*," I breathe.

Bennett pumps in again, grabbing my hip, capturing my neck, thrusting over and over until we're both letting out breathy exhales and moans. He leans in to bite my shoulder. I roughly run my fingers down his back, and he's going faster, faster, and I can feel my own warmth building, building.

I'm so close again.

Reading my mind, like he always does, Bennett moves one hand from my hip to down between my legs, where he rubs circles over me until I'm quickly falling apart around him in a mix of moans and gasps echoing through the trees.

"That's my sweet girl," he grunts, pushing in and letting out groans that get caught in his throat with each thrust.

"Come for me, Bennett," I whine.

He exhales against my shoulder, thrusting, growling, moaning until, finally—

"Damn," he groans out, shuddering as his legs shiver beside me.

He gently releases my neck, kissing along the place where his fingers were.

I let out a breathy laugh at the same time he does. "I could get used to that."

"Good. Then, I have an idea."

He looks down at me with that devilish grin and those taunting brown eyes.

"Go on," I say.

"How about I give you so many orgasms that you forget all the years we weren't together?"

"That's a lot of orgasms. We'll have to do a lot of sessions."

"Yeah, well, good thing I have forever to enjoy your pussy."

My face heats, and I shake my head. "You love saying that word."

"Forever?"

"Well, yes. But also the other one."

"Which one?"

I smile with an eye roll. "You know which one."

"Say it."

"No."

"Come on, Rubes."

"It's weird."

"I don't think so," he says, moving his fingers back between my thighs. "In fact, I like it quite a lot."

I let out a small whine. I hope I never get used to this. I hope we're always playful.

"Go on," Bennett coaxes, dipping two fingers inside me, causing my breath to leave in an exhale. "I'm waiting, sweet girl."

Sweet girl.

He sure knows how to convince me.

"Pussy."

"Perfect," Bennett replies with a rumble in his throat. "Now, come on. We've got many years to make up for."

60

Bennett

Four Months Later
Ruby & Bennett are Thirty Years Old

I love that Ruby's stuff mixes with my stuff in our new house. I love that we share toothpaste. I love how we don't have designated hooks on the coat rack, but just a jumble of both of our jackets. I love that we installed the wallpaper together even though both of us got irritated when we realized we hadn't bought enough paper to complete the whole wall.

I threw my hands in the air after our fifth attempt to "make it fit."

"Bennett Shaw, you are not walking away from this," Ruby said, following me into the kitchen.

I wasn't.

I turned around after shutting the fridge with a water bottle in each hand.

"Me? Walk away from you? Absolutely not. I just thought we needed hydration for our first fight."

She smiled, and I smiled back, and the fight was forgotten as we christened that kitchen counter for the third time that week.

Tonight, we grab our jackets off the coat rack near that same half-papered wall. I slide Ruby's on before mine, and we lock up behind us.

Hand in hand, we stroll down the sidewalk to The Honeycomb. I sold my mom's old house. I figured it was time to move on, to downsize to a space that would fit me and Ruby better. We have a little cottage a few blocks away from the bar with just enough walking time to debrief about our days, or to plan dinners for the week, or to simply just say hi to the clown in the sewer—the bit that Ruby still does and the one I will laugh at forever because it's just that good.

I open the door to The Honeycomb for Ruby, and she ducks under my arm to go in.

"The Dynamic Duo!" Theo calls, holding out her arms.

"Is that our name?" Ruby asks with a squint.

"Huh," I say. "I was really hoping for Terrible Twosome."

"Or the Cute Couple."

I shrug. "Or simply Rennett."

"Buby!"

"Nice!" I say as we exchange high fives. "*Definitely* Buby."

We take our usual seats at the end of the table, and when Ruby's seat is a bit too far for my liking, I grab the chair's leg and drag her closer.

"Okay, Buby, let's get our head in the game," Lorelei says. "I really think we can win it this week."

469

I chuckle. "Yeah, only because we insanely outnumber literally every other team."

Everyone at the table looks around. We sit at one of The Honeycomb's longest picnic tables, and we are packed to the brim. Lorelei and Emory are on one end; Quinn and Landon are on the side; Theo and our occasional guest from the bar, Orson, sit across from them; and then Ruby and I take up the opposite end.

"Okay, well, maybe we should split the group?" Lorelei suggests with a wince.

"Over my dead body," Quinn says. "Frank is a power-house of knowledge. He's worth four of us."

"True."

"Yep."

"The old jerk."

I'm not even sure who all vocally agrees. I just know that we jointly do, and not a one of us moves from the table.

Even with our collective brains, we still take second place. Frank is in fact some sort of genius. The geriatric table in the corner with him, Bill, Honey, Fred, and Mrs. Stanley all high-five.

"It must be great, being old and knowledgeable," Landon muses with his chin in his fist.

"Yeah, how's that feel, Emory?" Quinn asks.

Emory twists his lips to the side, giving her a sneaky middle finger as he scratches his ear.

Lorelei lets out a quick, "Emory!" and we all burst into laughter.

I could live the rest of my life, doing exactly this—hanging with friends every week at the local bar, losing at trivia, and joking as much as possible along the way. Sure, a small-town life might not seem like much to some people. But it's everything to us, and I like us.

I hold up my pint glass. "To our ridiculous friend group."

Quinn boos. "So sappy!"

"Whatever. I can get behind that toast," Theo says, raising her glass with me. "To us!"

"To us," Lorelei joins in, nudging Emory, who, with a side smile in her direction, raises his glass of water.

Quinn rolls her eyes but still raises her pint. Landon, giving her a wink, joins in.

Orson runs over from his place behind the bar, kissing Theo on the cheek and placing a hand on the opposite side of her glass since he doesn't have one himself. She laughs and kisses him back.

And then Ruby raises her glass too.

"To us," we all say in a staggered attempt at speaking in unison.

It's sappy.

But I wouldn't trade it for the world.

We clink our pints together, and when I take a sip of my beer, I glance over at Ruby, who simply smiles back.

Yeah, I could get used to a lifetime of this.

61

Ruby

Three Months Later
Ruby & Bennett are Thirty Years Old

We're at Honeywood Fun Park, per Bennett's request. But this visit is different from the others we've had in our life. We've become that gushy couple in the queue lines. We're dragging each other through the midway, hand in hand, journeying through crowds and bubbles of families, as if in a family unit of our own.

I love our specific bubble.

"Why do you have a backpack?" I ask at one point.

Bennett shrugs. "What backpack?"

I look at the very obvious black canvas rucksack on his back.

"Suspicious," I say. "I'm keeping my eye on you."

He grins. "I sure hope so."

He's got a secret. And I think I know what it is.

Near the end of the day, we sit on the rocky edge of the

Buzzy the Bear fountain. My head rests on his shoulder as water cascades down the statue's side. Before us, the sun sets, backdropping Honeywood Fun Park in a glaze of yellows, pinks, purples, and blues.

Bennett unzips the backpack at our feet.

"Mysterious," I whisper.

"Don't pretend like you don't know," he says with a laugh.

But when he pulls out a fistful of flowers, messy and wild, my breath catches in my throat.

I didn't know.

But now, I have a good idea.

"Handpicked for you," he says.

"For me?"

"For you," he repeats.

I take them from him, holding the precious gift close to my chest. My heart flutters like a caged bird, but it's getting set free real soon. I'm going to let it fly.

"I always told you I'd give you handpicked flowers at Honeywood. I promised to ask you a very important question at this exact fountain. And I am. Sort of. I promise I won't get down on one knee. I won't even ask for a legal piece of paper."

"Not a W-2?"

"Not even your Social Security card."

"Oh good. I don't want to give that up."

I grin at our joke. He does too, squeezing my knee.

"I love you. I want you. Forever. That's all I'm asking. And if you don't want to make it official, it won't change a damn thing about how I feel. I will still spend the rest of my life being with you. You're not getting rid of me, Rubes."

"Stalker," I whisper on the shaky exhale.

He laughs, chews the inside of his cheek, then nods.

"But, hey, Bennett?"

"Yeah?"

"You can get down on one knee if you want."

I can see the relief wash over his face in an instant. It's the lines on the sides of his face. The grin that reaches all the way up to his eyes. The squinting eyes—he's so happy that they can't help it. His best smile. The smile that belongs to me.

I decided years ago that I would marry Bennett if he ever asked. I've seen partnerships fail, but now, I've seen them thrive as well. Emory and Lorelei. Landon and Quinn. Orson and Theo. Heck, even Fred and Honey.

Marriage is what you make it. And if after months of officially dating—and of course, many years of friendship—my soul mate wants marriage, who am I to deny that to him? I wouldn't want to spend my life with anyone else. I'm not sure my soul would allow it.

With a tearful smile—because Bennett is such a softy—my best friend lowers down onto one knee in front of me. My hands are full of his handpicked flowers, and we're right next to the fountain at Honeywood. It's exactly as we promised nearly eighteen years ago.

My pirate opens his mouth to ask a question—*the* question—he closes it again and sniffs.

"I love you, Rubes."

I love you.

I want to hear it again.

Fifty times.

A million.

I drop one hand from the flowers to squeeze his. He reaches up to slide his palm over my cheek, tracing a thumb across my nose, right where my freckles lie—his favorite thing about me.

My legs bounce in anticipation. "Come on, Pirate. I've been waiting for far too long."

He lifts a single eyebrow—that devastating eyebrow—and grins.

"Will you marry me, Ruby?"

And like the woman in love that I am, I answer, "Yes."

He cups my jaw and pulls my lips to his. We kiss, soaking in each other like the sappy lovebirds that we are.

I believe this is the start of a very beautiful relationship.

62

Bennett

Five Months Later
Ruby & Bennett are Thirty-One Years Old

Loving Amelia Ruby Sullivan is easy.

Sure, there's the stress of wedding planning and engagement parties. But they're punctuated by jokes and close friends and car rides to catering companies, where we eat all their food.

Loving her is like breathing. Simple. Right.

Plus, she carries extra Tupperware to hoard more catering food.

I love this woman so much.

But there's also the day-to-day happiness.

God, the happiness.

Parties at Honeywood might be fun, but there's something about sitting on our couch, watching television, occasionally throwing popcorn at each other. Or even pausing the movie because we keep talking over it anyway. We've tried watching with subtitles, but sometimes, that's a lost cause.

If I could go back in time and tell seven-year-old Bennett that he was going to marry that shy redhead, that he would grow up to share strawberry shampoo, just for the smell, or that he'd wake up, kissing her from her dreams, I would.

Younger Bennett might whine, *Ew, gross, cooties.* Or he might just grin and say, *Cool. Every pirate needs a parrot.*

And he does.

I need my parrot like I need each breath of life, and Ruby gives that to me every day.

On our thirty-first birthday, I wake up to a treasure map on our kitchen table.

"Oh, no, you didn't," I say, running back to our bedroom and pulling a very similar treasure map I made for her from the bedside table.

Thankfully, our buried booty are in different spots.

We start with my gift. I tucked her treasure in our back-yard, near the garden we planted, and she follows the map with ease.

Sifting through the flowers, Ruby finds the handmade pirate treasure box I constructed in secret at my workshop in Honeywood. I tried to hide it before today, but the little twinkle in her eyes says she might have seen it at least once. But what she hasn't seen is the treasure inside.

All of our treasures in fact. A shadowbox full of her drawings, our prom picture, and even the PC disc for RollerCoaster Tycoon. And nestled at the bottom are the remnants of our two pink bracelets.

Her eyes well up with tears before she rolls them.

"You sap, you."

I shrug with a grin as she scrambles to her feet and

jumps into my arms, placing kiss after kiss on my cheeks, peppering me with the love I'm not sure I'll ever get accustomed to.

"Okay, your turn! Your turn!" she says, shoving a map into my hands.

I follow the map's path through our house and to our front yard with her trailing behind at each step.

When I reach the X at the end of our driveway, almost bumping into our car, I look up.

"There's nothing here," I say with a laugh.

"Isn't there?" she prompts, clicking the key chain that has our car unlocking.

"The treasure is the car? Are we taking a trip?"

"Oh, yes," she says.

"And to where?"

"Your favorite place."

I squint. "Between your legs?"

She snorts. "Hilarious. No. To the tattoo parlor."

I can't help the smile that grows on my face.

"Oh, yeah?" I ask. "And to get what?"

"Forever."

"To get forever?"

"Just get in the car, Pirate."

"Whatever you say, Parrot."

63

Ruby

Two Months Later
Ruby & Bennett are Thirty-One Years Old

"Hey, this is a little awkward, but that's my ship."

I kick my feet out from the branch, letting them swing below me.

"This one?" I ask, gesturing to the tree. My long white dress is overflowing down the sides, the train cascading onto the forest floor.

Bennett walks toward me with a devilish smile, hands tucked into his navy-blue suit jacket pockets.

"That one," he confirms.

"Guess you'll have to commandeer it, Pirate."

He steps between my legs with a grin.

"I'll commandeer you," he growls.

"That makes zero sense."

"Oh well. By the way, you look stunning."

I pull in a mock gasp. "You can't say that."

"No?"

"You're not even supposed to see me."

"Oh, right." Bennett snaps his fingers. "Superstition and all."

"Eh, it's fine, I guess. I've never been one for silly rules anyway."

My best friend, my fiancé, and my future husband—in T-minus ten minutes—places his hands on either side of my waist, caging me in where I sit on the tree branch.

On his wrist is the solid pink line he got as a present on our thirty-first birthday. A tattoo circling his wrist. It's the only pop of color on his skin below the tattooed sleeve. He looks good in pink.

"What a pirate thing to say, Rubes."

I scrunch up my nose. "Yarr."

He chuckles, leaning in for a kiss. I cup his face in my palms and let his lips explore mine. Even after a year, the spark hasn't left. Before pulling away, he tilts his head to the side, kissing my wrist and my own tattoo adorning it—a thirty-first birthday gift to myself as well—a solid pink line exactly like his, wrapped in a circle around my bone.

I watch Bennett absentmindedly run a thumb over my dress, across the intricate cream tulle and lace.

"You nervous?" I ask.

"With you? Never. But … I am worried about the reception."

"Orson and Landon?"

"Yeah, I'm second-guessing making them masters of ceremonies."

I exhale. "Probably not our brightest idea. Is Landon wearing the top hat?"

"Yep."

"Yeesh."

"Their speeches are gonna be unhinged. You know that, right?"

"Don't I ever."

But unhinged speeches aren't exactly foreign to us. There have been a lot of those the past few months.

First, there was Brittney's.

"Now, I should be angry that you didn't propose with me around," Bennett's mom told us over bacon and biscuits at Chicken and the Egg.

We nodded like two children getting into trouble —something that had happened too many times when we were kids.

"But, well ..." Brittney shrugged and smiled. "That anger is for another day. Now, come here, my precious gemstone!" She gathered me in her arms and whispered, "You've always been like a daughter to me anyway." She slapped Bennett's arm and said, "Took y'all long enough. Jesus."

Next, there was Emory, who asked if I wanted to travel to other countries to expand the company's reach.

"I mean, I'm not trying to drag you away from your happy life or anything, but—"

I was already texting Bennett.

"Are you kidding? It sounds like a dream."

Emory, Lorelei, Bennett, and I spent the following month in Europe. We ate our way through Germany, the Netherlands, and England, visiting every theme park nearby and networking with industry leaders. Lorelei spent this time gathering ideas for a sister Honeywood Fun Park she'd be pitching to the board in a few weeks.

Finally, there was the unhinged speech from my dad, who insisted that we get married in the little white chapel on Main. Bennett and I said no—mostly because he's banned from it. But also because we wanted a wedding in our new backyard. We wanted to be at home, a place where we had started our new life together, where we'd literally placed roots and grown flowers and made memories—not in the chapel downtown, where it seemed all marriages we knew went to die.

I went out to dinner with my dad and my mom a week ago—just the three of us, like we hadn't done in years—and told them how I felt. Finally. After so many years.

"I've never been your priority," I admitted. "But I forgive you for that. Because I think that need for someone is what gave me Bennett."

All my mom did was nod in silence—in what I assumed was guilt. Because, if it wasn't, I wasn't sure how I'd feel.

Then, my dad said, "Well, I'm happy you're marrying the man who treats you as his priority."

"He doesn't just treat me that way," I replied, straightening my posture because I refused to feel small around the parental figures in my life. "He really, truly sees me like that. I *am* his priority."

So, now, here I am, ten minutes from the ceremony, with my soon-to-be husband meeting me for a secret kiss at our tree. I thread my fingers through his rock-and-roll locks that are right back at his shoulders. He places a final kiss on my freckles.

"Ready to go?" he asks.

"Been ready for far too long."

I walked down the aisle, arm in arm with my dad. He walked slow, but I was too busy grinning at the man waiting for me at the end to notice. About halfway down, I completely dropped my dad's arm and ran. I ran away from the man who could never choose me first and toward my best friend—the man who always has—until I leaped into his arms with his palm splayed over my lower back. The crowd laughed, and my best friends *oohed* from the bridesmaid line, but I only had eyes for Bennett.

I honestly don't remember much after that. They always say your wedding day is so hectic that it becomes a blur of faces and songs and feelings. They're right.

I don't remember Lucas's best man toast about soul mates and true happiness, but everyone told me afterward that it made Miranda cry. If Lucas hadn't seen it with his own eyes, I'm not sure I'd believe it.

I don't remember Lorelei repeatedly turning down alcohol or Theo calling her out about it at the bridesmaid table even though Lorelei told me afterward that she really did try to hide how pregnant she was that day.

I don't remember Emory, Orson, and Landon sneaking off to decorate Bennett's motorcycle with empty cans and ribbons, saying *Finally!*, but I found out later that Landon had forgotten the string, so they had just stuck the cans on the handlebars instead.

But the memories I do have—the ones I will always remember—are the little moments of hanging out with my best friend.

I remember eating dinner together in our bedroom, how he made sure to sneak us a plate of wings before the reception started to ensure I got some of my favorite food.

I remember our first dance, how he kissed my neck and whispered the lyrics to Etta James's "At Last" into my ear, sniffing every so often because my tattooed pirate could cry if he liked.

I remember how, every time we passed each other for

even a moment, he traced his thumb over my new tattoo, and I mirrored the same to him.

But mostly, I will always remember how my husband smiled. How there wasn't a single second I looked at him and he wasn't beaming from ear to ear, proud that I was his wife.

We ended the night running between two rows of our friends and family as they clapped and cheered and threw random fistfuls of confetti at us. Bennett lifted me onto his motorcycle first, then climbed in front, tossing the random handlebar cans to the side and revving the engine.

I wrapped my arms around my husband's waist as we roared down the roads of Cedar Cliff. And on that ride, with my head leaning against his back, I had the best memory of all—the realization that I got to spend forever with my best friend.

Epilogue
Ruby

Nine Years after Ruby and Bennett's Wedding Day

Ruby & Bennett are Forty Years Old

"Why is it written in big letters like that?"

"They're huge," Bennett agrees.

"Massive," I say. "Some astronaut in space is in awe."

"Pretty sure I've aged even more, just trying to look at them."

Orson looks between us and sighs. "Do you mean the numbers four and zero?" he asks.

"Well"—I hop off the ladder and shrug—"and the rest of it."

Bennett finishes pinning his side of the banner and lands beside me. Both of us peer up at the sign that reads, *Happy 40th Birthday, Buby.*

Theo, hands on her hips, grins. "I kind of like it."

"Welcome to your forties," Orson says, clapping both Bennett and me on either shoulder. "The best years are ahead, I promise."

Bennett and I exchange a glance.

Debatable, we both think.

Our thirties were pretty fantastic. We bought a house. We got hitched. Bennett is director of maintenance at Honeywood, and two of the roller coasters I'd designed for the park won Golden Ticket Awards year after year.

I'm sure my forties will be wonderful, but they have a fantastic decade to beat.

It's been a beautiful summer day in Honeywood Fun Park, full of local families and roaring roller coasters and an abundance of pancakes from The Bee-fast Stop. But the party has barely begun. Lorelei closed the park to start decorating early. I'm not sure she's supposed to abuse her power as Honeywood's main shareholder like that, but I don't see a retired Fred complaining one bit.

"What's a booby?"

We all look down to a little girl with massively curly hair—a spitting image of Theo, but with the comforting grin of her father, Orson. Sophie is old enough to know what a *booby* is. She thinks she's being cheeky. She gets it from her mom.

Orson tickles her side. "You know what that means, you nut."

"I thought it was a trap," she says with a wide smile. "You know. A *booby* trap."

"Nice!" Bennett says, reaching out for a high five. She slaps her tiny hand against his with a beaming grin.

My husband likes to reward punny humor.

There's a tugging at the bottom of my shirt, and we both

look down to see a familiar blond boy with thick glasses. He's blinking up at me and Bennett, each of our shirts held in either tiny fist.

"Uncle Bennett? Aunt Ruby?"

"Hey, kiddo." Bennett swings down to grab him, resting him on his hip. "What's up?"

"I can't find Lou."

"Are you two playing hide-and-seek again?" he asks. "In the park? A *giant* park?"

Freddy rubs the heel of his palm across his nose. "Don't tell Mama."

Bennett hoists him over his shoulder. "Oh, you're in trouble now."

Freddy's panicked words immediately turn into a symphony of giggles as Bennett takes exaggerated steps toward the amphitheater, bouncing the boy on his shoulder.

"See y'all later!" I call to Theo and Orson.

I catch up with my husband, Freddy's giggles getting louder as Bennett tosses him into my arms. I hang Freddy by his hands, swinging him back and forth over the midway as we walk on. The continued childlike giggles are unstoppable. It's one of my favorite sounds.

Although we decided to have no children of our own, Bennett and I are obsessed with our surrogate nieces and nephews. I once described us as the "cool aunt and uncle."

Quinn said I was getting a big head, but then Bennett whispered, "Because she knows we totally are."

Bennett and I march Freddy to the railing near the amphitheater, where Quinn and Landon sit, hand in hand, legs swinging over the stage.

"Child delivery!" Bennett calls.

Quinn jumps off just in time for me to dump her child

into her arms. She runs a hand through his delicate blond hair.

"Mama, I lost Lou."

"Ruh-roh," Landon jokes through a very dad-like laugh. "Y'all playing hide-and-seek again?"

"Mmhmm."

"In a big park?"

"Yes."

Quinn shakes her head. "I swear you two will be the death of us."

Freddy quickly adds, "But Lou said I could find her with the twin thing."

Quinn's eyes swivel over to Landon, who bursts into laughter. A smile breaks out over Quinn's face, and then she's laughing too. She never stays mad at Landon for long. His joy is infectious, and her love for him is too strong.

"I'm not sure that's how the twin thing works," Landon says to his son. "But we'll work on it."

Freddy's eyes widen. "I could read her mind one day?"

Landon shrugs. "Maybe."

Quinn elbows him. "No."

He winks and whispers, "Maybe."

His wife is smiling once more.

Quinn was nervous to have kids for a long while, unsure if she'd end up a duplicate of her own neglectful mom. But we all knew Quinn was worried for nothing. She and Landon have a picturesque home anyone would envy with family s'mores nights, nightly strolls around Cedar Cliff, and makeshift children's theater performances in their backyard. One time, we watched them perform *Wicked*, and little Lou hit that classic high note at the end of the first act. Or she tried at least. Our friend crew gave a standing ovation anyway.

Quinn places Freddy down, linking her pinkie with him. "Let's go find her together, all right?"

"Family scavenger hunt!" Landon jumps off the stage and grabs Quinn's other hand. "Ah. I spy a clue."

With a nod of his head toward a bush in the corner, all of us adults eye two blonde pigtails peeking out from the directional sign near the midway.

"I wonder where Lou could possibly be," Quinn shouts in a fake, practiced tone.

"We'll take a look around," Bennett says, winking at Quinn and Landon.

"I can't imagine where she'd run off to," I say louder.

Giggling, Lou leaves her hiding space. Her parents see, but her twin is none the wiser.

The five of us follow her out of the amphitheater, taking opposite directions at the fork in the walkway and departing with a wave.

"Ten bucks she's running to the Bumblebee Greenhouse," Bennett murmurs to me.

I nod in agreement. Quinn and Landon's little girl has a penchant for plants, just like her grandparents. I'm pretty sure they assume she'll take over the family business, but only time will tell.

We cross over to The Romping Meadow, where Lorelei is pinning more balloons.

"Hey, Lore!" Bennett calls. "You've reserved a spot in the greenhouse for your niece, right?"

Lorelei laughs. "I told them she can have a whole garden here if she wants. There's room down by The Hornet."

Honeywood Fun Park's latest thrill coaster, The Hornet, is down by the edge of the park, near the refinished parking lot. Although it gets a lot of visitors, there's still a decent amount of blank land, where more installations will form in years to come. But at the present, new attractions are on hold while Lorelei and Emory jump between here and the third Honeywood park. Its grand opening in Colorado is only two months away. Never a dull moment for the Dawson family.

"Mom!"

The sound of sneakers slap on the blacktop of the midway. Following them is an out-of-breath, gangly, wavy-haired boy. He bends in half, resting his hands on his knees. When he finally straightens up, he's taller than me. Killian gets his height from both of his parents, but those eyebrows of his—thick like caterpillars—are definitely from his daddy.

"Catch your breath, Killi," Lorelei says. "What's up?"

Lorelei's son holds up a single finger and takes bigger breaths.

"Did you run all the way here?" I ask with a laugh.

"Racing," he exhales. "Sophie."

"Ah, right." Bennett chuckles. "As usual."

Lorelei's son loves running just as much as his parents. He's convinced he'll be in the Olympics one day. With his family's determination, I wouldn't be surprised. I see him most weekday afternoons, jetting down Cedar Cliff sidewalks. Bennett and I try to have lemonade sitting out on our front porch when he passes by.

Coming up seconds later is Sophie. There's about a three-year age difference between Lorelei's son and Theo's daughter, but they're stuck like glue. If Killian is there, Sophie is sure to follow.

"Got you!" she says, heaving.

"Did you run here for a reason?" Lorelei asks.

"Oh!" Killian throws a thumb over his shoulder. "Yeah. Dad needs you by The Beesting."

Lorelei tucks her clipboard under her arm. "I swear that ride is on its last leg."

"Race you again," Killian says.

Sophie is already darting off, but Killian's long legs soar past her.

Exchanging another look, Bennett and I shrug and accompany Lorelei to The Beesting.

Our world is a lot like this most days. Going where the wind takes us. Enjoying the company of friends. Following their active kids. Trying to soak in every moment of our beautiful life.

When we turn the corner to the highest free-fall ride in the park, Emory is by the control panel, a baby swaddled to his chest. I swear her eyebrows are just as furrowed as his.

Emory turns on the spot, the wide eyes of the baby taking in the new direction's surroundings. Lorelei kisses her baby on the head before placing another on her husband's cheek as well.

"You rang?"

Emory exhales. "This booth is on its last leg, beautiful."

Lorelei smiles. "I figured."

"Anything we can do to help?" Bennett offers.

Lorelei waves him off. "Nope. Go be birthday people. We'll get it cleared up before the party."

"Need help with the kiddo?" I offer.

Emory's mouth tips into a smile. "And give up my girl?"

"You'd have to pry her off him," Lorelei says with a grin. "She's a daddy's girl already. Okay, now, the last time I looked ..."

Lorelei's words fade out as she and Emory walk into the booth.

Then, it's just me and my best friend.

Bennett reaches for my hand as we stroll to the center of

the midway, taking a seat on the bench near the fountain, right back where we started.

"What do you think?" he asks.

"About forty?"

"Mmhmm."

"I'm ready for it," I say. "Bring on the gray hairs."

"I'm already one step ahead of you."

"More like fifty steps," I joke.

As of about two years ago, Bennett's shoulder-length hair started to get streaked with random strands of silver. It's only noticeable if you're close up, but I've never been more attracted to him. It only adds to his rocker look.

Bennett is still the same man I fell in love with, though different in all the best ways. The little check marks beside his eyes are more defined, and his laugh lines are deeper than ever. We laugh a lot. First thing in the morning, sometimes when we're having sex, and even when we're fighting. Because we promised to never be mad at each other, and we always keep our promises.

We look around the park at the collection of familiar faces—Honey sitting next to Fred on the far bench, arm around her and kissing her on the temple. Mrs. Stanley, still wearing crop tops after all these years, is in the grass with her old dog resting a head on her stomach.

Near the entrance, we spot my mother-in-law, Brittney, popping the leather jacket collar on her fiancé—some accountant named Dave, who is a far cry from her ex. He does have a motorcycle though. I think she's going for a subtle rebel nowadays. Dave proposed after three dates. Some men just know, I suppose. Some men don't make their women wait, like Bennett's dad did.

We haven't seen Bennett's dad since Florida, and at this rate, I don't think we ever will. Bennett seems fine with that fact, which means I'm fine with it too. He says he doesn't need someone around who won't put him first—not when he has someone who continues to choose him every single day.

That's me, by the way.

And he's right; I'd choose him first every time.

My dad isn't here either, but he never seems to come to these things, especially not now that he lacks arm candy for the first time in his life. Unlike my mom, Miranda was ruthless in the divorce, and I'm not sure he has enough money to woo another woman for the next ten years.

My mom doesn't attend my birthdays either; she's too busy, still traveling for work, as she always has. I'm not too upset about it. She's always known what she wanted out of life—never remarrying and only reciting vows to her job.

The Sullivan family is represented by Lucas instead, who Bennett and I both spot near The Bee-fast Stop, hammering away.

"Do you know what he's doing?" I ask.

Bennett shakes his head. "Absolutely not. But I trust him. He just finds things to fix, Rubes. I swear, he's gonna know more than me soon. I'll have nothing left to teach him."

My brother is now working at Honeywood, training for a maintenance position under Bennett's mentorship. I'm pretty sure he spends more time here than he does at home, but as long as he doesn't come home too late, I don't care.

After Lucas graduated high school and Miranda left Dad, Lucas didn't want to move away from Cedar Cliff, so we took him in. We've only seen him sneak out once, and it was unsurprising when we found him loitering outside The Honeycomb with Michael's oldest kid. They're a couple of knuckleheads when they get together.

"Oh boy, here comes trouble," Bennett jokes.

I follow his line of sight to the iron gates creaking open once more.

Even after ten years, Jolene still wears bright red lipstick to match her flaming hair, and I swear she's the only person I know who can pull off something so bold.

Jolene crosses the midway with Michael and their three children, the eldest already jogging toward Lucas. They place a wrapped box on the gift table, which Bennett and I said was totally unnecessary, but pretty much everyone has insisted anyway. We both give her a small wave. She returns it with a playful middle finger, which makes her husband laugh out loud.

Their crew disappears down the midway, and then it suddenly feels quiet. Calm.

But it's always peaceful when it's just the two of us.

Bennett reaches out for my hand, wrapping his two palms around it.

"Hey, Parrot."

I smile the same smile I have for over thirty years. The one that is so filled with happiness that it doesn't feel real. Maybe in ten more years, I'll finally believe I'm not living in a dream. But it's hard when every day feels impossibly perfect.

"Hi, Pirate."

I admire all the changes over the years—the new rides, the new families, and everything in between. But I also appreciate the consistency—the familiarity of The Grizzly's rattling roar, the '70s music pumping through the speakers, and the wafting scent of The Bee-fast Stop's pancakes hanging in the air.

We made the right choice, celebrating our milestone

birthday at the park. It's where we met. Where we had our first kiss. Where we gradually fell in love.

At the end of the day, this theme park is our favorite place.

Honeywood Fun Park will always be our home.

THE END

Also by Julie Olivia

HONEYWOOD FUN PARK SERIES

Romantic Comedy

All Downhill With You (Emory & Lorelei)

The Fiction Between Us (Landon & Quinn)

Our Ride To Forever (Orson & Theo)

Their Freefall At Last (Bennett & Ruby)

—

INTO YOU SERIES

Romantic Comedy

In Too Deep (Cameron & Grace)

In His Eyes (Ian & Nia)

In The Wild (Harry & Saria)

—

FOXE HILL SERIES

Contemporary Romance

Match Cut (Keaton & Violet)

Present Perfect (Asher & Delaney)

—

STANDALONES

Romantic Comedy

Fake Santa Apology Tour (Nicholas & Birdie Mae)

Across the Night (Aiden & Sadie)

Thick As Thieves (Owen & Fran)

Thanks, Etc.

When I started plotting the Honeywood series, I knew I wanted Bennett and Ruby to be the finale. It was a challenge to myself to see if I could plant hidden references that wouldn't get a pay-off until the final book, and I wanted that pay-off to be HUGE. I remember telling my husband, "Even if the last book flops, I just want to look back on this series and feel proud."

Well, here we are. All four Honeywood Fun Park books are finished. The series is complete. And am I proud? You bet your ass I am.

But, even though I've written a whole dang book series, I still somehow cannot express through words how special Honeywood Fun Park is to me. It feels like I'm closing a very special chapter of my life. Maybe I get too emotional about my own characters, but boy am I gonna miss this crew. I just hope they remember me, y'know?

Sappiness aside, this series was only possible because of the wonderful support network I've had throughout the whole journey.

First, thank you to all the Honeywood Fun Park readers! When I dreamed up this little theme park, I had no idea so many people would love it like I do. I still tear up every time I'm tagged in pictures of people wearing Honeywood Staff t-shirts. Y'all make this theme park feel real.

To my editor, Jovana. Working with you has been a dream. Thank you for always catching my continuity errors, especially when I mess up the actual title of Honey Pleasure's children's book series (because I clearly never remember what I named it)!

Jenny Bailey. My sister-in-law and best friend. Thank you for talking me off a ledge when I call in a panic, for always reading the horrific early drafts and insisting it's not really bad at all, and for simply being one of the best humans I know.

Dad. You've always supported my pie-in-the-sky dreams. If it weren't for your constant encouragement, I wouldn't have thought writing a single book was possible, let alone having an entire career as an author. Thank you.

My brother, Rusty. I will always look up to you, and I don't think I'll ever get over the fact that you read all of these books. Thanks for being the cool sibling I strive to be.

Allie G. Thank you for being you. I have officially clung to you like glue, and you cannot get rid of me. Sorry not sorry. kloveyoubye.

My beta team! Thank you to Jenny, Allie (Orson's Blueberry), Hannah, Angie (my PT Queen!), Carrie, Emily, Elizabeth, Rebeca, Erin, Beth, and Kolin. This book (and this series!) has changed so much thanks to your feedback and wonderfully unhinged commentary. I really do have the best beta reading team.

Special shout-out to Emily Henry for all the behind-the-scenes theme park maintenance knowledge! Thank you for being kind enough to hop on a phone call with me to discuss parks for well over an hour!

My reader group, the Feisty Firecrackers! You are the most supportive group of readers! Not just with me, but with each other.

To every fellow romance book lover I've met through

Instagram and TikTok. You've made every release in this series absolutely magical.

And finally, to my husband. I have a distinct memory on our wedding day where we walked through those cathedral doors hand-in-hand, and we couldn't stop laughing or crying. We probably looked ridiculous to everyone else, but we were both thinking the same thing: *I cannot believe I get to spend forever with my person.* I tried putting that joy into words for Bennett & Ruby's wedding day, but I don't think I could ever do the real feeling justice. Thank you for always believing in me. Thank you for showing me what true love is. Thank you for being my person. I love you.

About the Author

Julie Olivia writes spicy romantic comedies. Her stories are filled with tight friend groups, saucy bedroom scenes, and nose-snort laughs that will give you warm fuzzies in your soul. Her phone's wallpaper is a picture of the Veloci-Coaster. Her husband has come to terms with this roller coaster obsession.

They live in Atlanta, Georgia with their cat, Tina, who does not pay rent.

Sign-up for the newsletter for book updates, special offers, and VIP exclusives!: julieoliviaauthor.com/newsletter

facebook.com/julieoliviaauthor

instagram.com/julieoliviaauthor

amazon.com/author/julieoliviaauthor

bookbub.com/authors/julie-olivia

Made in the USA
Middletown, DE
27 October 2023

41515801R00285